"BRIGHT, MOVING, LARGER-THAN-LIFE . . . FILLED WITH HUMOR, COMPASSION, AND GENEROSITY."—*Publishers Weekly*

"AN INSPIRATION! Guy has a reporter's eye for detail . . . that captures the innocence of the times."
—*Dallas Morning News*

"HIGHLY ENJOYABLE . . . with believable characters."
—*Pittsburgh Press*

"Funny and touching . . . just right."—*Chicago Tribune*

"Humorous, with realistic characters in realistic situations . . . HIGHLY RECOMMENDED."—*Library Journal*

"Personal, poignant . . . genuine perception . . . with a sharp but pain-gentled sense of humor."
—*Washington Post Book World*

DAVID GUY was born and raised in Pittsburgh, and graduated from Duke University. He currently lives with his family in Durham, North Carolina. His two previous novels, *Football Dreams* and *The Man Who Loved Dirty Books*, were published to superb reviews.

SECOND BROTHER

David Guy

A PLUME BOOK

NEW AMERICAN LIBRARY

NEW YORK AND SCARBOROUGH, ONTARIO

Publisher's Note

This novel is a work of fiction. Names, characters, places, and incidents either are the product of the author's imagination or are used fictitiously, and any resemblance to actual persons, living or dead, events, or locales is entirely coincidental.

NAL BOOKS ARE AVAILABLE AT QUANTITY DISCOUNTS WHEN USED TO PROMOTE PRODUCTS OR SERVICES. FOR INFORMATION PLEASE WRITE TO PREMIUM MARKETING DIVISION, NEW AMERICAN LIBRARY, 1633 BROADWAY, NEW YORK, NEW YORK 10019.

Second Brother was published in a hardcover edition by New American Library and published simultaneously in Canada by The New American Library of Canada Limited.

Acknowledgment

"We had a family vase," by Paul Goodman. Copyright © 1947 by Paul Goodman. Reprinted from *Collected Poems*, by Paul Goodman, edited by Taylor Stoehr, by permission of Random House, Inc.

 PLUME TRADEMARK REG. U.S. PAT. OFF. AND FOREIGN COUNTRIES REGISTERED TRADEMARK—MARCA REGISTRADA HECHO EN HARRISBURG, VA., U.S.A.

SIGNET, SIGNET CLASSIC, MENTOR, ONYX, PLUME, MERIDIAN and NAL BOOKS are published *in the United States* by New American Library, 1633 Broadway, New York, New York 10019, *in Canada* by The New American Library of Canada Limited, 81 Mack Avenue, Scarborough, Ontario M1L 1M8

Library of Congress Cataloging in Publication Data

Guy, David.
  Second brother.

  I. Title.
PS3557.U89S4   1985   813'.54   85-5122
ISBN 0-453-00497-0
ISBN 0-452-25887-1 (pbk)

Designed by Leonard Telesca

First Plume Printing, September, 1986

1 2 3 4 5 6 7 8 9

PRINTED IN THE UNITED STATES OF AMERICA

For
Reynolds Price
and
Virginia Barber
and
Sherry Huber

THE VASE

We had a family vase
made in Bohemia of glass,
of ruby, of gold-leaf, with blue
eyes as I look at you:
a vessel used to show off
the bouquets that the suitors brought
to mother, bloody roses, or
when we came back home, we four,
(this was before Arnold died)
the cornflowers o' the countryside,
so many, hanging there like smoke.
Now this vase I was dared, and broke.
And now my art is never enough
tho I have wrote the Facts of Life
and have defined the Isles of Joy
and mourned for Arthur dead in the war.

—Paul Goodman

ONE

The only thing I disliked about having the paper route that summer was actually waking up. Having breakfast early and off by myself, getting out of the house in the cool of the morning, smelling the scent of fresh newsprint and assembling the separate sections, riding the back-heavy bike and stopping to fold the papers tight and fling them: all those things I rather enjoyed. But I detested the first harsh buzz of the alarm and being jerked awake, the long minutes when I stumbled around pulling on my clothes, my eyelids heavy, head full of cobwebs, muscles weak and trembling. I never did adjust.

There is a family joke about that, one of those old family stories that still get told once in a blue moon when we all get together. I had been allotted the guest room that June with the understanding that it was just for the summer, that once the school year started I'd move back in with Bennett. We were the kind of family that has guests all the time, stray musicians and visiting poets and guest lecturers from the university; a member of the family couldn't be taking up the guest room. But the summer was slow in that regard, and it did seem stupid to wake Bennett up at five forty-five for no reason, during his vacation, so that summer I was allowed to be my family's guest. They treated me like a member of the family!—my clothes in the closet and a bright new alarm clock on the table, even though Teddy said he was always awake at that hour and would be glad to get me up.

The kid was an early riser, no question about it. You got up to go to the bathroom in what you thought was still essentially the middle of the night, the dawn barely creeping over the horizon, and there was Teddy stretched out in the television room, maybe chewing on a fried pie, staring at the test pattern to warm up his eyeballs for a day of heavy TV watching. He looked as if he'd been awake for hours. I don't know where he got his energy. Maybe the fact that he was the youngest, so he had to jump around all day like a vaudeville performer to get what he felt was his share of the attention, gave him a certain drive that the rest of us didn't have. Or maybe those long hours in front of the television were not waking time, just another kind of slumber, his mind shut off and his consciousness at rest while his subconscious, feeding on a steady stream of images, was plugged directly into the tube.

Anyway, Teddy had said he'd get me up, but I didn't care to depend on that little twit. My first morning on the job, however, I had somehow remembered to attend to every little detail except pulling out the button on the alarm clock. Teddy waited for me to get up, he waited and waited—for some reason, the first day of my paper route had become a major event in the life of my whole family—and finally, about forty-five minutes after I was supposed to have appeared, he went in and woke up our mother. She came to the guest room with him, saw that I was deep in slumber—my mother was such a devoted and enthusiastic sleeper that it pained her terribly to have to wake anybody up—and told Teddy he should awaken me, but to do so very gently. He leaned down slowly, positioned his mouth very carefully just next to my ear, and shouted "Hey!" at the top of his lungs.

The story goes that I jumped up in bed and shouted "Hey!" right back, as if an echo, then writhed and bounced on the bed for a while, then sat there and shook uncontrollably for a few minutes while my mother held me. "Oh, Teddy!" I could hear her say as she patted my back, my body pressed to her large soft bosom. "Theodore!" I'm sure he was trying to look suitably chastened in the background. I had to drag myself out of bed after that and deliver the paper for the first time, with not much idea what I was doing and just a ragged list of house numbers for a guide. From then on, for the rest of that summer and a number of years afterward, I always jumped up, in bed when the alarm went off and looked wildly all around, as if to ward off an attack.

Cute kid, that Teddy.

But that's the way it was with my brothers. Probably is with most brothers. If he wasn't paying me back for something specific, he could have been getting at me for general grievances. There was certainly a long backlist.

Once I got over the shakes every morning, I really did enjoy getting ready for the paper route. I could take crowds of people at the table for other meals, I even enjoyed them, but breakfast was one meal I thought should be eaten alone, preferably off in a corner somewhere, in utter silence. I also found most breakfast foods disgusting. Soggily buttered toast, lukewarm pulpy orange juice, blobs of marmalade, the slowly hardening juice of a runny egg yolk: scrape it all into the garbage can. A large glass of chocolate milk (I mixed my own, none of that artificial store-bought blend for me), three or four carefully chilled powdered sugar doughnuts, and I was on my way.

We lived in the block of Thomas that is just above Westinghouse Park, and as I stepped out the front door a white film of dew lay across the grass down there; far down through the trunks of the high trees, a mist hung over the railroad tracks. A truck would have left the papers in a couple of fat bundles in our yard, first sections in one and second sections in the other, each wrapped in a strand of thick wire, and I assembled the papers first, kneeling in the dew of the lawn, then loaded them into the sacks that I draped on either side of my rear fender. The route took me less than an hour, and I had been told that if I had the last paper delivered by seven that was time enough, so all I tried to do was be on my bike at a little after six.

The summers all run together back there, of course, as all the years tend to run together, but I sometimes think of that as the happiest summer of my life, or maybe I mean the last happy summer. That was the first real job I ever had, the first time I earned a substantial amount of money, the first time I realized how much I liked the early morning—still my favorite part of the day—and, in all the confusion and hubbub of a family of six, it was a good chance to get off every day on my own. I was coming up on my eighth-grade year at school: I would finally be in the oldest class and, perhaps more important, I would be the only member of our family at that school (Teddy, as we all had, would be starting first grade at public school). Furthermore, though I didn't follow politics, a certain amount of passionate—if rather vague—political feeling had been passed down to me from my father, and, after a long bad time, things seemed to be improving along those lines too. The morning after the important night of the Democratic convention, it rained, so I couldn't throw the papers but had to walk up to the stoops to drop them, and each time I did the youthful confident face stared at me beneath a blaring headline, Kennedy Captures Nomination.

The route I delivered had plenty of variety. The houses on Thomas must once have been spectacular—one massive brick place, for instance, had high white columns, like an antebellum mansion—but now they were mostly run down, either broken up into apartments or owned by people like my father, who didn't give a damn. A lot could have been done with those houses, but people weren't about to do it, because they were afraid of the burgeoning black neighborhood that lay down beyond the park. Further up there was a street of smaller houses, rough little red brick places, or larger structures that had originally been built as apartments, but still further, on the other side of Penn, was a much newer neighborhood, only ten or fifteen years old, with quiet tree-lined streets and beautiful brick houses, nicely spaced, immaculately cared for. It wasn't necessarily the case, of course, that people in those houses tipped me more, or tipped me at all, or even paid the bill when I came to collect. My most consistent tipper, in fact, was a divorced harried mother of two in a scrubby little house on Meade Street. She always had to scrape around in her change purse to find something to give me, but she always found something.

The house that intrigued me most was up on that other side of Penn, though not on one of the side streets. It was white brick, the first white brick house I had ever seen, with trim of a dark brown and one wing of dark-brown siding. It seemed from the front to be split level, with a brick wall—also white—in front of the property and ten-foot hedges around the side and at the back, where there seemed to be a substantial yard; on the asphalt driveway, or tucked into the garage, were a long black Cadillac and a sleek Thunderbird. I think it was that summer, riding around, that I began to speculate about houses—a persistent habit, as it has turned out—wondering if you could guess at the people inside from what you saw outside, if you could distinguish a place that housed happiness from one that concealed sorrow, wondering what might be happening behind those doors when I flung the papers at them, or during the long hours when I wasn't there. Most of all I wondered about that white brick house that seemed so much different from all the others, and from my own house. But I wasn't to find out much about it that summer. Like only a very few other places in the neighborhood, the white brick house didn't take a morning paper.

II

I couldn't understand why Bennett wanted to come to school with me the first day. I couldn't believe he did.

"You have the day off," I said. The upper school started a day later. "Can't you for once in your life take the day off when you have it?"

"I'm taking the day off," he said. "Of course I'm taking the day off. I'm just stopping in to visit."

"You can sleep in," I said. "It's your last chance."

"I've been sleeping in all summer."

By which he meant he hadn't vaulted out of bed at six forty-five to the lilting cry of an alarm clock. He bounced out maybe ten minutes later, to the sound of no alarm. He didn't need an artificial device to remind him of the call to duty.

"You're through with this school," I said. "You're too old for it now. Don't you think you'll feel like a wimp going back there?"

"There's nothing wrong with stopping by to see your old teachers. It's a friendly gesture. They'll be glad to see me."

He'd be glad to see them too. To live for a few moments more in that scene of his greatest triumphs. The future was fraught with peril, alive with a new endeavor.

But that guy had an answer to everything. We could have launched into a twenty-minute debate on the subject, complete with pros and cons, rebuttals, a question-and-answer session, and concluding remarks, and he would have won hands down. It wouldn't even have been a contest. It was the same with any subject.

I don't want you to come! I should have shouted, but I had long since learned not to express a wish. Anyway, he had that cross-examination down pat. Does it somehow reflect on you, just because I'm along, just because I'm your brother? Can't you be your own person? He didn't understand, he would never understand, what it was like to follow a guy like him through a school.

"You can go if you want," I said. "We don't have to go together."

"How would that look? Two brothers going off to the same school and not even going together."

"You're not going to the school. You're just dropping by for a visit, like you said. Anyway, I don't care how it looks. I don't care how anything looks."

I did, though. I cared deeply. That was the way I was raised.

"Come with me, Henry. I'd feel like an idiot going to that place alone."

"You've gone to that place a million times."

"But I don't belong there anymore. I don't go to that school. I *would* feel like a wimp going in there alone."

An interesting situation. For once the older brother needed the younger.

That was the way things went in my discussions with Bennett. If I expressed a wish, what was essentially a feeling, he took it as an intellectual proposition and beat the living shit out of it. But if he expressed a wish, I saw it as a feeling, and had a hell of a time saying no to it. He was my brother, after all.

"I'll introduce you to Mr. Friedman," he said. I think that

was his fondest hope, to pass on the intellectual tradition. Here's another fine scholar for you, sir. Not up to my level, but still, not all that bad.

"You will *not* introduce me to your teachers." On this I was going to be firm. "You will not appear with me in the presence of your teachers. You will not mention that you have a brother." They knew who I was, of course—it was a small enough school that the teachers knew everyone—but I didn't need it emphasized that I was Bennett Wilder's brother. I was hoping to have one year off from that.

"Okay." His eyes bore a hurt look. He just didn't get it. "But at least let me ride over there with you. At least let me go to the campus with you."

Very clever. He was giving in and still getting what he wanted.

"All right." He had worn me out. "If it means so much to you."

"I want to have plenty of time to talk. We'll need to get an early start."

We were on his schedule now.

I almost have the feeling I can look back through the years and see those boys. Both are what you call, in boys, towheaded; their hair has been bleached almost white by a summer in the sun. Their faces and arms are a deep brown. One is half a head taller than the other; he is obviously older, but he will always remain, even into adulthood, that half a head taller. The taller one is thin, and hard, and serious. He has reached that adolescent thinness that precedes the body's filling out: he is just starting, with no particular effort of his own, to acquire clearly defined muscles. His hair is dry, and stiff, and has a cowlick, so it hangs over his left eye as if coming to a point. His face has a look of self-importance, of dignity, as if he knows he is made for some remarkable destiny. (Many adolescent faces wear such a look. Few human beings achieve a remarkable destiny.) He is riding a new three-speed Raleigh bike—he has just had a birthday—a bike that, in comparison with others from those days, is bright, and sleek, and shiny. He rides with ease.

The other boy is pedaling a rusted, tarnished, American bike, a Schwinn. It has fat tires, wide fenders, a heavy body. It is just an accident, of course, that he is the second brother and that he is riding a secondhand bike. Nobody is trying to make him feel bad by giving him a hand-me-down, but who wants to waste a perfectly good bike? The peculiar thing is that he also seems to have a secondhand body. His hair is lighter than his brother's, softer, not stiff, though he too has a cowlick. At the moment his face is red and he wears an expression of dull pain, trying to keep up his brother's pace, but most of the time he wears almost no expression, as if he is not wearing a face to meet the world, but is dwelling inwardly on himself. At times he wears a broad bland smile. He is, as I have said, shorter than his brother, and he is also . . . I would not like to call him fat. Most people probably would not call him fat, and I can see, looking back at pictures of him, being objective, that he is not really all that fat. (Personally, at his most savage moments, he would have called himself fat fat fat.) But he is definitely soft. Though just fifteen months younger than his brother, he is not even starting to acquire the other boy's leanness, and in fact he never will. He will grow harder, he will lose what he hates to hear described as his baby fat (at least let my fat be my own age, he wanted to say), but he will never really be lean, and he will certainly never feel lean. All his life, even when he acquires the thinnest of ten-speed racing bikes, it will always look like a fat secondhand clunker to him.

The boys have ridden their bikes to a street that dead-ends into a playing field beside the school. There is a fence at the dead end, and beside the fence a hedge; they have to get off their bikes and walk them down to a break in the hedge where they can enter the field. At their end of the field, as they walk out, a man is holding a football, tossing it in the air and spinning it; far down the field, perhaps fifty yards away, is a cluster of boys.

"Hi, Tom," I said, as we walked out toward the man.

"Hello, kiddo," he said. Old Tom wasn't too hot on names. "Don't ride them bikes across my field."

"We're walking, not riding," I said. I had received this warning hundreds of times.

Tom did a double take, seeing Bennett. He *was* pretty good with faces.

"Dint you get enough of this place?" he said. "You back for more?"

"Just came by for a visit." Bennett was looking vaguely off in the distance, as if he couldn't stand even to lay eyes on the man. He looked as if he would like to turn on him savagely and correct his grammar.

"Maybe you could make first-string basketball this year."

That was the last thing Tom should have said. He had picked the one thing Bennett thought exposed the man's stupidity for all time. The gall Bennett had sometimes, his sheer belief in himself, was incredible. The year before, when the basketball lineups had been posted, he had gone to Tom and tried to persuade him to change the first team. Bennett had all his arguments marshaled; he had tied the man into knots verbally. Any jury in the country would have found for Bennett. He still didn't make the first string.

"Yeah," Bennett said. He loaded the word with sarcasm.

"One of the finest quick jumpers from the corner I ever seen, kid. Really." He looked at Bennett, his face the picture of sincerity. "If you could just work on that defense. Benny, isn't it?" His face was all screwed up with the effort of remembering the name. "Benny Wilder."

"Right." No one else had ever called Bennett that.

"I wish you all the success in the world, son." I don't know how the man restrained himself from stepping over to shake Bennett's hand, or at least pat him on the ass. Gym teachers loved that pat on the ass.

Tom was the kind of man who somehow wound up teaching gym at a school like ours. No other teacher was quite like him, which we acknowledged by calling only him by his first name. He was a physical marvel, or at least he once had been. He looked now as if he belonged in the corner of a boxing ring, or, if you could scare up a dinner jacket, maybe on the stage of a small nightclub in Vegas. He had jet-black hair that always looked as if it were soaking wet, and that was always immaculately combed, in waves. You could see the tracks of the comb. You could also see the comb, sticking up out of his back pocket.

He was around five-six—near in height to the kids he coached —and blockily muscular, with arms that he held out to the side a little, pectoral muscles and deltoids that swelled his T-shirt. Only in the past couple years had he started to put on weight, adding a small paunch, a little loose bulk to his muscles. He still had all the moves, he was just half a step slower.

Now he took two quick strides—the classic move; he had even tossed the ball up in the air and caught it, as if taking the snap from center—and got off a booming punt, his knee coming up nearly to touch his big beak of a nose, his left foot giving the little hop that really delivered the power. The ball took off in a tremendous arc, spiraling far down the field.

"Oh!" one of the kids shouted from down in that little cluster. "Oh!"

It was as if they had just witnessed the launching of a satellite. They stood around in a little group, as if commenting on it; one of them might have raised an arm and gestured, as if noting the arc. It was an interesting phenomenon. They had nothing essentially to do with it.

Except for one of them. One had stood out from the group, apart from the rest, looking at the ball in a different way, his body crouched, hands out a little from his side; he stared at the ball as if he were about to take aim with a rifle and shoot it.

"He's not going to *catch* that," I said.

He looked smaller than the others, and as a matter of fact he was, a little shorter than I (from the distance of years I can add details I could not see then). He was lean, but not as lean as Bennett; he had brown hair that was fairly short, though he kept enough to comb; he had a thin face that came down to a square chin. He stared at the ball with a deeply serious expression, almost solemn—it seemed to hang up there forever—his feet stepping lightly in a little dance.

"He isn't going to *catch* that ball," I said.

"We don't know yet, son," Tom said. "We have to wait and see."

An astute comment if there ever was one.

The ball swooped down out of the air like a hawk and the kid caught it, taking it against his chest, clutching up his arms; it knocked him a couple of steps back, almost knocked him down, but he caught it.

"Oh!" the guys shouted from down the field. "God!"

"Who is that kid?" I said.

"New kid," Tom said. "New boy this year. I had him down at the gym this summer, teaching him to box. He's a good little athlete."

Down the field, one of the other kids had gone out for a pass, and the new kid faded back, pump-faked, delivered a perfect spiral. The receiver started the long trek to bring the ball back.

"I don't believe he caught that," I said.

"It ain't all that hard. All it takes is a little nerve. Whyn't you go down?"

"Not me." Not without a suit of armor.

"Let's go," Bennett said. He was still not looking at Tom. He hadn't deigned to watch the punt, or at least to acknowledge that he had. He was making gradual progress toward the academic building.

"I want to stay," I said.

"It's time to go."

"School doesn't start for twenty minutes."

"We came here to talk." Bennett always assumed that if you came with him, you came for the same reason he did.

"I'm talking. I'm talking to Tom here."

Bennett looked back at me darkly. Everybody knew that wasn't conversation.

"We came to talk to your teachers."

I think Bennett honestly thought, in his heart of hearts, that the old scenes were going to repeat themselves, him taking me around to my teachers, just to make sure they knew whose brother this was, them saying things like "Are you as good a student as your brother?" and "I see the resemblance in the face. You're built a little different." As determined as I had been at home, those scenes probably would have repeated themselves. I sleepwalked into those things. Something in me wanted them.

But not now. "You go ahead," I said.

Bennett looked back at me with an air of honest surprise. A

person like him isn't insensitive to other people's feelings, exactly. He just can't believe they're different from his own.

"My teachers will figure out who I am," I said. "I'm going to be here all year."

And you aren't, I might have added.

For a moment he looked as if he might say something—he was staring at me as if he didn't quite understand—then he shrugged and walked off toward the building, his face wearing that solemn dignity that covered so much. You might have thought I'd have felt bad, but I don't think I did. I probably felt a small mean satisfaction.

There was a lot I didn't understand about people's feelings in those days. Probably still is. But I wasn't much thinking about how Bennett felt at that point. I wanted to stay and watch the new kid.

It is hard, looking back on it, to decide how much I actually realized that day. In my memory that moment stands still in my life, when I finally let Bennett go off alone, when I stayed behind as if I knew something important was about to begin for me. Any veteran of the school passing by would have noticed the new kid, of course. Any person, for that matter, would have noticed the kid who kept stepping out to catch the punts. Nearly anyone my age would have stopped for a moment, seeing him, and thought, "I'd like to know that guy." But in my memory it is something more. It is as if everything around him, the other kids and the rest of the field, the fence at the end of it and the trees beyond that, are a blur, but he—that first time I ever set eyes on him—stands out in sharp focus; it is as if I could tell by the way he set himself, by the calm intentness of his upturned face, that he had something to show the rest of us; it is as if I knew just by looking at him that he would be important to me, he would be a person in my life.

I couldn't have known all that then. I must have just admired what he did.

In any case, it happened again and again, on and on until the bell finally rang and we all had to go in. There was the ominous pause as Tom held the ball for a moment, hefting it; the swift powerful rhythm of his steps and the boom as his foot connected and the ball sailed high into the air; the slow high arc it described as it traversed the length of the field; and, down at the other end, the new kid: face upturned, hands poised at his sides, feet shuffling in their little dance, as he stared up at the ball, and waited.

TWO

"It's not like the other places up there," Sam had said. "You wouldn't put it in that neighborhood. It's built in a different style. Got more grounds."

It was funny that I couldn't picture the house he was describing. I just didn't want to put him in it.

"You'll know it when you see it," he said.

Fortunately, he also gave me the address.

I enjoyed just taking that walk in those days, on an afternoon early in autumn, the sun still bright but not strong, the air crisp and clear. Along our tree-lined block of Thomas, the leaves were just starting to turn, only a few on the ground. I turned the corner there and walked the little hill up to Penn Avenue.

I was carrying a baseball mitt, bouncing it off my thigh as I walked. Pittsburgh in those days was not quite the football town it is today; even so, most years, I would have been wearing my pads at that point, not carrying a mitt. But that was the incredible season when—for the first time in thirty-three years—the Pirates not only won the National League pennant, but went on to beat a great Yankee team in one of the most bizarre and exciting World Series ever played. All the Pittsburgh boys were carrying mitts that fall. Even at school, where the fall sports had started, we played baseball after lunch way into October.

It was also the year when I started playing a new position. Up until then, I had always played with my brother's friends, older kids, and I wasn't about to request a particular spot; I was glad they were letting me play at all. Right field, first base, I even caught sometimes: didn't matter to me. But that year there were no older kids around, and one day when Sam had picked up—even though he was new, you could see he should be a captain—he turned to me, when he was figuring out his lineup, and said, "What do you play?"

"Doesn't matter," I said. "First base. Outfield. You name it."

"We got an outfield," he said. "You're a little short for first."

"I don't really care," I said. "Put me anywhere."

Even a few weeks later, when I had gotten to know Sam a little better, I wouldn't have said that. He had a moody side to him, an impatient side, and if there was one thing he hated it was indecision. He didn't care how stupid your opinion was, as long as you had one. But you had to have an opinion.

"You must want to play something," he said.

"I do. I just don't care what it is."

"Tell me what you want to play! What am I, a mind reader?"

He had taken a step in my direction. I don't think he was threatening me, exactly. . . .

"I want to pitch," I said.

I wasn't sure why I had said that. I would never have said such a thing around my brother's friends.

I haven't made a study of it (I'm not much of a man for research, so it's up for grabs), but I have often wondered if superior control-pitchers might not have been a little heavy as youngsters, or might even have been younger brothers. In those games with my brother's friends, I never got to do much—when a kid came up who was likely to hit to right field, they made me change places with the left fielder—but after the games, after my one accidental chance in the field and my two or three times at bat, I would go out back for a while and throw a rubber ball against our garage door.

There was always a strong element of fantasy involved in that—it's the top of the ninth and the bases are loaded with the Pirates ahead by a single run: we need a man who can throw a strike—but it was also the case that our garage door was designed in squares, so that if you threw the ball in the middle of a square it bounced right back to you, but if you missed the middle it might bounce to one side or bounce crazily over your head, over fences into other yards that surrounded our own. Some quick and agile kids might have liked those crazy hops, but I wasn't out there to jump around, and I had never been much of a fence climber, so it wasn't long before I developed pinpoint control. I could hit any square on the garage that I wanted to, dead center. I also, once I had developed that kind of control, picked up a lot of speed. I liked the whirr of the rubber ball, the dull loud *pock* as it hit the door, the always-true bounce as it came back to me. It wasn't like those unpredictable games with my brother's friends where, when somebody did hit me the ball, I was so surprised I might muff it anyway.

"Can you get it over?" Sam said.

"Sure." I knew I could get it over.

Sam didn't look so sure. "Okay," he said. "You can pitch," as if calling my bluff. He grabbed a catcher's mitt. "I'll warm you up."

For the most part, in our games, pitcher wasn't an important position. Nobody was especially good at it, we didn't even want anybody to be good at it; we just wanted a guy who could get the ball over and wouldn't hold up the game too much. Sam dropped into a crouch—whatever position he played, he looked as if he'd played it forever—and held up a fat target, dead in the center of the plate. I leaned into a windup and burned one in there.

Sam looked at his mitt as if some accident had happened. He had hardly moved it. There had been a loud crack.

"Okay." He tossed the ball back. He tried not to look fazed. "Inside corner. Low." He held out a slightly more difficult target, just in front of one knee.

I burned the ball in there.

He looked at his mitt as if something had stung him. Something had.

"Let's try the other corner," he said. "High and away."

It wasn't anything to me. I was just out behind the garage, picking my spots, throwing to the center of the square so the ball would bounce back true.

Sam had a way, when anyone else would have been wearing

a big grin, of stifling a smile, his teeth digging into his lower lip, eyebrows crinkled and sleepy. As you got to know him, you saw that expression as broad approval.

"Okay," he said. "I guess you can get it over. You can pitch."

The game was positively boring. After years of hitting the lobs most pitchers threw, nobody could touch my fastball. They couldn't even foul it off. I could throw for the corners, drill one down the center of the plate, it didn't matter. By the end of the game I was lobbing it in myself, trying to give our fielders something to do.

It wasn't strange to me to be doing well. I'd always been a pretty good ballplayer, at least around guys my own age. What was strange was to be doing conspicuously well. Most of the time we were on the field, I was the only guy doing anything, while the players around me shouted encouragement, the guys on the other team tried to bait me. It was strange to me to be noticed.

"Why didn't you ever pitch before?" Sam said, afterward.

"I never got the chance," I said. "I never asked."

"You shouldn't have been asking. You should have been telling." He shook his head. "We've got to get some competition."

"It's that or start pitching underhand," somebody said.

"Why don't we challenge the ninth grade?" Sam said.

"Jesus," somebody said. "We just got rid of those guys."

"We never beat them before," another guy said. "We never even came close."

"You never had a pitcher before," Sam said.

"We had a pitcher before." Dirk Spaulding had spoken up. He had pitched for us in the past. Everybody looked at him. "Kind of," he said.

"I don't think they can hit Henry's fastball," Sam said.

"How do we get them in here?" somebody said. The upper school was in the suburbs, twenty minutes away.

"We challenge them for a Saturday morning," Sam said. "This field. If they can get a team to show up, they can play us."

"They'll get a team to show up," somebody said. "They'll get two teams to show up. Shit, they won't believe this."

Even I was feeling a flutter of nervousness. Sam had never seen the ninth grade.

"Most of the lineup's got to strike out," Sam said. "We'll just have to take care of the rest."

That was the way it was for Sam. It wasn't fun for him, as it was for everyone else, to play a laugher and walk all over the other team. He wanted a challenge. As soon as he beat one team, he was looking for another that would make it closer. He was never satisfied.

"Just in case," he said. He was looking at me, almost smiling. "I think we better teach you a curve."

That was why I was walking to Sam's, on that Sunday afternoon in the middle of September, the first of many times I would take that walk. It seems funny now that I would have drawn a blank on that house when he described it. It just goes to show the strength of a prior assumption. I had imagined so much about that house that I would never have seen it as the place where Sam lived. There were too many things in the way.

It was the house of white brick and brown siding, high hedges around the yard, fancy cars in the driveway.

My feeling that I could look at the exterior of a house and imagine what was going on inside was severely shaken. For that house I had pictured an aging businessman as the owner, silver-haired, deeply tanned, immaculately dressed in a gray suit. He drove that battleship of a Cadillac while his young wife—his third, and young enough to be his daughter—tooled around in the Thunderbird. She was the kind of woman who played tennis and played golf and kept horses somewhere and owned a sailboat. All day long she occupied herself with physical pursuits while her husband went out and piled up the money.

Such a couple would never have encumbered themselves with a child.

As many times as I had stopped to stare at that house, I had never stepped on the property. It was like violating sacred ground. The door was high and heavy, and didn't seem the kind that a knock could penetrate. I rang the doorbell beside it. Nothing happened—it wasn't like some newer houses, where you can hear the bell outside about as well as in—but in a few minutes the door was tugged open, and a woman stood there.

I had been expecting a servant of some kind, perhaps a French maid in a frilly uniform. That wasn't exactly what I got. The woman who answered was roughly my height. She wore a house dress that was faded and ragged, and her skin was a black that approached the shade of ashes. Her eyes were sleepy, her mouth twisted and somehow askew. Above it was a thin mustache that would have done a man proud. She looked as if she had no idea what I could possibly be doing at that door.

At that point I was beginning to wonder myself.

"Is Sam here?" I said.

"Come in." She stepped back from the door. "I see."

She seemed to mean she would inquire around the place to see if such a person existed.

If anything, I felt less comfortable standing inside the door than I had walking up to it. The front hallway was small and dim. The carpeting was a pale beige, thick almost to the point of being bouncy. There was an oriental rug in front of the door. An antique table stood beneath a large gilded mirror, in which I stood and stared back at myself, disheveled, rumpled, my sweatshirt twisted, the mitt a piece of dried cracked leather in my hand. I looked fat. Must have been some distortion in the mirror.

What really struck me about that house was its quiet. Our house, with four children, two large and flamboyant parents, bare hardwood floors, was never anything like quiet. Even when no one was there but me, the wood gave off all sorts of groans, cracks, and creaks, as if complaining about the punishment it took all day. But this place was dead silent. It felt as if the floor wouldn't give off a sound even if you jumped up and down and pounded on it. It was as if the floor, like the outside of the house, were also made of brick.

It still didn't seem to be the house a young person would inhabit.

The silence of the place seemed to hold a secret.

From the room more or less in front of me—the hallway moved around to the left, and there was a doorway beside the mirror—I thought I did hear a sound, maybe something being placed on a table, and for a moment, in the doorway, a woman appeared. She was tall, but not especially thin; she wore a skirt and a sweater, a pin on the sweater; her hair was black, lightly flecked with gray. I would not want to give the impression she was old, but she was slightly older than I had expected. She was not what I would have called pretty, but not quite plain; I think she was what people call a handsome woman. She wore almost a haughty expression, a little strained, not friendly. "Hello, dear," she said. Her voice was a deep alto.

"Hello," I said. Sounded like the squeak of a mouse.

When she stepped back into the room she said, to someone, "A friend of Samuel's."

From the stairway beside me, Sam came running down, hardly making a sound. He carried a fielder's mitt, and a catcher's mitt, and a ball. He moved as if someone were chasing him. "Let's go," he said, stepping out the door.

To the side of the house, behind the hedges, was a long wide yard, and there was another one just as large behind the house. Even after a scorching month of August, the grass was still green and thick. It seemed strange to be playing in such a large space where nobody, because of the high hedges, could see us.

Sam was all business, as usual. "Warm it up," he said, tossing away the catcher's mitt, pulling on a fielder's glove. "We'll throw easy for a while. Then we'll pitch."

I have seen many athletes, in many sports, before that day and since, but I have never in my life seen a more natural athlete than Sam Golden at the age of thirteen. Even just doing simple things, warming up his arm, he was smooth and easy, and he had a seriousness about him that you almost never find in a kid that age: he concentrated all the time. Playing ball never felt stupid or lazy with Sam. "Grounders," he said after a while, and he was the picture of an infielder; he went down on every one effortlessly, his mitt just brushing the grass, and when he came up on the hop he was already going into his throw, sidearm or three-quarters. Once he started feeling loose, he took up the catcher's mitt, still making me go easy— "Throwing isn't pitching," he said. "You've got to warm that up too"—then harder and harder. When he finally thought my arm was ready, he trotted over to show me the new grip.

"You hold the curve different," he said. "Across the seams, not with them. You hold it with your two fingers tight together, and the ball jammed into your hand. Then you throw it different. You snap your wrist." He showed me the motion, flipping his hand. "The ball comes in slower, and it kind of whirrs along, then it curves." He winced. "Sometimes."

"Who taught you?"

"I don't know." He shrugged. "I picked it up. You take the catcher's mitt. Let me try one."

For sheer velocity, I probably had it on Sam—I know I did—but even at that he might have made the better pitcher. He had good speed, good control, and he'd have had wonderful sense out on the mound. He had a mind for the game. Now he took an easy windup and threw: the ball had a funny spin, floating in, and just before it reached me, it dropped.

"It works!" I shouted.

Sam nodded, satisfied. "Now you try it."

We jogged to change places, picked up the other mitts. When I got in position I tried a couple of fastballs. I held the ball for a moment, looked at the new grip.

"It feels like it's going to fall out of my hand," I said.

"It is, kind of. That's the idea."

"I'm not sure I can do this."

"Give it a try. You've got to try it."

As long as I knew Sam, it was always the same, me being reluctant, him urging me to try something.

From behind the house, around the side, a man came walking out, his face wearing a little smirk of amusement. If I had been wrong about the lady of the house—and I certainly had—I had missed the man by a mile. He was tall, and wore beautiful clothes, gray slacks, a white shirt, a pale-blue cardigan sweater. He was almost completely bald, just a fringe of dark hair around the side of his head, and his body rounded into a big soft belly. He was the shape of a ripe pear. He carried his weight gracefully, though, didn't walk like a fat man. His hands were stuck in the pockets of his slacks. His face was fleshy, didn't look much like Sam's. In a corner of his mouth sat a short black cigar.

As soon as Sam saw him—from that far side of the yard, he saw him before I did—he seemed to redden, or darken, and frown, and cringe a little. He didn't look at the man, seemed not to want to look at him, as if he might go away if we just ignored him. Even though I had been about to pitch, Sam didn't give me a target. Everything was going to stop for a moment. The two of us just waited while the man came walking out.

"Your mother thought I should get out of the house for a while," he said. "Get some fresh air. A little exercise." He still wore that smirk, talked around the cigar. "She really just wants to get me away from the liquor cabinet. I thought I'd see what you little assholes were doing."

"He doesn't mean anything by it," Sam said. "He calls everybody that."

"That's right, kid," his father said. "No offense. The whole world's an asshole."

He was walking vaguely in our direction, walking, actually, toward Sam. His cigar gave off a light trail of smoke.

"Let me see it," he said. "It's my mitt." Sam still wasn't looking at his father, but gave him the catcher's mitt. "He's more than happy to give up his mitt," his father said. "To the man who taught him everything he knows."

Sam smiled sheepishly. He wasn't looking my way either. It was as if we had stumbled across a harmless derelict, just had to humor him for a while.

"See, kid"—Sam's father turned toward me, fingering the mitt—"where I grew up, it wasn't like this. You didn't have nice thick grass and hedges all around and a big long yard to play on." He was walking slowly in my direction. "You didn't have a big beautiful house and a maid to cook your meals and a room of your own full of books and records and a big double bed. You had a dirt field, with oil on it to keep the dust down if you were lucky, and rocks and stones and broken bottles all over the place. You had a bunch of guys who didn't have money for a lot of equipment, so a ball was a precious thing, you taped it when the cover came off and played till nothing was left of it. Some of the guys didn't have mitts, but they went ahead and played barehanded, and the catcher, he had a mitt, but nothing else. No mask or shin guards, none of that crap."

He had gotten close to me by then, was standing over me, swaying a little. "See this beak?" He reached up and touched his nose. "Pure rubber." He pushed it down, pressed it flat to his face.

I stared, dumbfounded. I had never seen anything like that.

"Go ahead, kid." He leaned down. "Touch it. The freak show of the century."

I reached up and touched. It looked like a nose, but it didn't feel like one. You could push it down, twist it around. It was more like an ear or something.

"It got broke so many times, foul balls and fights and thrown bats and all that, that there wasn't really a bone in there anymore, just a collection of little bone parts. When I breathed it sounded like a wind symphony. I snored so loud I shook the walls. Finally I went to the doctor, I said, don't try to put it back together. Just take it all out and throw it away. Fuck it."

It's hard to remember, in these days when things have changed so much, how shocking it was for somebody to talk like that. I had never heard the father of a friend use such language.

"So," he said. "I learned in a tough school. And I learned good. Not like this little asshole." He had turned away, walked back to where Sam was standing. "You got a good catcher to throw to now, kid. Let's see what you got."

Despite his huge size and shape, he dropped easily into a crouch, just like Sam; he had been there before. A part of me was nervous—this wasn't exactly throwing against the garage door, or even throwing to Sam—but a part of me was loose, too. The man was funny and scary all at the same time. He gave me a target, and I didn't miss by much. I could do it, that was all.

"Hey," Sam's father said when he caught the first pitch. "Do that again."

I did it again. He had held the second target a little lower, just like Sam.

"You got it, kid. You got a hard one, as the woman said to her husband. Now let's see your curve."

I stopped, reddened. "I never threw that before. That's what Sam was teaching me."

"*He* was teaching you. What the hell's he know about it?"

"He can throw it." You could talk back to this man.

"I bet he didn't tell you who taught him. Did he?"

"He didn't."

"Every fucking thing he knows. Okay, kid. Show me your curve."

I was trying the grip, jamming the ball into my hand. "I'm not sure I can do this."

"You probably can't."

"I never even tried it before."

"Jesus, kid. Just throw the fucking thing."

I gave it a try. It wasn't easy, snapping my wrist in the middle of the pitch. The ball spun wildly out of my hand, dove into the ground. It missed Sam's father by ten feet.

He rose slowly out of his crouch, his smirk spreading into a smile. He took the cigar from his mouth and tossed it over the hedge. "I think you better stick to the hard stuff, kid."

Sam had gone chasing back to the hedge after the ball, and his father turned to watch him. "You want to see how I made this kid tough?" he said to me, back over his shoulder.

"Sure." I'm not sure I would have said that if I'd known what he meant.

"Tried to, anyway. It never took." He was staring at Sam. "You ready?"

Sam was standing in front of the hedge, the ball at his chest, his right leg bent slightly and poised on one toe. "Anytime," he said.

"Then hit me," his father said.

Sam whirled and uncorked a terrific peg, straight at his father's chest. It threw him off balance, he had thrown so hard. The ball went whizzing on a line. His father picked it out of the air like a gnat.

"That all you got?" his father said.

Sam was watching him, poised and alert.

His father did the same thing, reared back and unleashed a

wicked throw. He threw like a catcher, from behind his ear, and was throwing down a little, caught Sam about waist-high. The ball cracked into the mitt.

"Put something on it, next time," Sam said.

That was the game, apparently, it was all part of it, the hard throws, the taunts, the one-handed grabs as if there were nothing to it, the deadpan expressions. Each throw, if anything, was harder than the last; with each catch they took one step toward the other. It was a game of chicken, seeing who would give in first. The closer they got the faster they moved, shortening the taunts, shifting their feet to throw before they even made the catch. "*Hit* me, I said." "*Throw* the ball." Sam's hands were incredibly fast, faster than his father's, but he couldn't throw as hard, and I don't know how his glove hand took the punishment. Finally, when they were about eight yards apart, Sam threw one his father almost missed: it bounced off the edge of his glove and struck him in the chest, bounded into the air. With a bellow of rage, like pain, he snatched the ball out of the air and threw it at Sam's head. The boy ducked, hit the dirt; the ball sailed over him and flew into the bushes.

"I knew it!" his father shouted. "I told you! Who's tougher, kid? Who's tougher?"

The man was standing over his son, his fist raised into the air. Sam lay belly down, not moving, his face buried in the grass.

His father turned back to me, red-faced, staring wildly. As awful as it was, you still almost had to laugh.

"Jesus, kid," he said. "It's a good thing he ducked when he did. That thing had hit him, it would've killed him."

II

It wasn't just that evening, with Sam; it was lots of evenings, with lots of people, maybe every evening I ever played ball. After we had worked on my pitching for a while—I never did learn a curveball; I just couldn't get the hang of twisting my wrist—a couple of his friends from the neighborhood showed up, and we wound up playing different things: run-down, in Sam's yard, a little Indian ball in the street. We took some batting practice, playing on and on, while dusk fell all around us. For a while when I was batting the pitcher was a little hazy out there, the ball a bit of a blur, and finally the time came when he seemed to throw but nothing happened, then all of a sudden the ball was five feet away and coming hard, as if out of nowhere. "It's too dark," I said, after a feeble swing. "Yeah," somebody else said, and only then did I realize how tired I was, my muscles leaden, a little ache in my lungs from the cold air, a scrape on my shin starting to sting when it hadn't before. "Good game," somebody said, and we all answered, "Good game. Good game," as we picked up our stuff and went our separate ways. It was as if each game were the last, each evening the last chance we would ever have to play ball, so we got slightly desperate at the end, playing a little faster, playing a little harder. We always went on too long.

The night around me was dark, the air snappy and cold, as I hurried home. Down on Penn the motors roared, the cars whizzed by. Houses back from the street were alight.

I don't know how another kid would have reacted to what I had seen that afternoon. I wonder how Sam, for instance, would have felt, if he had witnessed such a scene between a father and son. As it was, he had stood slowly from the ground, brushing himself off. His father was razzing him the way another kid would have—"What's the matter, Sam? Can't you catch the ball? You afraid of the baseball?"—and Sam was grinning a little, taking it, but also holding something back, the way you would with an older kid who you knew was too much for you. That was more like what I had seen. It wasn't between a father and a son. It was a competition between two men, not equals, but moving toward being equals. One of them had lost, but he was plotting his revenge.

Myself, I was aghast. I didn't like competition that was personal like that. I didn't like conflict that was naked and raw. I couldn't understand the simple acceptance of it, the acknowledgment that it would go on existing.

It was with some relief that I arrived back at my own house, walked around to the back door, by the kitchen, where we always entered.

Our kitchen was high, wide, and spacious, counters all around. There was an enormous double sink, a wide stove, a high double-doored refrigerator, long shelves of dishes, cups, bowls. Utensils hung everywhere. My mother liked to fix huge dinners, for many people, and she needed lots of space to work in. That evening there was a leg of lamb in the oven, and potatoes roasting to a golden brown. Tiny green peas were boiling on a burner. On a sideboard were fresh loaves of bread. Two apple pies cooled on the counter. My mother stood beside them, fixing a salad.

You couldn't miss her. She wore an apron that was fire-engine red and hung down the length of her. She had ash-blond hair that touched her shoulders in waves, a complexion the color of heavy cream and absolutely flawless, eyes just a touch to the blue of turquoise, cheeks with a blush of color, a small pert mouth that dimpled into a smile. And a body that was as great as all outdoors.

A few weeks later, Sam would try to put into words what everyone essentially felt about this woman. "Your mother is so . . ." he said. "She's so . . . she really is . . ." What *was* the word? "A mother."

Exactly. In the large billowy dresses my mother wore—you never saw the precise outlines of her body, because there were always yards of material around it—she glided about our kitchen like a blown-out ballerina. She was an extremely graceful woman, so you did not immediately think of her as fat. She carried the extra weight well, as they say in the sports world. While she glided she sang, very softly, in an exquisite soprano trained by the finest teachers of voice. Her dresses were cut low, showed the top of her alabaster bosom. Though many boys, in those days, had never seen any part of their mothers' breasts, I had seen every bit of my mother's, because she had been—unusually, for her day—a conspicuous baby nurser, flopping out a breast at the slightest provocation. I had often seen her feed Teddy a few years before. That little bastard had sucked away to his heart's content.

I've gotten even with him for that since. I know I have.

As I walked into the kitchen, the cabinet beside the door conveniently opened. Something about the suction from the door made it do that. Strictly as a reflex, I reached in and pulled out a box of Triscuits.

"Don't eat those crackers," my mother said. "You'll spoil your appetite."

My father was standing beside the cabinet, mixing a drink, and as I pulled out a handful of crackers—I got about nine; those things have a way of clinging together—he took the box from me with a broad smile.

"We're not spoiling our appetites," he said. "We're whetting our appetites."

My father was also enormous. He stood about six-four, tipped the scales at God knows what, but his bulk was different from my mother's, slightly more solid, more a part of himself. Not that he wasn't pretty damn fat. In my parents' wedding picture, he had been a brawny athlete—a fourth-string tackle on the Pitt football team, until he discovered that his real talents lay in the field of literature—and my mother had been a mere slip of a girl. It had almost been grotesque, the difference in their sizes. The two of them had joined forces and eaten themselves into compatibility.

My father reached into the box and pulled out a handful of crackers that made mine look pitiful. He had the hands of a fourth-string tackle, of course. He was standing there holding on to about half a box of crackers.

"You *will* spoil your appetite." My mother glided at us menacingly. "After I've spent the afternoon baking pies and baking bread. Fixing that lamb."

"We'll eat the lamb," my father said. "We'll eat the pies. We'll eat every little morsel you set before us."

He wrapped her in his massive arms. He held her there, tilted her head back, and—the ultimate gesture of affection between these two—popped a cracker into her mouth.

I turned away from that spectacle. That kind of thing was starting vaguely to bother me.

It was only about a year, actually, since I had heard what were euphemistically referred to in those days as the facts of life. A friend had told me rather rapidly while we stood around during the recess after lunch. "And that's what people mean when they talk about fucking and everything," he said, in conclusion. I found his information fascinating. I had actually been somewhat misinformed at first; my friend had neglected to mention the in-and-out friction that produces ejaculation, so I had assumed that the penis was inserted and then somehow knew to ejaculate itself, as if it had a little mind of its own (in a way, of course, it does). A few months later, however, I had discovered that friction accidentally on my own.

There was still one question that bothered me, however. I finally asked Bennett about it one night when we were in bed, in the dark.

"Do you think they do it?" I said.

"Of course they've done it." He had started thrashing wildly around in bed as soon as I brought the subject up. "How do you think we got here?"

What a strange way to get here, it seemed to me.

"But do they do it?" I said. "Do they do it now?"

"How would I know? There's Teddy." Obviously he had given the question some thought.

"That was eight years ago," I said.

"Why don't you ask them? Why don't you listen at the door if you're so interested?"

He seemed to mean that just bringing the subject up was about on a par with listening at the door.

How do they do it? was the question I really wanted to ask. I didn't see how those two bodies could join at that particular spot.

No one mentions this question peculiar to the children of fat people.

Oddly enough, it was Teddy who eventually discovered at least one answer. I have never figured out how he learned about sex so much earlier than Bennett and I had, or why he was so much freer about discussing it.

"I finally found out how fat people fuck," he said to us one day when he was eight years old.

"Shut up, Teddy," Bennett said.

"The woman stands up and bends over the bed," Teddy said. "Then the man sticks it in from behind."

"Shut up!" Bennett said.

"Like dogs," Teddy said.

It was a good thing Teddy had found out when he was only eight years old. If he had been much older when he said those things, Bennett would have killed him.

Anyway, I really didn't care to see my parents hugging and feeding each other out in the kitchen. The whole thing made me edgy.

Once my mother had wrested the Triscuit box away from my father and me—she might as well have thrown it away, for all the good it would have done anybody at that point—the two of us walked out to the living room, munching away. Parts of two Sunday papers lay scattered around on the floor. I picked up a sports section. He was reading the *New York Times Magazine*.

I think it was some homespun American philosopher— though it may have been an ancient Greek; I haven't bothered to check—who first stated the adage "When a family sits down to dinner, the whole of their lives sits down around them." In our family, that was just about as true of the period before dinner. Since he wasn't out shooting baskets—the same obsessive jump shot, again and again—Bennett was almost certainly up in his room, reading some book with enormous concentration. Teddy was off in the television room—I could hear the faint sounds of voices snarling, gunshots blatting—lying on his back, soaking it in. Susan was up in her attic room, doing whatever it was she did up there. She had her own bathroom, and all her things up there, so she rarely came down except for meals and to practice the piano.

All her life Susan would be apart from the rest of us, doing God knows what. Bennett would be studying some author with enormous concentration. Teddy would be taking things easy, soaking it all in.

That left me reading rather dreamily in the massive presence of my father.

I haven't mentioned his beard, which he did not yet have in that wedding picture; it was brown and gray and bushy, though trimmed in his own rough way. It dominated his face. He smoked a pipe, always a large bent pipe (though not always the same one; he had a huge collection) packed with a strong English tobacco. Its harsh acrid odor filled the house. Always he sat in the same chair, and always he was reading, in the afternoons a newspaper or magazine, in the evenings a book. Nearly always he was drinking, scotch in the afternoon, beer after dinner, though he sipped what he drank, and never showed its effects. There was the sound of pages turning, the heavy sound of a big man breathing, the tinkle of ice in his glass and the little "Ah!" as he drank, the burble and splash from the pipe as a trail of smoke floated away. All that was somehow soothing to me. I never got enough of it.

"How was your game?" he said, while he was reading. He had only a vague idea where I'd been.

"Fine." It was great. Sam's father tried to kill him.

"That's good."

We didn't communicate much by words. But there was something going on. Just sitting there, breathing the same air.

"Dinner's ready!" my mother sang from the dining room.

"Ah!" My father beamed over at me. "At last!"

As he always did when she announced dinner, my father walked to the dining room and kissed my mother loudly on the mouth.

I have often wondered if there was some method to the way we sat at the dinner table, whether my parents planned it that way or whether it all just happened by chance. I have even wondered if we became the people we did because of the way we sat at the table. Anyway, my parents sat at either end. To my father's left sat Susan, then me; to his right, Bennett and Teddy. If you drew a diagonal from the proper corners—you could have drawn all kinds of lines at that table, of course, but I swear this was the way things stacked up—you had three males, Teddy, Bennett, and my father, facing two females, with me wedged in between them.

"He's his mother's child," people often said about me, and I wondered what they meant (I wondered if they meant I was fat). Did they mean I was blond and fair? that I had my mother's temperament? that she had particularly influenced me? that I was in some way under her thumb?

At the dinner table, in any case, I was on my mother's side.

"I don't want too much," Susan said, as soon as she sat down.

"Teddy, sweetheart, sit straight in your chair," my mother said.

Teddy had a way of sitting on just the right front corner, say, as if he were ready to bolt at any time. He slid around, tipped the chair from side to side, practically fell off it now and then. You could have gotten motion sickness sitting across from that kid.

"What you don't give to Susan," I said, "give to me."

"Yes," Susan said. "Give it to Henry."

Susan was a bit of a mystery in our family, at least at that point. She was the oldest of us, six years older than Bennett, and nobody knew her especially well. She was a mirror image of Bennett, tall and thin, but with long pale hair that hung straight down her back. She seemed to have his intensity without anything to focus it on; she didn't, to my knowledge, shoot baskets obsessively or read voraciously. She was a talented musician, but rarely performed. Most of her men friends were other musicians, who came to the house and—pardon the expression —played with her. When they weren't making music they just sat down in the living room and—very seriously, it seemed— talked.

She was a quiet person. She had what amounted to a positive fear of food; she ate almost nothing, sat at the dinner table doing nothing, while everyone else was choking it down. She had been around when the rest of us hadn't, must have recoiled early from the spectacle of our parents grotesquely bloating themselves.

What she most wanted in the world, I think, was to get away. She was coming up on her junior year at Oberlin, was home at that point because her summer in Europe was over and her school year hadn't begun. Two years later she would be married and out of the house altogether.

Beside my father, having settled himself in his chair and waited for silence, Bennett spoke.

"The magnificence of Mencken's prose overwhelms me," he said. "It absolutely overwhelms me."

"That's too much for me," Susan said. "If it's for me."

"It's for your mother," my father said.

By all means, then, pile it on.

"It overwhelms me," Bennett said.

From beside him, leaning his way a little, Teddy pressed his teeth to his tongue and made the sound of a short wet fart.

"Teddy, please," my mother said.

"Who put you on to Mencken?" Father said.

"Mr. Edmond. He says it's time for a Mencken revival."

Mr. Edmond was Bennett's new English teacher that year. Already the kid idolized him.

"He was a first-rate journalist," my father said. "An interesting stylist."

"He was more than that," Bennett said. "Far, far more."

Down the table was passed a plate heaped with lamb, ringed with four small potatoes, smothered in thick gravy. Two hands, everybody. It's our mother's plate.

"Thank you, dear," my mother said.

"You're seriously undervaluing him," Bennett said.

Every evening was the same. My father looked forward to dinner more than to any other meal, probably any other moment, of the day. Through the late afternoon he sat sipping whiskey in anticipation while, all around him, the house slowly filled with the smells of cooking. Finally the great moment arrived, and at the crucial point, just as he was starting to serve, a voice began speaking to his right with whom he could not quite agree.

"That's too much for me," Susan said.

My father cut in half the already small slice of meat he had carved for Susan, beside it placed a miniature roast potato. No gravy.

That was all she could take.

"Throw that extra chunk on my plate," I said. "When you get there."

"He was extremely popular in his day," my father said.

"He had an enormous influence," Bennett said, just as if he had been there himself. "He saw so much about this country. And that prose!"

Teddy, by not using his tongue, simply pressing his teeth to his lip, made the sound of a somewhat drier, somewhat louder fart.

"Really, Theodore," Susan said.

"Teddy," my mother said.

H. L. Mencken was a typical writer for my brother to admire. Bennett loved writers who had definite, even outrageous, opinions; who employed an elaborate prose style that somewhat distanced them from experience (pile up enough words and they'll never get at you); and who wielded an essay as if it were a bludgeon, felling victims all around. Bennett wielded a similar style. If words could kill, he would have been a mass murderer.

Within a couple of months, of course, Bennett would think of H. L. Mencken as a cigar-chomping primitive who should have been hauled to the outskirts of Baltimore and drowned in a vat of beer. Bennett was a literary enthusiast, cooling off to a writer as quickly as he had gotten fired up. At the time he was reading a new writer he praised him extravagantly, as if to justify his time in reading him at all.

He also may have employed such extravagant praise just to annoy my father.

My father's dilemma was difficult. On the one hand it was Sunday dinner. Roast lamb! and tiny green peas! On the other hand, he was a specialist in twentieth-century American literature (was it any accident that Bennett was making his way through that very period?) and had dedicated his life to forming responsible opinions, stating them in a reasonable way. To some extent, his vocation was at stake.

"He's really a kind of minor figure," he said. "He *was* extremely influential for a few years. Partly because of one of those lucky confluences of the man and his time, partly because he did have an original, if somewhat limited, voice. He's great fun to read. But he does not have deep insights. He will probably go down in the history of American literature, if he goes down at all, in a rather short paragraph."

"A rather long chapter," Bennett said, "if I'm the one to write it."

There seemed to be no doubt in his mind that he would be.

Using more pressure from his teeth, more force from his mouth, Teddy made the sound of an extremely dry, probably painful fart.

"That one hurt," I said.

My mother said not a word.

Needless to say, there was a quiet side and a rambunctious side to our table. At the opposite corner from me, a struggle was taking place between a father and son that, in its own way, was as vicious as if they were trying to decapitate one another with a baseball. Beside them, the youngest child, who would spend his life wanting to enter into the spirit of the family and never quite making it (what the hell did he know about H. L. Mencken?), was trying to draw the action his way by making himself a royal pain in the ass. At the opposite corner from him was the oldest child, a girl, who had seen the family become what it was and was doing her best to stay apart from it. She took in as little as she could.

The major peacekeeping force was down in my corner. My mother kept a hand—a rather ineffectual hand, to be sure—on Teddy. She kept an eye—what she hoped was a soothing eye, a cautionary eye—on my father. No peacekeeper on earth could have had much effect on Bennett. She arranged the table harmoniously; she sang soothing melodies all day long; she cooked large amounts of delicious food, as if to smother the fires that were smoldering everywhere.

All her efforts, unfortunately, did not have much effect, except in one case. One member of the family sat at her end of the table, calmed by her spirit, watching the conflicts in the family but not entering into them, and eating, eating.

If I really was my mother's child, as everyone said, I don't think it was because I was fat. I don't think it was because I was blond and fair, or greatly influenced by her, or especially under her thumb (though all those things, to some extent, were true). I think that the first son is the father's child, that he bears the burdens and hopes and responsibilities of the family, that he meets life head on, develops earlier than the other children: he is the one to take on the father. The second son is likely to be a watcher. He sits back from the situation and sees it all happen, he doesn't enter into it because it is happening too soon for him, and because he sees how awful it all is, he sees the consequences of it all. He would like to stop it if he could; he makes vows (in secret concert with his mother) never to cause such an uproar when he is older; he does what he can to keep the peace, to defuse a potentially explosive situation and release the tension.

In my case, he tried to defuse the situation by making jokes. Laughter being a notorious tension releaser.

A well-known aphorist—also famous, as a matter of fact, as an only son—once said, Blessed are the peacemakers. He may just have been stating an opinion, of course, making what we call a value judgment, but if he intended a statement of fact I'm not at all sure he was right. The peacemakers often have ulcers, for one thing. I wouldn't be surprised if they tend to be overweight (got to throw something down there to soak up the gastric juices). Even worse, I think, is that the peacemakers are often trying to keep something from happening that needs to happen. They are avoiding conflicts that they themselves need to go through. And they become stunted. Afraid of life. They grow out, so to speak, instead of up.

It wasn't just a father throwing a baseball at a son that left me aghast.

"I don't think we should be having this argument at the table," my mother said.

Right. Let's all stuff ourselves instead.

"We're not arguing," my father said, his face giving off a slight tremor. "We're just discussing."

"Then how do you explain that knife in your hand?" I said.

He looked my way and smiled weakly.

"I don't see why you never see my side," Bennett said.

Because it's always wrong, dummy.

As if every other sound had been a prelude, an omen, a prefiguring, Teddy actually farted.

"Oh God," Susan said.

"Theodore!" my mother shouted.

"And there goes the bell for round three!" I shouted.

"I just don't see how you can sell a man short who has such a way with words!" Bennett shouted.

Did he never hear anything?

Sharply, and clearly, my father struck his water glass with his fork. "That's enough now, Teddy," he said. "And everyone. It's time for the blessing."

He stood above us, saying one of the short and simple prayers he always composed on the spot.

"Father. We thank you for a bountiful harvest." No thanks were ever more heartfelt. "We thank you for this day." Especially that it's almost over. "We thank you for each other." In the abstract. "We pray that we will always be together." I can state unequivocally that this prayer was answered. You could go to the South Pole and not get away from that family. "Amen," he said.

"Amen," we all said.

He sank back in his chair and gazed at the woman who had spawned this family. "Darling," he said. "This looks like another wonderful meal."

III

"I think it's wonderful the way Bennett works," Father said. "Dinner's over, things are cleaned up, and no sooner do you turn around than he's up in that bedroom studying."

"Yep," I said. Could you keep it down, Dad? I'm trying to read *Sports Illustrated* here.

Everyone had resumed his previous place after dinner, Bennett and Susan and Teddy upstairs, I in the living room with my father, who had taken up his book. My mother had joined us, doing needlepoint; she and her work were spread out all over the chair opposite him.

"Henry studies," my mother said. She stabbed at her needlepoint. "He studies enough. Not everyone was meant to be a straight-A student."

"I never said a word about Henry." My father looked up innocently. "I was just marveling at Bennett."

"I thought you were implying something."

"Of course not."

My mother took a sip from her beer. My father also had one. They were amazing. All that dinner, ice cream with the pie, a shared pot of coffee afterward, and they still found room to sip beer throughout the evening. It took years of hard work to achieve such powers of ingestion.

"I sometimes think Bennett works too hard," my mother said.

"I know you do." In other words, don't bring it up again.

"It isn't necessary, at the age of fourteen, to be studying far into the night. It isn't healthy, in my opinion. I hate to see a boy who's barely a teenager working as if he's a first-year medical student."

It was true. Sometime within the past few years Bennett's teachers had introduced him to the concept of homework: a fearful yearning had come into his eyes as he began to grow fangs and snarl. He spent all evening at it, every evening; he was still bent over the table sometimes when my parents were ready for bed (my father pried him away with a crowbar). There was an infamous history teacher in eighth grade who gave wicked quizzes, the bane of every eighth grader's existence; at the end of that year, Bennett's quiz average stood at 9.87. They lowered the flag to half-staff when he missed a question. That same year, one May evening when we were out shooting baskets, Bennett's French teacher had called after grading his exam—apparently she was too overcome to go on—to say that on a two-hour exam, testing three years of work, Bennett had missed not a single thing. Not one accent wrong. A hundred percent.

I was only surprised he hadn't done better.

It was the same with other things. Several years before, he had read an article about the eccentric teaching methods of a basketball coach in the eastern part of the state, and that afternoon he was out on our backyard court in a bulky sweatshirt, heavy boots, winter gloves, his sunglasses down on his nose and covered with tape so he couldn't see the ball, while he dribbled through an obstacle course of folding chairs on his way to the hoop. In the same get-up he practiced his jump shot from the corner, the single dribble, the little leap, the flick of the wrist. Swish. Again and again. The kid had enormous energy.

Nobody mentioned the psychic energy it took to be the brother of this person.

"You make it sound as if I encourage him to study that hard," my father said.

"You do encourage him. You push him in that direction."

"I want my sons to do well in school. I want them to get good grades, so they can go on and have interesting careers, and be happy. I don't see anything wrong with that."

"Staying up every night to the point of exhaustion and ruining his health isn't going to make Bennett happy."

This was not, of course, a discussion that had never taken place before. It took place often, in fact, on evenings when I was sitting around downstairs and Bennett was upstairs studying. My father was a plodder, a self-made man who had taken average ability and fashioned a fine career out of it. He had written important monographs on several minor American poets and was about to be made a full professor at the age of forty. My mother, on the other hand, was a woman of unusual and far-ranging abilities. She painted, she sang, she played the cello, she was a wonderful cook, she had raised four children by the most progressive methods, she acted in amateur theatricals, she had written two unpublished children's books. She had taken extraordinary talents and managed to spread them out into mediocrity. She was someone who did not so much care to be an artist as to act the artist, the center of attention, the three-hundred-pound diva whom everyone fluttered around in admiration. She didn't seem to care that it was just one more little-theater production of *Oklahoma!*

All our lives these two influences would pull us in opposite directions. The plodding scholar who knew he had a great deal to do, a great many hours to study, before he ever accomplished anything. The prima donna who thought she had already accomplished a great deal just by being alive.

"I don't encourage Bennett to stay up late," my father said. His face wore a pained, vulnerable expression. "I often suggest he take it easy. Get some sleep."

"I don't want to see another of my sons pushed into being a compulsive worker."

I solemnly swore at that moment never to give my mother cause for such worry.

Still, it was easy enough to see what was creating tension between my parents. The proper road for a peacemaker was clearly marked. Anyway, the pleasure of reading a sports magazine in the presence of my father had been severely diminished.

"I guess I'll go up and do some homework," I said, standing.
"Might as well get an early start." My father beamed at me.
"*Enjoy* your work, darling," my mother said.

And if you don't enjoy it, she seemed to be saying, don't do it.

I should have told her, sometime, that it was she who was laying an impossible burden on me. It was hard enough just to do that stuff. I could never have enjoyed it.

Upstairs there was a peculiar silence. Susan was in her attic suite—she never made any noise up there—and Teddy, in the television room, had the volume way down. Bennett had probably stepped in to lower it about sixteen times. In the vicinity of the bedroom hung the odd hush that one finds in the vestibule of a chapel.

I opened the door and entered. "Don't make any noise," Bennett said. "Close the door behind you. Don't take a lot of time getting settled. I'm working."

No kidding. Apparently hell hadn't frozen over yet.

Bennett was hunched over his work at our study table the way a bulldog hunches over a beefsteak. Step within lunging distance and you can say goodbye to your leg. He always sat in precisely the same position, on the edge of the chair, his back straight as a die, while a stream of light shone over his shoulder from the lamp. He stared down at his work, but also kept flipping his eyes up at me, to let me know his timer was running.

"Lift it, will you?" Bennett said. I had started to drag my book bag to the table. I lifted. "You're not going to write, are you?"

"I don't know."

"It jiggles the table. I've got reading to do."

He was running through his mind the hundreds of ways I might be about to disturb him.

Actually, I had no idea what I was going to do. It was Sunday evening, and I always tried—very successfully, I might add—to keep all thoughts of homework out of my mind over the weekend. Let it come as a surprise. There was probably a term paper due the next day.

I lifted the massive ancient history text out of my book bag and put it on the table.

"Jesus!" Bennett bolted from his chair as if I'd dropped the book on his balls. He started snatching books and papers from all over the table, holding them to his bosom as if they were his child.

"What's wrong?" All I had done was put the book on the table.

"What's wrong?" Already he had gathered about twenty pounds of material, was headed toward the door. "Jesus!" He slammed his way out.

It didn't really matter, of course. Sooner or later it happened every evening. This was the same kid who had once moved away from me in a movie theater because I was breathing too loud. Without his example to shame me I forgot about the table, dragged my books over to the easy chair, and plopped down there.

My theory of studying that year was that you started with what you didn't like, that what you enjoyed would act as a lure to draw you through what you detested. In practice, that was like sitting down to a bowl of sawdust before you began a sumptuous meal. I sat in the easy chair to read a chapter of my ancient history text (Bennett's specialty) but began to realize things weren't going too well when I was still on the third page an hour and fifteen minutes later. I turned to the back and looked at the first of fourteen study questions (we were to answer them all in full), but it seemed to have nothing to do with what I'd read. I figured I'd copy somebody else's before school. The math assignment concerned fractions. Halfway through I ran downstairs for a snack (Bennett glared from the dining-room table), whipped up a quick chocolate sundae and at the last minute threw on a few peanuts. All those fraction problems were basically the same, but I still managed to get stuck on the last three (dashed downstairs for a few more nuts). The French assignment was the irregular verb (give it a laxative). List after list of bizarre endings. I stared at them for a while. I decided the English assignment would go a little better with a few oatmeal cookies. I went downstairs and got five. Halfway through "The Luck of Roaring Camp," I realized it had also been in the previous year's short-story anthology (it would also be in the following year's), but I finished it anyway, after running downstairs to get some milk to go with the cookies (grabbed three more while I was down there). "It's no wonder you never get anything done," Bennett said during this fourth trip. "You're never up there." His major sustenance through a long evening of study was bottle after bottle of Vernor's ginger ale. The fizz firing up his nose probably kept him alert. I enjoyed "Roaring Camp" so much that I read three more stories from the anthology, then reread two from the previous year's. I would have liked to have some more cookies, but didn't want to give Bennett the satisfaction. Anyway, it was time for bed.

Far into the night, when most of the world was fast asleep, a solitary visitor crept into my room. "Henry?" he said. "Henry? You're not awake, are you Henry?" Actually, it was this question itself that often woke me up. Sometimes I answered and sometimes I didn't. Either way, the same thing happened. A lamp was turned on, and Bennett began a slow tour of the room, the same elaborate journey, in fact, every night. The books placed in a particular spot on the dresser, turned always in the same direction. A trip to the bathroom for ten minutes of tooth brushing (sometimes I got up and shifted the books slightly, in the hope of driving him out of his mind), followed by a visit to the jar of hand cream beside his bed (all that outdoor basketball left the hands chapped, to say nothing of the eighteen times a day he washed them), where he followed a ritual as elaborate as the Eleusinian mysteries. Finally the books were checked, the clothes, the watch (and tapped eleven times, or whatever it was), the lights snapped out. With all his rituals completed, Bennett fell asleep immediately.

Sometimes I lay awake for hours.

IV

On the day of the big game with the ninth grade, as it turned out, nobody could hit my fastball. They had showed up with eleven guys, grinning and confident, while we came up with seventeen—it meant more to us than it did to them—though we only used nine. I never had learned a curveball, but I probably wouldn't have used it if I had, my fastball was hopping so much. Sam was dancing around and chattering back at shortstop, shouting encouragement, up on his toes with every pitch, but he only had one ball hit at him all day, a little nubber that anybody could have made the play on.

Unfortunately, there were two other hits that nobody could have made a play on. The ninth grade had a big left-handed first baseman named Lampley, a dumb kid with a jaw like a bucket, who finally flunked out at the end of that year. He was a good-natured guy, a little slow-moving, who wore a genuinely friendly smile as he lumbered up to the plate, laid his bat on it to measure his stance. He wasn't slow with the bat, though, hit two towering shots way over the head of the right fielder. They were almost as impressively high as they were long. His third hit almost tore the glove off our second baseman, bounded into center field. Poor Lampley had to settle for a double.

After the game, in all seriousness, Sam looked me in the eye and said, "You pitched a three-hitter."

"Yeah," I said. "But what hits."

Our team couldn't do anything with their pitcher. Sam got a single and a double, stole two bases, but nobody else even got on. It ended 2–0.

Bennett played right field for the ninth grade. He had not gone to the game with me, but showed up later, on his own. There was a lot of hooting and hollering from both sides when he came up, brother against brother. Bennett wasn't much of a batter anyway—striking out almost anyone else was more of a feat—but I had never beaten him at anything in my life, and every time he swung and missed I felt a gaping hole like a pain in my chest. I could see him visibly tighten with every strike. He fanned three times. The last time, he almost fell down on the third swing, and then he threw a fit, bouncing around behind the plate as if he were on a pogo stick. Everybody was shouting, screaming with laughter, but when Bennett wanted to throw a fit he threw it, he didn't care who was watching.

Eventually, as a grand finale, he took a roundhouse cut at a side of the backstop, caught it down around the bat handle, and split the bat in half. That brought the house down (it was our bat). All over the field people were laughing until they cried, holding their stomachs, falling down—it was the funniest thing they had seen on the field in years—while I stood on the mound trying to grin, and trembled, trembled.

THREE

It didn't seem strange to me at the time, of course—friendships bloom naturally and artlessly among boys— but as I look back on it I can't help wondering at the fact that Sam and I became such good friends. I have no doubt it looked odd to people around us. There was Sam, small and dark and quick and good-looking, for whom every physical action, even the most intricate of maneuvers, was done with ease, and beside him he dragged this plump red-faced boy who looked as if he'd have trouble bending over to tie his shoe. I was funny, of course—I'd had all that training around the dining-room table—and I would take any kind of joke, come back with a harsher one at my own expense. You might have thought Sam kept me around because he looked good beside me, but Sam would have looked good beside anybody. I think Sam took me for a friend most of all because I was there, because I lived just a few blocks away and was glad, anytime, to come over and do something. He was the kind of kid who made the most out of what was around. He would have made a friend out of anybody.

He was also a kid who knew how to get around. That fall we traveled all over the city, and he knew the whole network of streetcars and buses. "This one'll get us pretty close," he'd say, stepping out onto Penn to flag a streetcar down, or, "We can transfer into town from Oakland." He seemed never to want to let a car go by, as if that showed some lack of imagination on the part of the traveler.

Sometimes we were just going into East Liberty, to one of the ancient movie theaters down there, where rats scurried after stray popcorn in the aisles, and the roar of a passing freight momentarily drowned out the soundtrack. Or we went the other way, into Wilkinsburg, which for some reason was still a little haven of duckpin bowling, those fat little pins that didn't explode when you hit the pocket, just scattered politely all around. We traveled into Oakland, where the universities were, for football games on Saturday—that long walk down the hill in the autumn air after the game, through crowds and dead leaves in the early dusk—but also to an athletic association where Sam's father belonged and where we could shoot baskets, or to a bowling alley down on Forbes where you had to take an ancient open-air elevator up to the lanes.

Downtown was even better, with department stores and novelty shops and pool halls and just the streets to wander through. We tried to get into burlesque houses—you were supposed to be eighteen—and if that failed tried movie theaters for the children's price (under twelve). In the novelty shops you could deposit a quarter into a machine and watch a bare-breasted woman do what seemed to be an exercise routine, pouting at the camera all the while. Squirrel Hill had the best places to eat. "Great corned-beef sandwiches in here," Sam would say, ducking into a door, or, "The best slice of pizza in Pittsburgh." Sometimes I thought he just read those things off the signs. But we ate in a great many places that autumn, went through a huge variety of foods. Sam was game for anything.

Our favorite place to bowl was down a little side street halfway to East Liberty, on the second floor above a car-parts shop.

I was genuinely surprised the first time we went. I'd passed that street hundreds of times, never noticed a bowling alley there. It was just like Sam to have found it. You walked in a little door around to the side, up a cement stairway that was dim and dingy and spattered with urine, stepped into an intimate establishment that was surprisingly well kept. There were eight lanes, painstakingly waxed and polished. At the back were food machines and drink machines and pinball machines and a jukebox. The lanes had automatic pinsetters, which were fairly new in those days, and little blowers where you could push a button and dry your hand. There was chalk, too, and a towel, and a little plastic ball that you spun around to produce moisture. Wet, dry, warm, chalky: any way you wanted your hand, you could have it.

On the counter below the register was a sign. "All Day Bowling. 11:00 A.M. to 6:00 P.M. $2.50. It's the Only Way to Go."

We thought All Day Bowling sounded like a hell of a deal.

The first time we bowled there, Sam mentioned one thing about the place as we approached it. "This is strictly a spade joint," he said.

"What?"

"It's colored guys who run it. Colored guys who bowl there. Even the owner's a dinge, as my father would say. That doesn't bother you, does it?"

"Not if it doesn't bother them." I'd never been to such a place.

"No. They like little white boys like you."

"I bet."

"Your money's green. That's all they're worried about."

All that autumn it became a rallying cry for us, one of those things you say to a friend just for the sake of saying something. "All Day Bowling," I'd say, passing Sam in the hall at school.

"It's the only way to go," he'd say.

When Bennett, in the evening, was hovering over the table in his solemn pose of concentration, I'd walk in on him and say, "All Day Bowling is the only way to fly."

"Don't take too long getting settled," he'd say.

Finally Sam and I had talked about it so much that we had to do it. We never really asked ourselves if we wanted to. We chose a Saturday early in December. There had already been a couple of substantial snowfalls that week, then on Friday night a cold spell set in, so the sidewalks were treacherous, but the streets pretty clear, as we trudged our way down. When we told the proprietor we wanted to go All Day Bowling he didn't know what we were talking about. We had to bring him around to the front of the counter to show him the sign. There wasn't another soul in the alleys when we started; they were all dark except for our single lane, at the far end.

At first we were perfectly serious—we saw this as an opportunity to work on our game—and we bowled four straight games, the most that I, at least, had ever bowled in a row. The third games were our best; the fourth was down a little. We took a break for lunch, told the proprietor we'd be back. Sam knew of a little hole in the wall down that way that made its own hot dogs, long and thin and tough-skinned, so you had to bite them hard; we both had one with sauerkraut and one with chili and cheese. By the time we got back the alleys were starting to jump. It was Saturday afternoon, and kids were there, families, working men in big loud groups.

It was a bit of a bizarre feeling, being the only white kids in a black establishment. We did have that far lane, so we were out of the way. Black bowlers were different from the white bowlers I'd been around. They made a lot more noise for one thing, shouting at strikes, screaming in hoots of laughter at a bad shot. They danced around at the line using body English. They took more time over the game, discussed what each frame meant before they rolled it, stood around analyzing it afterward. Men clustered around the scorer's table smoking, talking, and laughing. Long clouds of smoke drifted above the lanes.

Sam and I might as well not have been there. The other bowlers took no notice of us at all. They never watched, no matter what we did; they never spoke to us; if they happened to glance our way they didn't seem to see us. We could have thrown our clothes off and bowled naked for all they cared. The first lane just seemed to be vacant that day.

I had never known how tiring bowling could be until I had bowled four games and still had a whole afternoon of it staring me in the face. Our scores were steadily going down. My fingers started to bleed after a while, and my back ached; my lead foot was starting to go on me. By five o'clock I thought I never wanted to see a bowling ball again. We had been taking frequent breaks for grape drinks, potato chips, Milk Duds, ice-cream sandwiches. Sometimes we stopped to watch the people around us. We bowled an entire game left-handed, rolled the ball with two hands, between our legs, we ran up together and bowled two balls at once. Finally, at five-forty—twenty minutes short of our goal—we got kicked out, because Sam rolled the ball before the automatic pinsetter had finished. The ball made a terrible metallic crunch, hitting it. Sam always insisted afterward that he had not hit the thing on purpose.

"That All Day Bowling," he said. "It'll do something to you."

We were a little giddy by the time we stumbled down the cement steps to the door, our bodies aching and bloated with junk food. My face felt swelled and puffy, the way it gets when you've been inside by a heater all afternoon. We pushed through the door and were hit by a blast of arctic air. The slush and old snow lying around had frozen solid. All day long the sky had been gray and overcast; now the early winter dark had fallen, so the streetlights out on Penn were on. They shone on the frozen sidewalks with a silvery sheen.

As we walked down the three steps to the sidewalk, two guys stepped out from the side of the building and stood on either side of us.

I'm not sure at what point I realized what was happening. Two boys who have been out bowling all afternoon, having a big time, do not expect things suddenly to go wrong. They certainly don't want things to go wrong. I'm sure at first I tried to think there was a perfectly reasonable explanation for the sudden presence of those guys.

"You boys got any money for the streetcar?" one of them said.

The one who had spoken was standing beside Sam. He was taller than we were, but only slightly, looked about fourteen, wiry and thin. The guy on my side seemed older, lazy-eyed, snub-nosed, huge. He had wide shoulders, long arms, seemed to tower over us. He was crowding me a little, touching me with his body, so I was bumping into Sam.

My reaction to their presence had been to freeze, all my senses numbing, to curl in upon myself like a worm. In a couple of minutes I'd be lying on the ground in the fetal position. Sam, on the other hand, had grown suddenly alert, and also, oddly, relaxed, as if we had just bumped into a couple of casual acquaintances. The young man had asked a perfectly reasonable question under the circumstances.

"Nope," Sam said. "We don't have any money for the street-car. Don't have a cent, as a matter of fact."

"You seemed to be spendin' pretty good in there."

Experienced All Day Bowlers would have cased the joint for suspicious-looking characters.

"That's true," Sam said. "That's the whole problem, actually. We spent so much in there we don't have a thing left for the streetcar."

"How was you gettin' home, then?"

"Walking. Straight up Penn. Five or six blocks."

"Ain't you kinda young to be walkin' all alone after dark?"

Perhaps these two kind gentlemen had arrived to help us on our way.

The four of us had been moving—very slowly, of course, but moving, nevertheless—in the direction of Penn, toward the glare of the streetlights. Now the guy beside Sam put an arm on his chest, stopping him, and the guy beside me grabbed my arm—it felt as if his hand encircled it completely—and held it tight. Our procession came to a halt.

"Ah wont de money," the guy beside me said, slowly shaking my arm. "Ah wont it now."

I reached into my pocket for a handful of change and gave it to him.

Sam glared at me furiously, as if deeply ashamed that I had exposed him as a liar in front of those guys.

"Ah wont it all," the guy beside me said. He shook me harder. The next step was to pick me off the ground and bounce me up and down for a while.

At that point, I was convinced I was a dead man. My pocket—contrary to what Sam had said—was full of change, but I was certain that no amount of money I could pull out would satisfy that guy. I would keep handing him change, and he would keep shaking me harder and harder, and when I had finally given him everything he would snap my neck like a stick and leave me there as a warning to any other white kids who ever wanted to go All Day Bowling. Before me stood the wide avenue I had traveled hundreds of times in my life, past it the high brick wall of the National Biscuit Company—those incredibly fragrant smells of baking—but all was changed, the landscape that once I had known was altered beyond recognition, and I was standing on the spot where I would lose my life.

"Ah wont it all," the guy said, shaking me again.

I reached deep into my pocket and handed him every cent I had.

Sam's father, with his slum upbringing, had not wanted to raise a son who could not take care of himself. He was afraid that the boy, accustomed to luxury, would grow soft, and would not be as fit for the world as a less fortunate background would have made him. So he had arranged to have Sam take boxing lessons. Once a week, Tom Cognetti—our gym teacher from school!—came to the house and worked with him on the basics. He taught him to use the light bag, the heavy bag, to shadowbox; he sparred with him a little. He also taught him emergency self-defense—that was really the point of the thing—and imprinted in Sam's brain, in case he was ever stopped by a gang of kids, one basic strategy: hit the biggest one on the point of the chin with everything you've got, and run like hell.

I would have said kick him in the balls, but let's not quibble over technicalities.

Sam had to improvise slightly in this instance, to give himself some room. He turned to the kid who was standing beside him and gave him a quick smack on the shoulders—pop!—with the palms of his hands. The kid skidded back on the ice, stumbling; he must have been leaning back already. Sam whirled, like pivoting on a double play, and threw a straight right at the kid who was holding my arm. The kid's grip loosened. Sam had missed the point of his chin, struck him instead in the middle of the face. A spurt of blood gushed from his nose. Large tears appeared at his eyes.

"Awww," he seemed to say. "Gawww."

"Run!" Sam screamed.

I realize now that everything had depended on keeping us where we were. Nightfall or not, a side street toward East Liberty or not, you couldn't chase somebody down and mug him in full view of the lights of Penn Avenue. It was only about five steps we needed: once we were out of the shadows we were all right. At the time, however, I thought those guys would chase us to our doorsteps. Unfortunately, we were running on ice, the kind of ice that freezes from slush, with peaks and valleys, gaping crevices to twist your ankle in. Sam was doing pretty well, flatfooting along to keep his balance, but I was spinning like crazy, taking about four steps for every one I advanced. By the time we turned the corner onto Penn, Sam was fifteen yards in the lead and gaining fast. I did pick up some speed there, and noticed—Sam was shouting at it and waving his arms—that a streetcar was passing us. At almost the same moment I noticed I had slipped, was sailing through the air roughly parallel to the ground. "Ah!" I heard myself shout, as if hearing someone slightly behind me; I pitched forward onto the ice, crashed belly first, and—the impact was too much— threw up, a whole long afternoon's accumulation of junk food. I must have skidded ten yards. They wouldn't have any trouble picking up my trail. By the time I had scrambled to my feet and started running again, the streetcar was waiting for me. Sam was standing at the doors, making sure it didn't leave.

"I don't have any change," I said, as we climbed on.

"That's okay," he said. "I got it." He looked at the driver. "If you can break a ten."

I stared at him.

"You didn't think I was going to let that son of a bitch have ten dollars, did you?" he said.

He got the change and deposited the fares. We walked back to the sideways seats behind the driver.

For a while we didn't say anything, just sat there and caught our breath. Fortunately, since I had fallen slightly sideways, I wasn't all covered with vomit. I don't think Sam even knew I'd thrown up. I actually felt better for having thrown up, and for my brisk run in the cold evening air.

"That kid started to cry," I said, finally.

"Yeah," Sam said.

"I couldn't believe he started to cry."

Sam shrugged. "I hit him pretty hard."

We were quiet for a while. Sam was examining his knuckles.

"I wonder if that was their first time," I said.

Sam frowned, considering. "Might have been."

"That one guy looked a little nervous."

"They didn't exactly have their technique down."

There is a lot I can put back in that moment from the perspective of years, a lot I didn't know then. I can imagine the lives those boys might have come from, the difficult backgrounds. I remember the flimsy jackets they were wearing on a bitterly cold night, their bare hands. I can guess how they might have felt about us, spending freely money that would have meant a great deal to them. I can imagine the humiliation and desperation that lay behind what they did. In a way, though, I think I realized all that then, without being able to put it into words. In the moment of seeing the blood spurt, hearing that awkward cry of pain, I knew that guy wasn't a nigger, a mugger, some dark incomprehensible force. He wasn't someone far beyond my experience. He was a kid, like us.

The car approached our block, and we walked to the front and got off. Sam was heading one way from there, I another.

"Well," he said, standing under the streetlight, his hands in his jacket pockets. "That was quite a day."

"Quite a day."

He did something then that seems strange as I look back on it—two thirteen-year-old kids after a day of bowling—but at the time it seemed natural, and appropriate. He reached out to me and, rather solemnly, we shook hands, like two middle-aged business executives closing a deal.

"All Day Bowling," he said.

"It's the only way to go," I said.

We grinned. He turned and walked back toward the hill.

He hadn't made a big deal of it. That might have been the thing I liked most about Sam. That fall we'd been to pool halls, lunch counters, delicatessens, novelty shops, places I'd never been before, kinds of places I'd never been. I'm not sure Sam had either, but he took them in. He didn't act afraid, or scornful, or embarrassed, or superior; he didn't seem to be doing things just to widen his experience; he took it all in, watching, listening. It was his attitude toward experience—open and attentive—that seemed new to me.

Even walking back to the house seemed different. I was glad to be heading home, of course—I still liked the place—but always in the past it had been a haven for me, something I hurried back to. I wasn't in such a hurry anymore. As I picked my way over the icy sidewalk, I was glad to be out on that frigid night, to be breathing in the harsh air, glad to see the bright lights in the houses all around, even glad to be arriving a little late. I didn't think I'd explain myself. Somehow I knew Sam wouldn't be talking—I had the feeling he told his parents almost nothing—and I thought I'd keep that evening to myself, a little pocket of experience all my own.

Approaching my house, I knew my whole life didn't take place there. I was beginning to be at home also elsewhere.

II

My father never lost faith, never seemed in any way to lower his expectations. At the end of the week, I walked into the living room early in the evening, and he looked up at me and beamed. "It's Friday, Henry."

"Yep," I said, smiling weakly, as if he had named any old day.

"This is our night."

"Yeah," I said, vaguely.

"Susan's been practicing all afternoon. She and your mother are doing a new song."

"Oh," I said, looking through a pile of newspaper, "*that* night," though I'd known all along what he was talking about. "Friday night again." I didn't look at him. I picked up the sports pages and walked elsewhere to read them. Friday was the one night I didn't like to sit with him.

I don't know why I couldn't have been nicer about it. It wouldn't have taken much to pretend to be enthusiastic, or at least indifferent. There was something about the intensity of his expectations. I could never have lived up to them.

Some years before, my father had read—probably in *Time* magazine or someplace—that Mormon families were always close because they had a family night each week. The article he read was rather vague about what they did, made popcorn balls or bobbed for apples or performed some other suitably

American activity (perhaps they chatted about excluding women and blacks from the hierarchy of their church, another suitably American activity), but he thought it sounded wonderful. Not the content of the evenings, but the idea that one evening a week would be reserved for a family get-together. On a higher plane, in our case, than making popcorn balls.

My father's dream for his family was that it would be a cultural paragon. As he sat in the living room, sipping scotch or beer and reading his book, what he would have liked to picture was one child off in his room doing a pirouette, another composing a poem, a third practicing the flute, the fourth studying the lines of a play (the closest he ever came was when my mother was upstairs doing all four things at once). He never pushed us into such activities—he was far too progressive a parent for that—but he held them up as so plainly being admirable that we couldn't have missed.

It is interesting how we had all reacted at that point. Susan had a vague interest in all the arts; she could sit slouching around—a cigarette burning in her hand, her long hair hanging straight, a bored weary expression on her face—and discuss John Cage and Picasso and Cocteau by the hour. Whether or not she actually knew anything about these people was another question. She also constantly practiced the piano—she always seemed to be pecking at it—but she never did much with her talents; she never gave recitals. Bennett, on the other hand, had set about systematically absorbing all the arts. Already, at that age, he was reading through Shakespeare—he had finished the histories, moved on to the comedies—and was also listening through the symphonic repertoire; the next year he would move on to opera. He regularly visited the museum. I was an indiscriminate reader, but mostly of baseball and football and basketball magazines. Occasionally I stumbled across a work of literature. Teddy was devoted heart, soul, and eyeballs to the television.

Nevertheless, none of us could have claimed we hadn't been exposed to culture. The arrival of the Wilder family at a Friday-evening performance in Pittsburgh was a regular event; people actually looked for it. We went to symphony concerts at the Syria Mosque, sitting in the back toward the left or up in the first balcony. We attended free evenings at both universities: piano recitals, string quartets, poetry readings, plays. We went to dramas at the Playhouse, eating dinner first at the plush restaurant that adjoined it. We never missed Christmas performances of the *Nutcracker* and the *Messiah*, or performances by any dance troupe that came through the city, or the Civic Light Opera, or Jazz in the Park, or touring theater companies. As children we didn't have to enjoy such things—we could take along a book, or a pad and pencil to doodle with—but we did have to attend; we had to sit through them. The recent evenings when Susan was home from school, and Teddy was old enough to go—so that we all, all six of us, trooped into some cultural hotspot together—must have been among the proudest moments in my father's life.

Even more, though, I think he enjoyed those evenings when we stayed home and made culture for ourselves.

Such evenings took different forms. We had a long and difficult recorder period, during which we tried to make music together, everybody from my mother and Susan, who had studied for years, on down to me, who didn't know what the hell was going on. Within a few months those recorders were gathering dust in a closet somewhere. My secret ambition was to split them up for kindling. There were times we tried to do rather complicated sing-alongs with my mother directing. She could never be satisfied with a tune like "Row, row, row your boat"; she always had to drag out a Bach aria or something. Other times we all took parts and read a play aloud. That was probably the most fun. Teddy, strictly improvising, provided sound effects.

More often, those evenings were a kind of amateur hour. Susan would play whatever she had been practicing on the piano. My mother would sing a melody from *South Pacific* (Mary Martin two hundred pounds later). Bennett would read a poem he had composed. Teddy would act out a scene from a TV show. My father would read a classic American short story. For the most part I declined to do anything. It always seemed appropriate to me, in any setting, to be in the background, taking potshots at what was going on (I often did make amusing comments about the performances people were giving). Anyway, what the hell would I have done? Read aloud from a baseball magazine? Throw a fastball? Maybe I could have made everybody a chocolate sundae! My parents, at least, would have considered that a worthy art form.

On one occasion that winter, though—the first winter I knew Sam—our Friday evening was to be quite special, because Susan was home on vacation. She and my mother had cooked up an appropriate performance.

"The men will clean up tonight," my father said, pushing himself back from the dinner table. Before him sat the remains of two roast chickens that had been utterly demolished. "We'll do the dishes too." Speak for yourself, Pop. "But later. Right now you ladies need to get ready to perform."

"On a full stomach?" my mother said.

Was there any other kind?

"You can get yourselves ready," my father said. "Take as much time as you like. But I don't think our headline performers should be troubled with domestic duties."

"Bennett'll do it all," Teddy said.

Bennett didn't even deign to glare at him.

My mother must have been acting coy. She was ready to perform anytime, could probably have given a creditable performance even between courses, like a gypsy violinist, all the time clearing the table and preparing the next dish. That night she was dressed in a bright shift, a garment that just seems to be a long piece of cloth (in my mother's case, a very long piece of cloth) that is wrapped around a person repeatedly. I always wondered if maybe you laid the thing out and rolled yourself into it, like rolling up a rug. It was an ideal garment for my mother, since its many folds served in a way to conceal her massive bulk.

The one thing I never understood about these performances was how Susan felt about them. She always consented to perform in the living room, anytime she was home, though she never gave performances in public. She actually seemed to prefer performing with my mother, being in the background as an accompanist. She was always utterly impassive. She sat very stiff and straight before starting to play, and never looked at the audience; she always read music, even when she knew the

piece perfectly. She swayed around some when she played—
Teddy and I made fun of that, secretly—but she always just
seemed to be up there with the music, never projected to the
audience. She was playing for the sake of the music, not for
any people who might be there. She gave a polite little nod
when we applauded at the end.

That night she accompanied our mother in a medley of
songs. "Summertime" was the first word my mother sang, very
long and drawn out, and for a moment we started to laugh—
the temperature outside had dipped into the teens—but she si-
lenced us with a glance, and from then on we sat enraptured.
We really did love to hear our mother sing. She had a throaty
and genuinely beautiful soprano, not like the shrill amateur so-
pranoes you sometimes hear. She sang several more songs from
Porgy and Bess, and we had seen the movie, so we all felt a
little sad when she got to "Oh Lawd, I'm on my Way." On a
lighter note, she said, "Now I'd like to sing a few songs by a
man born right here in Pittsburgh," and broke into some tunes
by—not Henry Mancini, but—Stephen Foster, whose song
about the Sewanee River may actually have been inspired by
the muddy Monongahela. My mother's closing number may
have been a mistake. Even at its quietest, her voice was not a
soft sexy whisper, and Susan had trouble with the idiosyncratic
rhythm, and the overall texture of the song was marred by the
absence of Stan Getz's silky saxophone. All in all, it was something of a high-opera version of "The Girl from Ipanema."

"That one needs some work," Susan said.

"It was wonderful. Wonderful," my father said. He was definitely in his element, applauding loudly, clutching a huge
pipe between his teeth.

The rest of us, sitting on the floor, also applauded.

Next to perform was Bennett, who moved to the chair beside
the fireplace. He wore a solemn expression, as if he were about
to read from the scriptures; he did not look at us, but kept his
eyes fixed on the handwritten page. "I'd like to read a short
story," he said. "Mr. Edmond suggested I write it. It may be
part of a larger work. But it is also complete and self-con-
tained. It's called 'A Long Soft Jumper from the Corner.'"

"Wonderful," Father said. Everything was wonderful that night.

Teddy and I strained to keep from laughing.

Bennett's story leaned in the same general direction that all his writing did. It concerned a fourteen-year-old boy who was new at a school, who was lonely and scorned because he played the violin and wrote poetry and was more sensitive than everybody else. He also played basketball, had played it all his life—it was a sport that one could practice alone, while thinking lofty thoughts—and he had a wonderfully accurate jump shot from the corner. It was so good that he actually made varsity as a freshman. Unfortunately, either because he was sensitive or because he was so talented, his teammates didn't like him; they resented his extraordinary jump shot and conspired to make him look bad in practice.

Even at the age of thirteen, I knew something was wrong with the manner of Bennett's story, though I couldn't have said exactly what. The problem was that it was told at one remove, like an anecdote, and never broke into dramatic scenes. That would always be Bennett's problem as a writer of fiction; he could never get the story outside himself. He was born to be a lyric poet.

The story did hold my attention, though, and it dealt effectively with the emotions of its central character, and it had what struck me as an ingenious ending. As might be expected, the protagonist emerged as a star in the most important game of the season; his teammates forgot their petty jealousy and kept feeding him the ball for one perfect jump shot after another from the corner. With his team down by one, in the waning seconds of the game, he once again broke for the corner, and they fed him the ball. Unfortunately, a defender made a wild lunge, committing a glaring foul that for some reason the referee neglected to call; in any case, it delayed the play, so that when the hero was at the top of his leap, in the little pause that all the great jump shooters have, the buzzer sounded. The ball took off in its perfect arc and unerringly found the hoop, but the team lost anyway. The kid just stood staring at the basket in disbelief, while his teammates and coaches and all the people in the stands walked off and left him there.

Bennett was always happiest when he was miserable.

While he sat there looking deeply moved, we all applauded wildly.

"We want to do something," Teddy said.

"Who?" Father said.

"Henry and me," Teddy said.

"Wonderful!" Father said.

At that point, although I had thought the whole thing up in the first place, I would have chickened out. I had seldom done anything on the family evenings, but that week I had gotten an inspiration, and adopted Teddy as co-conspirator, since he was really the only one available. Actually, he was a born performer, and always would be; even at that point he could have done a medley of farts that would have brought the house down on *Ted Mack's Amateur Hour.* Now he ran to set things up—we needed two chairs and a card table—and I reluctantly went to help him. I wasn't sure we should be doing this.

In my defense, I will say that I had set up a more elaborate skit than the one we actually presented. It was to be slapstick and exaggerated, but I was hoping to make it a little more subtle, and I would certainly have made it last longer than seven seconds, or however long it actually did. Also, I would have reversed the roles: things would have looked more appropriate, and I think we would have given better performances. Teddy, however, insisted on being the star. He wouldn't perform at all if he couldn't be the center of attention.

The whole thing went very quickly. Teddy knelt in his chair, trying to look taller than I, and made mock carving motions. "Teddy, sit square in the chair," he said. "Teddy, stop making those noises."

Even when he was playing someone else, he directed attention toward himself.

Everyone laughed politely, no one with more delight than my father.

"An extra potato for my middle son," he said, handing an imaginary plate to his left. "Pass that down to fatso."

He was improvising, the little bastard.

I was not playing myself, however. I was sitting to his right, just beside him, and now spoke my first line. "I think H. L. Mencken is the greatest writer who ever lived."

"You crazy idiot!" Teddy shouted. And utterly departing from the script—I never found out whether he forgot his lines or what—he stood in his chair and took a flying leap at my head, knocking me out of my chair and sending us both to the floor.

"Teddy!" my father shouted.

"Boys!" my mother shouted.

Great comedians are born anarchists, who will tear down a whole room, or an entire culture, for a laugh.

I was all right. The living-room rug was thick. Teddy himself had a rather soft object to fall on (me). Only he, of everyone there, was really laughing, pushing himself off me with his hands on my face.

Bennett sat in the chair with his arms folded, shaking his head, muttering to himself.

We ended the evening on a lighter note, as always. My mother sat doing needlepoint in one of the chairs by the fireplace. Susan sat in the other, reading a book. Our little radio on the table in the corner was tuned to an FM station broadcasting a Haydn symphony. The four men of the family sat around the card table playing blackjack.

My father liked to ham it up at our card game. Somewhere he had bought the kind of green visor that card sharps wear; he was wearing that, and smoking a cigar. Teddy, in imitation of him, was wearing a baseball cap. It took Teddy forever to add his cards up, of course, and he inevitably—despite all the advice we gave him—kept shooting for twenty-one, no matter how high he got, so he nearly always went over. "God," he'd say, counting up on his fingers and shaking his head. "Over again."

When he wanted another, Teddy picked up his down card and brushed the table. Father rapped the table with his knuckles. I did that also, or said, "Hit me." Bennett, forgoing all idioms, said, "I'll take another."

As luck would have it, Bennett was having a rough time that night. At first he had tried to win by bluffing, sticking with a

high face card and low down card; when that didn't work he
played more conventionally and kept going over. He still
seemed moody, staring darkly at the table and not looking at
anyone, as if he had really been bothered by our skit (I had
trouble believing that) or as if he had really lived through the
experience he described in his story. He still seemed to be staring in disbelief at the basket while everyone walked away.

We had all started with the same number of chips, but his
pile was rapidly dwindling. Toward the end, though, he had
won two straight hands, and on the third was going for five
cards and under, which, according to our rules, would have
won him double the chips; we would all have to kick in again.
If he lost, however, he would have to kick in extra. I was deal-
ing, with Bennett to my right, Teddy across from me. Bennett
sat with his hands under the table, staring at his one card down
and three up.

"You got twelve showing," I said.

"I'll take another," he said.

I dealt him the queen of hearts.

"Strike three," I said.

"Christ!" Bennett banged the table in anger. Unfortunately,
his hands had been under it, not on top, so the table jumped,
tipped—cards flew, chips scattered everywhere—and fell into
Father's lap. Bennett bolted from his chair.

"Bennett!" Father shouted, clutching at the table as if it
were a life preserver and he were going under.

Bennett was already out of the living room.

"Here we go again," Susan said.

"Come back here, Bennett!" Father shouted.

Teddy and I had burst into whoops of laughter. Bennett was
dashing up the stairs, shouting bizarre sounds over his shoulder
like Hoo! and Ha! as he went.

"You wait a minute, Bennett!" Father was trying also to bolt
out of his chair, but he did, after all, have a card table in his
lap, and he was also weighed down by the huge dinner he had
eaten. In his struggle to rise, he was actually pulling the table
back on himself. Finally, however, he pushed it away and
stood.

Bennett had long since disappeared to his room.

"Let him go, dear," Mother said.

"Let him go? He ruined our whole game."

"His feelings were hurt. He's been battling his brothers all night."

At that moment, in fact, we were tasting the fruits of victory, rolling around in our chairs and laughing our heads off.

"All he did was lose a hand," Father said. "This was our Friday evening."

His dream of a harmonious cultured family had been shattered again.

"His brothers hurt his feelings with the skit," Mother said.

"No," Susan said. "He likes that kind of attention. I think he was disappointed with his story."

"But we loved his story," Father said.

Mother stared at Susan. "Did he say he was disappointed?"

"I could just tell."

Susan, who never gave the slightest hint of how she felt about her own performances, could tell about Bennett.

"That doesn't seem any reason to upset our whole game," Father said.

"Would you quit talking about your game?" Mother said.

Father seemed abashed. "I'll certainly go speak to him. I really did admire his story."

"I think Susan should go," Mother said, stabbing at her needlepoint.

"*Susan* should go?"

"They understand each other."

Father looked bewildered. Up until then, he had probably thought he understood Bennett.

"Well. All right. Do tell him I liked his story, though."

"Tell him we all liked his story," Mother said.

"I thought he should have let the kid win the game," Teddy said.

"I'll talk to him," Susan said. "I don't think he'll come back down."

Later, in the kitchen, I was washing, Teddy was rinsing, and Father was drying.

"Maybe you shouldn't have done that skit," Father said.

"Okay," I said.

"Not that I didn't think it was good." Far be it from him to stifle our creativity. "And I was delighted you wanted to do something." Now pat me on the head, Dad. "But it might have hurt Bennett's feelings."

"He hurts our feelings all the time," Teddy said. "He calls Henry fat."

"Shut up, Teddy," I said.

"Bennett's sensitive," Father said.

I was never sure what everybody meant by that. I wasn't sure they knew what they meant. Maybe they meant Bennett was nuts.

"Like the kid in the story," I said.

"He was trying to tell us something with that story," Father said.

I had meant my remark to be ironic, but Father hadn't noticed.

"He's no more sensitive than I am," Teddy said.

Nobody mentioned—though I had certainly noticed—that Bennett's extraordinary sensitivity had once again gotten him out of washing the dishes.

III

Our school made a number of subtle statements about our lives, about where we lived and what we lived for. The building had once been someone's house, which was a not so subtle statement in itself. It was an enormous eccentric place, with three wings, narrow hallways leading to rooms of assorted sizes. In the body of the building was a sweeping staircase, wide enough for eight or nine people to walk down abreast. It slowly made a forty-five-degree turn, and as it did it passed a window that must have been a story and a half high and about that wide—squared off into smaller panes, of course—that looked out on the front courtyard. That was an ideal stairway for a couple hundred early adolescents to run up and down on between classes, but it was a little hard to imagine someone actually living with it, tripping down those stairs in the morning, say, for a fried pie or a few chilled sugar doughnuts. At the bottom of the stairs was a marble-floored room that we used as a study hall—rows of long tables that drowsy kids sat around, trying to work—but that the owner of the house must have used as a drawing or sitting room. It was terribly cozy. All he had to do, for instance, if he wanted to check on the weather was run halfway up the stairs and look out the story-and-a-half window.

The students dressed in jackets and ties. As early as the age of eleven. We stripped ourselves of them rather easily (that first day, for instance, Sam hadn't been catching punts in a jacket and tie), and we didn't always act as if we had them on—sprinting to get somewhere, or breaking into scuffles in the hall—but we did wear them. We also carried briefcases. There were so many books to transport that you had to carry something, and briefcases were somewhat in style for school kids in those days, and our briefcases hardly looked neat, stuffed sometimes so full of books and papers that the seams were starting to split. But they were briefcases. At eleven, and twelve, and thirteen, and fourteen, we were already wearing jackets and ties, carrying briefcases, preparing ourselves for the careers—as doctors, lawyers, corporate businessmen—that would someday allow us to live in houses just like that.

One morning that winter, however, I was standing at the railing above the sweeping stairway, staring out the huge window at a gentle snowfall, blinking back tears, as if I were the poor little rich kid who occupied the place, all dressed up and nowhere to go.

"What the hell are you crying for?" Sam said.

"I'm not crying." I sniffed slightly as I spoke.

"No. You're not crying. You're not crying at all. Excuse me while I get a mop. I don't want anybody to slip in the puddle here and fall over the railing."

We were standing essentially alone up on that landing. Now and then some poor lost soul would wander past, but not often. Furthermore, the building around us was quiet. That was an ominous sign. We had four minutes to change classes, and during most of that time there was a rumbling throughout the building as if the place were about to blow apart. When that rumbling finally stopped, the bell was about to ring.

We were going to be late.

The thing of it was, we had gotten out of our previous class with minutes to spare. Our ancient history teacher, Mr. Friedman, had finished early and—not seeing any reason to put off his cigarette between classes—told us we could leave as long as we promised not to make any noise in the hallways. We promised.

I didn't recognize it then—I hardly knew anything about politics in those days—but I can look back on Mr. Friedman now and see him as a classic early-sixties liberal intellectual. If he didn't know Allard Lowenstein he knew someone exactly like him. He sported the kind of clothes that I think of now as Ivy League—the light sport jacket worn very casually and always left unbuttoned, more like a cardigan sweater; the necktie all of about an inch and a quarter wide—and smoked filter-tipped cigarettes, holding the end between his teeth like a little cigar when he lit up. The man was cool. He was light-haired and quite bald, just a fringe of short hair around the sides and at the back, but he had a distinctly handsome and youthful-looking face. He invariably wore a relaxed and friendly smile.

His course, however, was an absolute bitch. The text was a six-pounder that played a major role in bursting the seams of those briefcases, and twice a week we had wicked quizzes on our reading. The tests were also killers, complete with true/false, short-answer, multiple-guess, and essay questions. That spring we were scheduled to do a term paper. In short, we were taking a college course at the age of thirteen. Nothing I did in school would ever seem as hard again.

The day he let us out early, while everyone else crept out of the room in relief—he wasn't going to pop a quiz on us, thank God—Sam leaned back in his chair and turned my way. "Let's stay a few minutes and bullshit with Friedman."

It was all right with me. I liked the man fine once class was over.

"Hey, Mr. Friedman," Sam said, when everybody else was gone. "Who was that girl I saw you with the other day?" He slid out of his chair and walked toward the front.

"Girl?" Mr. Friedman already had the cigarette between his

teeth, was grinning around it as he applied the lighter. "I don't remember any girl."

Mr. Friedman was known for escorting glamorous women. Students had seen him all over town. If a knowledge of ancient history brought that kind of reward, bring on the textbook.

"Downtown. On Saturday. Over around Mellon Square."

"Mellon Square. Downtown. Saturday." Mr. Friedman rubbed his chin, utterly mystified. "You're sure this was me."

"It was you all right. I saw the glare two blocks away."

Friedman didn't mind jokes about his bald head. He made them all the time himself.

He was still touching his chin. "I think it's coming back to me. A woman about my height. Stunning blond hair down to her shoulders. A navy-blue overcoat. Hazel eyes."

"I didn't see her eyes. But the rest of her sounds about right."

"That was no girl," Friedman said. "That was my sister."

We were both standing in front of him by then, while he sat back on a corner of his desk, filling the air with smoke.

"That was no sister," Sam said. "That girl was goyim."

Mr. Friedman broke into a broad grin.

That was where I started to get lost. I understood the joke about seeing a teacher with a woman. After all, you never really expected a teacher to have a life outside the school. He stayed around his class all weekend, sleeping on a cot in the corner, cooking his meals on a hotplate, until it was time for class to start again on Monday. Anyway, what would a teacher do with a woman? Would he give her a quiz, or what?

The thought of a teacher actually screwing a woman was absolutely hilarious.

But this new word that the two of them were starting to use threw me off. (It did not, incidentally, sound like a real word. More like a mispronunciation. The result of a speech impediment.) It apparently had some major significance. There seemed to be a little sexual innuendo going on here.

I just stood there grinning, though. Far be it from me to admit ignorance.

"She was a friend of my sister's," Mr. Friedman said.

"You let your sister go out with goyim?"

"As long as she's careful. We wouldn't want her living next to one."

"Some of my best friends are, though."

"Goyim? Or living next to them?"

"Both."

This word was about to drive me nuts.

"To tell you the painful truth," Sam said, "my father married goyim."

"Your father's not Orthodox?"

"He's not much of anything. But some of his family is. It's been quite a hot topic around our house, through the years."

"I bet. So you're a man without a country."

"A school like this is about as comfortable as I get."

There was a broad acceptance of anyone with money at that school, a liberal sprinkling of Jews among the rest of us. I had finally figured out that was roughly what they were talking about, though I still didn't know what that word meant. I didn't even know how Sam was so sure Mr. Friedman was Jewish. That was how little such things were discussed at my house.

Though the two of them had been talking to each other, I had the peculiar feeling they were making fun of me.

"Anyway, Rabbi Friedman," Sam said, "how about telling us our midterm averages?"

Uh-oh. This was where I came in.

"You know I don't give out those averages."

"Not to just anybody. But to your special friends. The kind of kids you sit around and talk to after class."

"As if I had any choice."

Mr. Friedman was still grinning, though. Sam could charm anybody.

I turned and headed for my briefcase. "We'd better get going, Sam."

"I don't want to get going. I want to hear my average."

"You can figure out your own averages," Mr. Friedman said.

You certainly could. That was why I wanted to get going.

"I want to hear you say it. The voice of authority."

"If I say this thing, will you let me finish my cigarette in peace?"

"We won't even tell Mr. Hollings you let us out of class early."

Mr. Hollings was the headmaster.

"It's a deal," Mr. Friedman said.

He was already looking through his little blue book. "Goyim, Sam," he said. "I mean, Golden, Sam." He stared, frowning. "Looks like about a B plus."

"B plus! That's what you always say! What do I do to get an A around here?"

"Practice, practice."

"I did practice. I studied my fool head off."

"It's close. It really is very close. I may have to get my dart board out on this one."

As a matter of fact, Sam was as excellent a student as he was an athlete. He was equally competitive about both activities—he checked the honor-roll list as avidly as he did the basketball stat sheet—and he went about the two in much the same way. In study hall, while everyone else was staring off into space, plotting to steal one another's books, conducting a spitball war, he actually took out a book and did an assignment. What a novel idea!

I, on the other hand, was one of the kids staring around aimlessly (I noticed Sam's strange behavior out of the corner of my eye). I had managed somehow to struggle through the first term of Mr. Friedman's course with a C. Having been emphatically warned by Bennett, I hadn't gotten killed by the early quizzes (as other people had, not knowing how picky they would be). I had also studied myself blind for the exam. But early in the winter term I had slacked off—so relieved was I not to have flunked the fall—and I let a couple of reading assignments go by altogether. That didn't help the old quiz average any. I was actually in deep dread of that midterm report.

Still, I was standing back by my briefcase hoping against hope that Mr. Friedman had forgotten to record the bad quizzes, that he liked me so much he would just overlook them, that he knew I was basically a C student and would give me the benefit of the doubt, that he would look at the wrong line and give me some other student's average, anything. We never really believe a catastrophe can happen to us, even when the runaway truck is only a few feet away.

"Looks like a D." Mr. Friedman had reddened, biting his lip.

I nodded, picked up my briefcase, and walked toward the door. Instantly, as if someone had slapped my face, tears came to my eyes.

"A *D*?" Sam stared in disbelief. "How the hell did you get a D?"

"It was easy." I looked vaguely toward Mr. Friedman—that bald guy on the other side of the waterfall—while my face collapsed all around me. "No chance to bring it up?"

"Not before midterm. After that, of course. But you had that one low quiz."

"Yeah."

"How low was it?" Sam said.

"A one," I said. My face convulsed into a feeble smile. Please pass the shit. Mr. Friedman and I weren't mentioning the four.

"A *one*?" Sam started quietly to laugh, as if one of us had farted. "How the hell did you get a one?"

"I forgot to do the reading."

"But there's always reading. That's like forgetting to put on your pants."

I was already out the door and in the hall. I couldn't stand to face those guys.

"You'll pull it up after midterm, Henry," Mr. Friedman called after me.

I walked through a door out to that main landing of the second floor, stopped there to collect myself.

People from stupid families won't understand—I'm sure that in some households a D in ancient history is an honorable tradition—but I just couldn't imagine what would happen in my house when that report card arrived. Screams of terror from the front hall where my parents read the mail. The sickening sound of dead flesh meeting wood as my mother collapsed. My father's measured strides back to his study, a brief period of silence, the sharp report of a pistol shot. Teddy's screams from in front of the TV, Susan's hurried footsteps down from the attic, Bennett's fury at having his schedule interrupted.

Actually, I wasn't at all sure my parents would understand that notation on a report card. They had heard of it, but never seen it. It was as if I had brought home a report from the public health department. Syphilis. I'm sorry, Mom. I forgot to wear a rubber.

I don't know what Sam and Mr. Friedman were talking about—I pray to God it wasn't me—but they were at it a long time. I stood out there while classes changed, everybody hurrying by. (It was nothing at that school to see somebody standing in the hallway in utter despair. Nobody even noticed.) It wasn't until I was alone out there that Sam finally came out, and asked me why I was crying.

"I can't go home with a D," I said.

"Why not?"

"Nobody in my family ever made a D. Susan never did. Bennett."

"How do you know?"

"Bennett never made anything but an A."

"Bennett Bennett Bennett. That's all you every say. I'm not sure I even believe he exists. He's just an excuse you use to keep from doing anything."

It was an odd thought, at that point, but Sam had never actually met Bennett. The three of us never did anything together. The closest they had come was when the eighth grade played the ninth in baseball.

"Listen, Henry. You got some kind of block. I don't know what the hell it is but you got some kind of block. A history book is just words. Words on a page. You read them and they say something. You remember what they say. If it was baseball you'd remember. If it was bowling you'd remember. If it was how to make a banana split you'd sure as hell remember. But I see you sitting in study hall. You'd think the book was radioactive. You sit there with it open but it's like you're afraid to look at it. You call that studying?"

"I try," I said weakly.

"You do not try. That's what I'm saying."

"It's not that easy."

"You're telling me it's not easy. Don't I do the same thing as you?"

"It's easy for you."

"It's the same for me."

"Guys like you and Bennett."

"I just told you. I don't believe in Bennett."

"I don't know why I can't do it."

The buzzer sounded.

"Oh God!" I said. "We're late."

"Now you're going to tell me you've never been late."

"Never."

"Holy shit! Two firsts in one day!"

I figured the thing to do was just throw myself over the railing. I probably wouldn't be the first suicide that house had seen.

"All right, dammit," Sam said. "Being late and getting a D, they don't mean you're a criminal. You won't necessarily go to hell for those two things."

Hell sounded preferable to returning to my house.

"We're going to walk into that class. We're not going to act stupid. We're not going to act afraid. We're not going to make excuses. We'll say we were talking."

"*Talk*ing? He'll kill us."

"Henry. You do what you do. You don't read the book, you flunk the quiz. You stand around in the hall talking, you're late to class. That's the way it is. It's what life is all about."

"This is Mr. Tash. We can't walk in there and say that."

"Just do what I do. Follow my lead. But you're going to be the one to say we were talking."

Mr. Tash was our math teacher. He was actually a very good teacher, saw to it that you did your work; he was a perfectly reasonable man in a way. But he was five feet nine and weighed a solid two ten; he wore the same brown suit every day and the same brush cut; he had a square reddish face with a notch between his eyes that looked as if it had been put there with a chisel. In short, he should have been one of the legendary seven blocks of granite at Fordham University in the 1930s. I once ran into him full-tilt when he was refereeing a basketball game and found myself suddenly flat on my back, the wooden floor very hard against the length of my body, the lights very bright in my eyes. He hadn't moved. One day when we were practicing feats of strength with pencils—entwining them in the fingers of one hand and snapping them in half—he did the same thing with a wooden ruler. I was only thankful it didn't have one of those metal strips in it.

As Sam and I walked in, he was standing at the board, and turned (that neck wouldn't turn; he had to move his whole body) to face us.

"Golden. Wilder. We're glad you could make it today."

We nodded, standing there in front of him.

"I wonder if I could trouble you to tell us where you've been."

Sam glanced vaguely in my direction.

"We were talking," I said.

"Talking?" He pronounced the word quietly, as if he must have heard wrong.

So you were talking. Just talking, eh? He would step in front of me, arms at his sides, then a hand would suddenly flash out and wave at my face, as if to brush something away; my head would flutter back and forth as if on a swivel, to the muted sounds of flesh meeting flesh. Now what were you really doing? I would lean forward, before answering, to spit out a mouthful of blood.

"What were you talking about?" he said.

What's the answer to that one, Sam?

"It was a personal thing," Sam said quickly. "We were out in the hall talking and lost track of the time. The bell rang and we came straight to class."

"I see." Mr. Tash seemed almost disappointed. We were apparently telling the truth. "That's what you say too, Wilder?"

"Yes, sir."

"All right." He heaved a sigh. "That's a mark for each of you." He turned back to the board. "Take your seats."

Sam looked at me and nodded once, smiling.

IV

The year I was in eighth grade, the basketball game with the ninth grade took place at our gym.

I was on the basketball team, as unlikely as that may sound. I wasn't quick, and my personal best in the standing vertical jump was all of about two inches, and I was virtually useless as a defensive player. But I had killed a lot of hours out on the same backyard court where Bennett practiced, and I had a pretty deadly jumper from as far out as twenty feet. Of course, anybody who could jump three inches could block it, but occasionally when our opponents were playing a particularly tight zone I was sent in to loosen it up (keep shooting till they stuff it down your throat). I also usually got in if we were way ahead or way behind toward the end of a game.

Just to eliminate any needless suspense from the outset: I did not play in the big game against the ninth grade, though I did have an excellent view of the action from the bench.

Our gym was the kind of massive frigid old place that a gym should be, red brick on the outside and tan on the inside, with high wide windows—each covered by metal caging—running along the walls, an immensely high ceiling crisscrossed by a network of steel girders, light bulbs protected by wire (so kids wouldn't take potshots at them during dodgeball). Those lights, well up toward the ceiling, only illumined the place when it was quite dark, and even then not very well. On the gray winter day when our game took place, the lights cast a feeble yellowish glow, and what was coming through the windows had an odd dark quality, like when you've stared at a snowbank too long. The whole game had a ghostly air, as if it were being played by phantoms.

My feelings about the game were bizarre. On the one hand, I was on a team, and supposed to be ready to give my life for it. On the other, I wouldn't be playing, and I knew in my heart (this was part of my problem) that it was just a dumb little game between two grades of the same school. All my life I had been cheering Bennett on, watching him do the things I couldn't do, largely living through him. We had played against each other in pickup games, but now, in a major event, that was important at least to him, I was supposed to root against him. I could pretend, of course. Anybody could pretend. But I didn't see how I could really do it. It would be going against the habits of a lifetime.

The presence of my family at such a game was a foregone conclusion. My mother would have driven through a blizzard to see her sons perform (you know the type), and my father had actually rescheduled classes for some games earlier in the season. She was wearing a hooded belted parka that day that made her look like a stylish Franciscan monk, and he was wearing, along with his full-length camel's-hair, a Tyrolean hat—he loved to exhibit his collection of hats—and carrying an old army bugle, which he brought to all sporting events to give an earsplitting blast at appropriate moments. Teddy was also there, roaming the bleachers and carrying a tin can to bang against any metal he could find. The presence of the Wilder family could be felt all over the gym.

Just from the appearance of the two teams as they stepped out on the court, you would have expected the eighth graders to get slaughtered. The ninth graders were taller than almost all our guys; they were leaner; they looked more confident. There was something almost indefinable about their bodies that was different; their muscles were etched, shaded by dark lines, while the eighth-grade bodies were still soft and smooth. The ninth graders also looked much better organized: they took the opening tip, set up an offense that got our zone overbalanced, used two quick passes to get the ball to Bennett, who was open for a jumper on the other side. Swish.

A blatt from the bugle. "Bennett! Bennett!" my mother shouted, standing and waving. From somewhere across the court—it would keep wandering from place to place—the tin can clanged.

I felt a thrill too, I had to admit. That kid had a shot.

The game was starting out just like his story.

At the other end of the court, we looked like a bunch of kids in a schoolyard game, trying to force the ball in against the big guys. The first three times we took the ball down we lost it without getting a shot off, once because we took steps, twice because our passes were intercepted. All three times the ninth graders scored, twice on jump shots by Bennett. Two minutes into the game, he already had six points.

Down at the end of our bench, Coach Tom was all dressed up, blue suit, white shirt, dark tie. He looked as if he should have owned a funeral parlor on the North Side. He was already starting to sweat, though, as if he had sprinted up and down the court a few times himself. The man was excitable. After that eighth point, he leaped to his feet and called a time-out.

The eighth grade did have one kid who matched the ninth graders in size. That was understandable, since he had flunked twice. He was a big blond guy named Anthony Frazier, with tight stringy muscles, long lank greasy hair that flopped around on his head, one front tooth that was chipped and another capped in gold. He was our center. He rarely sank a shot, and he had a way of batting away passes that were meant for him, and he often seemed to get overly excited, hopping and jiggling around out there for no good reason. But he could get up in the air and pull down a rebound, and sometimes, we hoped, get it out to our guards to start a fast break. So far, unfortunately, there hadn't been any shots to rebound. They had all gone in.

"We got to stop that jump shot," Coach Tom said. He looked as if he wanted to slap us around a little. He stepped in front of Tony. "When that kid gets the ball, that Bennett"—he glanced my way for a second, as if trying to remember how I fit into all this—"I want you to get on him. Let him get the ball, and let him take the dribble, but then go out on him. Forget the zone. It's always the same shot, from the same place. I want you to block it."

Tony was nodding so fast his teeth should have been clicking. "Yessir."

"That's your job on defense. For a while, anyway."

I had to get word to Bennett. If I could just locate Teddy . . .

"And you." Tom stepped in front of Sam. "You got to calm your offense down. Quit making so many mistakes."

"I will." Sam wasn't looking at Tom. He seemed impatient to get back on the floor.

It wasn't Sam who had been making mistakes. The other guys were throwing the ball away.

The new strategy on defense worked. The next time the ninth grade came down, Tony stepped out of the zone almost before he was supposed to—it looked as if he were headed over to the bench for a drink or something—but he did let Bennett get the ball, let him go into that single dribble and go up, then soared into the air like a plucked eagle and swatted the ball almost to midcourt. Sam got there about the same time the ball did, and took it in for an easy lay-up.

It was along in there that the game began to change. We didn't exactly take control, and they were still a better-organized team, better-coached, but every time Bennett went up for his jumper—and he went up for it on six subsequent occasions—Tony was there to knock it away. Down at the other end, Sam was a whirlwind. He seemed to have decided that taking control of the offense involved keeping the ball himself, since anybody else who touched it found a way to hand it over to the ninth grade. He was very low to the ground, seemed to dribble just a couple of inches off the floor, and waded into the big crowd, got them moving around; he'd give a foot here, show the ball there, look with his eyes another way, and get them so faked out that either he could take a shot or somebody else would be wide open. I don't think he had any idea of what he was going to do as he brought the ball down the floor. He just dribbled in there and let it happen. There was a kind of genius involved in what he did with a basketball. We didn't win—it ended 34-28—but it was the closest game anybody had seen between the two grades for years, and Sam scored sixteen points, a new eighth-grade record. After the game, the ninth-grade coach walked straight up to him and said, "I don't care if you don't grow an inch. I can't wait to have you on my side next year."

Though he was on the winning team, Bennett looked deeply chagrined after the game. The last couple of times he had gone up for his jumper, there had been an almost audible groan from his side. Finally the coach had taken him out. "You can't keep taking the same shot if it doesn't go," he said. "You got to try something else." (Teddy had been there for an on-the-spot report.) Bennett never did get back in.

My shirt was about as soaked after the game as if I had played the whole thing. I couldn't help rooting for our team—- almost everybody in the gym was by the end—and I was amazed by the exhibition Sam was putting on. I had even felt an odd thrill when Bennett went up and got his shot blocked, as if at the thought that such perfection could have a flaw. On the other hand, he was my brother. I didn't like seeing him humiliated. I didn't like the bewilderment on his face when those shots were blocked, the pain when the crowd was groaning, his obvious embarrassment when he was taken out. There also seemed something patently unfair about what had happened. It should have worked out for him. He had had things so carefully planned.

There was an odd awkward moment after the game. The spectators had poured out of the stands, and the teams cleared the benches—a small crowd had formed around Sam, including even some ninth graders (Teddy was at the outskirts)—but my parents were off to one side with Bennett and a man I had not seen before. He was short, slightly shorter than I, and had brown hair thinning at the temples. He wore a tan corduroy suit—I was not familiar with the corduroy suit—and a greenish tie, held a cloth cap and umbrella together in his hands. As he listened to my father he leaned back slightly and tilted his head to one side, as if skeptically, and when I stepped up to the group was saying, "Yes. Well. It was an exciting contest. This young man did a fine job."

The guy obviously knew nothing about basketball.

"Mr. Edmond," Bennett said, "I'd like you to meet my brother Henry."

Bennett looked as if he would rather be anywhere just then

than out on that floor. But he had badly wanted my parents to meet Mr. Edmond. He had spoken for several days of the possibility that the man might be at the game.

"Hello, Henry Wilder," Mr. Edmond said. "I believe I detect a resemblance."

Beneath that flabby exterior another Bennett Wilder was waiting to be discovered.

"Hi." I was always rather shy at these meetings with Bennett's favorites.

"I understand you'll be out with us next year."

For a little guy, he had a hell of a grip. As we shook hands I experienced a brief moment of agony, prefiguring the full year of agony I was anticipating at that school the next year.

"I guess." Another chance to be Bennett's brother. I dreaded it.

"We can always use another Wilder at that school."

If all the teachers were like this guy, I wasn't sure I wanted to go.

"We're awfully proud of our basketball players," Mother said that night at the dinner table.

"We certainly are," Father said.

Bennett and I said nothing, picking away at our plates.

"Two greatest bench warmers in the world," Teddy said.

"Teddy. Such a thing to say," Mother said.

"Your friend is certainly quite a ballplayer," Father said, looking at me.

Bennett dropped his knife loudly on his plate. He was staring off at the ceiling in disgust.

"He sure is," I said.

"I thought he should have given some of the other boys a chance," Mother said.

"The other boys stank," Teddy said.

As it turned out, not much had really changed around the house since I got that D in ancient history. My parents had been concerned, but also sympathetic. (Especially my mother. "*Everybody* forgets an assignment now and then," she said.) They decided I should spend a full two hours in the room every evening, studying. I already did that. Spent the time, anyway.

When I walked in that evening, Bennett didn't immediately start surrounding me with restrictions, as he usually did. He had a more solemn task. He looked up from his books and said, "You've seen the last of me on a basketball court."

He was always ready with the perfect phrase. I was sure he was hoping I'd remember it for his biography.

"Jesus, Bennett," I said. "You scored six points."

"I didn't get a shot off after the first two minutes."

"Your team won the game."

"*They* won the game. I wasn't a part of it."

He was saying this to me? who had collected splinters in his ass from benches all over the city?

"Your six points made the difference, when you think of it," I said.

I didn't know where that had come from. For a moment it almost seemed to console him.

Why was *I* consoling *him*?

"No," Bennett said. "I'm not going to keep playing a game where some ignorant cretin who doesn't even know anything, who probably has to get the coach to lace up his shoes, can come spazzing out of a set defense and ruin a whole offensive plan."

That was just like Bennett. We should have stayed back in our zone and let him take the shot.

"The kid can jump. What can you say?"

"That's all he can do. He didn't score a single point."

It was true. If somebody could have taught *him* a jump shot . . .

"I'm going to find a sport where that kind of thing doesn't happen," Bennett said.

"Like what?"

"Where the kid who has the most talent, works the hardest, where he wins the game."

It seemed to me he was describing most sports.

"You should work on another shot," I said.

"What's wrong with the shot I have? I mean had." He really was serious about quitting.

"There's nothing wrong with it. But to always do the same thing. Shoot from the same spot. If you had thrown one fake, Tony would have gone sailing into the bleachers."

"No." Bennett never was one to profit from criticism. "I'm through with basketball."

"You should play more like Sam."

I should never have said that. (I couldn't help it, though. It was bursting out of me.) Bennett knew how much I liked Sam. He knew I almost idolized him. I must have seemed to be growing disloyal at the worst possible moment.

Anyway, it made no sense. There are people in the world like Sam, loaded with talent, bursting with confidence, who rely on their own inventiveness and the inspiration of the moment, and there are others like Bennett, who put their few outstanding talents at the service of an iron will. One wades in dribbling and lets it happen; the other takes the shot he practiced thousands of times. It makes no sense to ask one person to become the other.

"Your little friend," Bennett said.

"He is my friend."

"Denizen of pool halls. Frequenter of burlesque houses."

"If you haven't tried it, don't knock it." One of Sam's favorite expressions.

"I want to tell you something. You won't believe it but I'm going to tell you. I've seen a lot of kids come and go. Older kids than you. I've heard about a lot more. That Sam Golden is the kind of kid who winds up no good."

I just laughed. "You don't know what you're talking about."

"You won't believe me now."

"How would you know, anyway?"

"I just do. I understand about people."

"He's one of the best students in our class."

"I don't doubt it."

"The best athlete I've ever seen."

"I've seen a number better."

"Bigger. Or older. But not better."

"Better."

"He's more fun to be with than anybody I've ever met."

"I'm sure."

"Everybody's crazy about Sam. He's the most popular kid in my class."

"They always are. That's the first thing you hear. But you remember what I said. Mark my words. Sam Golden's the kind of kid who winds up no good."

FOUR

Spring came early to the city that year, like a dinner guest who's inside the door before the table is set. I can remember walking with Sam along Penn, on a Sunday early in March that was more like May, when there was a border of dirty snow along the sidewalk and the grass was oozing water, sidewalks tracked with mud. There we were in light sweaters, but also wearing gloves, making what looked as if they would be the last snowballs of the year (they were real iceballs too, with that fast-melting snow), pegging them at cars and taking off down a side street.

We were headed toward a drugstore at the end of that long block of Penn, down by the fire station. It had apparently once been a good store, but the druggist who owned it had died, leaving it to a wife who couldn't seem to handle things. She kept hiring and firing one druggist after another, so the pharmacy was often out of commission. All the nondrug items were ancient, shelves of cosmetics covered by a layer of dust, a rack of comic books that were fast becoming classics. Mrs. McCarthy spent her whole day going over inventory, standing in the back shuffling through papers, shaking her head with what seemed to be a tremor.

The fountain, however—leave it to Sam to have found out—was run by the same person who had always run it, a middle-aged black man named Chester. It was bright and clean, its silver fixtures gleaming, and had a light scent of vanilla over it, as all the old fountains did. Even Chester seemed to gleam back there. He was a deep chocolate color, almost completely bald, with just a slight paunch; he always wore a white shirt and narrow black tie. He seldom smiled. Smooth, was the word you thought of when you looked at him; his skin was smooth, and his motions as he worked were smooth, and the things he served were always smooth. He leaned to scrape and scrape for ice cream, until the scoop he came out with was perfectly round, then stood to deposit the scoop in a dish while the silver lid slammed lightly shut. If you ordered a soda he mixed it elaborately, a little syrup with a little soda, some careful stirring, more soda and more stirring, one of those large perfect scoops of ice cream, more soda and a flourish of whipped cream.

He served everything the old-fashioned way, so if you asked for an ice-cream sandwich, he took out a little block of ice cream—vanilla, chocolate, or Neapolitan—and surrounded it with a couple of sugar wafers, served it on a sheet of wax paper. When he made a milkshake he always left it going exactly long enough, so it was without lumps and whipped into a light froth; he poured from a foot above the glass, so the shake came down in a long stream, and stopped so it just came over the rim. He served you the glass with the canister beside it. He never hurried, never made anything to less than perfect specifications, and served everything with style. He was a gourmet soda jerk.

"You ever had a *malted* milkshake?" Sam said to me, that first day of spring.

"I've heard of it. I don't think I'd like it. I had a malted milk ball once." Give me a malted mothball any day.

"It's nothing like that. Not the way Chester makes it. Just a light taste over the chocolate. It's fantastic."

That was where we were headed on our walk down Penn, to get a malted milkshake.

Though he was normally the sanest of men, Sam did have his moments, even that first year I knew him. I never knew what they were, those odd moods that came over him, and I never seemed to notice until it was too late. He'd be unusually quiet for a while, as if pondering something, then suddenly start acting disagreeable, as if that were some decision he'd made.

"What fastball?" he'd say, if the subject of my pitching came up, or, if we were talking about basketball, "It would help if you could get off the ground." There was a custom, among the four or five of us who walked home together that winter, that if you could get a foot on a certain cigarette pack you could slug anybody within reach (yelling "Lucky Strike!"), and I can still see him—in one of his moods—taking a quick step for a pack and throwing a straight right that would leave a bruise on somebody's arm for days, twisting his wrist and digging his knuckles in. You couldn't get away from him in one of those moods. Anything you did, he wanted to come along. He seemed to need somebody to pick on.

One of those moods seemed to be coming on that afternoon we went for the milkshake; he clobbered me once from a Lucky Strike pack and just missed another time, when I lunged out of the way. Once we were in the drugstore and had ordered we were quiet; I didn't want to bring anything up, and he was staring silently at the counter. When our malts came we just sat there sipping, like a couple of steelworkers having a shot and a beer.

Sam was right. Chester's chocolate malted milkshake was exquisite.

"You know," Sam said after a while, to Chester, "a chocolate malted milkshake is about the most fattening thing you can eat."

"They good." Chester was wiping things off behind the counter. Nobody was at the fountain but Sam and me.

"I know," Sam said. "But I was looking through my mother's diet book. A chocolate malted milkshake is right at the top of the calorie charts. Up there with an avocado."

"I never eat no avocado."

Who ever heard of going to your neighborhood soda fountain for an avocado?

"Speaking of which." Sam turned to me. "I've been wondering lately. Meaning to ask you. Do you really want to be fat, or does it just run in your family, or what?"

I felt myself redden, looked up. Chester was gazing at me, as if genuinely interested in my answer to this question.

"What the hell are you talking about?" I said.

"Your brother isn't fat. The famous Bennett. And your little brother isn't either." Sam had seen Teddy at the basketball game. "How about your sister? Does she carry a lot of blubber?"

"She's skinny." I looked down at the counter. "Like Bennett."

That was my first mistake, treating his words as a serious question, instead of the ravings of a lunatic.

Up until then, my favorite thing about Sam had been that he never mentioned my weight. Most guys said something, if only in passing. Sam never had. It was as if he hadn't noticed.

"So it's some kind of hobby of yours," Sam said. "You don't get it from your parents."

"Actually"—a little wistful humor seemed in order—"my parents didn't used to be fat. If you look at their wedding pictures. They're like two normal people. My mother was almost small."

"No kidding." Sam sipped at his shake. "Were her tits as big as yours are now?"

"All right, Sam." Humor wasn't working. I'd try anger. "Keep quiet about my mother."

"I wasn't talking about your mother. I was talking about you. *Your* tits."

"Just shut up, would you? Just shut the fuck up."

"Now, boys. Mizz McArthur don't like no language."

Why couldn't black people ever pronounce anything right? It was *Mrs.* McCar*thy.* He'd been working with her for twenty years, for God's sake.

"There's nobody else here," Sam said.

"Mizz McArthur in the back."

"She can't hear you, is the thing," Sam said. "She never hears a word you say." He raised his voice slightly. "I want you, Mrs. McCarthy. Your firm, ripe, wanton body."

We all looked back. She was staring down at the inventory sheets, shaking her head.

"See?" Sam said.

Chester's face hadn't changed. He didn't look happy. These dumb little motherfuckers, he was probably thinking.

"So what's the story?" Sam said to me. "You like these unsightly rolls of blubber, or what?"

"You say one more thing," I said. "You say one more thing about being fat, and you'll be sitting here alone. Drinking two milkshakes."

"You frighten me."

"You think he can drink two, Chester? You think Sam can drink two milkshakes?"

"Can't nobody drink two. Can't nobody drink two my shakes."

Good old Chester. He was on my side.

"Not even somebody as fat as Henry?" Sam said.

"That's it." I slid around on my stool.

"I'm sorry." Sam grabbed my arm. He was stifling a smile, looking off toward the counter. "I won't say anything more."

"You got to promise, dammit."

"I promise."

"Not another fucking word."

"I promise, already. Jesus, Henry. Just sit back. Sit back on the stool." I slid around. "Don't leave me here with two milkshakes. God. I can't drink two of these things." He took a long swallow, staring at himself in the mirror behind the fountain. "I might get fat."

"Goddammit."

Chester walked to the back and disappeared through a door. Stupid little white motherfuckers driving him crazy.

Sam had grabbed my arm again, was holding me against the counter.

"If you don't like being fat, why the hell are you sitting here drinking a chocolate malted milkshake?"

A question fat people have been asking themselves since the malt was invented.

"You asked me to come drink this milkshake."

"I wanted to see what you'd say. I wanted to see if you had any willpower." He let go of my arm. "You could diet, if you want to lose weight. You ever go on a diet?"

"Once."

"For how long?"

"Three months."

"I don't believe you."

He was right. I'd only lasted four days. "How would you like to eat cottage cheese at every meal?"

"You could start a program of exercise. Do roadwork."

"Now there's an idea. Why didn't I think of that?"

"Long slow miles of roadwork. It's the best way to lose weight."

"What the hell do you know about losing weight?"

"I read an article about it. Archie Moore. The Old Mongoose. All fighters do roadwork."

"All right. All right. I'll do roadwork. I'll start tomorrow."

"Only if you want to lose weight."

"Of course I do. I'll go out in the morning. Just like a fighter. Now will you shut the hell up?"

"It's all up to you."

We went back to our milkshakes. Mine suddenly tasted flat, and seemed to blow me up like a blimp. (I kept drinking anyway. I enjoyed the pain.) All my life, whenever I have eaten anything fattening, I have felt instantly fatter, as if fat cells formed in seconds.

"What time are you going out?" Sam said.

I looked at him in the mirror. He was staring down at his shake, sipping it.

"What's it to you?"

"I thought I might go out with you. Start to get in shape."

"You're in shape. You've always been in shape."

"For short stuff. Like basketball. But I can't run any distance. I've never been able to. There's that All Comers Track Meet in May."

I turned slowly to stare at him. "So you want to start doing roadwork too. By some coincidence."

"I thought it sounded interesting. Something I haven't tried. And you have to lose all that unsightly blubber. I figured we could go out together."

On the one hand, I could have killed him. That whole long scene, that had hurt me deeply, embarrassed me in front of Chester, was just to get me to do something Sam had planned before we even came in there. On the other hand, I was intrigued. I hadn't really been planning to do any roadwork, of course. I had just said that to shut Sam up. But I knew fighters did roadwork to get in shape, and I did want to lose weight, I'd always wanted to (now that somebody mentioned it). It almost sounded possible with Sam along. I pictured us working up to five miles, seven miles, no problem at all, while fat melted off me like snow in the spring sun.

Any plan for losing weight sounds good, as long as it doesn't start until tomorrow.

"Either you want to be fat or you don't," Sam said. "It's as simple as that."

"No it's not. Nobody wants to be fat."

"Then come out with me and do roadwork tomorrow morning."

"Okay. I'll give it a try."

"None of this crap about trying. You'll do it."

"I'll do it. I'll do it."

I felt a flutter in my stomach, fear and excitement all at the same time.

"Finish your malt. Your new life starts tomorrow."

Sam was right. I'd never eat another fattening thing as long as I lived.

"Why didn't you just ask me if I wanted to do this?" I said after a while. "Instead of giving me all this crap."

"You wouldn't have done it."

"I might have."

"You might have." He shrugged. "It was more fun this way."

"I don't like the sound of this," my mother said that evening at the dinner table. "I don't like the sound of it at all."

It went by the old saying, blubber loves company.

We were sitting in our usual configuration, though with Susan gone I was the only one on that side (and therefore had to eat for two). The entree that evening was a steaming concoction of ground meat, tomatoes, and macaroni.

"There's nothing wrong with it," my father said. "A little fresh air and exercise."

"God knows he needs it," Teddy said.

"He won't get enough sleep, getting up early like that. He'll be tired all day. His schoolwork will suffer."

If it suffered any more, it would die.

Actually, I was beginning to feel a little trepidation about the whole thing myself. It had sounded rather wonderful in the drugstore, when Sam was beside me with his enthusiasm, but now six-fifteen was sounding pretty early, and the whole concept of roadwork suddenly seemed bizarre. I wouldn't have minded if my mother had vetoed the whole thing.

A mother in general does not want her son to change. Her first instinct is to protect her child, and she can do that best if he will remain small, and soft, and round, so she can hold him in her arms and feed him at her breast. When he moves beyond that, the trouble begins.

"He can go to bed earlier," my father said. "The exercise will make him sleep better. He'll probably spend the day feeling more refreshed."

"He'll be exhausted. All the time."

"Your body adjusts. You get used to these things. That's what getting in shape is all about."

A father, too, sees his son as an extension of himself, but more like a revised version, a second draft. He thinks his son should be better than he, and he hates to see his own faults appear in his son, out there where he can't (though he tries to) do anything about them. He *wants* his son to change.

"I just think it's an extreme way to go about losing a little weight. I'm not going to say he can't do it." Oh, hell. "But I'm going to be watching very closely."

Maybe she'd run along behind us.

"I wish you'd do it another way," she said.

"He could try eating a little less," Teddy said.

"I think it's a fine way," my father said. "I think he's going to enjoy it. It's a wonderful idea."

"He won't last three days," Bennett said.

"I hate this," I said.

"You haven't even done anything," Sam said.

It was true. We were heading down the walkway to the sidewalk, getting ready to start. It was six twenty-two A.M.

"I'm already tired. I was tired before I even got out of bed. And I know how this is going to feel."

"You do not. You've never done it before. Don't talk yourself out of it before you even start."

Sam was dressed in cut-off jeans and a T-shirt. I was wearing gym shorts, a T-shirt and sweatshirt, and a towel around my neck. My father had told me fighters always wore towels that way, to absorb the sweat.

"All right," I said. "But we've got to stop when I say."

"We'll stop when you say. I've told you a million times. Let's just get going."

We took off at the blazing pace of two old ladies on the Atlantic City boardwalk. Sam ran with easy motions, a gentle footfall. I was flop-flopping along like the clown with big feet at the circus. My body felt leaden. By the time we hit the corner I was ready for a breather.

"I've seen you sprint further than this," Sam said.

"That was when I knew where the finish line was. I don't know how far you're taking me."

"We can talk about it. It doesn't have to be far. But we've got to do better than this."

Already he was breaking his word about letting me stop when I wanted.

As we ran, and walked, up Lang and in the direction of Reynolds, he talked about what had made him want to take up running. It turned out the whole thing had recently become an obsession of his (Sam was known for his intense enthusiasms) and he had done a lot of reading about it. A band of Australian runners had recently invaded our country, carrying off all the prizes in the long and middle distances, and their training methods were the rage of the track world. Whereas American runners worked out once a day and took it pretty easy at that, these Australian runners trained all the time, two or three workouts a day, all different kinds. They took long runs on the beach in the early morning, finishing up by splashing through a foot of surf for a while and taking a long swim; they did speed work on the track; they lifted heavy weights and tossed around a medicine ball; they ran repeatedly up a high dune until they dropped from exhaustion. They lived out in the wild together in primitive shacks, ate health foods like rolled oats and raw wheat germ; they wore several days' growth of beard and seldom saw anybody except each other. Their trainer was an eccentric old guy who worked out with his runners, a former hard-driving businessman who had had three heart attacks and given up on civilization altogether. He had rehabilitated himself through running and the simple life, and frequently ran that sand dune to the point of exhaustion himself. For his boys, those little half-mile, mile, and two-mile races in the States were simply a lark.

Sam had also come across an article in an old *National Geographic* about a tribe of Indians in New Mexico who were absolutely phenomenal runners. They ran barefoot, along rocky soil, all the time—it was their primary means of transportation—and covered distances that, to the rest of the human race, seemed incredible. Just for fun, sometimes, they ran competitive races that lasted all day and all night, two teams moving together and kicking (barefoot) a ball made of juniper wood, one man from each team carrying a torch after it got dark. One factor in their phenomenal abilities was that their land was utterly barren, their methods of farming and hunting extremely primitive. "So if they want to eat something, like a rabbit, say, they can't really catch up to it—nobody's that fast—but they run along behind it till the poor little fucker drops from exhaustion. Then they pick it up and carry it home."

That did sound like a primitive method of hunting.

"Next time I see a rabbit I'll try it," I said.

We had finished our jaunt by that time, were sitting on the steps that led up to my house. We hadn't made it very far—just up to Reynolds—and had walked about half the way. We weren't quite ready to take on the Tarahumara Indians. But I wasn't totally exhausted. I actually felt a little better than when I had gotten out of bed.

"You're missing the point," Sam said. "They don't think about what they're doing. When their legs hurt, it's just the muscles stretching. When their chests hurt, it's the lungs expanding. All in a day's work. Nobody's told them they're running distances no human being can possibly run. Nobody's told them they can't do it."

"Nobody's told me either."

"The hell they haven't. Somebody must have. You were ready to stop this morning before you even got started. People tell me all the time. I mention to somebody, I swear to God, I mention to anybody that I'm thinking of running the mile in this All Comers Track Meet in May, and the first thing they say is, you can't do that."

"You really want to run the mile."

"See? Even you do it."

"I'm not saying you can't."

"Just name it. Anything. That you really want to do. Just talk about it a little, and you'll find somebody to tell you you can't do it."

I was a little stiff the next morning, and getting out of bed, if anything, was harder than the first day. Sam wanted to go further, but I made him stop at the same place. The third morning was the real shocker. I heard the alarm from far off, I'm not sure how long it had been buzzing (I was occupying the guest room again, so as not to disturb Bennett), and when I reached for it was convinced I had suddenly come down with a case of infantile paralysis. This was not stiffness. This was blinding pain. I eventually hobbled down the steps, wishing we had one of those stairway elevators for heart patients, and showed up at the front door in my pajamas.

"I just can't do it," I said. "I hurt too much."

"This is the day we have to do it. If we quit today we'll never go out again."

"I need a couple days to rest. So my muscles aren't so sore."

"If you rest today you'll just get sore the next time you start."

"I don't think I *can* run. I'm not doing a real good job of walking."

"We'll start off walking. We'll walk the whole way if you want. But we've got to go out there today. You go up and get dressed or the whole world's going to see those pretty pajamas of yours."

He had that hard glare in his eyes. I went up and got dressed. We did walk most of the way that day, and the next day we didn't do much better (much later, Sam told me he had gone back and run some after we had finished, just to get a work-out), but I found that just getting up and moving around was good for the aches, better, anyway, than sitting still. Friday morning it rained, a steady gray pelting, and I was just about to roll over and catch up on my sleep when, to my astonishment, I looked through the window and saw Sam trotting down the sidewalk. "If we let the weather stop us it'll always be something," he said, when he met me at the front door. "Too wet, too cold, too hot. Get dressed." The rain, as a matter of fact, made us want to keep moving, and kept us from getting overheated; that morning, though we covered the same route, we ran more of it than ever before.

Gradually we extended our distance. Before long we were going down Reynolds to the traffic circle, swinging around and heading back, but it was a big step to continue past the circle, up that hill to the wide green where Italian men played bocce on Sunday afternoons. From there it was easy to go on to school. When we got to the field, I would sit around while Sam did something else, either ran sprints or ran up and down the big hill we liked to sled on (he had progressed much further than I had, was ready for more work), then we trotted home. About a month after we had started, I managed to run the whole way, with that break in between.

I don't know when it was in there that I began to realize that all Sam had said was true, that much of the fatigue you felt while running was strictly mental, the result of years of people telling you (and you telling yourself) that you couldn't do it; that what you initially felt in your muscles was not pain or fa-tigue, but simply stretching, and would go away; that the scary feeling of being out of breath was not really dangerous because you'd drop before you could hurt yourself (like that crazy old man on the Australian dunes); that even real fatigue, real pain, were things you could take a lot more of than you had thought. It wasn't talk, of course, that convinced me, but the actual experience of getting out and running. I could feel myself change, my horizons expanding.

I cannot say it was exactly that March, or that April, that I stopped being fat. I wasn't running along one day when I saw twenty pounds fall off my body and roll down a sewer. I never really knew I was losing weight, because it's hard to see that happening; I was getting taller at that point too, so my weight probably didn't change all that much. But if you look at two pictures—the eighth-grade basketball team, say, and the ninth-grade track team—the change is dramatic. I hadn't become exactly svelte, and my torso wasn't etched in muscle, but my body went from being one you thought of as fat to one you didn't think of one way or another. That was an enormous change for me, after a lifetime of being overweight, and it took me a while to catch on to it (in some ways, of course, a person who is fat when young will be fat forever, no matter what he weighs). My body was reflecting a change that had taken place in my life.

By the first week in May we were both running the whole distance at a steady pace. At the school field I ran the hill a couple of times and jogged a lap in between; Sam either did that with me (or rather, ahead of me) or ran sprints by himself, then we ran back together. I'm not sure what the exact distance was, but it was close to two miles.

I don't think I looked at that point like a kid who could run two miles—after a lifetime of being one way, the body is slow to change—but the fact was that I could. I could do it easily. I did it almost every day.

II

"He's building a *swimming* pool up there?" my father said, when I told him about it at the dinner table.

"He's already got it built, practically," I said. "Ready for the first warm day."

My parents had strange, stricken looks on their faces, as if Teddy had farted at the dinner table (nothing unusual about that, of course) when the department chairman was over. They could not put their feelings into words, exactly, but the feelings were strong, nevertheless.

"I've never heard of a swimming pool in that neighborhood," Father said.

"There's no reason not to," I said. "They've got a huge back-yard. Hedges all around."

"What about the noise?"

"There won't be any. Sam can only have two friends over at a time. That's the rule."

"I don't mean that kind of noise. Like a lot of people. But in that location. With all those little houses around. It's just kind of . . . knowing it's there."

Father wasn't normally so vague about things.

"It doesn't belong in that neighborhood," Mother said.

"It does now. They're pouring the concrete. It's practically a swimming pool already."

I didn't like my parents' reaction. I was telling them what I thought was wonderful news, and they were treating it as a grave misfortune.

I understand now what they were talking about. I think I even understood it then. That neighborhood is still one of the oldest and prettiest in the city, quiet shady streets, brick houses on both sides, modest cars in the driveway. Families from those houses earn decent livings and bring their children up right and send them to public and parochial and occasionally private schools and keep the yards mowed and raked. A swimming pool no more belonged there than did the Goldens' house, with its white brick exterior, broad expanse, the sweeping asphalt driveway with its luxurious Cadillac and sleek Thunderbird.

I liked it, though. I liked the thought of something totally new. To think that you might walk up to what seemed just the front door of a house, step through that door, and emerge a few minutes later from the back in a bathing suit and dive into a swimming pool! What a bizarre idea! I was thinking just that, as I stood out back one raw wintry afternoon with Sam and his father, and watched a small bulldozer dig the hole that would eventually be the pool. I liked it that they were breaking ground for something that might shake up the old neighborhood. Out with the old and in with the new.

Mr. Golden was wearing a gray herringbone overcoat and a fedora, his ever-present cigar in the side of his mouth. We stood transfixed, the way children are, by that burrowing persistent machine that seemed to have a mind of its own. We might never have left if Mr. Golden hadn't stepped back and said, "They won't get this hole dug in one afternoon. I'm going in."

"Yeah," Sam said.

Mr. Golden whacked my arm with his evening newspaper. "A man's got to have some pleasure in life, doesn't he, kid?"

"Henry," Sam said. "His name's Henry."

"I know his name," Mr. Golden said. "I don't have to use it for every little thing."

Sam always complained that his father didn't pay any attention to his friends. That people under a certain age—forty, say—were garbage to him, because he couldn't do any business with them.

"A man deserves a little pleasure in life, doesn't he, kid?"

"Sure," I said.

"What the hell's a backyard for, if not to put a swimming pool in?"

Sam and I were the first two people to use the pool, diving in one brisk morning in April when it was first filled, swimming a couple lengths at top speed, then jumping out and running back into the house. It was far from Olympic size, of course, and it wasn't—much to my regret—even quite rectangular, rounding itself off slightly at the corners. But it was fifteen yards long, and had a deep and shallow end, with a rope of floats in between, and if you swam between the two points that were farthest apart it was almost like swimming in a regular pool: you could get some exercise. Not that that was what we used it for. We just wanted to screw around. Sam even got one of those little baskets and balls so we could play water basketball, and it was fun to launch yourself out of the water like some kind of sea monster, palming that little ball and stuffing it through the hoop.

We had thought of starting our morning runs a little earlier so we could finish them with a vigorous swim, like the Aussies in the surf, but that seemed to be complicating matters unduly; the morning air was a trifle brisk, and we really didn't want to wake up any earlier than we already were. Our Saturday runs started a little later, though—Sam showed up around eight—

and by early May the mornings were starting to get warmer, and we had the whole day before us, so we finished our workout at Sam's with a swim. We usually didn't do much, just lay in the water and let it soothe our aching muscles, but it was a nice way to end a long run. After we had been in the pool awhile, the Goldens' maid brought out breakfast, fried eggs usually, and bacon or ham, and stacks of hot buttered toast, and a pot of hot chocolate. We ate it slowly, and I could stay around all morning, or the rest of the day if I wanted to.

Sometime along in there Sam's father would come padding out, in a bathing outfit that included a shirt that buttoned down and matched his suit and a little beach hat on top of his head. Whatever time he came out—this was before his breakfast—he was already smoking a cigar, and sometimes it would be smoked pretty far down, as if he had been smoking in his sleep, or as if he had lit up a leftover butt from the night before. He too was served breakfast out there, usually just some toast and a large pot of coffee, and after he had eaten would take off the shirt (but not the hat) and ease himself into the pool, his arms up on the side, the cigar still plugged into a corner of his mouth. Sometimes he propelled himself around, in what could best be described as a modified breast stroke, but he never removed the cigar or the hat, and it wasn't long before he was hanging at the side again. Often enough Sam and I were resting there too, because we had strict instructions not to splash around while Mr. Golden was in. The three of us just sat there, utterly silent most of the time, bobbing around like buoys.

"Nothing like a little exercise first thing in the morning, is there, kid?" Mr. Golden might say to me.

"Nothing like it," I'd say.

He never seemed to address his words to Sam when I was around. He always spoke to me.

One morning when Sam had gone inside for a minute, Mr. Golden said, "I got a beautiful house, kid. The pool's fantastic. I worked like hell for all this and I'm glad to have it. But some days. I swear to God. Some mornings I'd give the whole thing up for one healthy bowel movement."

I nodded wistfully, staring off into the distance. I didn't know quite how to reply to such a remark.

Mr. Golden never seemed in a particular hurry to get anywhere—after his swim he might get out and read the paper, light up a fresh cigar and have another pot of coffee—but he didn't spend the whole morning around the pool. Sooner or later he'd rise from the chair, fold up his paper, and head toward the house. "Got to make a buck, kid. The boss got to put in an appearance." Eventually he emerged from the house in dark slacks and often enough an incredibly loud sport jacket, a summer straw hat on his head, to glide away in that quiet Cadillac.

It is not quite accurate to say Sam's mother never came out in the morning—she did show up around eleven if the sun was hot—but she did not eat breakfast out there, and she never came out when her husband was around. There was an entirely different feel to the pool when she was there. We weren't supposed to fool around when Mr. Golden was actually in the pool, but it was okay to do anything while he was sitting at the side; he liked to see us have a water battle or go one-on-one in basketball. When Mrs. Golden was out there, though, we could hardly move. "Hello, dear," she would say, as she walked out (she no more knew my name than her husband did, but at least she didn't call me an asshole), and, "Hello, Samuel," in her quiet throaty voice. She would lie on one of the chaise lounges—face up, eyes tight against the sun, or face down, as if she were sleeping—and Sam and I would stay in the pool and quietly talk, or get out and sit talking in a couple of the chairs. We never talked to her, and never got close enough so she could hear what we said. We were just three people sitting out by the pool, as if it were a private club and Sam and I didn't know her very well.

In the families of kids I knew (and probably in my own family, for other kids), the parents were very much a part of the experience of going to visit; they greeted you at the door, or shouted at you as you went by the living room, or drove you places and did things with you. Sam's parents were not that way. They were off in the house somewhere, or Mr. Golden was at work, his wife at some social appointment. Sam came pounding down out of the second floor as if he rented rooms there, and never said much to them, or they to him. They hardly seemed to know one another.

They didn't even look like each other, didn't seem to belong together. Mr. and Mrs. Golden seemed somehow too old to be Sam's parents, and he didn't look like either of them, and she didn't seem the right wife for the rotund man who swam in a beach hat while smoking a cigar. Not that I would have expected someone correspondingly dumpy. It would have seemed appropriate, for instance, if he had been married to some glamorous starlet type whom he obviously wanted for her body, while she craved his bank account. But Mrs. Golden was what you might have called dignified, distinguished. The ugly one-piece bathing suits women wore in those days didn't show much, but her legs were shapely, her breasts large, and her belly flat; her body, at least, seemed young, and supple, and tan. I find that her face as I think back on it is almost a blank. It was lightly freckled, with eyes that were set deep, fine bones to her cheeks and nose. But it is almost without expression, in my memory. She lay on the chair, eyes closed to the sun, and her face didn't move, or speak, or change.

Often on weekends she had friends to the pool, just one or two women, and they were served lunch out there under a round white table with a huge umbrella. They sat around and talked, sometimes floated in the pool a little. Like Mrs. Golden, her friends took no notice of us whatsoever. We couldn't wrestle around, play water basketball or just throw the ball, even swim hard. Apparently we were supposed to sit there and have quiet cultivated conversations, as they were.

It was on one of those days—an unseasonably hot Saturday in May—that I said something to Sam about his mother. It was almost customary in our circle of friends to pay another kid some harmless compliment about his parents, so he'd know you didn't think they were too weird. That day she and a couple of friends were having iced tea under the umbrella, while he and I were at the opposite end of the pool, where it was bright and hot out on the cement. Sam was staring at the women pretty hard, so I said something to let him know it was okay, that I didn't think his mother too strange for making us be that way.

"Your mother's nice," I said.

"What?" Sam said.

I think he heard me. He was just being difficult.

"Your mother's nice," I said. "I like her."

He turned to stare at me. "What do you mean?"

He wasn't supposed to say that. He was supposed to take it as a polite little gesture, say "Thanks" and let it drop. It was rude, trying to pin me down with that kind of question.

It was also just like Sam on a certain kind of day.

"I don't know." It wasn't going to be real easy coming up with something. "She's friendly, and she always says hello to me, and she doesn't get after us to do things, the way some parents would."

Sam had turned and looked back at the pool.

"She beats me," he said.

"What?" Now it was my turn to play dumb. It wasn't that I hadn't heard the words, exactly. More that I didn't believe the way they went together.

"She beats me. With a belt."

"Oh." That's what I'd thought he'd said.

Somehow I had wandered into a place where I had never intended to be. A part of me was scared, wanted to step back. Another part—I didn't understand this part—wanted to go on.

"Why?" I said.

"How would I know? You could ask her. You could walk over to that table of ladies and say, I really hate to disturb you, I'm terribly sorry to interrupt your little chat, but I just wanted to ask Mrs. Golden why she beats her son."

He was not looking at me, still staring at the pool.

"I'm sorry I brought it up," I said. As if I had.

"She never talks to me about anything, for days at a time. She's off in her room, or she's down in the den, or she's out somewhere. She's probably out more than in. She never has meals with me, she never does anything with me, but then sometimes, when there's nobody else in the house, she comes in my room and starts telling me about something I've done wrong and says she's going to punish me. She gets this big leather belt, it's more like a strap, and she makes me stand up and take off my pants, then she tells me to lie across something, like the bed, or the back of a chair, and she beats me."

My heart was pounding as I heard those things and I felt breathless, could hardly speak. "Does it hurt a lot?"

"God yes it hurts. You wouldn't believe how it hurts. She whips me on my ass, and she whips me on my legs, and I scream and yell, and beg her to stop, but that never does any good, she just keeps on beating me, as long as she wants, then when she's through she tells me not to do whatever it was anymore and walks out. She never says another word about it. But she's been doing it since I was a little kid."

"Jesus."

"I never told anybody. But I thought I'd better tell you. Since you think she's so nice."

I didn't know what to say. I'd never felt so utterly speechless in my life. I could have said I was sorry, but Sam didn't seem to be asking for sympathy. I could have said I hadn't meant what I'd said, that I didn't know what I was talking about, but what Sam had told me didn't seem to have much to do with that; it could have come up after anything.

We didn't say anything, either of us, for a long time, just stared at the water, heard the light patter of conversation from the other end of the pool. Finally Sam said, "This is stupid. Let's get dressed." We got up and walked into the house.

What happened next seems in some ways so strange that I hesitate even to mention it. It only happened once, nothing like it ever happened again, and in that way it seems uncharacteristic of my friendship with Sam. At times, on the other hand, it seems the logical end of our friendship. It seemed somehow to follow from the things we had said at the pool, though we didn't mention them again; we didn't make the connection.

There is something else I should probably mention, though I also don't think that it had any direct connection with what happened next: I don't think Sam noticed. While Sam was telling me about his mother, while my heart was pounding and my lungs felt empty, I was also sexually excited. I had an erection. No doubt that has some vast significance in my psychic life. I know now, of course, about men who like to be beaten; I know about men who like in other ways to be dominated by women. I don't think I am especially that way. But something in the thought of that woman, that quiet distinguished woman, doing something in a violent passion; something in the thought of her cold-bloodedness, telling the boy to strip, telling him where to lie; something in the thought that it only happened when they were alone in the house, as if she were waiting for them to be alone; something in the thought of shouts, and screams, and entreaties, and a woman who paid no attention to them; something in all that excited me. There was a closeness about it, a passion, that my family never had, just as we never had the distant silence that was the other side of it.

I feel sure that Sam had not noticed my excitement. We were quiet in his room, sheepish, as we peeled off our wet suits. Before he started to dress, though, he turned to me, reached down and touched himself, said, "I got this caught in my zipper the other day. Gave it a little nick."

Sure enough, there was a small red mark partway up his cock.

In addition to everything else—and I'm not sure this was unrelated; he may just have been more mature than the rest of us—Sam had what must have been the biggest cock in the eighth grade. We had all entered puberty, or nearly all of us, but Sam had a man's cock on a body that in many ways was still a boy's. It was long, and thick, surrounded at its base by dark hair, his balls were also heavy and hairy, and as I looked down at it—this was just like everything else—that was the cock I wished I could have, just one more way that I wanted to be like Sam Golden. I had never felt such an urge before, but for some reason I wanted to hold it, to heft it, to see what it was like. It was as if touching his cock would make me more like him.

"Touch it," Sam said, as if he could read my mind.

I reached down and took it in my hand.

We were not looking at each other. We were both looking down. It was as if there were three presences in the room, me, and him, and his cock, and we were concentrating on that third presence to keep from looking at each other.

His cock began to stiffen and grow hard.

"Have you done it?" he said. "Made yourself come?"

"Yes," I said. Only about eight times a day.

"Do it to me," he said.

There was a great deal we were not saying. He did not say, for instance, "I want you to do it to me," had not said, before, "I bet you want to touch it." We did not say, "God, this is weird," or, "I don't believe we're doing this"; we did not say— what we both knew—that what we were doing had some connection with what had been said at the pool, was all part of the same strangeness. We did not say we liked each other, we loved each other, that we were best friends. In a way all those things seemed part of what we were doing, and in a way they seemed to have nothing to do with it; it was just happening.

He stepped over and lay across the bed, and I lay down beside him. By that time his cock was fully erect, and I started to stroke it, slowly and awkwardly. It felt strange to be reaching over to touch somebody else, propped up on my arm the way I was; it felt strange to be so close to him. I could feel the heat come off his body, see a little trickle of sweat roll down his chest. He was lying on his back with his eyes closed, his teeth pressed to his lower lip. His cock felt huge and hot. He came very soon, spurting way up on his belly, and groaned and shuddered on the bed. I kept stroking until he finished.

He opened his eyes and smiled up a little sheepishly, as if embarrassed, reached for one of the towels from swimming, and wiped himself off. "Lie back," he said, tossing down the towel, then stood and stepped over to my other side, lay down, and started to touch me. By the time I had finished with him I had an erection myself. His hand was quicker, and more knowing, than mine had been (the kid was even better at jerking off!); it was the first time anyone had ever touched me there, and it felt warm, and smooth, and terribly intense. I also came very quickly, the strongest orgasm I'd ever had. It felt as if I wouldn't want to do it again for weeks. A couple of hours, anyway.

I wiped off with the other towel, then Sam took them both out and put them in a hamper. When he came back we started to get dressed.

"It doesn't mean you're queer, Henry," he said.

"I know," I said. Though I didn't know. I didn't know the first thing about it.

"It's normal for this age. I read it in a book."

"Okay."

I didn't particularly care at that point. Normal or abnormal, queer or not queer. I just knew it felt better than anything else I'd ever done in my life.

"Not that I want to get in the habit of it," he said.

"No."

"Maybe it would make you queer, if you did it too much."

We never did do it again, as it turned out, never even spoke of it. I think I would have done it, but Sam never brought it up. It remained the strange thing we had done on that hot May morning, just like the strange conversation we had had down at the pool. We had never mentioned the conversation again. I don't think I ever said another thing to Sam about his mother in his life.

Though Sam did say something before we left the bedroom that morning. "That stuff about my mother. I didn't really tell you because of what you said. I'd been wanting to tell somebody about that for a long time."

"Okay."

"I told you because you're my friend."

III

The All Comers Track Meet in May was the ancient idea of some administrative higher-up; it had been a school tradition for years. All Comers was right: every kid from the eighth grade was required to attend, and all the ninth graders from the upper school. There was no rule that you had to participate, but there was a definite suggestion (pounded into us for days ahead of time) that as long as you were going to be at the upper school the next year, and as a little token of your willingness to join into the spirit of things, you should at least enter one event. It was supposed to be more like a field day than an athletic competition. All our teachers came out, and the ninth-grade teachers from the upper school. It was a time for people to meet each other, for the eighth graders to see the campus and get used to the idea of being there.

In actual fact, of course, it was none of those things. For one thing we already knew, if not everybody, then at least most of the important guys in the ninth grade; we had been at school with them the year before. For another, the ninth graders didn't feel any compulsion to enter events; they had already been at the school a year, and everybody knew what fuck-offs they really were. The eighth graders stayed in nervous little clumps, and the ninth graders hovered around their perimeters, like sharks around a school of tuna. The ninth-grade teachers, no doubt shy people themselves, just stood around talking to the eighth-grade teachers. Whom they already knew. Only the talented ninth graders—those who had been on the track team, for instance—chose to enter, so it was really just one more chance for the older class to stomp us into the dirt. A worthwhile introduction, as it turned out, to the whole method of the upper school.

It was just like Sam, of course, to take what looked like an occasion for humiliation and turn it into an opportunity, to train for the track meet that everyone else just sat around and dreaded.

The afternoon of the track meet, late in May, was genuinely miserable. No doubt that was a school tradition too. It was not cold at that point, but terribly windy, leaves flapping and tree limbs shaking, the sky alternating between pewter gray and billiard-ball black. It didn't actually rain much for as bad as it looked; it would look like rain, then look as if the world were coming to an end, then sprinkle a few drops and go back to looking like rain again. We had changed at our locker room, into the bulky gray sweatsuits that everybody wore around a track in those days, and as we rode the bus to the upper school the sky just got darker and darker. In the still of the bus those sweatsuits were hot, and the day was terribly humid. Nobody talked much.

If the middle school was modeled on the elaborate marble-floored mansion we were all one day expected to own, the upper school was a miniature of the Ivy League college we were expected to attend. It really did look like a place where you'd go away to school (which many people did, boarding there just to get the practice even though they lived within commuting distance). To get there we drove down the wide boulevard—a medley of bumps and cavernous potholes—that led to the Allegheny, then crossed the river and passed through a small town into the exclusive suburb where the school was located. All around us, on the road to the school, were rolling green lawns, immaculately cut, and huge impressive houses, mostly Colonial in style, not the tightly packed dirty brick houses of the city. The most impressive rolling lawn, and most substantial brick structures, were those of the school itself, which you entered through brick and black iron gates toward the end of the road. The driveway wound up past the steepled chapel and the main academic building, entered a quadrangle to where four dorms were located, one on each corner, then ran down a hill on the other side of the quad to the gym. The track ran around the football field below the gym, and below the football field, on successive terraces, were soccer fields, baseball fields, beyond them even a golf course.

There was a real beauty to the place, as we stepped off the bus and stared down at it; beyond the track, and beyond the lower levels of fields that we could not actually see, were high hills of trees, amid the trees an occasional mansion (who lived in such places? I was often to wonder), against the deep green of the trees the dark sky of scudding clouds. Down on the track, guys were standing in packs, looking up at the bus and grinning, or they were jogging around the track, doing exercises to loosen up.

"We've got to warm up," Sam said, as soon as we got off the bus. He was rolling his head around, shaking his arms. "Got to get loose."

"I'm plenty warm already," I said. The bus had felt like a steam bath. "If I get any looser, my arms'll fall off."

I was feeling a little weak at the knees, if the truth be known.

"We should jog a couple laps," Sam said. "You get stiff on a bus ride like that."

"A couple laps. Jesus." Until a couple of months before, that was as far as I'd ever run.

"You don't run well until you're loose. You don't get loose until you've run pretty far."

Try as he might, Sam couldn't convince me that what I needed was to jog half a mile. I let him go, walked around the infield some, even trotted a few steps, imitated the ninth graders in the exercises they were doing. Mostly I just tried to keep my stomach from vaulting up through my throat and out my mouth.

I had never intended to enter the track meet seriously. Even in my training, I had thought of myself as trying to get into shape, not preparing for anything special. My intention for the meet had been to do what most of the other guys did, enter some inconspicuous event and hope I wasn't noticed.

"I took up running to lose weight," I had said to Sam a couple of weeks before, when we discussed it. "Not to compete in it."

"You get bored if you just try to lose weight. You've got to have goals."

"I do have goals. So many pounds." I didn't really, but it sounded good.

"I mean real goals. Not like some old lady. Running's an athletic endeavor."

"Anyway, I don't want to enter the mile." That was what he was suggesting. "I'm not sure I can run a mile, when the chips are down."

"You run two every day."

"I'll enter the half."

"You don't have the speed for the half."

I didn't have the speed for the mile, when you got right down to it.

"You don't have a chance in the half," Sam said.

"I don't have a chance in anything. Jesus Christ. Who's talking about chances here?"

"You've got to enter the thing where you have the best shot. At least act like you're serious. What's the use of even doing the thing, if you're not going to be serious?"

All right then, if that was the way he felt. I wouldn't do it.

I never seemed to see that the thing Sam insisted was best for me was also always the thing he wanted me to do.

There was a larger field in the mile than I might have expected, a couple of other eighth graders who thought they could last the distance, several ninth graders who had run cross-country or the distance events that year, seven guys in all. We were packed together at the starting line, bunched into about two and a half lanes, and in the crowd that was wandering around in the field I heard a couple of people say my name and laugh. I definitely wasn't listed as the early favorite. That was the first time I had ever seen the start of a distance race; I'd had no idea we'd be jammed in together like that. When the gun went off I must have jumped three feet, and I took off like a sprinter. It wasn't long, though, before the seven runners had strung themselves out, and I was back at the end of the string.

I think it was on that day that I actually caught the track bug. I had found in the past couple of months that I enjoyed running more than I had ever thought I would, that once I got in shape it wasn't all dull throbbing pain, but falling in love with the sport of track and field was a slightly different thing. The sky was still dark when the race began, the wind still gusting—shouts of the spectators seemed to be blown about—and as we headed into the first turn we were splattered by a few drops of rain; the weather lent a certain drama to the race.

I had never actually run on a track before, and I liked that surface that gave a little, the bite of the cinders under my feet. I liked the way the curves came up and you banked into them slightly, giving the illusion (in my case) of speed. I liked it that a few guys were dashing around the infield, running to selected spots to shout encouragement to their friends, but especially liked the way the bulk of the spectators pulled further and further into the background as you ran, so their shouts were distant echoes.

There was something intimate about running the mile, only you and the other runners off on that backstretch and with any real idea of what was happening. Feet pounded and puffs of dust and cinders arose; you could see a runner labor and begin to falter, hear if you got close his hoarse deep breathing. Track, I always thought, was simultaneously the most relaxed of all sports and the most nerve-wracking; most of the time you just lay around on the grass watching other people do things, or stretched your muscles waiting for your event to start, but when your moment finally came it was you all alone, everybody seeing how you did, as you came back to the homestretch and ran through those spectators again. I also found track to be the friendliest of sports; guys between races sat and talked to guys from other teams, and there was the instant camaraderie of meeting a guy from your own event: you had that experience in common. I didn't discover all those things that first day, of course. I discovered them gradually, through the course of several years. But they all somehow seem to be present in that first experience of running the mile.

What I did discover that first day was that running a race was not nearly as hard as I had thought it would be. I discovered the terrific jolt of adrenaline that came at the start of a race (the flip side of the yawning lassitude that precedes it), so that with a little experience you learn to hold yourself back at the beginning. I discovered that Sam had been right, I should have warmed up, because I did run much better when my muscles were loose. I discovered I could run way faster than I had on my mornings with Sam. I discovered a certain strength, or endurance, it might best be called rhythm, once the pace was established. I discovered I had a lot more left over at the end than I had ever thought I would. I can still see myself coming around the last turn and passing the two other eighth graders who were in the race; both of them were binding up and dying, one looking as if he were about to fall. I didn't run any great race, but finished strong, and came in fifth, better anyway than I had thought I would do.

Sam had employed a different strategy: he took off with the leaders and ran their pace, saw how long he could stay with them. He was more confident of his conditioning. He had never been a threat for first, but there was a real battle for the next three places; he stayed with the ninth graders until the very end. He eventually did pass one of them, nipped him at the tape for third, but he was far more tired at the end than I was, walking around with his hands on his hips and his chest heaving, bending over from time to time to catch his breath.

"I should have gone out faster," I said, once I had recovered some. "I should have gone out way faster. I didn't know how much I'd have at the end."

"It's hard to tell. You probably wouldn't have finished any higher."

That was true. I would never have finished up there with him.

"You ran a good race," Sam said. "We both ran a good race. Let's walk a lap."

The guys at the finish line were still grinning—they'd grin at anything—but I could meet their stares now. Most of them couldn't have done what I did.

The one other feature of the mile that was interesting that afternoon—possibly the most interesting feature in the long run—was that it was won by Bennett Wilder, who had broken five minutes for the first time. He had been on the track team that spring, was the best freshman miler and one of the best freshman distance prospects they'd had for years. He had apparently found the sport where the best man won, where they couldn't take it away from you if you had the most talent and did the most work. While Sam and I were walking a lap, catching our breath and talking, he was trotting around the backstretch, warming down like a fine thoroughbred—his head lolling, arms dangling—all alone.

IV

"So it's North Carolina, is it?" Sam said.

"Looks like it," I said.

We were out in his side yard throwing the ball around, the same yard where, nine months before, he had tried to teach me a curveball. It was the last Saturday in May. Exams began the next week.

"What the hell's in North Carolina?"

"That's what I'd like to know. I think it's just another one of my father's damn fool ideas."

That spring, a little over a month before, my father had been at a Southern university giving a paper, and on a sudden impulse had rented a car and driven to the seashore. Just wanted to smell the salt air, he said. It was still out of season, and the whole coastline had been pretty much deserted; for a

man, however, who had spent his whole life vacationing in
New Jersey, it was a revelation. Whereas his summer beach experience had always been to wade through a mass of heavily
oiled bodies until he found a patch of sand that was unoccu-
pied, to stake it out with an umbrella or a large quilt—while
all around him, as far as the eye could see, were boardwalks
and game arcades and hot dog stands—all he had found in
North Carolina was the basics, sand and sea and wind and
wood, rather weather-beaten wood at that. All along the
beaches—and the beaches included spectacular massive dunes
—was nothing but cottages, many of them up on stilts. An occasional restaurant. Although it was April, and the place was
deserted, you could see it would never really be crowded.
There were not places enough to house people to crowd it.

We had never stayed more than a couple of weeks in New
Jersey—that was all we could take—but in North Carolina,
standing down on a dune, my father had a sudden vision of another kind of vacation, a working vacation, where we didn't
just sit on the beach all day but actually occupied a beach cottage, made it our home. He would enjoy the beach—we would
all enjoy the beach—but he would also work there, and finish
the monograph he had been writing on several obscure
nineteenth-century American humorists.

On an impulse he put down a deposit to reserve a cottage for
ten weeks.

The whole family reacted differently. Mother immediately
said it was no vacation for her to live in a scrubby beach cottage somewhere and do the cooking with makeshift utensils all
summer; Father said we would go out all she wanted, that
things were cheap and we could afford to be extravagant. Susan flatly refused to go. She had been making other plans anyway, having just graduated from college, and decided to take
this opportunity to set up an apartment on her own. For someone who had been trying to break away from the family, the
thought of spending ten long weeks with them in the same cottage must have been sheer hell. Teddy was ecstatic, but immediately wanted to know what kind of TV the place had; though
Father had envisioned a primitive existence, wandering the
beach and taking our food from the sea and sleeping at night to

the sound of the surf, he agreed to take our portable. To deny
Teddy that would have been wanton cruelty, and might have
resulted in withdrawal symptoms. Bennett was guardedly op-
timistic. For a person with genuinely hermetic tendencies, the
situation sounded ideal.

I wasn't sure how I felt. On the one hand, I loved the beach,
loved to fish and swim and sunbathe and eat seafood. On the
other hand, I had a life outside the family that I hated to lose.
Two and a half months. I was a little like Susan, I suppose, just
starting to pull myself away from the family. I hated to be
thrown back in again.

"Maybe you could come," I said to Sam, right off the top of
my head. It sounded a little crazy—how would he get along in
the family? (how would he get along with Bennett?)—but it
would have solved all my problems.

"I've got to stay here and take care of the pool," he said.

"You couldn't leave it for a week?"

"I couldn't leave it for a day. You wouldn't believe how that
thing gets. Anyway, if it wasn't for that, my parents would be
sending me to camp."

Sam's father was actually going to employ him that summer,
pay him quite a lot of money. ("If it wasn't for him I'd just
have to get some other asshole," he said to me. "Cost a lot more
money. It's always cheaper to keep it in the family.") It
sounded great to be making a lot. Unfortunately, he'd also
have to hang around that house all the time.

As it turned out, that Saturday in May was the last time we
threw the ball around all summer. There was something fundamentally different about the way Sam and I were playing
catch from the way it had been before. For one thing, of
course, we were really just out there because the pool was
being occupied by Mrs. Golden and her friends. We had finally decided it was less frustrating to stay away than to sit
there and not be able to do anything. But we were also somehow playing in a different way, or at least Sam was. Just nine
months before, we had always had some purpose in mind. Sam
was teaching me a curve, or he was working on grounders, or I
was learning how to go back on a pop fly. We weren't doing
those things anymore. We were killing time, something we had

never done much of. If I threw a tough grounder Sam made a halfhearted stab, or he took off his glove and threw it at the ball. When he got it he threw an even tougher one at me.

"You looking forward to next year?" Sam said to me at one point.

Maybe that was the problem. We had just spent a year as eighth graders, top men on the totem pole. We weren't looking forward to getting pounded down again. Things didn't seem to have as much point if you couldn't do anything with them.

"I don't know. It's kind of exciting, I guess. Also kind of scary. I guess I am."

There came a time when the old middle school looked pretty small.

"If you want my opinion"—Sam leaned back and let fly a long lazy peg—"I think it's going to be the same old crap."

He would say that. Sam's big thing was debunking, those days.

"Every year they make it sound like a big thing," he said. "You're in the eighth grade now and you've got a lot of responsibilities. Set an example for the younger kids. Then you're in the ninth grade. You are one of the younger kids. You've got to live up to the great example the older kids are setting. I admit the place looks a lot different. That big campus, and all those facilities. But I swear to God it'll be the same thing. English class'll be English class, and math class'll be math. Freshman sports will have the same old guys in them, and the same kind of half-ass coach. The big game of the year will be when we have the immense privilege of playing the tenth grade. Who we've only played about a zillion times."

All that was easy enough for him to say. He wasn't returning once again to the school where his genius of a brother was one year ahead of him. The endlessly repeating nightmare.

"I'm tired of all that crap," Sam said.

"*You're* tired," I said. "How can *you* be tired?"

"It's easy. Just watch me."

It didn't bother me that Sam could do all he could. I thought it was great that somebody could do all that. But it sure as hell was going to bother me if he could do all that and then complained about it.

"You've got what everybody wants," I said. "You're the best athlete in the school. Captain of all the teams. You get great grades. The teachers all like you. The students." You've got the biggest cock in the class!

"It's not that easy being me."

"I wouldn't mind trying it for a few days."

"You say that now. It's easy to say. But how would you like it if you had these exams coming up . . ."

"I do have these exams coming up."

". . . if you had these exams coming up, with all we've got to study, and if you didn't get a ninety-six or something everybody would give you all kinds of shit."

"My heart bleeds for you, Sam. Honest to God."

"You got a ninety-two. That stinks. How would you like it if every time you're on a team, no matter what team you're on, every time you're on a team they want you to do the whole thing. If we lose, it's your fault. If we win, that was what they expected. You've got nothing to gain. It used to be fun when they laid the whole thing on me, I liked the challenge, but not anymore. It's just the same old thing. You've got to do it again."

"I'd love to be able to do what you can do."

"I would too, if I could just do that. If all this other stuff didn't go with it. I'm tired of the other stuff. I'm tired of being me."

Let me be you, I wanted to say.

"Next year *will* be different," I said. "A bigger challenge."

"Thank you, Joe Upper School."

"You can try out for the varsity. Or at least the JV."

"*And* play on the same team as your big *brother*. Whoopee."

"It's not just my brother. There are all kinds of guys out there."

"Maybe." He unleashed a vicious peg. "But I've got to stay here all summer. Hanging around the house. Before I get to that. I've got to take care of a swimming pool for a bunch of old ladies."

There was no getting around that. Maybe Sam was really mad at me, was trying to tell me something with all that other talk. Maybe it was because I wasn't going to be around—there was no one to work with—that he didn't want to work at anything.

"I'm burnt out," he said.

"You're *not!*" I shouted the words.

"It's not all that surprising. It happens all the time."

I had tried to throw him a grounder, but put too much on it; it wound up a wicked one-hopper, but he swooped down and picked it up effortlessly, as if the ball had been lying dead on the ground. He just had those great hands.

"What a tragedy," he said. "Fourteen years old, and already over the hill."

FIVE

My father always wore a straw hat at the beach, and a sleeveless T-shirt (what my friends and I called a cement-mixer T-shirt, in honor of the men who most often wore them), so he somehow looked like a bather from the roaring twenties. Along with his canvas-backed chair he brought out a huge bent pipe with a lid on the bowl, a tin of tobacco, a box of kitchen matches, and a massive paperback; he never seemed to read a thin book at the beach. He sat in the chair (which gradually sank deep into the sand under his weight), and smoked, and read. His salt-and-pepper beard was full, but somehow, in the strong breeze off the ocean, looked scraggly; his hair hung stringily out of his hat, windblown and disheveled; his rolls of fat folded up under his shirt, so he looked even fatter (if that was possible) than usual; he sat nearly motionless for hours at a time—his paperback folded back as if he were trying to destroy it—and read. After a particularly long session his muscles tended to stiffen, and getting up from the chair could be an elaborate process. I tried not to be present for it.

Mother's beach problem was one of fashion. Given the situation and clothes of her choosing, where she could calculate the effect, she was an absolutely stunning woman, for all her size. Sometimes even at the beach, when she had had a little too much sun (every third day, it seemed), she could come out in a billowing and blindingly white sundress, and a wide-brimmed straw sunbonnet, and be positively dazzling. The rest of the time, however, she was a mess. No bathing suit in the world made her look like anything but a fat lady, and often she came out in that sunbonnet too, so she looked like a Mexican squaw on a holiday. Her big thing was magazines, not books, and she always brought out two or three, turned to the middle of some article. She also brought her needlepoint, or knitting, or sewing, to get sand all over that. Her skin was fair, and never seemed to tan; it was white, or pink, or a garish red that was painful to behold. She never gave up, though, was forever out there applying suntan lotion, so her body was greased like a heavyweight's in the ring. She was terribly restless at the beach, would sit there making lists. She never sat forty minutes that she didn't think of three hours' worth of errands to run.

Bennett was in his big reading period then (actually, it had begun a couple of years before and hadn't ended yet); being at the beach hardly altered his life at all. He did take one swim every day, after his early-morning run (which he took back on the soft tarry roads, not on the sand). Most of the day he sat in a rocking chair in the shade of our porch, and read. He was continuing to make his way through Shakespeare that summer, seemed to have the huge black volume in his lap all the time. He read with his usual intense concentration, rarely looking up from the page. When he did look up, it was usually to intone some lines from what he'd read. "Oh, what a rogue and peasant slave am I!" he would say, if he felt bad about something (couldn't have put it better myself), or, when Father had a complaint, he would shake his head and sympathize, "Uneasy lies the head that wears a crown." (Teddy also went around the cottage repeating these phrases.) Late in the afternoon Bennett took a long bicycle ride by himself—we had all rented bikes for the summer—and sometimes he took a swim after that. At night he played miniature golf with us, or cards, or Monopoly; if he had read any more his eyeballs would have fallen out. But he kept an iron-tight schedule that ruled his day. Even at the beach he could have punched a time clock.

Teddy also kept a rigid schedule, but his was printed on the television page of the newspaper. I don't know whether it was because the South was backward or because the little television station at the beach took whatever it could get, but it had an incredible collection of ancient television shows, like a history of the tube. *"My Little Margie!"* Teddy would shout, dashing out of the surf and in the direction of the house, or *"December Bride!"* He seemed to have learned to tell time by the sun. The reception on the little portable was fuzzy and faint, but he lay there watching contentedly anyway. Between shows he ran back into the water, or built elaborate structures with wet sand, or begged for money to go play miniature golf; he also spent a great deal of time around the pinball machines at the fishing pier. You could argue with what Teddy did, but never with the energy he had. That kid knew what he wanted.

To my father's credit, I should also mention that he accomplished a lot of work that summer. He had set up a study in a spare bedroom, and on regular occasions, especially when the sun was too hot on the beach, he went there to work. Often down on the sand we could hear the clacking of his portable typewriter. He did finish his monograph—*Vaudeville on the Prairie: Three Nineteenth-Century American Humorists*—and it was published the next year by LSU Press, where it remains in print to this day.

Myself, I loved that summer at the beach. There must be things I'm forgetting—the odd tinny taste of the water, the sand we could never manage to brush out of the beds, the green-headed flies that came around the beach late in the afternoon expressly to bite the backs of our thighs—but my memory is that it was a wonderful summer and I loved every minute. I liked the New Jersey beaches—I still like the New Jersey beaches—but that summer I decided I liked North Carolina beaches better. There wasn't as much to do, but the things themselves were better.

My life was scheduled by the tides. When the tide was low, at its lowest ebb, it had left a stretch of hard-packed sand, and that was when I took my run. Sometimes it was early in the morning, when there was not quite a fog, but a haze, over the water, the sun rising slowly to burn it away, gulls gliding low over the waves (which always seemed to be gentle at that hour) looking for food. Sometimes it was in the blazing heat of mid-day, when the sun was high in the sky and glittered on the water like silver, the surf full of swimmers. Sometimes it was

on toward evening, with the sun sinking back toward the
sound and people starting to pack up their gear and head toward the cottages, a few evening fishermen starting to arrive.

The beach at low tide was a great place to run. I ran barefoot, and really learned to heel-and-toe it that summer, which
is the best way to run distance. The surface was just right,
hard-packed but with a little give as your foot hit. As I ran one
way (and for a long time I didn't know which way it would be,
though eventually I learned to tell by the direction of the
waves) there was a breeze at my face; the other way it seemed
to die off completely, which meant it was at my back. The sun
always seemed suddenly hotter in that direction. The wind and
sun, in fact, were real factors at the beach, the sun especially
(it is rare to run anywhere else and not find shade somewhere
along the way). If you began to get hot you could move into the
surf, cooling off your feet at least, or stop to splash water on
your body. I ran strictly by time down there, since there was
no way to measure distance (though I did, eventually, have
certain cottages as landmarks); by the end of the summer I was
running forty-five or fifty minutes, which is a hell of a way on
the sand. Afterward I took a walk in the surf, then a long
swim.

High tide, or at least the time when the tide was getting high
and coming in, was the best for fishing. The fishing was wonderful there. I had taken all our equipment, including a lot of
heavy tackle we used for bottom fishing in New Jersey, but
what proved to be the best was the freshwater spinner I had
taken as an afterthought. You could use shrimp for bait,
though the sand fleas that skittered around in the surf by the
dozens were just as good, and you hardly had to cast any distance at all, just out to where the waves broke, which was
where the fish fed. There seemed an unlimited number of
spots, and some mullet, and sea trout, and flounder (sometimes you would step on a flounder when you walked out for a
swim); in early August the pompano arrived. Fishermen with
heavier equipment cast way out for bluefish. The fish I caught
were rarely large, but they were plentiful, and if I fished long
enough (alternating with Teddy) I could catch a real meal of
them. More often we caught a few, and would have them as a

side dish, or Father would eat them as a special treat for breakfast.

I had a huge appetite that summer, never seemed to get full—something about the salt air seemed to do that—but I didn't gain weight because I was swimming and running so much. I ate at the pier, hot dogs and cheeseburgers with chili and slaw and all the other strange garnishes they have down South; I ate sausage and country ham biscuits, new delicacies to me; I sampled the incredible variety of cakes and fried pies and ice-cream treats that they stocked at the pier. There was a diner not far away that served breakfast pancakes with a thick blueberry syrup, and that served, unasked-for, delicious fried potatoes with your eggs (the grits I cared for less). Sometimes in the evening we went to a seafood restaurant where they had benches and wooden tables and huge seafood platters, bluefish and shrimp and scallops and oysters, with a bowl of clam chowder for openers and a huge basket of hush puppies (also new to me) on the side. As we finished our meal we could look out on the sound, at the back of the restaurant, and see the sun set over the water.

I think of that summer as the turning point of my life, though the real turning point had come several months before. When I got back to Pittsburgh I was a deep brown, my hair bleached almost white; I was in terrific shape and running every day; my body was as thin as it would ever get, and starting to sprout some muscles; I was full of plans, looking forward to the coming year. I felt ready, even anxious, to start the upper school. Bring it on.

II

My family had come home by way of Washington, stopping for a couple of days to visit the Smithsonian and the art museums and to experience firsthand the hottest, most humid August city on earth. The last day, we decided to drag it out and see a few more things, so we didn't make our usual predawn start; we rode on the turnpike through the heat of the day and arrived in Pittsburgh in the middle of the afternoon, staggering out of the car as if from a sauna (it would be impossible to describe the ordeal it was to ride in the backseat with Teddy). The city was hazy and overcast, the way it seems to be every day in August; a slight breeze stirred. We all pitched in to unload the car, and I went upstairs to unpack—throwing things down the laundry chute, mostly—then hurried outside, headed up toward Penn. It felt great to be back. It felt great to be out of that car.

If you had asked me, I would probably have said I was going to see Sam. Actually, I was going up for him to see me.

When I got to his house, he was working on the grass; he had finished mowing, was raking the clippings. He was at the end of a row, looked up at me as I approached and looked back down, then looked up again. His jaw fell open as if I were floating on air. He actually dropped the rake.

"Jesus Christ," he said. "You're skinny."

If I'd had a rake handy, I would have dropped it too.

The problem isn't just that you don't see changes in a person day by day. It's that when you've known a person for months, the way I'd know Sam, then don't see him for a while, you tend to remember him the first way you ever saw him. I was expecting that short quick kid with the marvelous coordination who had stood bravely beneath that booming punt a year before.

That wasn't exactly what I got.

He looked bigger, for one thing. Way bigger. He was wearing a blue oxford-cloth shirt—Brooks Brothers, it looked like to me—with the sleeves rolled up and the shirttails untucked; they nearly obscured the ragged madras shorts he had on underneath. On his feet were battered penny loafers that didn't seem to have been shined for months. No socks. He seemed to be bursting even out of those clothes. His shoulders were broad, his chest thick; his arms looked long and his hands large. You would not have described him as short anymore. Somehow he also looked shaggy and overgrown, and it was a while before I noticed—what a woman, for instance, would have noticed right away—that his hair was much longer, probably hadn't been cut in a month. He looked mature, that was all. He looked like a young man.

He had probably looked the same way the previous spring. I just hadn't noticed.

"What the hell have you been doing with yourself?" he said.

"I don't know. The usual beach stuff. Swimming a lot. Fishing. I also kept up with my running. I did a lot of running."

"I believe it."

"What about you?"

Sam grinned, shrugged. "I've been loafing around. Different stuff. I sure as hell haven't been running."

Which brings up the question, in a way, of why I had. It seems perfectly natural to a person like me; I took up running after a casual encounter over a malted milkshake one afternoon when I was thirteen years old, and have been at it ever since. But it wouldn't have seemed natural to a guy like Sam, who—like the rest of the world—might take something up for a while, then drop it, maybe take it up again after a few months.

The truth of the matter was that I was running scared. The act of running had made me take possession of my body in a whole new way. A year before, my torso had been surrounded by a layer of blubber that had a life of its own, added to itself at will while I stood back and stared at it with some alarm. Now the blubber was gone; I was all me. Something in the act of running had done that for me, the act of standing up and walking out the door and doing it. I didn't want to stop. I was afraid I'd lose my body again.

"There wasn't a whole lot to do at the beach," I said, lying a little. "It helped kill some time."

He seemed a little edgy, as if even talking about the summer made him restless. That edginess was new to him.

"Why don't we take a walk?" he said.

"A walk?" That wasn't anything we had ever done. "What do you want to take a walk for?"

"Just to get away. I get tired of being around the house all the time."

"Me too. But I just got here."

He shrugged. "Let's take a walk."

"Don't you have to finish the grass?"

"It'll be here when I get back."

"I'm hot. I've been in a car all day. I'd like to take a swim." I had even brought my suit.

"We'll swim later. I want to get away, for Christ's sake."

I didn't get it, particularly (taking a walk! It sounded like something a couple of old ladies would do), but Sam really seemed to want to, so I left my suit there, beside his rake and the grass clippings, and we started to walk, down to Reynolds and over toward school, the same general direction we had used to run. That first block of Reynolds was positively dim, it was so thick with leafy trees, but the lawns were mostly burned out, the way they get toward the end of August.

While we walked we talked, about our summers, though Sam said there wasn't much to tell about his. Every morning he had gotten up to do the pool first thing, about a two-hour job, fishing out dead bugs and other debris, cleaning the filter, checking the composition of chemicals. It wasn't a hard job, just boring, the same exacting tasks seven mornings a week for three months. He didn't have much to do the rest of the day. He could swim, of course, but that wasn't much fun alone, and he hadn't found anyone else he really liked to do it with (I wasn't entirely unhappy to hear that). Half the time, anyway, his mother was out there. There didn't seem to be any good pickup ball games, the way there had been the summer before. It was funny, you'd have thought that if you lost interest in one or two things you'd take up with something else, but for Sam it seemed to be all or nothing: if he lost interest in one thing he lost interest in everything. Mostly he had just sat around all summer listening to the radio.

"And singing along," he said. "I know the top forty by heart. Want to hear it?"

"Another time," I said.

In comparison, I felt guilty about all I had done. I didn't tell him how great it had been, how clean and uncluttered the beaches were, how the water was clear and almost green in color, how easy it was to fish. I made the pier sound like a dump. I did talk about my running, but tried to play even that down.

"It was natural to keep going further. Like you said last spring. You get bored staying at the same distance."

"So how far did you end up going?"

"I don't know. I can't judge distance at the beach. Maybe three miles. Four." Probably further, actually.

"Jesus."

"I'm going out for cross-country in the fall. Bennett too. He says it's the only sport that's JV and varsity, there's no freshman team. Everybody runs together."

"If you make it."

"Everybody makes it. If you don't make either squad you run with the JVs. At least at home."

"Huh."

"And I'm going out for track in the spring."

"We're already planning for the spring?"

"It goes with cross-country."

"And you're giving up baseball."

"I'll do better in track, eventually. That's another sport where everybody runs together. At least in the distances. I don't think I'd be that good in baseball. People were starting to catch up to my fastball last year. Even you got a few hits off me."

"I owned you, Christ. You didn't even look fast to me."

By that time we had reached the entrance to Frick Park, a gray stone building with an archway to it; Sam led us through. I hadn't entered that park for years. I had gone there on walks with my parents when I was a kid, but had never gone in alone because they had told me vagrants hung out in the park who hurt little children. More recently I had realized they meant queers hung out there looking for little boys. Vaguely I pictured myself getting groped by a hobo.

I didn't see anybody as we walked down the path. The way my parents had talked, I would have expected a man behind every tree.

As if he had done it thousands of times, Sam took a pack of cigarettes from his pocket and offered it to me. "Want one?"

I stopped in the path and stared at him. "What's this?"

"A bar of soap. Wash your face."

"You smoke?"

"Of course I smoke. What else would I have these for?" Sam was blushing, half smiling. "Do you want one?"

I just stared. "What the hell do you want to smoke for?"

"Do you *want* one? Answer my question."

"No I don't want one. I wouldn't even know what to do with it."

"I could show you."

"I don't want one."

He shrugged. "Up to you."

He took out a cigarette and put away the pack (the pack, I had noticed, was battered and nearly empty, which somehow made things worse), then took out a lighter (a lighter!) and lit up. The motions seemed entirely practiced. He inhaled deeply, expelled a stream of smoke with a bored grimace. You would know it. He was even good at smoking.

"Why the hell do you want to do this?" I said.

"If you haven't tried it, don't knock it."

That fucking saying again.

"Smoking stunts your growth," I said.

"Do I look any shorter?"

"It cuts your wind. It ruins your lungs."

"I haven't noticed anything."

"You haven't done anything. All summer. You told me."

All he had done all summer was listen to the top forty and systematically rot his lungs.

"Most professional athletes smoke," Sam said. "I hate to tell you."

"Do your parents know you're doing this?"

"I have no idea. It hasn't come up. I didn't run home first thing and tell them."

They didn't know. His mother would thrash him to within an inch of his life.

"I just don't get it. You never smoked before."

"Give me time. Jesus. I was only thirteen years old."

By that time we were walking down the leafy path that led to the woods, then up the one that led out. Fast trip through the park. We apparently hadn't come there just to appreciate nature.

"It was so boring this summer," Sam said. "You wouldn't believe how boring it was. How nuts it drove me. Smoking relaxes you. Or at least it makes you nervous in a different way. Gives you something to do. Especially when you don't have permission. Getting out of the house for your first cigarette of the day. Sneaking off somewhere after meals. Smoking in your room with the window open. Even just finding a way to buy the things. It exercises your wits. You can build a whole day around smoking cigarettes."

"Like running." I tried to lace my voice with sarcasm.

"Right. You ran. I smoked. No difference."

"Next thing you'll tell me that you drink."

"I've been known to have a few."

"Jesus Christ!" I threw up my hands.

"No hard stuff yet. Just beer and wine."

I stared at the trees and shouted, "Smoking and drinking!"

"For all I knew you were doing it too. How did I know you weren't down at that beach smoking your head off? I kind of figured you were."

"What a hell of a summer you had."

"It was kind of interesting"—he frowned, considering—"in certain ways."

"Where do you get this beer?"

"You've got to be careful about that." Sam dropped his cigarette, ground it into the dirt. "My old man keeps track of his. The best thing is if you know some really far-gone drunk. Who couldn't count his beers if he wanted to."

"You meet them in the park here." Drunken child molesters. If you really want a beer, kid . . .

"I mean the parents of some of your friends. Like Cindy's."

"Cindy's." An alarm went off in my brain.

"You remember how smashed they used to be. Picking us up from dancing school."

Sam was definitely blushing now. He had tried to slip Cindy's name past me unnoticed.

"And that's where you get your beer," I said.

"She's been looking forward to seeing you again. She said to bring you around when you got back."

"I'm surprised she even knew I was gone."

Sam was gazing toward the ground, trying to make his face very matter-of-fact.

"I thought we might go over there now, actually. She just lives in the next street."

What a coincidence.

It was beginning to look as if there had been a little more to Sam's summer than he had been letting on.

I forgot to mention that Sam and I had attended the same dancing school the year before. Probably wanted to spare myself the pain. At the time it seemed a coincidence that we both wound up there; I can remember the stunned look on his face when he walked into the ballroom and saw me standing across from him. Neither of us went to the really posh dancing school in town, Sam because they wouldn't accept Jews (what if I only dance from the waist down?) and I because my father wouldn't patronize a place that had such a restriction. Sam, on the other hand, did not attend dancing school at the Jewish club in town. The place we went, I suppose, represented some odd middle ground. Protestants who were almost, but not quite, in the upper echelons of society; Jews who did not want to confine themselves to their own kind; Catholics (though a really wealthy Catholic could go to the posh dancing school). There seemed to be a lot of ethnic Catholics at our dancing school.

I actually think we had more fun at our dancing school, though none of us, at that age, would admit we had any fun at all. At the posh dancing school, I happen to know (I visited the place twice in my romantic career), the boys had to wear blue suits, and the girls correspondingly dressy dresses. *Both* boys and girls—I found this utterly incredible—wore white gloves. The music was provided by a long, lean, cadaver-like man at the piano—one had the feeling he never left the bench from week to week, just raised his arms to the keys on Friday evenings—who played music that had apparently been popular when he was young. The instructors were teachers from the local schools. That kind of moonlighting was acceptable (just don't let us catch you down at the shoe store). As people entered the room in two lines (boys and girls, and keep your hands off each other, too), an aging dowager by the name of Mrs. Hardwick shook their hands, extending her arm to its fullest length to keep them from getting too close. At the midpoint of the evening she walked to the center of the dance floor, diamonds glittering, jowls sagging, to deliver a lecture on etiquette, while everyone sat on the ornate chairs that surrounded the place. The rest of the evening, they danced to the lilting tunes of the corpse at the piano, doing the waltz, the fox-trot, and, when things really got hot, the rhumba. Shake it, Mrs. Hardwick.

Our dancing school was a faded bourgeois imitation of that. No white gloves, for one thing (thank God), and no blue suits. They boys wore sport coats and ties, the girls skirts and blouses. We met in a smaller, less formal room that had folding chairs around the outside in place of that ornate furniture, boys on one side and girls on the other. We did not have a dowager. Our music was also provided by an older man, who happened also to be bald and thin, but he fancied himself as keeping up with the times, smiled at the dancers as he played and tapped his foot. Our instructors were not moonlighting teachers. They were full-time dance instructors, who did only that for a living.

The male instructor was a guy named Jack McHale. He was a real man, unlike the succession of fairies they had over at the other place. He was probably six-two, with a heavy upper body and long slender legs. He would have made a hell of a light heavyweight. He wore a suit, had a high wave of slick black hair on top of his head. He looked like a small-time nightclub singer, the kind who might invite a heckler from the audience to step outside, then take him to an alley out back and bloody him up pretty good, leaving him bruised and unconscious in a scarlet-stained mud puddle beside the building, wiping the blood from his own knuckles with a silk handkerchief. To me, at least, he was something of an exotic—it was like being instructed in dance by a small-time hood—but to the Catholic kids he was no doubt a logical role model.

The man could dance, I'll say that for him. Our repertoire of dances was considerably larger than that at the posh dancing school; it included the cha-cha, the jitterbug, the bunny hop, balling the jack; it also extended into all the new dances that were springing up in those fertile days. One time when McHale was giving a little lecture on the new dances somebody yelled, "Pony!" and he started galloping around the room like the baddest-assed dago on *American Bandstand*. As a matter of fact, when he did them, the most traditional of dances—even

the waltz—looked like natural, manly things to do. Jack Mc-
Hale made you want to dance.

When he was introducing a new dance, he stood in the middle of the room talking about it for a while, slowly turning to
take everyone in. Once he had finished, he would say, "Miss
Hart?" and extend his hand to the wings; from the next room, a
little annex to the one we were sitting in, his partner would enter.

Miss Hart was not pretty, exactly. She had a plain face,
tastefully made up, brown hair that was reddish and done into
one of the little permanents women wore in those days. She
had a nice body, slender, not spectacular. Like bad Jack, of
course, she was a fantastic dancer. But the thing you noticed
was her immense poise, and his immense poise, and the way
they were so much together. Under the gaze of several dozen
thirteen-year-olds, many of whom were quite flustered by the
situation, they came together without a shred of embarrassment, and danced as if they were one person. His prizefighter's
hand on the small of her back, and her small white hand in his
other big paw, they moved about the room as if in a dream.
There was nothing sexual about the dances they did, but there
was definitely something sexual about the way they came together. "Every Friday night he takes her home after dancing
school and puts it to her," Sam once leaned over and said to
me, and I had the same feeling. I had originally, of course,
been told that sexual intercourse was something married couples did, but I was aware early on that other couples did it too,
and I was absolutely sure those two people did it. They did it
like nobody else had ever done it before. They gave off sparks.

Our dancing school was fun, then. Once we had learned all
the traditional steps, we were allowed to move on to the new
ones, and twice a year we had sock hops, where we brought
our own records and kicked off our shoes to dance to them. At
Christmas there was a big party that began with a roast-beef
dinner downstairs, then moved to the ballroom, where there
was a huge Christmas tree and where we drew for the presents
we had all brought, dancing afterward to a jazzy combo that
accompanied the pianist.

The thing of it was, we had to pretend not to like it. Nobody liked dancing school was the official party line in those days, just as nobody liked girls. Actually I liked dancing school. I liked girls too. I made jokes and snickered about them just like everyone else, while we were sitting on one side and they on the other, but once McHale told us to make a choice, I was glad to do it. I especially—I might as well admit it—liked Cindy.

How exactly we got into a dancing-school carpool with Cindy McCann I'm not quite sure. Once Sam and I had met on the first night, it seemed logical for us to start driving together; I think Cindy's parents were friends of Sam's parents, and had already arranged something with them. Since Cindy rode in the car with us, it was natural to ask her to dance, and I often did. She was a short girl, slightly plump (you knew that as soon as you danced with a girl, put a hand on the small of her back and felt the fat there), and rather pretty, with pixieish blond hair and white-framed glasses. She was always dead silent when we rode in the car, but very friendly, even talkative, while we danced. Something in her manner made her a pal almost immediately. She didn't distance you with flirting. She was your friend.

Sam was right about her parents. On the nights they drove, they always both came, as if it took the two of them to make out the road, and though they were usually just happy, or a little silly, on the way to dancing school, they were totally out of it on the way home, smiling broadly and slurring words and forgetting to end sentences and falling all over each other. It was pretty dangerous, I suppose, but also pretty funny (not to Cindy, as she sat there in her stony silence). We took it as part of the evening's entertainment. They always seemed to get us home.

Cindy lived on a side street not far from the park. Most convenient. You could go to the park for a cigarette, hang around long enough to get molested by a vagrant, then head over to Cindy's for a beer. Hers was a little two-story brick place on a modest lawn. Just enough for her and her parents, and a fully stocked bar.

"Henry!" she said as she opened the door. You'd have thought we were long-lost cousins. "You're back!"

I hate to keep going on about the changes we were all going through, but in many ways hers were the most spectacular of all. The first thing I noticed was that her outfit seemed an imitation of Sam's; she wore a blue oxford-cloth identical to his (I had never seen a girl in such a shirt), also with the sleeves rolled up, also with the tails untucked, and under it a pair of Bermuda shorts. She was barefoot. Her hair was longer than before, and seemed blonder, curling up slightly at the shoulders. She had abandoned her glasses. Her cheeks wore a light blush of makeup. She seemed taller than I had remembered, and not exactly thinner, but her shape had changed. Whereas once her body had been what you might describe as chunky, now she had a waist, she had hips, she had a bottom; most noticeably of all, she had breasts! Not enormous breasts or anything, but breasts nevertheless.

"You're so brown!" she said, as I walked in the door. "And so thin!"

You have tits! I might have said, but I didn't.

There was something secret, conspiratorial, about visiting a girl's house for the first time. Almost wicked. You hoped nobody saw you go in.

A faint scent of luscious perfume lingered in the air around Cindy.

"The parents are both out," she said, as we drifted down the front hall. "But we can only spare two beers." They seemed to be falling into a routine they knew by heart.

"Only two!" Sam's voice was torn with disappointment.

"There are four left. Mother's vague, but she does remember when there's only one left. Or none. I don't think she'll notice the difference between four and two."

This woman was in serious trouble.

"Probably by tomorrow we'll have a whole case to work on. I bet she's out buying it right now."

"Old Henry here doesn't even drink," Sam said. "Or smoke."

"I never said that," I said.

The whole question seemed to take on a new significance with Cindy present.

"He might not have had the chance," Cindy said.

"That's right," I said.

Sam gazed at me, wrinkling his brow.

Down some stairs was a gameroom that was simple but substantial; it seemed to extend under most of the house. It had couches along a couple of walls (beds with back cushions, actually), a Ping-Pong table at the far end, a hi-fi system on a battered cabinet, a small refrigerator. The room was low, with acoustical ceiling, which somehow made it seem more extensive than it was. The floor was a checkerboard of black and white tiles. As soon as we went down there, Cindy put on a record, Sam lit a cigarette, and she stepped over to the refrigerator to get the beer. In a moment the three of us were on the couch. Cindy had sat next to me, and Sam to her; our three bodies touched.

The record was an assortment of fifties ballads, a piano in the background lightly keeping the rhythm, above it a group harmonizing with various dips and werps, in the foreground a tenor doing acrobatics with the lyrics. Already these songs were considered classics.

"This is where Sam spent the summer," Cindy said.

"That isn't what he told me," I said.

"Maybe he's embarrassed about it. Maybe he's ashamed of me."

"I didn't want to shock him too much at once," Sam said. "He just about died when I started smoking."

"Sam made it sound like such a sad, lonely summer," I said. "Nobody around."

"It would have been," Sam said. "Without old Cindy here."

"It's nothing romantic," Cindy said. "We're just pals."

"Good buddies," Sam said.

Things seemed to be moving pretty fast. Who said anything about romantic?

"We've got to split everything even with Henry," Cindy said. "When we get a sip, he gets a sip."

"Henry doesn't drink beer," Sam said, taking a long swallow. "He's too moral."

"You don't know that," Cindy said. Her mouth was just

touching the top of her bottle, as if musing on it. "Wouldn't you like a sip of this?"

Just hold it where it is. Don't move.

"I would," I said.

Actually, I had tasted beer before. Since the time I was a little boy, my father had given me sips of his beer, and I had always like it. It was just the thought of Sam's sitting around all summer wasting himself that disgusted me.

I took a sip from Cindy's bottle. Delicious.

"How immoral," Sam said.

"Now the cigarette," Cindy said, holding up one she had lit. "Want to try it?"

"That looks a little harder," I said.

"I'm a great teacher," Cindy said. "I taught Junior here everything he knows."

"Even the French inhale," Sam said.

"Shut up, Sam," Cindy said.

"We've been having lessons all summer," Sam said. "First she French-inhales me . . ."

"Don't listen to him," Cindy said. "The man is dreaming." She turned my way. "The thing you have to do, to learn to smoke, is this." She touched a hand to her chest, and sucked in air, as if she were gasping. "That's an exaggeration, but it's close. Do it."

I did it.

"Just right. That's all you have to know how to do. Taking a drag is just like sucking a straw. Only you've got to suck harder."

"Now when you're talking about sucking . . ." Sam said.

"Just shut up." Cindy glanced back at him. "He's not always like this," she said to me. "It must be for your benefit."

"You're in the presence of an expert," Sam said.

"We'll ignore him," Cindy said. "The thing I'm trying to say is, it's inhaling that messes people up. That makes them cough, or start to choke. You have to do it hard. You have to be bold." She took a drag and demonstrated. Smooth as silk. "Want to try?"

"Does it make you sick?" I said.

"That's an old wives' tale. It never made me sick."

"Chewing does," Sam said. "If you swallow any of it."

"I really wouldn't know," Cindy said.

"Smoking *will* make you high," Sam said.

"It'll do more for you than beer," Cindy said. "The first time. All fuzzy and funny. Here." She held out the cigarette.

It was true I'd been disgusted a few minutes before when Sam said he'd taken up smoking. That was when I'd thought he'd embarked on a new life, that he'd be different from me (that was exactly what he'd done, as matter of fact). But now that I was in this basement, with Cindy beside me, her thigh against mine and her face only inches away, I could see the attraction.

"Do just like I showed you," she said, as I took the cigarette. "Be brave."

It seemed strange even to be holding one of those things. The cigarette felt hot against my fingers. I sucked on it, just the way she had, then gasped; a harsh hot pain flooded my throat.

"Blow out," Cindy said.

I blew out.

"Perfect," she said. "First time."

"Hooray," Sam said. "Another candidate for the cancer ward."

"You did even better than Sam," Cindy said.

"Just wait till you try the French inhale," Sam said.

I held the cigarette back to Cindy.

"Keep it," Cindy said. "Sam's got more." He had another whole pack, as a matter of fact.

So we sat together on the couch, the three of us, listening to ballads, touching bodies, smoking cigarettes, drinking beer. As many a teenager will attest, these things went together wonderfully well. Cindy held an ashtray in her lap. When I finished the first cigarette she lit me another.

"I'm having a party this Friday, Henry," Cindy said. "Girls from school. Guys from your place. I want you to come."

"Sure."

I would have agreed to anything at that point. My head was floating vaguely somewhere above my body.

"You'll get to meet Sam's girlfriend," she said. "That sweet little thing."

Sam's girlfriend?

"God," I said. "I feel strange."

"Isn't it great?" Cindy said.

"It is." Her perfume seemed to mix with the feeling.

"You just lost your cherry," Sam said.

"Don't be disgusting," Cindy said. "Don't ruin it." She had turned my way, spoke a little wistfully. "It'll never be this good again."

"I believe that," I said.

"The man is floating," Cindy said.

"We got him high," Sam said.

"He's turned on," Cindy said.

One of the things I always wondered about my mother was how (also why) she performed some of the cooking feats she did. The evening after we had gotten back from the beach, when anyone else would have opened a can of beans and boiled a few hot dogs, Mother had bought and cooked a roast beef (rubbed in garlic), mashed some potatoes and stuffed them back into their skins with a sprinkling of cheese, and shelled and cooked a bowl of fresh lima beans, lightly peppered and swimming in butter. She made a massive Yorkshire pudding and a thick beef gravy to cover it. She also created a mammoth garden salad out of late-summer produce, and topped it with a thick Russian dressing (God, we ate heavy in those days). All this in order to have Susan over, the first night back, for a special dinner. Susan, who never ate anything anyway.

Susan's absence from the family had been a sore point all summer. After she had declined to spend the whole ten weeks with us, she had been asked at various junctures to come down for a couple of weeks, or a week, or a few days, or a weekend, and though at the time of her first refusal she had made it sound as if she would be down for any number of shorts stays, she had never showed up. She claimed she couldn't get away from work. I was never sure whether she had known from the start she wouldn't come, or whether she had just decided as she went along (the longer I do this the better I feel). Anyway, she held out for the whole summer.

She looked as if it were she who had been on vacation. She was tan, and her hair was blond and bright; she had a glow to her. She seemed profoundly rested. She smiled frequently, which was extremely unusual for Susan. She had escaped the family, in so subtle a way that almost no one had noticed, and now she was sitting at the table as a guest. A small distinction, but important to her.

"I don't understand," my mother said to me, after I had brought up the subject at the table. "What kind of party?"

I fought back a massive belch, pondering this question.

I suppose that, strictly speaking, Cindy was right when she said that smoking for the first time wouldn't make you sick. I wasn't sick, exactly. I had also never heard that drinking a single beer for the first time (we had finally decided to open a third. Cindy's mother would just have to wonder) would make you sick. I did feel slightly strange, however, and though that feeling may not have been nausea, it was certainly the next best thing. I had been dizzy and pretty silly for much of the afternoon, was just touching down. I was ravenously hungry, tearing into that roast beef pretty hard, but not entirely sure I should be eating it. It tasted delicious, which seemed to be a good sign.

I don't know why I brought the subject of the party up under those circumstances. Probably just a case of blurting out the one thing that was on my mind. It was on my mind because I was trying to remember not to say anything about it.

"I don't know," I said. "Just a party."

"What's the occasion?" Father said.

"No occasion."

"Is it a swimming party?" Mother said. "Will you take your suit?"

"Oh!" I had intentionally blurred the details in bringing the subject up. "It's not at Sam's. It's at Cindy's."

"Cindy's?" Mother said. The word fell on the table like a cannonball.

"A boy-girl party," Susan said. "How exciting."

"Since when?" Mother wore an expression as if she, and she alone, had just seen a cockroach emerge from a fold of the beef. "This is so sudden. Since when have your friends been having parties with girls?"

"All summer, it sounds like. I didn't really ask."

How did she think I felt? I had gone away with my friends playing baseball and following sports, and when I got back I found them smoking, drinking, listening to the top forty, and having girlfriends. I had spent one of the most important transitional passages of adolescence in absentia.

A pain twinged in my stomach like the plucking of a bass.

"This is so fascinating," Susan said. "Who is this Cindy?"

"Somebody from dancing school. I hardly know her." You know me. I don't like girls.

"We hardly know her either," Mother said. "That's the problem."

"You remember," Father said. "The little girl from over by the park."

"I remember the little girl." Mother's voice was rising perceptibly. "I don't know who she is."

"That all-important question," Susan said. She seemed to be enjoying this discussion in a way that no one else was.

"All we know is that her parents are friends of the Harrises," Mother said.

"That sounds like a pretty good credential." Father was trying to smile. He was wearing roughly the same expression as when Bennett brought up the subject of American literature.

"We don't know where he works," Mother said. "Where their social life is. What she does."

She drinks.

"I think he works for Sam Harris, actually," Father said.

"We don't even know if this is a real party. There's hardly been a proper invitation. We don't know if her parents know it's happening."

"Of course they know. Under their own roof."

They wouldn't know if it was under their own noses.

"Probably while they're off somewhere," Mother said.

"That's the best kind," Susan said.

This discussion was evolving into a real conflict. Had *I* caused it?

My dinner heaved in my stomach like a whale blowing for air.

"We're making far too much of this," Father said.

"I'm just not ready for it," Mother said. "We no sooner get through with Susan . . ."

"Yes," Susan said. "Well. At least you're through with me."

"We're not through with you," Father said.

"I didn't mean it that way," Mother said.

"What do they do at these parties?" Teddy said. "Make out?"

"That's what Henry hopes," Susan said.

"It is not," I said.

"But it depends on *who Cindy is*," Susan said.

"It just doesn't seem fair," Mother said. "Our first night back."

From over at his place Bennett was glaring darkly. "He's far too young," he said.

III

We all got dressed up for parties in those days—strange as that may seem now—even the informal kind of gathering Cindy was having. "It shows respect for the parents," we would say to one another rather solemnly. As if Cindy's parents would notice. Sam had told me, so I was prepared, in dark slacks and a pale-blue seersucker, and showed up at his house in plenty of time. In fact, he wasn't ready yet. I had to wait in the den, where his parents often sat.

It had that odd, almost eerie hush, as if sealed off from the rest of the place. Maybe it was soundproofed. The white carpeting was thick, and the furniture plush, so you sank way into it as you sat down. The tables were glass-topped—there was a half finished drink on one of them—with silver frames, and there were two paintings on the walls, large abstract pieces with garish colors. There was a small bar, and behind the bar a mirror. Most of one wall was taken up by an elaborate hi-fi system playing the cool jazz that was popular in those days, a combo with vibes, a piano, a bass, brushes on the drums. Sam had told me his father was a fanatic for such music, that he owned the best hi-fi system money could buy. It made even a warped record sound good.

I had sunken into the couch, listening to the music—as soothing as the hush of the house—when Sam's father came in.

"Oh," he said. "Hello, kid."

I said hello. He had spoken casually, as if it were no surprise to run into a stray person in that house.

"You're stepping out tonight," he said.

"Yes."

"Me too."

The summer had agreed with Mr. Golden. He had a deep tan, which he had apparently acquired through weeks of vigorous exercise out at the pool. His whole head was tan, in fact (must have discarded that rain hat of his). He was wearing charcoal-gray slacks that evening, and a blue dress shirt, carrying over his arm a bright madras jacket with a lavender tint. He had come into the room to tie his tie. He smelled lightly of after-shave, a bracing scent that was soon obliterated by the smell of his cigar. He put his jacket over a chair, walked to stand in front of the mirror, talked to me while he did his tie.

"I understand you kids are smoking now," he said.

Quite a conversation opener. I felt myself redden, muttered some cross between "Huh?" and "No." Before I could elaborate he continued.

"That little asshole thinks I can't tell. But I know all the tricks. Used to sneak around a little myself."

I decided not to say a word. Nothing I could say would help.

"He did okay at first. But it's getting obvious. Running up to his room all the time. These walks he supposedly takes. When did he ever take a walk? Half the time, hell, you can see the pack in his pocket. You got to hate that kind of carelessness." He shrugged. "I guess it's the age, isn't it, kid?"

"I guess."

"All these things burning up inside you."

That was the way we talked, Mr. Golden and me. Two casual observers commenting on the youth of the day.

"How do you like it yourself?"

"I've hardly done it."

"You don't have to hide things from me. My lips are sealed."
With a cigar butt.

"Really. I've been away all summer."

"Yeah. Well. You take it from me, kid. I've done it all. Cigarettes are made from scrap tobacco. The stuff they sweep off the floor in the cigar factory. You want to smoke something good . . ." He took a cigar from his pocket and threw it to me on the couch. "That's the real thing."

It wasn't a long cigar, but it was pitch-black, and very hard. It looked as if you'd need a blowtorch to light it.

"I'm not saying now. Wouldn't want to make the wrong impression at that party. But when you're in the mood for something good. I'm telling you, kid. You'll never look back."

I grinned. "Thanks."

"Anytime."

He was having a surprising amount of trouble with his tie, was trying to fasten under it one of the pins men wore at their collars in those days. He had done the whole job completely twice.

"So you're going over to what's-her-name's house," he said. "That little kid from the carpool."

He made it sound so romantic. "Yes."

"Nice-looking girl. Little on the heavy side."

"She's lost weight over the summer."

"Her loss is your gain. But she'll be a sweetheart when she grows up. You can see that already. And she's got the hots for you guys. I can tell."

"Oh?"

"Really, kid. She was squirming around up there in the front seat. Dying to dive into the back."

For some reason, no matter who drove the carpool, Cindy rode in the front seat and Sam and I in the back. A subtle form of sex discrimination.

"I'm not a great one for giving advice. Never liked it when I was young. Hell. Some old fart telling me what to do. But you don't mind, do you, kid? One little piece of advice?"

"No."

"Get all you can while you're young."

There was a long pause. That was the advice? That was all of it?

"I know you're scared. You're bashful, embarrassed. What the hell. Everybody is. Eventually you get older. You got money. You got influence. It's all right there for you. But you find out. It's never as nice as when you're young. Know what I mean?"

"Sure." I didn't, though. I had figured out the general subject matter.

"So don't be serious all the time. And don't pass things up when they're there. It's never the same again."

A profound philosophy. Maybe we could get this man to come out and give a lecture at our school.

About the time he finished with his tie, Mrs. Golden came in. She was wearing one of the gowns women wore in those days—strapless, clinging tightly to the contours of her body—and a single string of pearls. She, too, was deeply tanned. She was also more dressed-up than I had ever seen her before, an odd mixture of the elegant and the sexual. The low cut of her gown showed the tanned tops of her breasts. She looked beautiful.

"Hello, dear," she said, as if she had just seen me the other day. She didn't do a double take, but seemed, for a moment, actually to look at me. She had finally noticed me.

"My, Sam," she said. "Isn't he getting tall?"

"Yeah," Mr. Golden said.

"And thin. Quite the young man."

"He'll be quite the young man," Mr. Golden said, "if he'll just take the advice I'm giving him."

There was something about Mrs. Golden that seemed slightly aloof from her husband. They were right there together, and they were husband and wife, but they were not quite a unit. It was as if she would hear, or fully acknowledge, only certain things he said.

"I'm sure you've given him some wonderful advice," she said. "But it really is time we were going."

"Yeah." He picked up his jacket from the chair, and just before they were out the door turned to me. "Remember, kid," he said. "While you're young."

I nodded.

When Sam came down, I said, "Your father knows you're smoking."

"I know," Sam said. "The other day he walked over and tapped the pack in my pocket."

"He thinks cigarettes are crappy. He gave me one of his cigars."

"The man is out of his mind," Sam said.

We were going to Cindy's slightly early—walking over, the way you could still do in those days—because Cindy's mother had asked us to, or at least asked Sam to. She was apparently worked up at the awe-inspiring responsibility of having a party at which teenagers would be present.

There were a lot of questions I would have liked to ask Sam at that point. How did these parties get started? I wanted to know. Who finally broke the ice? It seemed a terrific coincidence, an incredible stroke of bad luck, that I had been away when all these changes had happened. I would have loved to know how they had come about. Along with the changes, however, there was a new solemnity about Sam. We weren't supposed to question things—especially jokingly—the way we once had. It was hard enough to have made all those changes; to make them stick we were going to have to pretend the past hadn't existed. Don't look back. We had decided to mature in one fell swoop, in the course of a summer.

Mrs. McCann was an older version of Cindy, or at least of what Cindy had once been, short, plump (big wobbly knockers on this woman); she wore silver-framed glasses, had hair that—almost completely gray—looked as if it had been chopped short with a meat cleaver. She wore a nondescript skirt and white blouse. The blouse was well on its way toward becoming untucked.

"Oh, Sam!" she said as we appeared at the door, as if we had just showed up at the mass funeral of her family, as if, in fact, we were the only people to have showed. She threw her arms around his neck and mashed her lips against his face. "You remember Henry, don't you?" he said, emerging from this embrace and trying to look nonplussed. "Of course," she said, stared at me vaguely and rather wildly for a moment, then treated me to the same greeting, wiping her lips halfway across my face and practically dragging me to the ground with a hug. I knew my neck would be stiff in the morning.

We walked in and sat on some chairs in the dim living room, just one weak lamp lighted. Mrs. McCann hunched over a coffee table, where there was a cigarette burning in the ashtray and, beside it, a can of Iron City. In fact, two cigarettes were burning. Cindy was right. Numbers were not this woman's strong point.

"God," she said. "This party has me all aflutter."

She drew on a cigarette as if for dear life, guzzled at the beer can. Her glasses kept slipping down her nose, and she pushed them back with an index finger.

"It won't be bad," Sam said. "Not much happens at our parties." Not much we're going to let you know about, anyway.

"I'm just glad I have two strong men" —she stared at us over her glasses, which had started their downward slide—"to help me."

This woman was more out of it than I had thought.

"I know you boys and girls have your little things . . ." She paused, I swear, at exactly this point in the sentence. No telling how this thought might develop. We waited breathlessly for its completion (". . . that you like to play with and put into each other") while she fought back a belch. ". . . that you do," she said finally. Thank God. "I really don't care what you do. As long as you keep it . . ." She winced, and made a violent pushing motion, as if forcing something to the floor.

"We'll keep things quiet," Sam said. "You can depend on us."

"No." She started shaking her head violently, as if Sam had made some dreadful mistake. Her eyes were closed. Her head just kept wobbling back and forth. For a brief terrible moment I was afraid she wouldn't be able to stop. Finally she did, and looked up slowly, as if to pose one of the world's grand philosophical questions. "How can you possibly keep a group of teenagers quiet?"

"I don't know." Sam shrugged. "Ask them to keep it down.

Down" —he brightened at the familiar witticism— "to a dull roar."

"No." She started to shake her head again. Please, Mrs. Mc-Cann. I think I'm going to be sick. "You can't."

"We can't?"

"You can't keep teenagers quiet. I don't ask that. I don't expect it. I just ask that you keep them . . ." She screwed up her face for a terrific effort. Once again she strained at the neck, and made that pushing motion toward the floor. It was as if a large animal were rising up to overwhelm her.

"You mean downstairs," Sam said. "Down in the rec room."

She looked at him with one eye shut, as if sighting him at the end of a rifle. "Exactly."

"No sooner said than done," Sam said. "You won't even know a party's going on."

"You boys are so . . ." Mrs. McCann started to shake her head. "So . . ."

We quietly made our way out. She might be planning to reward us with a kiss.

Cindy was waiting for us downstairs. She seemed considerably calmer than her mother. There was an outside door leading into the backyard from the rec room; Sam went out front to direct people back that way, so we could leave Mrs. McCann to her Iron City and her dreams. There was a table set up with bottles of Coke and a spectacular array of snacks—sandwiches, pretzels, chips, cupcakes, cookies—and Cindy had put on a thick stack of albums, all of them, like the one we had listened to a few days before, oldies from the fifties. There were any number of such collections around in those days.

Guests mostly arrived in clusters and stayed in clusters. Everyone came over to speak to the hostess, and Cindy introduced me around. A few of the girls looked familiar, from dancing school, but most of them I didn't know. Cindy stood beside me making comments at their arrival. Most of the girls who she said were nice were the less attractive ones. The boys she liked, on the other hand, were generally good-looking. I thought Cindy herself looked smashing that night, in a simple white summer dress and with her blond hair bright and hanging in a curl at her shoulders. The color of her face was slightly heightened by makeup. Somehow she looked older than she had a few days before. Her lips wore just the palest blush of color. She stared at the arriving guests with a knowing look, a small smile. Finally she brightened as if at a joke. "This is her," she said. "This is Sam's little ballet dancer."

Sam's girlfriend turned out to be named Renee, an unusual name in those days. She was extremely dark, almost oriental-looking; her eyes did slant, but just slightly. She had jet-black hair that she wore straight and very long, way down her back; on her full sensual mouth—though most of these girls wore makeup very sparingly—she wore bright-red lipstick. She was thin, rather tall, did not seem to have the soft burgeoning body that most of these girls had. While the other girls stood in groups, she stood alone, though she didn't seem self-conscious. "None of the girls like her," Cindy said. "I'm sure you can see why." I couldn't, particularly. Once Sam came in from directing traffic she had him to stand with. He stood beside her immediately, smoking, talking to her, while she mostly watched him with her lips pursed into a smile. Occasionally she took a drag from his cigarette. Once the dancing had started he danced with her every dance, and stayed with her in between them.

Cindy had started dancing with me just to get things rolling, and I soon found out that whatever lessons we had learned in delicacy and decorum at dancing school had been utterly forgotten. The dances were just prolonged embraces, during which boys and girls—even total strangers—stood pressed together head to toe, not moving much. There were various ways of enacting these embraces, some more stylized than others. Sam and Renee, for instance, held hands with their arms hanging straight at their sides. Other guys cradled the girl's hand at their chests. A few couples held their hands slightly out from their bodies at about shoulder level, in the traditional style. Others had somehow agreed to embrace with one or the other's arm behind the back in a hammerlock (I Surrender, Dear). One last couple had given up pretense altogether; they stood virtually motionless with both arms wrapped around each other, eyes closed, expressions of bliss on their faces.

Cindy really looked after me, danced with me often and saw that I danced with other girls. ("Just ask them," she said. "They have to say yes. They're dying to be asked.") One novel interesting body after another. Once we went over and pried Sam loose from Renee, swapped partners with them. Renee said not one word to me, but danced with me in a very particular way, with what seemed to be her lips (could this be?) pressed against my neck. Her body felt light in my embrace, as if it might drift up and float away. She wore absolutely breathtaking perfume, which mingled gently with the scent of her skin. She gave me a knowing smile when we finished, still not saying anything (she did open her mouth as if she were going to say something). Then she went back to Sam.

Perhaps the most noticeable person at the party was Cindy's cousin Thomas, who was related to her on her father's side. Her parents had made her invite him. Thomas was tall and thin, hunched slightly at the shoulders, with a narrow bony face and dark eyes. He wore his black hair wet and slick, with large curls at the front that fell over his forehead. He was more than a little out of place at the party. Not only was he two years older than the rest of us, but he also—while all of us attended private schools—went to the local Catholic high school. He had arrived that evening in the kind of sport jacket hoods wore in those days, one that did away with lapels and buttoned up all the way to the neck, leaving just an inch or so of necktie showing. It was something like a straitjacket, without the special sleeves. To the best of my knowledge this style has since disappeared from the face of the earth, like the Edsel.

During most of the party Thomas just stood in front of the refreshment table, watching the crowd and chain-smoking unfiltered cigarettes. He held his cigarette pinched in his thumb and first two fingers, sucked on it as if in pain. He also, quite unobtrusively, ate about half of the refreshments. He put away one of the small crustless sandwiches in one bite, as if it were a cracker. A cupcake went down in two. A few guys went over to talk to him, apparently with Cindy's encouragement (she didn't ask Sam and me. She liked us), and came back with the gratifying news that he really was a nice guy. He wasn't suddenly going to whip out a switchblade and start carving people up. He was just like us.

Except in one particular. The news soon traveled around the party—it spread like wildfire among the boys—that Thomas had actually been laid. Two times, with two different girls (apparently he had failed to establish a lasting relationship with either one), one on the couch in her living room and one "in the tall weeds beside the railroad tracks," wherever that was. He had used a rubber on this second occasion, or, as he preferred to call it, a "safe" (no one knew what this expression meant at first; we finally had to consult Sam). Thomas had a safe on him that night, just in case. He might as well have blown it up as a party balloon.

How Thomas managed to introduce all this information so easily into a casual conversation I never found out. Soon whole groups of guys were walking over to stand in front of the refreshment table. Various other details of his experience gradually came out. Both of his partners had been girls from the Catholic girls' school who were just known to do it (names? phone numbers?). You didn't have to do anything special, just go over to their houses and ask them. The girl whom he had had at the railroad tracks sounded much the more interesting, blond and thin and with a reputation at the girls' school as a fist fighter. She had just wanted to jerk him off until she saw the safe. He had humped her during a gentle rain, with nothing as a bed but those tall weeds. Her box (all these were his terms) had been burning hot; he had half expected to see himself steaming when he finally pulled out, or to see the rubber burned to shreds. He had left it there by the railroad tracks, to give some bum a thrill.

He went on record as estimating that eighty percent of the girls at that party would have done it by the time they were sixteen. He wouldn't be surprised to hear that some of them had done it already (he had obviously never heard the etiquette lecture at dancing school). His most startling piece of information, however, related to what a girl supposedly smelled like just before you fucked her. It was a fact as odd and mysterious as the thought of those two compliant Catholic girls. No one who attended the party ever forgot it. Even in these far more permissive days, I can hardly bring myself to record it.

He said the girl smelled like dead fish.

After a while Cindy went over to her cousin—I think she had gotten nervous seeing everyone talk to him—and said, "Why are you standing around like a zombie, Thomas? Why don't you dance?" Immediately, as if there were no question in his mind who the most desirable girl at the party was, he walked over right in front of Sam and asked Renee. She stared very seriously into his eyes for a moment, then accepted. Thomas had a novel technique for dancing, his arm extended straight like a lance. It was a lot like Groucho Marx doing a tango, except that Thomas and Renee didn't have their cheeks pressed together. He moved around the room rather differently than other people, more quickly, for one thing, but also tilting a lot, spinning and swaying. "God, how embarrassing," Cindy said, standing beside me. All around us people watched with fascination. The only person who didn't seem shaken up was Renee, who followed his odd steps easily, as if she danced that way all the time. When they finished she looked him in the eye again, smiled, and nodded. She did go back to Sam.

"That's the last time I tell him to go dance," Cindy said.

"Maybe he'd like to dance with his favorite little cousin," I said.

She closed her eyes in pain.

Eventually the party began to spill over into the backyard, the windows and doors open, so the music drifted out on the air. According to Sam's interpretation, we were still satisfying Mrs. McCann's request that we keep the party "down." "She's probably passed out anyway," he said to me. The McCanns had a surprisingly large backyard, bordered by thick bushes and leafy trees, so you could easily slip into the shrubbery unnoticed. It was a soft balmy evening, more comfortable out than in. You could see couples dimly, girls in their white or yellow dresses standing out beside their shadowy partners. Drags on cigarettes glowed like fireflies. Cindy and I walked out after a dance and found Sam standing alone.

"Where's your little girlfriend?" Cindy said.

"Peeing," Sam said. "Or whatever it is girls do in the middle of a party. God. It takes forever."

"It's your only chance to be alone," Cindy said.

Sam shrugged.

"The separation will do you both good," Cindy said.

Sam looked very smug as he stood there, taking deep drags on a cigarette and staring at the ground as he expelled the smoke. He wasn't really looking at us.

"Are we going for our walk in the park?" Cindy said.

"Not tonight," Sam said. "I don't think."

"I'm sure Henry would look after Renee."

I'd get Thomas to look after her.

"I just don't feel like a walk," Sam said. "Particularly."

"You always feel like a walk when Renee's not around."

"True. But Renee is around. Tonight."

Sam and Cindy were pretending to joke, talking lightly, smiling a little, but there was more happening than they were letting on. Cindy was blushing, as if in anger, and Sam was looking away from her.

"Maybe I'll just go with Henry," Cindy said.

"Suit yourself."

"Let's go, Henry. He might not want to be seen with us when Renee gets back."

I frankly didn't know what the hell was going on. Things had been happening too fast since I had gotten back from the beach. Sam looking so much older, and smoking and drinking, and acting sometimes so solemn, and being such good friends with Cindy (Cindy! whom we would not even have admitted to knowing a few months before), and being accustomed to parties, and having a girlfriend. Now, it seemed, he was actually arguing with Cindy, as if he knew her that well. And she was using me against him.

It was as if I had been involved in their friendship all along; it had developed in my absence, but they had considered me a part of it. Now I was supposed to fall right into step. Unfortunately, I didn't know where we were. There was nobody to ask, either. I had to play it by ear.

I certainly hadn't anticipated walking with Cindy away from her own party that evening. Lots of people had gone outside, but no one had actually left. What about her obligation as a hostess? The street itself was quiet, houses on either side softly alight. At the end of the street, lights shone silver on the pale top of the bowling green. From behind us came the sound of party music, and of voices.

For a while we didn't say anything. Finally Cindy spoke.

"What do you think of Renee?"

"I don't know. Hard to tell." I acted as if I were asked such questions all the time. "She didn't talk when we danced. Didn't say a word."

"She never talks to me either. She never talks to anyone." Cindy was silent for a few steps. "Do you think she's pretty?"

"In a way. She's kind of odd-looking."

"Yes."

"Sort of exotic. Not like anyone else. I guess she is pretty."

What I really thought was that she seemed mysterious, a girl who might know things the rest of us didn't. She was the kind of girl you might dream about knowing and meeting in private. It took a hell of a confident person to hang around her in public.

"Why do you think Sam likes her?" Cindy said.

He wanted to solve the mystery. "I don't know."

"He could have anybody. Any girl at that party."

Including Cindy?

"Why is that?" I said.

Cindy smiled. "It's hard to describe." She was blushing a little, contemplating the question. "He *is* good-looking, of course. But it's not just that. Lots of boys are good-looking."

Me, for instance.

"And he's got those funny ears," she said.

"Funny ears?"

"They stick out. They're almost pointy. You hadn't noticed?"

I hadn't. But I checked it out later. She was right.

"It's nice to have a flaw, though. Especially a funny one. The thing about Sam is, he's so relaxing to be around. So sure of himself."

That was the truth.

"He makes you feel good when you're a girl. More confident. Prettier. So what does he want with Renee?"

"Beats me."

"The most confident girl I've ever met. The one girl at that party who doesn't need what Sam has. She is weird-looking, in my opinion. Those strange eyes. And that positively ugly mouth. She has nice skin. But she doesn't have any friends. She's always alone at school, and at parties. Standing by herself like she knows all there is to know. All those girls all around who would love to have Sam. And he walks up to her."

"Yes."

"Who doesn't need him at all. Why does he want her?"

"Maybe for the same reason Thomas wants her."

"God. Don't say that."

We had reached the park by then, had walked, with Cindy leading, around the outside of the bowling green. Finally we stood in shadow just above the path that led down into the woods. Not another soul was around. Cindy stopped walking, turned to face me.

"I hate to see the summer end," she said.

"Yes."

I wasn't sure what she meant. I didn't know what the summer had been.

"Sam and I are just pals, Henry. Nothing between us."

"You told me."

Was it entirely necessary to keep repeating this fact?

"But sometimes in the summer we used to take these walks together. Almost every night, in fact. Just to get out of the house. And to get a little practice."

"Practice?"

"Kissing."

I looked up at her. I would have expected a smile, but she was staring at me rather seriously.

"Just in a friendly way. Just for fun. It was his idea."

I bet it was.

"Anyway." She started to step toward me, then hesitated. "I wish he were here now, watching. I wish he were here to see us."

She stepped to where I was, and put her arms around me, and kissed me.

With profound apologies to all the other women I've kissed —the many thousands who are angrily reading this—that was the best kiss I've ever had (still accepting challengers). No other kiss has even come close. Cindy's lips were full, and soft, and warm; they were positively hot. Simply a reflection, in my opinion, of her warm loving heart. Her arms were bare around my neck, and held me tight; her mouth seemed to melt against mine. Without even seeming to, her lips made mine open; her tongue entered my mouth and gently fluttered. She's just not trying, I have often thought since, as I kissed a woman and her kiss did not match up to Cindy's, but Cindy was trying: she was kissing me well because she was trying to. That was what I prefer to call my first kiss (I don't count those from preadolescence), and it has spoiled me for any kisses since. It seemed to go on and on. Finally a salty taste joined it; I pulled back, and saw tears rolling down Cindy's face.

"I'm sorry, Henry," she said. "It's nothing about you. I just hate to see the summer end."

"I know."

"I don't want to see it end. I don't want to go back there."

"Okay."

"I want you to stay out here and hold me. For a long time. We can kiss."

"Sure."

"We'll be buddies too. Pals."

That was what we did. We stayed out in the park for some time, hugging and kissing. Hugging, mostly. None of her later kisses matched that first one, but no one else's have either. After a while we could see cars arriving at her house to pick people up. Nothing too specific, of course—it was a long way off—but we could see a flurry of activity. People were prompt about picking their children up at a party. By the time we got over there, the only one left was Sam.

"You took your time getting back," he said.

"We knew you were here," Cindy said.

"I had to handle the goodbyes myself."

"I'm sure you did a good job. Especially with Renee."

"Your mother staggered out at one point."

"God."

"Just looked around at all the headlights and went back in."

"I hope she left us some beer."

"I checked. There's plenty."

That was how we ended the evening, sitting on the couch and drinking beer, Sam and Cindy smoking cigarettes. The music played, but softly. There wasn't much food left— Thomas had seen to that—but we ate what there was, Cindy holding a plate in her lap and Sam and I munching from it.

"Smoking's so good after kissing," Cindy said.

"I know," Sam said.

"The best cigarettes you ever have." She turned to me. "Wouldn't you like one?" A glance back at Sam. "He's been kissing."

"So I gathered," Sam said.

"Maybe I'll try this cigar," I said.

"Good Lord," Cindy said.

"Sam's father gave it to me. He says it's great."

"If you smoke those things, you wind up looking like him," Sam said.

A fateful moment. I took the cellophane off the cigar, inhaled the scent, removed the end ("You can bite it," Sam said. "But I've noticed the old man just pinches a little off with a fingernail"), and lit up. I held the cigar in the side of my mouth, let the smoke drift out as I drew on it. I knew better than to inhale. "Hey," I said. "This is good." A cigar had substance in your mouth, wasn't just a little piece of paper you were sucking at; it had a rich strong taste, not the harsh bitterness of cigarettes; it revealed its taste in your mouth, so you didn't have to suck the smoke into your throat. From that evening on, strange as it seems, I was a confirmed cigar smoker. Even when I was still just an adolescent, even when I was in training for teams, when I was the brother of the cross-country captain and later the cross-country captain myself, I spent a good bit of time and a great deal of money (I had started off with the best) sneaking off to cigar shops downtown and looking for safe places to smoke. Good cigars became one of the passions of my life. I never smoked a cigarette again.

The three of us sat there smoking, holding our beers and now and then sipping from them.

"Do you think it's true?" Sam said. "What Thomas said about girls."

"I don't know." I wasn't sure precisely what he was referring to. I didn't know if any of it was true.

"I didn't see you two talking," Cindy said.

"He didn't say it to me," Sam said. "But it got around to all the boys. It's something about the way girls smell."

"I don't want to hear it," Cindy said.

"It's not all that bad." It was, though.

"I still don't want to hear it."

"I just wonder if it's true."

"Thomas is dirty and disgusting. He always has been. Ever since he was a kid."

"I heard he was a pretty good guy."

"He's a disgusting slob. I don't want to hear what he said."

That seemed to settle that. We waited for a few moments in silence.

"You're not going to make me jealous," Sam said. "About doing something with Henry. Not matter how much you say it."

"I was just explaining where we'd been," Cindy said.

"The hell you were. But you can kiss Henry all you want. You can kiss anybody all you want. It won't change things between us."

"I know."

"We're going to be buddies," Sam said. "The three of us."

"Yes," Cindy said.

"Friends for life."

Sam was not making a prediction. He was telling us the way it would be. He had apparently decided that, sometime during the summer. We all sat in silence for a while, contemplating, I suppose, what we thought he meant.

SIX

It was one thing to say you were ready for the upper school, to have big plans for the year and think you couldn't wait for it to begin. It was another thing to feel that way on the day classes started.

At the breakfast table it was just the three of us, Father, Bennett, and me. Mother fixed breakfast, but said she didn't eat it (I couldn't believe that. She had to be sneaking something out there), and Teddy ate either on the run or in front of the tube. The three of us were looking distinguished that morning, in our shirts and ties. I wasn't hungry myself. Father, on the other hand, had made his way through freshly squeezed orange juice, four scrambled eggs, two sausage patties, God knows how many pieces of toast. Now he was nursing a pot of coffee and lighting his pipe, that harsh English blend that lent its aroma to the whole house.

"I don't understand," he said, "why two brothers from the same house should go to different bus stops."

"I'm not going to a bus stop fifteen minutes early just so he can stand there and hold hands with his girlfriend," Bennett said.

He was referring to Sam.

The bus went along Reynolds, over near Sam's, then cut over to Penn and made a stop on Braddock at the middle school, drove back on Penn on its way out to campus. Bennett always caught it at Penn and Dallas, the last stop. It did arrive there later, and the stop was closer to our house. But Bennett really liked it because he didn't want to mix in the action in the middle of the bus, preferred to get on later and sit down gingerly toward the front.

"Sam says it's better to get on early," I said. "There aren't as many seats left by the end."

"How would he know?" Bennett said. "There are plenty of seats."

"I told him I'd meet him at that stop," I said. "That's where I'm going."

His pipe clenched in his teeth, a look of vague bewilderment on his face, Father raised a hand to each side of the table. "I wish my sons could agree on the simplest thing."

I had to hurry to get to Sam's stop on time. He had on all new clothes—olive-green khaki slacks, a greenish plaid jacket —but he looked a trifle pale, standing there. He wasn't talking about how it was all going to be the same old crap that morning.

It was mostly a feeling that made the upper school seem so much different from the middle school. The middle school was plenty difficult, after all. Most of the teachers were men, and we wore jackets and ties, and had a great deal of homework, and there was a full-scale athletic program that included competition against other schools. At the same time, however, the middle school was right there in the city, and you reported to home room first thing, and the place did have the feel of a house (even if it was a monstrosity), and you always had the feeling people were watching you. You couldn't get too far out of line at the middle school.

Heading out to the upper school was another thing altogether, a twenty-minute trip out across the Allegheny to the suburb where the school was. The bus would eventually become quite a spirited place, full of storytelling and practical joking and outright brawls, but it was pretty quiet that first morning, everyone off in his own thoughts. Bennett had looked back to see that I was there, but afterward sat in the front and took no notice of me at all. When we arrived at the campus everybody just piled out, the freshmen gathering in a cluster. No delegation of older students came rushing over to welcome us to the school.

It was a beautiful piece of property. From the brick-and-iron gates where the bus entered, you gazed at a broad expanse of green, gradually rising, a clutch of pine trees in the foreground about halfway up, and above their tops the high steeple of the chapel. Dew lay on the morning grass like a haze. The bus had wound up to the left, and beside the pine trees on sunny mornings the golf coach (who turned out also to be my history teacher) practiced his medium irons; he shaded his eyes with a hand that first morning as he watched the bus pass. Where his shots had hit the grass there were green streaks in the dew. As the bus went up the hill it passed a small brick library on the left, the adjacent chapel and academic building on the right, then stopped at a long quadrangle that had a dining hall at one end, a dorm at each corner. The bus brought only a few of the school's students. Many others traveled by car, and about half of the students boarded.

So part of the newness of the place was just the expanse of it, the fact that you weren't in one building all day with teachers watching but were spread all over a large campus. There was an apparent freedom to the place. The students, too, looked different. Whereas a year before we had been running down hallways with a bunch of preadolescents, now we were on campus with what looked like adults, guys with broad shoulders, heavy beards, bass voices.

There was also something almost indefinably different about the upper-school faculty. The middle school seemed to have a unified group, people who had gone to teachers colleges all over the state and had chosen education as their profession. The upper-school crowd was more like a college faculty, a collection of cranks with peculiar interests who for one reason or another had wandered into jobs at that school. They were eminently qualified in their individual disciplines. They just didn't seem to merge into a faculty.

My French teacher, for instance, was a soft lumpy Englishman with a high forehead, a delicate mouth, and a thin tracery of weblike veins on his cheeks. His face wore a weird vacant smile. He had abominable posture, one unique feature of which was that he stared constantly into the sky; he would have been a great candidate for falling down an open manhole if there had been one on campus. He wore rumpled clothes, often with his jacket buttoned askew, and smelled like the room down at the gym where they hung the sweat clothes out to dry them. He had terrible difficulties with names, often combined one guy's first name with another's last, so you didn't know who the hell he was calling on. His French was excellent, however—it was one of seven languages he was fluent in—and his exams were absolutely legendary. Every paper I ever handed him came back with red all over it. To top it all off, he was said to be an ordained minister. How he could call himself a Christian and still slash up my papers that way I never knew.

For history I had a man possessed by a mania. Every spare moment found him out by those pine trees practicing his medium irons, and the school day was barely over when you saw him striding across campus with a golf bag on his shoulder, heading for the course that was adjacent to the school. He was a short slight man, dry and pallid, with rust-colored hair and a freckly face. He moved very rapidly and had a number of tics and twitches, most no doubt acquired during spells of deep concentration on putting greens. His passion for history nearly matched his passion for golf. He gave only one lecture all year—it started in September and ended in June—and began class each day by asking somebody what his last sentence had been, then took off from there without consulting a note. His lectures were dramatic, accompanied by multiple hand gestures, clenched fists, facial tics, roars of exasperation and approval, shoulder shrugs, nose picks. Often he addressed an imaginary ball with his pointer (other times he picked his ear with it), and occasionally, while we were staring down at our notebooks writing for dear life, a sound rent the air like the cracking of a whip. He hadn't been able to resist, and had taken a swing. He stared out the window as if at the flight of a ball.

My math teacher was a school institution, a trim neat man with a girlish walk and a face that always smiled; in fact, it always beamed. He had taught at the school for over forty years and hadn't apparently been bored for a moment. Though he was nearing retirement age, his hair had only small patches of gray. In class he spoke in a singsong voice that sounded like a parody, and he carried an ancient pointer that was held together by rubber bands and that he used for effect, scraping it across the board so it squeaked, dropping it lifelessly from his hands when someone gave a wrong answer, holding it high above his chair and letting it crash down point first to punctuate his remarks (the chair looked as if it had been attacked by a woodpecker). He could also, if need be, skewer an absentminded student with his pointer; after once seeing him work over a student who had given him a hard time, I wouldn't have been surprised to hear he could kill a man with it. He had a long tough thumbnail that he applied to the collarbones of students who were having trouble concentrating. You learned math from that man or wound up with marks all over your body.

The man I most remember from that year, however, taught me English.

Mr. Hirtle was a new teacher, and had been given a room that, in my opinion, was never meant to be a classroom. The basement of the academic building had a hallway full of ancient lockers—battered gray metal structures up on little stilts—and in the midst of all the lockers were two doors that pushed open, like the doors to bathrooms. One led to the business office, the other into Mr. Hirtle's classroom. Its windows looked out on window wells, past which, if you got at just the right angle, you could make out a small patch of sky. The ceiling was bumpily plastered, had pipes of various sizes running along it. The walls and ceiling were painted a loud beige. There was a desk for the teacher, a heavy wooden object that looked as if somebody had decided to get rid of it, taken seven or eight hard whacks at it with an ax, then changed his mind and given it to Mr. Hirtle. The chair he had did not go with the desk. It was the kind of high narrow chair that swivels around and that people sit at when they work behind a counter. He perched on it behind the desk like a bird on a post.

You would not have said Mr. Hirtle looked young, exactly; his age was indeterminate, though we knew he was just out of college. He was light-haired and balding; his face was thin; he had a jutting brow and dark eyebrows that formed a single heavy line above his eyes. He was thin, and might have looked athletic except that he was extremely swaybacked, so his belly stuck out like a baby's. His clothes were straight out of the Ivy League, button-down collars and all, but he also wore a beret into class, which he took off as he walked in and placed on the head of a bust of Zeus which occupied the front of the room with him. He said he had found the bust at Goodwill. He was a spectacular athlete—the state slalom skiing champion that winter without a day of practice, and as the backfield coach on the football team he sometimes took a turn at quarterback and swept past the defense easily with long loping strides—but he also drank coffee all day and smoked excessively, unfiltered Camels, which he drew on for what seemed at least twenty seconds and then, apparently, swallowed the smoke. Only wisps came out when he exhaled.

"I don't believe it," Sam said. "It disappears."

He was doing a study of smoking techniques, and had never run into that one before.

Somehow, already, Mr. Hirtle had three small children and a wife who looked uncannily like him, complete with that fierce jutting brow. They lived in a dormitory apartment but seemed apart from the rest of the faculty. On nice afternoons you might see them walking by a stream down past the athletic fields, or taking a picnic supper there.

As a teacher he was unique in my experience, especially in those days when teachers taught strictly by the book. He didn't even seem to have read the book. While most classes went through grammar gradually, doing it two days per week and keeping it up all year, he gave us one week of intensive lectures, during which we were assigned the entire text to read. "Grammar isn't that complicated," he said. "It's made hard by the way it's taught." After that week of lectures, we started class every day with what he called a grammar baby, or a rhetoric baby, long involved sentences that he mimeographed onto short sheets of paper and that might have any number of mistakes in them, or none at all. We were to correct any errors we found. At first we all flunked these quizzes, but you could read up on the things you missed, and pretty soon we learned to find the mistakes. Before long we were making perfect scores on the rhetoric babies.

Everyone else followed the vocabulary program in the same text, but he let us bring in our own words on flash cards every week, any twenty words one wanted to know. He went around the room quizzing us individually, picking three words at random (you got an A, D, or F), and the cards were cumulative up to two hundred, so at the end of ten weeks he might ask you any three of two hundred words. The system kept you on your toes.

Studying Shakespeare, we approached it as drama and acted out the scenes, holding the little Penguin texts and reciting the lines. We often had impassioned discussions about how we would direct a scene or how we would stage it (you had to have a deep understanding of the scene before you could discuss such things, but we hardly noticed that). Sometimes we translated scenes into modern situations and improvised around them. At the end of the unit we acted out one scene for real, complete with memorized lines, improvised props, desks pushed out of the way. When other classes studied short stories, they wrote turgid boring essays about them (must have been preparing for graduate school) while we wrote stories in imitation, or adapted the stories into screenplays. When we studied essays we classified them according to type (the Broadly Satirical, the Autobiographical Discursive, the Here's the Information) and wrote such essays of our own, or wrote parodies of them. When we studied poetry he invited a poet in to recite his own poems, and let us write poetry for extra credit (it didn't have to be good). He read us poems he had written.

Early in the year, he walked in at the beginning of class and asked us to write a sentence of fifty or seventy-five words describing the ocean. I had just been to those North Carolina beaches, and described the slate-gray early-morning tides— and the gulls skimming above them—that I had sometimes fished in. He told us to write the sentence again, adding more detail. A third time, to make the detail particular. A fourth, to pay attention to the diction and add variety to the syntax. All in all we must have spent thirty minutes on that sentence. "There," he said when we finished. "Your last sentence is better than your first." ("No it isn't!" three guys shouted at once. He ignored them.) "That's what writing is all about. Rewriting. If you took that kind of care with your themes you'd be great writers. You'd write masterpieces."

After we had handed the sentences in we did a rhetoric baby (a long involved sentence about the ocean; the man had a sense of humor), and at the end of the class he said there was one sentence he'd like to read. It was mine. I felt myself blush ("It's Henry's," Sam said, noticing) and heard three or four more things I would like to change as he read. After class he asked me to stay, and said he'd like to submit my sentence to the literary magazine as a prose poem. If that was all right with me.

"I guess," I said. "If you'll let me write it one more time."

"All you want," he said.

As impressive as he was in front of the class, Mr. Hirtle seemed shy of personal encounters. He kept looking down at his desk, wouldn't meet my eye.

"You must like the ocean," he said.

"I was just there this summer," I said.

"You noticed a lot."

"You stare at it while you're fishing. You get to know it pretty well."

If Mr. Hirtle had been standing in front of the ocean, he would have looked down, afraid of embarrassing it.

"Noticing's the first key to good writing," he said. "It's the hardest part to teach."

"It's funny," I said. "I never really thought I could write. I always thought Bennett was the writer in the family."

He looked up in puzzlement. "Who's Bennett?" he said.

II

Whatever else I may have expected from school, cross-country was all I had hoped it would be. Finally at the end of the day I could take off the jacket and tie I'd been sweating in; I could quit hurrying; I could quit feeling like a freshman (there was an elitism on the cross-country team, but it was an elitism of talent; there was also a real respect for anyone who would put himself through the rigors of the sport, however lousy he was); I could relax. There was a certain irony to the fact that it wasn't until cross-country practice began that I had the feeling I could quit running around.

It is hard to remember—nowadays when everybody and his grandmother is a runner, in fact when everybody and his grandmother has run a marathon together—what an oddball sport cross-country was in those days. There were just eighteen of us, dressed in scruffy blue sweatsuits (but each sweatsuit was a badge of honor; it was issued to indicate you were a member of a varsity team, however peripheral you might be), sitting on the infield that surrounded the pole-vault pit, or the one beside the broad-jump runway. All around us guys hurried to other fields, to the soccer fields down on lower terraces, to the football field that was right there encircled by the track. While the football team barked out their calisthenics like an army drill team, shouted and groaned as they pushed the heavy sled along the grass, we did our exercises in silence, slowly stretching each part of our body. The captain might name a new exercise, or he might just start doing it—he's touching his toes for a while, then he leans to stretch out his groin—and gradually, one by one, all the rest of us would start doing it too. We didn't look like an athletic squad. We looked like a flock of birds.

We did various workouts once we had warmed up. Some days we did interval work, four-forties mostly, more like track workouts than cross-country. We went for long runs, so long they would have been boring even on the cross-country course, so we ran on the tarry roads that surrounded the campus. We did intervals on selected portions of the course, especially the two wicked hills that were its most memorable features. But the workout that we all considered the hardest one, that we did once a week without fail and ate lunch lightly in preparation for, the workout that every cross-country runner took pride in, because it showed what he was made of, was running flags.

The flags themselves were small and red and on short wooden posts; they didn't stay out all the time, but were brought out once a week and driven into holes one hundred ten yards apart, so they divided the track into quarters. As the workout began, a small cluster of runners stood at each flag, and in the tower (the high metal scaffolding used by spotters at football games) stood our coach, holding a stopwatch in one hand and an air horn in the other. He slowly surveyed the four posts while we stared up at him, tensed and ready to start, then he raised the horn, and it sounded (oh, shit), and we started to run.

From then on, as long as the workout lasted, the horn sounded every twenty seconds. If in that interval you had made the next flag, you kept running. If you hadn't, you stopped. You waited until the horn sounded, and you started again. The trick, obviously, was to pass each flag just before the sound of the horn. The workout was in part an exercise in pacing. For that reason, there was at least one experienced runner in each pack, to lead the rest.

There was no real reason that flags should have been so difficult. The problem was the particular kind of person who chose to run cross-country. In any other workout, you ran a given distance. You were running four-forties, say, in seventy-five seconds, and each time you ran you either made it or you didn't, but in any case that interval was over. You jogged awhile and started again. But flags involved an inverted value system. Instead of being rewarded for success and punished for failure, you were punished for success (you had to keep going) and rewarded for failure (you got to stop). It was the perfect workout for the dedicated masochists that all true runners are. Either you could stand around the track castigating yourself for not making it, or you could congratulate yourself, in the midst of searing pain, for succeeding. Either way, there was plenty of pain to go around.

It was a study in the psyche of a runner. Anyone on the squad could make one flag (a twenty-second one-ten). Anybody could make four (an eighty-second quarter). Anybody but the very slowest could make eight (a 2:40 half). But the further you went, the more you upped the ante. Could you run a 5:20 mile? A 10:40 two-mile? In a race you could do it, but could you do it in a workout, and keep going afterward? Did you want to? Today? It was as if you were setting out on a race, but you didn't know how long it was going to be. That depended on how you did. And as you reached your limit, ap-

proached the flag that might be your last (or might not), you
felt your lungs burning, your calves aching and almost numb,
and knew that if you let up just a little, if you barely missed
that last flag—all but made it, really—you could stop, whereas
if you hurt just a little more, reached back for that little extra
that is the difference between champions and also-rans, you'd
have to keep going. It was like chasing a mirage, running a
race where the finish line kept moving back. It bore an un-
canny resemblance to nightmares many people have.

"So what's your best?" Sam said to me, about a month into
the season.

I was no all-star runner. Even on that small squad, I was
only a good JV. I still didn't have the build of a runner. I
hadn't done enough running. But everybody was proud of the
number of flags he could do.

"Thirteen," I said. "Two weeks ago. Last week I slipped up
at eleven. I don't know what happened."

"Thirteen." Sam was calculating in his mind. "That doesn't
sound too good."

"I'd like to see you do it." He couldn't make eight.

"I'm not in that kind of shape." There's a good excuse. "But
sixteen would be a five-twenty mile. You ought to be able to do
that."

"In a race, maybe. But this is a workout. Besides, you've got
to run again after you rest."

"Goof off when you run again. But at least try for a, five-
twenty mile. It'd be something to have done."

That was easy for Sam to say. He hadn't come out for cross-
country. But he was my unofficial coach that fall. From the
first day, he'd taken a real interest in me, asked about my
workouts, time trials, races. He was the only one who was interested in a JV runner who ran back in the pack. I was glad to
have him around.

Sam could have gone out for any sport, of course. He'd
played them all, one time or another, had always been good at
whatever he did. At the beginning of the year, I'd harbored a
secret hope that he would come out for cross-country. I had
three months of training on him, and he was smoking now,
and I thought I could beat him. I'd have enjoyed beating him

at something. He talked for a while about coming out. "I'd like to get into shape again," he said. "Really good shape." He also talked off and on about playing football. He'd played in a youth league a couple of years before, and with his good hands and all his know-how had been a great pass-catching end. He'd also played some quarterback.

I honestly think that on that first day of athletics, as we walked down the hill to the gym, he still didn't know what he was going out for. Somehow or other he wound up on the soccer field. That was the sport he'd played the most of the year before, and he was a natural; he could have played any position. In football he would probably have played on the freshman team, because you had to have extraordinary ability and pretty good size to be moved up from that, but in soccer he went out for JV and made the starting team, at right halfback. He was one of the stars, in fact. All signs pointed toward the varsity for the next fall, which would have been quite a feat for a sophomore.

On a Wednesday early in October when we were doing flags, he stopped on his way down to the field to speak to me. "The five-twenty mile," he said. "I'm counting on it."

"Only if you run too," I said.

"I might have to start getting in shape. Somebody's got to do it."

The fact of the matter was I'd decided Sam was right. I was going to run a 5:20 mile that day. The effort would exhaust me, and it was somewhat contrary to the spirit of the workout, since it was felt that the later runs, after you'd stopped once, were just as important as the first one. Still, I wanted to try. I felt in great shape, and I hadn't been timed for the mile since the All Comers Track Meet the previous spring. I wanted to see how I'd improved.

As soon as we'd started I felt sure I could make it. There was something instantly debilitating about running flags, even the first few steps, not knowing how far you would go, but that day I did know, I was setting out to run the best mile of my life, and I had a good track man to pace me. I wouldn't be able to vary my pace, and I wouldn't be able to sprint at the end—that would be too obvious—but I still had plenty of confidence I could do it.

I think I would have, if, as I approached the half-mile mark, a couple of soccer players hadn't been standing there with an injured player draped over their shoulders. They didn't get in the way, they could see that an important workout was going on, but I stopped anyway. I didn't even think of continuing. The player they were holding was Sam.

"What happened?" I looked from one of them to another. All three were sweating, they looked as if they'd been through hell (actually, they'd just run laps, done exercises, and started a soccer scrimmage), but Sam looked the worst. He was wincing, his eyes closed in pain.

"What the hell are you stopping for?" he said.

"He hurt his knee," one of the other guys said. "Got it twisted when somebody kicked him. No broken bones."

"Just keep running," Sam said. "What do you want to do, kiss it and make it better?"

"We're taking him to get it looked at," the other guy said.

"Go!" Sam said.

I started running, but I'd lost my rhythm. The horn sounded almost immediately.

"You stupid ass," Sam said. "Never stop running."

We were all so hard-nosed in those days.

I heard the story later, when some guys were talking in the locker room. It wasn't too unusual a thing to have happened in soccer. Sam and another guy had been going for the ball, and it had taken a funny bounce. The other guy had launched a kick just as Sam was changing directions, and his foot caught Sam flush on the side of the knee, a little behind it. The knee buckled, but buckled sideways. It was extraordinarily painful at the moment of impact—his shout stopped the scrimmage dead in its tracks—and when he tried to stand up he couldn't begin to. The knee hurt too much, and was too weak.

The problem was in the cartilage, not the bone, though the doctor said there must have been a bone bruise too, it was so painful to the touch. It shouldn't have been serious, but somehow it was. Sam was to stay out of athletics until it was completely better, and I can still remember, two weeks after it

happened, seeing him stand up from his study-hall desk and almost fall flat on his face. "God," he said, wincing and red-
dening, not looking at me. "I don't believe how much this
hurts."

He started going to physical therapy, and the doctor said
that if the knee wasn't better in two months (two months!—
soccer season would be long gone) they should consider an op-
eration. The knee was better in two months, but by no means
entirely well. Surgery would have sped up the process considerably, though they were naturally reluctant to do it (this
wasn't the NFL). By the time the knee was really better, basketball season was over too.

I have always thought that despite the activities of the summer before, it was Sam's knee injury that really changed him. I
won't say it ruined him, though that was how I felt at the time.
He hadn't changed his life much for the soccer team—he still
smoked and drank when we got together with Cindy, and he
still smoked when I saw him on weekends—but after he hurt
his knee he gave up on sports altogether. He started to smoke at
school, which he hadn't done before. First thing every study
hall he'd limp back and sign out for the bathroom, which
meant he was going to sneak to a spot behind the chapel stage
and smoke. After lunch he took a walk out to a little pine forest
behind the library and smoked. He smoked at the bus stop in
the morning, cupping the cigarette in his palm when a car
passed, and lit up first thing after we got off the bus in the afternoon. His fingers were stained a deep yellow—for some reason he was terribly proud of those stains—and he smelled of
cigarettes all the time, despite the clove Life Savers he sucked
in profusion. He even had a considerable smoker's cough. In a
few short weeks he transformed himself into a dyed-in-the-
wool cigarette addict.

Once he had become one of the school's sneaky weeders, he
began to join them in the other things they did. He joined the
literary magazine, partly at the encouragement of Mr. Hirtle.
He went out for the Glee Club, became a member of the
Dramatic Society. That was the thing about Sam. If he
couldn't be on the soccer team he'd join the Bridge Club and
beat the pants off everybody at that. There was nothing wrong

with those activities—though people on athletic teams tended
to look down their noses at guys who joined the artsier clubs—
but there was something about them I resented, because they
were introducing Sam to new friends, taking him away from
me. I'd gotten so involved in sports myself partly at his encouragement, because he was a good athlete himself and I was
competing with him. It was Sam who had gotten me started
running, after all. Now he could barely walk. That wasn't his
fault. But there was a kind of willed quality to his condition, as
if he had arranged the accident, or was drawing out the
convalescence. He had quit too easily. It was as if he had just
been looking for a reason to give up sports.

My image of Sam from the year before was of him catching
that punt, or taking a grounder at short, or throwing all those
classy moves on a basketball court. But when I think of Sam at
the upper school I see him limping down the long aisle in the
study hall, leaning on a desk sometimes for support, walking
back to sign out of the place so he could sneak off somewhere
and smoke a cigarette.

III

The tradition of daily chapel must have been left over from
the days when schools were founded by ministers. Every morning, first thing in the morning, we spent twenty minutes at it.
We entered to a mournful introit, sang a familiar Episcopal
hymn, prayed, and listened to a meditation, something between a short sermon and a lecture. The headmaster—a rotund and extremely short man, whose closely cropped head
and jowly face were just visible above the podium—seemed to
delight in giving the meditation, booming out an important
phrase, quietly echoing an afterthought, pausing significantly
for effect while he stared slowly at every face in front of him.
Chapel would have been shortened by ten minutes if he had
cut out those pauses. Often enough they caused him to run
over.

The assistant headmaster, on the other hand—a much taller
man, balding and softly corpulent, with a splotchy red skin

condition, a weird wild light in his eyes—seemed to die a thousand deaths up at the podium, trembling uncontrollably for the first ten minutes, pretending to stare down at us while actually his eyes were shut tight, finally calling the whole thing off with about five minutes to go. Teachers who were asked to speak also seemed to hate it, and even outside speakers—those who were brought in and paid to speak—looked with distaste and trepidation at the two hundred sixty faces spread before them. Almost nobody liked chapel. I don't know why we continued to have it.

Except on Friday. Friday was different. That was the day when students were in charge of chapel.

Often on Friday there was a skit, and often it portrayed members of the faculty, and always on that day (they might get a little lax on other days) the entire faculty attended. Already that year we had had a parody of chapel meditations, representing their two most common perpetrators (one guy walked out on his knees, and required a stool to make himself visible behind the podium); no one laughed louder than, at the back, the headmaster and assistant headmaster. Four students in the school had formed a rock band, and sometimes they gave an early-morning concert, whipping the student body into a frenzy. One morning some poor sap who had always wanted to give the "Friends, Romans, countrymen" speech from *Julius Caesar* was allowed to wrap himself in a bedsheet and give it, while other guys stood around in their own bedsheets and made appropriate responses. The kid was perfectly serious, and the guys around him did their best to keep straight faces, but the audience, from the moment the curtain rose, screamed with laughter. Sometimes he had to wait thirty seconds to get out the next line. Every line seemed funnier than the last.

One Friday late in October, the stage when we walked into chapel seemed not to be set up for anything special. Usually the podium was removed, and often the front curtain down (concealing some impending atrocity), but that morning the curtain was up and the podium sitting as usual out in the middle of the stage. Everyone who entered the chapel on Friday did so with great anticipation—there was no mournful organ introit, so the sound of conversation grew louder and louder—and the very fact that there was no special setup seemed to indicate that something spectacular was about to happen. As more and more people entered we set up a rhythmic clapping, the way audiences used to clap for a movie to start.

Seats were assigned in chapel—we sat in alphabetical order—but on Fridays after roll was taken nobody cared, so in the midst of all the clapping Sam came limping back to sit beside me, wearing a sneaky grin. Guys were milling around all over the place.

"What's on for today?" he said.

"Nobody knows. At least not that I've talked to."

The applause was getting louder, more insistent. People yelled things out in the midst of it, stood up and danced to it. At the back of the stage the curtain started to move, somebody fumbling around for an opening. It seemed to go on for a long time. Finally the curtain opened, and the fumbler stepped out, carrying a book. He walked toward the podium, sat down on the chair beside it. A huge roar went up from the crowd.

The guy who had walked out was Bennett.

"Jesus Christ." I felt myself sliding down on the seat.

"You knew about this." Sam was staring at me, smiling.

"I did not." I would never have entered that room if I had.

"You had to know. Your own brother taking the program."

"He never said a word to me."

Bennett was just sitting there, pale and quiet and serious, staring at the audience. He gave no indication of planning to do anything at all. After the first roar, people had started to applaud again; one huge football player, in fact—dark and sullen, with thick black sideburns and a heavy-lidded stare—stood up and led the applause, pounding out the rhythm with broad gestures. Every clap was like a body blow. Other guys stood up to accompany him. Eleven or twelve were standing around the room.

Maybe we would just applaud the whole time. Bennett would stare at us.

Sam was still smiling at me, trying to figure out what the hell was going on. All around the freshman class, heads were popping up and turning around, looking to see how I was taking it. If only I'd had a slingshot.

"What do you think he's going to do?" Sam said.

"Make a total ass of himself."

"What *can* he do? Sing? Dance?"

"Maybe he'll sit there and read to himself. He's pretty good at that. Maybe he'll put on hand cream for twenty minutes."

There were still a few people straggling in. Bennett hadn't even looked at the podium.

"He might just be introducing something," Sam said. "A movie."

"Why Bennett? Besides, the screen's not down."

Sam was still staring at me, biting his lip. He was trying to be sympathetic, I could tell. He could see I was in agony. At the same time, it was all he could do to keep from bursting into insane laughter and breaking into applause. He and I were probably the only two people in the room who weren't clapping. We had been, but we weren't anymore.

"I don't see why you really care," Sam said. "It isn't like it's you up there. It's your brother."

I just stared at him. There was no way to explain. He didn't have a brother.

Maybe there are brothers who don't have the same problem, who can be who they are and pursue their own interests without worrying who their brother is. I never could. Bennett had always seemed a part of me, one, to be sure, that I had little control over and seldom understood. All my life he had preceded me, astonishing people with the powers of his mind, amusing them with his eccentricities, absolute in his devotion to what he was doing and absolutely unconcerned with what anyone else thought of it. After people saw the first act, they always looked to the second. Was my mind as remarkable as Bennett's? (It wasn't.) Was I half as much an eccentric? (I swore I never would be.) The effect on me, in fact, was to make me want to go entirely unnoticed, merge with the crowd. I wanted just to be one of the guys.

I never could be one of the guys, though. I was always also Bennett's brother. There was a peculiar mixture of feelings about him around the school. He was admired (also resented; that kind of guy ruins the curve) for his intellect, somewhat scorned as an aesthete (the arts were appreciated around that school, but only once they were institutionalized. You could admire Dickens and Shakespeare, monuments carved in marble, but you were a trifle suspect if you had a thing for a living author, and if you went so far as to write poetry yourself you were practically branded outright as a faggot), admired and also resented (he's such a grind) as a runner. All those feelings bounced off Bennett—he was used to them, loved being the center of controversy—but they fell on me like boulders. We were like the celebrated Siamese twins. He got drunk, and I got the hangover.

"You wouldn't understand," I said to Sam.

At about that time, Bennett stood up and walked toward the podium. Another huge roar went up from the crowd.

"Oh God," I said.

Sam looked away from me. Couldn't bear the pain.

The applause continued, accompanied by the roar. I honestly think it might have gone on and on, he might just have stood there for twenty minutes and never said a word, except that the football player turned around and held up his arms (huge moons of sweat under there), silencing the crowd. He looked at us all for a moment, as if stunned at what he had done. Then he turned to Bennett, gestured toward the crowd.

Bennett's voice was weak. You had to strain to hear it. "This morning I'd like to read a short story," he said.

The roar broke out again. That football player could forget it. With one simple remark Bennett had provoked a reaction that even "Friends, Romans, countrymen" hadn't touched.

Sam glanced at me, but I wouldn't look his way. I was praying, praying, that the story wasn't "A Long Soft Jumper from the Corner."

The roar continued, but you could sense after a while that it was dying down. If Bennett was going to keep dropping howlers like that, the crowd was certainly going to quiet down to hear him. They were quieting down now.

"It's by a writer who"—Bennett's voice was still uncertain— "never received much credit from the critics."

"And with good reason!" somebody shouted.

A roar of laughter.

"He never got the credit he was due."

I didn't like this. I didn't like it a bit. This writer was sounding more and more like the author of "A Long Soft Jumper
from the Corner."

"He was enjoyed by the people, but never really picked up
by the intelligentsia."

"Intelliwhatsia?" somebody shouted.

Why did Bennett have to use such words? The crowd was
screaming again.

What he was doing—only I really knew—was taking up his
old argument with Father. He was once again championing a
popular author who had not been appreciated by the academic
critics. He was always discovering such people and bringing
them up at the dinner table, as if the whole thing were Father's
fault.

Did he have to present his side in front of all these people?

"His name is Ring Lardner," he said.

The name brought the house down.

"God Almighty," I said. "I don't believe this."

"This better be one very short story," Sam said. "He only
gets a line out about every two minutes."

"Who in the world but Bennett," I said, "would ever be such
an ass as to think he could do this? What kind of crazy bastard
does it take to think he can read a short story to a crowd like
this at Friday chapel?"

"Beats me."

Sam was still having a hell of a time to keep from laughing.

"The story's title," Bennett said, "is 'The Golden Honey-
moon.' "

The crowd went wild.

Anyone who knows Ring Lardner, of course, will understand by now what Bennett was doing. He wasn't half as dumb
as he looked. The whole thing—his fumbling around with the
curtain, his innocent walk out onto the stage, his long stay in
the chair while suspense built up, the football player who led
the applause (he was a friend of Bennett's; he had a brother
on the cross-country team)—the whole thing was calculated.
Bennett had known the reaction he would get. He had known
people would laugh at him. They would have laughed at anybody who walked out on that stage. Instead of trying to do

something like a speech from *Julius Caesar*, he was about to read at least a candidate for the funniest story in all of American literature. He hadn't wanted to wait for his audience to catch on. He had wanted to get them laughing before he started to read. It was like a talk-show host who sends out a comedian before the show to warm the audience up.

Bennett began to read, haltingly at first—they were still interrupting him at practically every line—then with more confidence. You could feel the mood of the audience change. At first, as before, they were laughing at lines just because he said them, they would have laughed at anything (he continued to read, deadpan, as if he didn't even hear). After a while, though, the laughter began to change, directed not—in effect —at Bennett, but with him. People were beginning to listen to the lines, to realize they were funny in themselves. After loud bursts of laughter the crowd dropped into an attentive silence. Pretty soon they weren't roaring at all the lines, even all the funny lines; they were laughing hard, but also listening for more, for the ongoing flow of the narrative. Occasionally they did break into a roar, as when a man named Frank Hartsell wasn't careful enough in his personal habits when he was playing horseshoes: "It seems like, when Hartsell pitches, he has got to chew and it kept the ladies on the anxious seat as he don't seem to care which way he is facing when he leaves go."

By the end of the story the audience was entirely won over, positively civilized; they gave Bennett a standing ovation, and when he went behind the curtain they wouldn't leave, just kept applauding. The football player finally had to go back and make him come out and take a bow. Three weeks later he read another story, and two weeks after that another. By the end of the year he was reading stories on a regular basis, once a month, and the last one he read—as if just to show he could do it—was a perfectly serious piece, without a laugh in it. Nobody in the audience even cracked a smile.

Bennett probably did more to promote the short story at that school than any teacher in its history. He was a born teacher himself; he proved it that day. He did not try to impose things on his students (a speech from *Julius Caesar*) that he thought they should have, but took what was alive in the situation and found something appropriate for that. All his life he would be a teacher, whether employed by a school or not. He was a teacher even in his daily conversation.

That night at the dinner table, after Bennett recounted what had happened (I had to embellish a bit; he was oddly modest about his accomplishments), Father said, "It was a stroke of genius to pick that particular story."

"I wanted to pick one that was funny verbally," Bennett said, "as well as in other ways. I wanted a writer who worked in the vernacular. Mr. Edmond thought Lardner was a good choice."

Once the crowd had calmed down, I had seen Mr. Edmond in the back, standing in front of the exit, smiling at Bennett to give him confidence.

"You couldn't have made a better choice." Father frowned, trying to stifle the professor in him. He couldn't. "Except possibly Mark Twain."

"I considered Twain." Bennett didn't miss a beat. "A superior artist, of course. But I didn't think he would appeal as much to a modern audience. At least not the one I had."

"Possibly not."

"Anyway, I'm not sure his best work is in the shorter form. I could have read an excerpt, of course. But Lardner is a master of the short story."

"That he is."

No argument that night. Father wasn't going to diminish Bennett's moment of glory. He also may actually have agreed with Bennett on this point. (If so, Bennett would soon change his opinion.)

"I wanted someone with appeal to a wide range of people," Bennett said. "I considered Lardner's frequent appearances in *The Saturday Evening Post*."

"Everybody read Lardner in those days," Father said. "Everybody."

"Even the academics?" Bennett was incredulous.

"They probably read him on the sly. They sneaked the *Post* into their briefcases."

"But they didn't write about him."

"God no. Not in those days. You didn't write about some-body who appeared in *The Saturday Evening Post*."

"I really enjoyed the story," I said. Had to admit it.

"There's your audience," Father said.

The common man, in other words. Not the intelligentsia.

"I'm glad you were such a success, dear," Mother said. A word from the performer in the family.

That day at school, when I had walked into English, Mr. Hirtle said, "So *that* is Bennett."

"That's him." In some ways I wished Mr. Hirtle hadn't seen him. I would like to have kept Mr. Hirtle to myself.

"He did quite a job." He shook his head in admiration.

The whole thing had been absolutely wonderful, of course. It had also come within about half an inch of being utterly dis-astrous. I still wasn't sure how I felt about it. Even when, in the chapel, you could feel Bennett's performance turning from failure to success, I was still a nervous wreck, poised on the edge of a precipice. After the reading I felt as if I'd been beaten by a club. My nerves were shot. I had nothing left for the rest of the day.

Sometimes I wonder if I hadn't actually wanted the whole thing to be a disaster.

People in chapel had been laughing to the point that they were rolling around in the pews, doubled as if in pain. I too had laughed until I was limp, tears pouring from my eyes. But it was largely the laughter of relief (Thank God I wasn't humil-iated again!), a very ambiguous laughter, that could just as easily have broken into sobs. More than anything else I would have preferred to forgo the whole experience. As I lay back in the pew, stomach aching, my face wet and sore, I might just as easily have been taken for a man in pain, my tears might have been those of helpless rage.

IV

From the center of the quad we stood in a cluster and stared up at the tower. The academic building loomed dark below it, dorms alight at each corner of the quad, but from the roof at all four sides spotlights were trained on the bell tower, so it was the natural focus of the view. It was a crisp evening, not bad for early November, and clear, stars scattered across the night sky. Sam and I were comfortable in our sport coats, the girls in their sweaters.

"It really is a beautiful campus," Cindy said.

"Until you go to school here," I said.

"I guess."

I had taken her hand; it lay limp and noncommittal in mine.

"I wonder how you get up there," Sam said.

"You haven't found out," I said, "in all your wanderings?"

I had the idea Sam had smoked in every nook and cranny on campus.

"I've been busy in all my wanderings." Sam frowned, considering. "I hadn't thought to look, actually."

"Why would you want to go up there?" Cindy said.

"Just to do it," Sam said. "See what it's like."

"I bet it's pretty grungy," I said.

"I want to do it because I'm not supposed to," Sam said.

The primary motivation in so much of Sam's behavior.

"Didn't you ever want to do anything," Renee said, "just because it's wild, and wicked, and wonderful?" Her mouth was pursed in a smile; her eyes held a glow.

"Jesus Christ," Cindy said, loudly and pointedly.

Cindy, of course, would have climbed to that tower with Sam in a minute. A single strand of rope, no safety net. It was Renee she was disenchanted with. All evening long, whatever Renee had said, Cindy had jumped all over it. Made a remark under her breath, if not a loud sarcastic comment.

"It may be crazy," Sam said. "I'd still like to do it."

We were in the midst of the major social event of the fall season. At one time all the dorms had held fall and spring dances, but the school had decided that was too much, that the whole fall calendar was cluttered with football games and dances, so the dorms' fall dances were merged into one. In the basement of the chapel—a wide low-ceilinged room where such events were often held—was a loud rock band to dance to (even on the quad we could hear the music clearly), and each of the dorms, in their commons rooms, also had receptions, and sometimes quieter bands. The whole campus was alive that night, music traveling on the air, people walking from place to place. The four of us were not alone on the quad. Couples passed us all the time.

I had arrived at the dance in what must have been one of the strangest triple dates of all time. In the front seat of our station wagon were my father—in a plaid sport jacket and an old cloth cap, puffing fiercely on a large bent pipe—and my mother, in a bright lavender gown with a fur piece around her shoulders. They had somehow been persuaded to chaperon the dance. In the second seat were Bennett and a girl named Nancy Shelby. She had a spectacular head of auburn hair that hung in curls at her shoulders, but she wore narrow brown-rimmed glasses that made her seem rather severe, and her face wore a constant intent frown, as if she were considering some question and readying herself to speak on it. I don't know how Bennett had done it, but he actually seemed to have found his intellectual equal from the local girls' school, both in the powers of her mind and the extent of her interests. All the way out in the car the two of them talked literature, Bennett displaying his overwhelming knowledge of Shakespeare, his intimate acquaintance with the byways of American literature (weapons in his Oedipal struggle), and Nancy didn't miss a trick; if she didn't know the minor play by Shakespeare or the obscure work of American literature, she knew of it. She could carry on a conversation with Bennett, take in the information he was spewing forth (all he ever really asked). She even frequently challenged his opinions, a fact which he very much enjoyed, challenges bringing forth his greatest powers. From the front seat, Mother turned partway around (no mean feat in itself), nodded and agreed, as if at polite tea conversation. Father stared at the road, streams of smoke drifting over his shoulder, and corrected Bennett only when he couldn't stand it any longer. Bennett leaned forward to rebuff the corrections.

In the third seat, Cindy and I sat and stared, dumbfounded.

I had seen quite a bit of Cindy that fall, though not as much as I would have liked. Often on weekends, Sam and I would go over to her house when we were together. Sam himself spent a great deal of time there, hours on weekends and even some weekday evenings. It wasn't just that he liked her, but also that her house was entirely unsupervised, both parents off somewhere in blind stupors with vodka bottles at their sides. What all Sam and Cindy did I don't know, but it included smoking ("Did you bring a cigar?" Cindy always asked when I got there), and drinking, and I think it also included a great deal of deep conversation about Sam's romance with Renee, which they alluded to—often rather mysteriously—around me, though not in much detail. When the three of us were together we mostly made small talk, gossiped about friends, listened to music.

Though I didn't admit it to Sam, I would have liked to be seeing Cindy alone. I was always glad when Sam suggested we go over there, but never went so far as to suggest myself that we go. That whole autumn I had only gone to see her three times. The first time, after I had spent literally hours getting my courage up, Sam was already there. We all somehow acted, in fact, as if I had just come over looking for him. The other times I myself acted that way, out of shyness, as if I were just staying on to see Cindy because there was nothing better to do. We chatted, were perfectly friendly. An outsider might have said we were polite toward one another. It was as if both of us—though I was sure I didn't—wished Sam were there, as if we were both waiting for him. The conversation fell flat without him.

The problem was that I was in love with Cindy. I was out of my mind with love for her. I know what people will say to that, that I loved her just because she was there, because I was afraid to get to know girls and she was readily available; that she had won my love by the way she had kissed me, or by the fact that she had kissed me at all; that I wasn't in love just with her but with that whole trio of Sam and her and me. I am fully willing to concede those points. Who knows why we fall in love? But it wasn't just some superficial crush. I was far gone. And that fact ruined our conversation. When there's something like that that you're not admitting, it tends to make all the things you do say sound stupid, or irrelevant (they are irrelevant). Your mind keeps banging into the one thing you're refusing to say.

I had not kissed her since the night of the party. That also seemed a strange fact, especially the times we were alone together, that there were those kisses between us that had seemed so passionate but that we never repeated and never said anything about. I kept thinking, those days I was with her alone, that I would like to have said something casual and suave and innocent, like "Could we try a few more of those kisses you gave me that night?" but I couldn't bring myself to, probably because my emotions ran so deep. If I had started to say anything I would have burst into tears and shouted that I was dying of love for her.

It never occurred to me that that might have been the thing to do.

I hadn't even actually asked Cindy to the dance. One weekend when Sam and I were over there (and I don't think the whole thing was prearranged between them; I think Sam was doing it on his own), he said, "You two *are* going to the Four-in-One Dance together."

"Nobody said anything to me," Cindy said.

"You've got to go," Sam said. "The three of us have to be there."

"And also that fourth person," Cindy said.

"Of course that fourth person," Sam said. "I get to have a date too."

"I do think we ought to ask Henry about this," Cindy said. "He gets at least one vote."

"As long as I have veto power," Sam said.

"Sounds all right to me," I managed to choke out.

"Don't act too enthusiastic," Sam said. "Cindy might think you really want to."

"Really. I'd like to."

"It's settled then. You'll pick her up around eight."

"Right."

There was a long embarrassed pause; we sat there listening to the music.

"God it's hard to get you two off your asses," Sam said.

The basement room of the chapel on the night of the dance was mostly darkened, a few tinted spotlights sitting in strategic spots. One shone on the refreshment table in the corner, where my parents stood grimacing, trying to pretend they were smiling. The blare of the guitars in there was deafening (though nothing compared to what it would be a few years later in the decade), and Cindy and I danced for a while, in that dim hubbub of music and voices and bodies, until Sam found us. He couldn't dance much with his leg the way it was, preferred to hang around the dorms' commons rooms. Before we left, though, he did ask my parents if he and Renee could have a ride home.

That sounded like an interesting carload.

It was quite a bit later in the evening, sometime after ten, when we were standing out on the quad and looking up at the bell tower.

"I imagine the entrance is somewhere down in back of the chapel," I said. "It wouldn't be easy to get to, with a dance going on. That building's crawling with teachers."

"I didn't necessarily mean right now," Sam said. "I was just thinking sometime."

"But let's do something now," Renee said. "Something exciting." She raised her arms and looked to the sky, as if reaching for the stars. "I'm tired of just walking from door to door."

The three of us stood there, trying to think of something for this prima donna to do.

"We could take a walk," Sam said. "We could stroll down to the athletic fields. That's always a gas."

"I don't think we're supposed to do that," I said.

"All the more reason to go," Renee said. She started doing some kind of dance step, pirouetting in the direction of the hill down to the gym. "Maybe we'll be pursued by the authorities. Maybe we'll lead them in a high-speed chase."

She leaped, spun, her arms extended as if in longing.

"I hope we don't all have to dance our way down," I said.

"We don't," Sam said. He was cupping the flame of his lighter, lighting a cigarette. "We don't even all have to go, if you don't want." He suddenly seemed sullen. He was not looking at Cindy and me.

He turned and limped after Renee. She was continuing to do those elaborate leaps, spinning and turning.

"God, what a fruitcake," Cindy said.

She and I did follow the two of them down to the gym. We tried to give them plenty of room. It was rather an odd procession.

I honestly don't think—and didn't think at the time—that Renee was the kind of person who wanted to do something wild and wicked and wonderful. I don't think she especially wanted to go to the athletic fields. I think she was the kind of person who said such things out of embarrassment, just to break a silence. Silences seemed to embarrass her. Standing still embarrassed her. She knew that when the conversation stopped people were looking at her, because she was such a rare beauty, and any way she stood—if she was standing still—felt like a pose. All her life, I imagine, she would say such things, propose wild actions just for the sake of saying something, and probably get into a lot of trouble for doing so.

In the same way, for the same reason, she was doing that crazy dance down the hill, making an utter ass of herself (though she did dance beautifully) because she was too self-conscious to walk down the hill and talk to us. Even Sam seemed embarrassed. He limped rapidly in pursuit of her, while Cindy and I, walking slowly, trailed both of them.

I think that if you had ever been able to get Renee off alone, if you had ever gotten her into a situation where she could cut the crap, you might have found quite a wonderful person.

It apparently isn't easy to be exotically beautiful.

By the time Cindy and I had made it down the hill, around the gym and to the steps above the football field, Sam and Renee were far ahead of us, halfway across the field. You could see her bright-yellow dress making its little leaps, and behind it could just make out the dark figure of Sam; sometimes you'd see his cigarette glow. You could also hear the voices, mostly Sam's, chattering and laughing. He sounded more relaxed since they had left us behind.

"Where do you think they're going?" Cindy said.

"I don't know. There are fields below this one. A golf course. There's a stream down there."

"We might as well let them go. I think they want to be alone." Cindy stared off at the darkness. "At least that's what Sam seems to want."

All evening Cindy had seemed in a strange, distant mood. It was as if she didn't want to be with me, though I couldn't believe she would rather not have come. It was much like the days when I had visited her alone. She was perfectly polite, but seemed to be waiting for Sam. Tonight Sam was already there!

"Do you want to stay here?" I said. "Or go back up."

"Either way. Whatever you want. We can stay down here awhile."

At least we were alone down there. I hated it when she seemed preoccupied in a crowd. It made me feel alone among all those people.

I don't know why I had thought it would be so much different. I had been around Cindy enough to know better. Somehow I had imagined we would have a wonderful time. She would be delighted to see me, brightening at the doorstep when I showed up, would snuggle close to me in the car and lean her head on my shoulder from time to time, would wear a bright glow when we danced, hold me terribly close and breathe into my ear during slow numbers, finally ask if there wasn't some nice thicket of bushes we could sneak off to somewhere. I'd had any number of preposterous fantasies about that evening. Now I stood there with a sinking feeling in my stomach, the date in ruins all around me. I didn't know how it had happened.

I didn't have anything to lose, either. There was nothing left to be ruined.

Cindy was standing in front of me, but she wasn't looking at me. She just kept looking down. Our eyes had hardly met.

"You don't seem to be having a very good time," I said.

"No, I am." She attempted a smile. "I'm having a good time. It's a great dance."

"You seem kind of bored. In a bad mood."

"I don't know why you'd say that."

Just the little things. The long yawns. The audible groans.

"I am a little tired of Renee," she said. "I don't like being with her."

She hadn't seemed exactly ecstatic before Renee arrived.

"We don't have to hang around with them," I said. "We can leave them altogether. Go back up the hill."

"They saw us coming down with them. They might wonder where we went."

What were we, their parents?

"Cindy." I stepped close to her. She still wasn't looking at me. "I know I didn't ask you to the dance very well. I really didn't ask you at all. But that doesn't mean I wouldn't ever have done it. I really did want to come with you."

"I know, Henry. You asked me fine."

"I'd like to come and see you more. Just by myself. I *will* come and see you more. I really like you."

The more things I said, the easier they came. At this rate I might even get to the truth.

"That's nice, Henry. It's nice of you to say that."

I touched my hands to her waist, and leaned to kiss her. For as tall as she was, I had to lean remarkably far. I did kiss her. There was no denying that our lips met. Nothing happened, but they met.

Cindy smiled slightly, looked up just a little. I kissed her again.

"I'm just crazy about you, Cindy," I said.

"Henry." She touched my face lightly with one hand. For a moment I was sure she was going to put her arms around me and kiss me with real passion.

"I'm in love with Sam," she said.

"Christ!" I stared up at the sky and shouted.

"I'm sorry." She was holding me by the shoulders. "I didn't know whether to tell you."

"Why is everybody in the world in love with Sam?"

"I thought it was better for you to know."

"Every girl loves him. Every boy loves him. Every teacher. Every sport. Every school subject loves him."

"It isn't fair, I know." Now she *was* leaning her head on my shoulder, and I was hardly noticing. "It's just the way it is."

There were exceptions, of course. Some people didn't love Sam. Bennett, for instance. Sam's own parents didn't seem to.

"This whole thing hasn't been fair to you," Cindy said. "I think I've been a little shy around you, I've been in what seems to be a bad mood, because I've felt bad about it."

"About what?"

"What happened at the party that night."

"Don't apologize for that. God. The greatest night of my life."

"Oh, Henry." Cindy gave me a little squeeze. "I wasn't really with you. I was with Sam."

"It sure felt like me."

"I was so mixed up that night. My feelings all jumbled together. I really did like you when I was with you, I mean I really do like you, you're a great friend. But that night I was kissing you because of Sam, because of all the things I'd done with him, because you were his best friend, because I was thinking of him. I was kissing you and remembering things."

"Let's remember them again."

"No." She laughed, put her head against my chest. "I wouldn't do that to you again."

"It's all right. Really." Walk all over me. Walk all over me with your mouth.

"I've got to get over this. I've *got* to get over it. I just don't know if I can."

I felt sorry for Cindy all of a sudden, hearing her talk that way.

"Maybe you don't have to," I said. "He might give up on Renee. He can't take much more of this." Dancing down the hill, for God's sake.

"I think he can."

"He likes you, Cindy."

"I wish somebody would tell him that."

"He knows it. In a way I think he likes you more than Renee."

"He does like me in a way. But it's a different kind of liking. Renee's a challenge to him."

If Sam couldn't play soccer, he'd find something.

"It's appropriate that he brought her down here on the athletic fields," Cindy said.

"What are we?" I said. "The spectators?"

"I know. I don't know why I wanted to come down here. I'm trailing after him like some kind of puppy. We should go back."

If we couldn't think of anything better to do than talk about them we certainly should.

The funny thing was that despite the fact of what she'd said, I felt closer to Cindy than I had before. I liked her even more. Now that things were out in the open, all the tension was gone.

She hadn't told me anything I hadn't already known, of course. I would have said I didn't want to hear it. But it was better to have heard. It was better to have the words between us.

"How about one kiss?" I said.

"Henry . . ."

"Just one! A consolation prize."

"All right. One. But don't you ask for another when I finish. That'll ruin everything."

"I promise."

She did it again. She was liking me again, happy that she had told me, and she gave me one of those incredible kisses, that a man would die for. I nearly fell to my knees.

"You're amazing," I said.

"I had a good teacher."

"Don't go into it."

Up at the dorm, when we got back, things seemed to be winding down. Guys who had been there a long time had opened their shirt collars, loosened their ties a couple of inches. Even the girls seemed to be flushed and wilting. Despite the brisk night the windows had been thrown open, but it was cool only right around them; stuffy air really collected in that basement. Nevertheless, people were still dancing. One massive football player, at the encouragement of the crowd, was dancing out in front of the band, his feet sliding as if they were on ball bearings, sweat glistening on his neck, his shirt opened about halfway. The band was playing endless variations on the same song. Cindy and I danced for a while, but finally got bored and gave up. When nearly everyone else had also dropped out, the football player turned to the band and shrugged. They stopped about in the middle of a phrase, began immediately to dismantle their equipment. They didn't even stop to sing "Goodnight, Ladies."

My parents were still standing in the same place, looking as if they'd spent three hours in a steam bath. Father, in particular, seemed far past the point of recovery. He wore an expression of profound dismay. Bennett was also there, with Nancy, talking animatedly, back from wherever they'd been all evening. They must have discussed the whole of Western literature by that time.

"I spent the evening trying to get your father out on the dance floor," Mother said. "He won't try anything new."

I would have given a lot to see the two of them shake it down.

"That isn't dancing," Father said. "It's mass hysteria. Besides. If I'd gotten any closer to those guitars I'd have gone stark raving mad."

"The music *was* a little loud," Mother said. She wouldn't have wanted to hurt anyone's feelings. It wasn't exactly her kind of music.

"I just want to get home," Father said.

"All we have to do is find Sam," I said, looking vaguely at Cindy.

It was surprising how fast things were coming to a close. The band was ramming things into their cases as if a mob were after them. The crowd had beaten it out of there as if at a bomb scare. Faculty members were cleaning up the refreshment table. My parents' responsibilities were at an end.

"Shall we?" Father's face wore a look of desperate hope.

"We've got to wait for Sam," I said.

"And where is he?"

"I'm not sure where he went."

"Things will be closing up all over campus," Mother said. "He'll get here."

"If he stayed on campus," Bennett said. "He's well known for his elaborate wanderings."

Father was frowning. "If he's not here in another ten minutes I'm going to leave."

"Dad. We said we'd give him a ride."

"We didn't say we'd wait for him all night." On Father's face was an expression of deep sorrow, slowly turning into anger, at the thought of the evening he'd missed with his books, his beer, his pipe. "I never wanted to chaperon this thing in the first place. I was talked into it in a moment of weakness. But I never agreed to stay past the appointed hour. Your friend said he'd be here at eleven. I'll wait another ten minutes. Then I'm leaving."

Cindy was standing beside me. "They should have some kind of warning system down on the golf course. An eleven-o'clock flare."

"People would come dashing in from all over the place."

"I don't suppose there's any use running down there and looking."

"I wouldn't know where to look. There are three more fields. Nine holes of a golf course."

While we sat around waiting, Mother helped with the cleanup. Father only grew more determined as we sat there, pondering the injustice of having to chaperon a dance at all. After ten minutes he stood.

"I'm sorry. But it was Sam's responsibility to be here when he should. He probably got a ride with somebody else."

The trip home was pretty grim. I think everyone felt guilty at what was happening. Bennett and Nancy seemed finally talked out, and my parents were also quiet. I'm sure Mother would have waited for Sam, but she knew when it was better not to contradict Father. Cindy seemed glum again, but she did let her hand rest in mine. At her door she said, "We shouldn't worry about Sam. He likes to get into trouble. He always lands on his feet."

The next morning, Father felt repentant (he had stayed up reading far into the night; I counted seven bottles of beer beside his chair) and called both sets of parents. Sam's hadn't even known he was late—they probably still didn't know whether or not he was in—but Renee's had been worried sick. Sam and Renee had finally showed up at about twelve-forty, in a cab, and Sam had even had to bum part of the fare from Renee's father. The whole episode hadn't apparently endeared Sam to the man. Renee wasn't to be allowed out of the house for a month.

I was apprehensive when I went to see Sam on Sunday—I didn't know how much trouble he was in—but when I found him, out raking leaves in the front yard, he shrugged the whole thing off. "I didn't get up there until quarter to twelve. I didn't come close to making it. It wasn't your fault."

"What's this about Renee being grounded?"

"They're always saying that. She'll talk them out of it. She'll cry her eyes out."

He acted as if he were concentrating on the leaves for a moment, creating a neat little pile. Then he looked up at me, biting his lip, stifling a grin.

"You know that thing Cindy's cousin said? The night of her party?"

"Yeah." I had answered automatically. I didn't know what he was talking about.

"I finally decided what I thought about it."

"Oh?"

He was grinning broadly as he looked at me. It dawned on me what he was saying.

He didn't tell me then—though he would later—about the long walk it had been down to the golf course, the ghostly quiet down there, once they had crossed the stream and climbed the hill beyond it, the cold air and bright stars as he and Renee had lain in the grass and looked up at the night. He didn't tell me how fundamentally shy Renee was (he didn't need to tell me that), how when they were alone she wasn't affectionate and friendly and sexy like Cindy, how she didn't even seem to like kissing that much, took a long time to warm up to it, but once she did seemed suddenly to change, clinging to your lips, taking long deep sighs between kisses. How the big thing in his favor (other than the fact that he was good-looking and charming and adored by everybody) was that she wanted to be exceptional, avant-garde and daring, the first to do everything. They had not taken their clothes off—it was way too cold—but he had laid his jacket down, and she had pulled her skirt up, and it was incredible, he said, how really wet a girl got, and how literally hot she got. It felt very harsh going in, and she had her eyes closed, telling him to go slowly, take it easy, but it had felt absolutely wonderful also, terribly intense, and he had finished right away. Renee had been happy afterward—she kept saying "I can do it! I can do it!" —and they had both felt talkative and exhilarated. They stayed down there forever, lost track of time completely.

He didn't tell me all that on that Sunday he was raking leaves. It came out later, through days of conversation. All he said that Sunday, a big grin on his face, staring me in the eye, was, "I do think the kid has been laid. I just don't think he has a real discriminating sense of smell."

SEVEN

That winter Sam and I started hanging around Mr. Hirtle's classroom during odd moments of the day. Often he wasn't there, but he was a teacher who left his classroom unlocked so students with time on their hands would have a place to go; he had brought in some old bookshelves and a number of paperback books to create an informal lending library. Sometimes he did come in, would sit at his perch in front of the classroom, smoking cigarettes and drinking coffee, so we and any other kids who happened to be around would talk to him about this and that. It was one of my favorite things, talking to teachers during spare moments. It made them seem halfway human.

The sentence I had written in Mr. Hirtle's classroom earlier in the year had been accepted for the literary magazine, and printed in the fall issue as "Dawn Over the Atlantic." Most of my family had been startled at this development. "You've been holding out on us," Father said, gazing down appreciatively at the magazine. Bennett, however, did not seem surprised. He had always felt that artful pieces of writing were perfectly natural, something anyone should be able to do. He welcomed me graciously into the company of the elect.

It was late in November, not long after the magazine had come out, that Sam and I were standing around in Mr. Hirtle's room, and Sam said, "I think Henry ought to join the literary magazine."

"You do," Mr. Hirtle said. Never a man to commit himself.

Sam himself was a member in good standing of the magazine. Anyone could join who wanted to, and you became a voting member simply by attending a certain number of meetings. He had voted for my piece, in fact, had spoken for it when it came up for discussion.

"He had that thing in the fall issue," Sam said. "And he likes writing. He's good at English. Besides, he's spending so much time at the gym lately he's turning into a real jock. He's got to broaden his horizons."

"*That* might be a good idea," Mr. Hirtle said.

"There are too many wastes on the literary magazine," I said.

"Wastes?" Mr. Hirtle said.

"Guys who smoke and drink. Who sit around letting their bodies fall apart. Who think that just because they write a few lines of free verse now and then they're doing something."

"I can't imagine who you're speaking of," Sam said.

"This guy used to be the best athlete in the class," I said to Mr. Hirtle. "Now he doesn't even go out for sports."

"I can't go out," Sam said. "I hardly have any cartilage left in my knee."

"You don't try to get better," I said. "You could soak it in the whirlpool at the gym. Go to physical therapy now and then. You could come down to the gym and work on your upper body."

"Those things are boring. My knee just needs time."

"It's been almost three months."

"The doctor says just a few more weeks."

"By the time your knee's better the rest of your body will be shot. Your brain will go soft."

"I don't see what all this has to do with joining the literary magazine," Mr. Hirtle said.

It disturbed me that he wasn't more interested in goading Sam. He couldn't see the kid was wasting away.

"I don't want to get like that," I said. "I don't want to be like the guys on the literary magazine."

"You don't have to be like them," Mr. Hirtle said, "to be on the magazine."

"We don't hold you down and pour wine down your throat," Sam said.

"People think you're like that if you join the literary magazine," I said.

That was one of my great fears, that if I associated with the wrong people—this feeling put a great strain on my friendship with Sam—I would be seen in the same light as they were. Teachers would avoid my eye in the halls, and feel constrained to lower my grades. Soon I would be banished from the cross-country team. Associates with the wrong element, my report card would read.

"Nobody judges you by what organization you belong to," Mr. Hirtle said.

Teachers might not, but students did. Sam knew it.

"I myself, however," Mr. Hirtle said, "don't think you should join the literary magazine."

"Why not?" Sam said.

"That isn't where his talent lies."

"He just had a thing in the fall issue! He was the only freshman to have one in there!"

It was Mr. Hirtle who had urged me to submit the piece!

"I don't mean he's not talented." Mr. Hirtle had frowned wearily, now turned to me. "I don't mean you couldn't write more pieces like that. Submit them to the magazine and possibly get them published. But you wrote that piece in the classroom. You wouldn't have done it on your own. And the thing that was good about it was the way it noticed small details. The colors of the sky reflected on the water. The gulls swooping down. It wasn't a poem, in a way. It wasn't essentially metaphorical."

Let's throw the whole thing out, hell. Find every issue of the magazine and destroy that page.

"It would have been a good background for a story. But writing a story's complicated. There's a lot to learn before you're ready for that. I think you ought to join the newspaper."

"The newspaper!" Sam said. "That bunch of grinds."

"Now you're going to whip out the stereotypes," Mr. Hirtle said.

"I wasn't looking for his perfect goal in life. I wanted him to work with me."

"You're a natural for the newspaper," Mr. Hirtle said to me. "You notice details. Write in particulars. You could sharpen your writing skills there. Gradually work up to more complicated things."

"He doesn't want to write for the newspaper," Sam said.

"Oh?"

"His brother Bennett writes for the newspaper. He hates to compete with Bennett in anything."

Sam was right. It had never occurred to me to work for the newspaper, because Bennett was already there.

"You run cross-country," Mr. Hirtle said.

"That's not the same thing," Sam said. "Bennett's varsity and he's JV. Besides. I'm the one who got him started running."

"When did you ever run?"

How the mighty had fallen. Mr. Hirtle didn't even associate Sam with sports.

"I used to be a hell of an athlete." Sam smiled wryly. "Just like he said."

Mr. Hirtle turned to me. "There are lots of departments on the newspaper. If you write for one you don't necessarily come in contact with somebody from another. You certainly don't compete with him. I think you should write sports. You seem to like them. And that would keep you from the artier crowd, which you apparently want to avoid. I just happen to know, as one of the advisers to the paper, that there might be an opening for a young sports reporter. If you volunteer right now I think I can get you in."

"The whole idea was to get away from sports," Sam said.

"He doesn't want to get away from sports. He just wants a chance to write more."

As far as I knew I didn't want either one. These guys certainly had a way of talking for me.

"Should I give your name to our editors?" Mr. Hirtle said.

"I still think you're missing out on a chance to know some great guys," Sam said.

* * *

Like many a charismatic teacher, Mr. Hirtle was a great ma-
nipulator. I have always remembered the specific remarks he
made that day about my talents. I have analyzed his words for
the bearing they might have on my future vocation. That was
the first time anyone had taken me so seriously, and it meant a
great deal. I hungered for such attention. But the fact of the
matter was that there was much superficial turnover on the
newspaper staff, that he had just lost two sports reporters from
the fall and was looking to replace them. He might have encouraged anyone who had been standing there to become a
sports reporter.

That isn't to say he didn't mean the things he said. Or that
they might not be true in a way.

In any case, it was because of what Mr. Hirtle said that I began my association with the newspaper, something that became as important to me as anything I ever did at the school.
The offices were on the third floor of a dormitory, an attic
where there were no student rooms but there was one faculty
apartment, that of my French teacher, the vague and rumpled
man whom we were constantly in danger of losing down a
manhole. On the weekends when we worked on the paper he
often cooked some dish that smelled strongly of onions, and
whenever he was in his room he played classical music—often
Brahms or Tchaikovsky—very loudly, and in the evenings or
on weekends he sometimes walked into the offices smelling of
beer and acting a little tipsy, to see how we were doing.

I loved those rooms. They were up in the eaves of the building, so the ceiling slanted sharply; if you stood up too quickly
or unthinkingly you cracked your head, suddenly remembering where you were. All three rooms were dusty and lit-
tered with trash, though we tried to keep the desks of at least
one cleared for work. The drawers were full, stuffed with old
articles and scraps of paper and layout sheets, and the desks
were chipped and hacked and gouged with messages. There
was a dank mildewy smell that reminded me of hotels at the
beach; the lights were fluorescent, buzzing and blinking and
covered with dust; the typewriters were ancient and enor-
mously heavy models whose keys you practically had to bang
with a hammer to make them do anything. In the corner of one

room stood stacks of the photographic blocks newspapers used in those days. I have no doubt that every photograph ever used in the paper was in those stacks somewhere, and occasionally when we were desperate for a filler we would find some ancient photograph—the dean, say, when he was a boyish young math teacher who still had his hair—and run it with an appropriate caption.

If the cross-country team was one of the most egalitarian institutions in the school, the newspaper was one of the least. The editorial positions carried a great deal of prestige, and they were won only after two or three years of nerve-wrenching labor, and once somebody had achieved one he considered himself a god who was entitled to order around any little kid he could get his hands on. A new kid on the staff was treated absolutely like dirt, handed the worst assignments and screamed at if he didn't handle them flawlessly. If he did a perfect job nothing was said. Silence implied perfection. Sooner or later, once you had done enough piddly little jobs, you were given an important one, or if you were really considered reliable an important one with a deadline, and if you did that job right you were suddenly an accepted member of the staff. The editor no longer yelled at you, or if he did you could yell right back (a lot of business was carried on by yelling at that place). When you were sitting around in those offices with nothing to do there was a camaraderie that you found almost nowhere else in the school. You could feel it in the air. The newspaper staff considered themselves one of the few groups at the school that was doing something real. There was a real distinction in belonging to that staff, if only in the minds of the staff themselves.

That first winter I did a little of everything for the sports page. Varsity sports were no problem, the editor and assistant editor took care of them, but there were also JV and freshman, basketball and wrestling, and everything had to be covered, if only with a box of results or statistics. At the height of the season every team had two matches per week. Every athlete in the school looked for his name on the sports pages—it was most important to get the names in—and every starting athlete felt worthy of special attention, if not some space in a headline. I spent the whole winter dashing to the gym to cover obscure contests. I got to know every sub-varsity athlete in the school. I went to practices and interviewed coaches and players; I traveled with teams to away games; I typed up articles (pecking away with two fingers) and composed headlines; I compiled statistics; I put captions on photographs. I'm not sure why I took to it as I did (I have sometimes thought that the abusive atmosphere seemed the way I should be treated, as the younger and inferior brother), but I loved newspaper work. I did as much work for the paper that winter as any freshman in the school.

Bennett's work for the newspaper was far more particular, though he worked for the feature page, which did not have such clear guidelines as the sports pages. It printed editorials, sketches, cartoons, poems, an occasional letter to the editor. Because that kind of item didn't require a tight deadline, and because the staff for the feature page tended to be artistic and temperamental, the feature page was not as savagely run as other departments. Bennett had never gone through a copyboy stage. He had always been treated as an honored guest columnist, who delivered his clean copy in plenty of time and required not a single change (at least you'd better not change it, you worm). He was genuinely appreciated as an invaluable asset. With his gift for words he could have filled the whole newspaper if he'd had to.

He had associated himself with the feature department primarily because he was disgusted with the drunken bums at the literary magazine (it was he who had told me they infested the place) but wanted to work with that kind of material. That year he had been writing a series of sketches about teachers on campus, opening with an exaggerated description, going on to tell a few stories—real or apocryphal—that surrounded the subject. The sketches were written in an elaborate rhetoric and were a huge success, as uproariously funny for the language they used as for what they were describing. The cartoonist for the paper did equally crazy line drawings to accompany them. Both he and Bennett worked under pseudonyms, and it was just as well, because a couple of the teachers whom they had manhandled swore revenge but didn't know whom to take it on. The real names appeared in the staff box, but people didn't make the connection.

The advisers weren't especially involved in the paper. They had to read everything before it was printed, and they gave help when they were asked, but for the most part students ran the show because they were fiercely proud of running it. Mr. Hirtle obviously helped staff the newspaper, but he rarely appeared in the offices. The other adviser, Mr. Edmond, didn't seem interested in anything except working on the feature page with Bennett.

As I had been around the school that year I had seen more of him, though of course I hadn't gotten to know him. He always wore corduroys, or tweeds, and shirts of odd off colors; often he sported a bow tie. He wore his cloth cap constantly, and carried a tightly rolled umbrella—swinging it jauntily as he walked—if there was any chance of precipitation in the next three days. That way he had of leaning back slightly and tilting his head was a mannerism; he used it often as he talked with the editors up in the office. To go with the strong grip I had discovered when I first met him, he had a remarkable voice, which came booming up the stairs as he and Bennett approached the newspaper offices.

At that point he was probably the leading influence on Bennett's life. Though he was no longer Bennett's English teacher, Bennett was still an ardent disciple. It was Mr. Edmond who directed Bennett's reading (he had outlined the Shakespeare project), he who encouraged Bennett's writing; it was he who had suggested Bennett read a story in chapel, and the summer before he had toured the country by bus and sent Bennett a series of postcards in calligraphy, which was the way he did all his writing (immediately Bennett bought the special pens and the book of instruction). He had a mottled brown bulldog named Somerset Maugham who was so well behaved he actually brought him to class; he had a Mercedes that ran like a clock with nearly two hundred thousand miles on it; in his apartment he kept a harpsichord and all kinds of interesting knickknacks and art objects. For a man who was basically eccentric he commanded enormous respect around the school.

He had a formidable intellect and a great deal of presence. Troublemakers got nowhere with him.

Of all the students at that school Bennett was the most likely to befriend teachers. Not the plodding state teachers college types (though he respected even them) but those who showed intellect and sensitivity. Bennett could form an intellectual partnership at the drop of a hat. At all kinds of moments around the school you would see him trailing a teacher, belaboring some abstruse point. He didn't really need any help making his way through an intellectual discipline, but he liked it. His discipleship often included a large measure of hero worship.

Bennett and Mr. Edmond didn't come to the newspaper office often, and when they did they didn't associate much with the staff, though they were always cordial about saying hello. Usually they repaired to an empty room, cleared off a space, and sat down to plan their page. They would go over things that had been submitted, ideas they wanted to assign. Eventually they would pick out a faculty member for Bennett and the cartoonist to rake over the coals in the upcoming issue.

II

There was no program of winter track at our school. There was a small core of dedicated runners—cross-country men waiting for track—who ran a little circuit of the roads and driveways around campus, taking it pretty easy, talking and telling stories to break up the monotony. We never ran hard, except for an occasional sprint up a hill. We were just running to keep our legs in shape, waiting for the winter to end.

I loved running with that pack. It lacked the competitive edge of a regular practice, so there was no real nervousness involved. We seemed a small elite, a lunatic fringe, devoted to that strange and lonely and demanding sport.

Bennett never ran with the group. He didn't care to run in packs. He was probably more dedicated than the rest of us, or at least more obsessive. He came up to the gym floor like everybody else to do his warm-ups, but stretched purposefully, the same precise routine every day, and paid little attention to what was going on around him. He worked on his upper body, as we all did in the winter, so many chin-ups, so many bar-dips, another repetition every eight days or whatever it was. Twice a week he also did some work with the weights, and every day—in his wool gloves, a red wool hat, Vaseline covering the sensitive parts of his face—he went downstairs and out the door to run, no matter how dark, dismal, snowy, sleety it might be.

He scorned the little course in the driveways of the campus. If it was light enough—if it was light at all—he took to the roads, long solitary runs through the suburbs, and he considered the traffic his enemy: it was he, with his brilliant career ahead of him, who had a right to the roads, and the drivers who should be on the lookout for him. He cursed viciously and at great length any car that had the effrontery to come near him. If it was dark, or especially messy, or if he just didn't feel like fighting the traffic, he actually went down on the cross-country course, ran through snow and patches of ice and often huge snowdrifts, wearing boots if necessary. That must have made his legs strong, but it always seemed to me that wearing boots would take all the joy out of running. Joy wasn't what Bennett was after, somehow. He got something out of running, he got something very important, but joy wasn't it.

As much as I liked it, I didn't get to run too often with the pack. That was when I was just starting out with the newspaper, so I often had to squeeze in a run after an assignment. I would have been up in the offices proofreading copy, or typing up an article, or down at the gym getting freshman wrestling results, and I would have to change into my sweats quickly, do a hurried warm-up and take a short hard run.

It was on an afternoon late in December that something happened almost unprecedented in my experience. A varsity basketball game was about to begin, and people were standing around watching the warm-ups: sharp hard passes, long strides to the basket, sudden leaps for a lay-up. People were gathering in the stands, including girls from the local girls' schools, and our cheerleaders—football players who didn't have a winter sport and who had donned letter sweaters to look like a squad—had stepped onto the floor to get the crowd worked up. It was the kind of day when I might have watched the first quarter, maybe the whole first half, stretching my body lazily until I felt like a piece of limp elastic, when something happened that should have made the floor shudder under my feet, a loud crack sound all around us, and a jagged split appear in the ceiling as a light shone down on me from the heavens.

Bennett had stepped up to me and said, "Want to go out for a run?"

I don't mean to make it sound as if we never did anything together. When we were kids, of course, we had played all kinds of games, and in more recent years had joined in pickup games when we were both in the vicinity of one. For the past few years, however, Bennett had been such a solitary—practicing basketball alone and running alone—that I had hardly ever done anything with him. He needed that solitude to concentrate in, needed it somehow for his overall well-being, but it hardly made for a close brotherly relationship.

More surprising than the fact that he was breaking his solitude was the fact that he was acknowledging me as a runner.

There was no special pleading in his eyes, no indication that this was a change from the policy of the last three years at least. He seemed so casual, not even looking my way, that I wasn't sure I had heard him right. I felt like banging my head a few times, pinching myself to see if I was awake.

"Where're you going?" I said.

"Out on the roads." He was bouncing up and down a little, stretching his calves. "Good day to go out on the roads. Clear. Not too dark yet."

"Don't you want to watch some basketball first?"

"Can't watch basketball. Gets too dark."

Bennett only spoke in so clipped a fashion when he was embarrassed at the encounter.

"We could run on campus if it gets too dark," I said.

"Can't run on campus. Hate to run on campus. Everybody runs on campus."

The whole thing was like Bennett in so many ways. Refusing to do what everyone else was doing, denying himself a small pleasure to do what he felt was his duty, coercing me—it was his oldest trick!—into giving up what I wanted in order to do what he wanted.

But there were concessions involved too. He was acknowledging my existence as a runner, actually condescending to run with someone, and with—of all people!—his own brother. He was giving up more than he was getting.

"All right," I said. "I'll come."

What I probably haven't revealed about my relationship with Bennett—what gets left out in a long story of rivalries, exasperations, and annoyances—is the enormous pride I felt in him as a brother. I suppose it's been inherent in much of what I've said. If I hadn't been proud of him I wouldn't have cared what an ass he made of himself, how much he screwed up in a basketball game, I would have laughed as freely and easily as anyone when he read that story in chapel. A brother is a part of you, and you want him to do well, just as he is your rival and you want to defeat him. So many of the difficulties between brothers reside in that ambiguity. You want him to win against everybody else, and lose to you.

But I well remember the swell of pride I felt when he sank his jump shots, the gap in my chest when he kicked in hard at a cross-country meet, and when he asked me to go out that day I felt a pride in myself as a runner that I couldn't have felt any other way. I wouldn't have felt any better if Paavo Nurmi had asked me to step out for a run.

That wasn't the only time we ran together. On days when we both worked late at the newspaper office, when I got to the gym on time and found him doing his obsessive warm-ups, on days when we happened to bump into each other in the locker room, we might run together. He asked me or I asked him. It didn't seem to matter.

As runners will do on long easy runs, we talked.

So for whatever reason—because I had entered the upper school and he felt I was mature enough, because I had lost weight and no longer looked like a little butterball, because I had started to write and shared that interest with him, because I had reached a passable level as a runner—Bennett and I started to spend some time together. We had personal conversations. We began to learn new things about each other. Out of nowhere, it seemed, we were acting more like brothers.

You don't look at somebody when you're out on the road with him, but Bennett never looked at anyone when he talked. Conversations with him were more like a lecture. A topic would come up and words started spilling out as if somebody had found a button on him somewhere and pushed it. He would stare vaguely ahead of him, delivering himself of an opinion that he had formulated sometime in the past (he had such opinions on everything), rethinking and clarifying points he had already settled on, rarely stopping long enough for anyone to say anything. That winter, while we ran on the roads, he delivered himself of any number of opinions.

On Mr. Hirtle: "I'm not sure he's really a first-rate mind. A first-rate mind, maybe, but not a first-rate intellect." (How did Bennett know Mr. Hirtle? The same way he knew everybody. He had latched onto him and formed an instant intellectual friendship, pumping him for everything he was worth.) "He's spent too much time skiing, and playing preppy sports, and hanging around with the cocktail set, and not enough time reading. He's never put in the thousands of hours at a scholarly library that you need to create a first-rate intellect."

"He's the best teacher I ever had," I managed to gasp out, more breathless at the unmitigated gall of his opinion than at the stiff pace we were keeping.

"I have no doubt he is. A second-rate intellect often makes a first-rate teacher. Not too far above the level of his students. But there's something whimsical about the man. Dilettantish. One day he said to me, 'I fully expect to wake up some morning and find myself a great poet.' You don't find yourself a great poet. You make yourself a great poet. Through a lot of hard work."

Take it from the man who knew. Who had already completed the first of many years of preparation.

On working for the newspaper: "You shouldn't let those people push you around. I know you think you have to put up with a certain amount of crap to advance yourself, but if you put up with too much you'll only advance so far. You'll be the person they keep around to do the drudgery, because he will do it."

"You've never done any of it," I said.

"I've never been asked to."

It was just like Bennett to hold himself above the plebeian crowd.

"You learn about the paper by doing those things," I said. "It helps to do the small jobs, so you see how the whole thing's put together."

"I have no desire to see how the whole thing's put together. I have no desire to be a journalist. Possibly you do. But I still think that before too long you should ask those people to give you a real assignment. Assign you an article that will be more than just a compilation of statistics. Make them treat you as if they want to keep you. If you don't do it now you may never have the chance."

On my track career: "You'll eventually be a two-miler."

(A thrill of pride went through me at the fact that he had given the matter any thought at all.)

"Jesus, Bennett. I hate long distances. The sooner a race is over the better."

"You don't have sprint speed."

"Who's talking about sprint speed? I'm talking about the mile. The half. You don't need sprint speed to run a mile."

"You can't be successful without it. A good high school miler has a kick. He's not a sprinter, maybe, but he runs a decent quarter."

"I run a decent quarter."

"You're talking about running back in the pack. You're still at the point where you're surprised at all you can do. Glad you can even finish things. That's fine for the time being. But if you ever want to be a first-rate runner—and what's the use of doing anything, if you don't try to be first-rate?—you've got to find the event that's right for your talent."

"I don't like the two-mile."

"You will. You like something when you're good at it. That's your event."

"And you?"

"The mile. Double in the half."

I was variously amused and astonished at the things Bennett said to me, and at the certainty with which he said them. He spoke as if he were a world authority on every little subject. The fact of the matter was, though, that on those three topics at least, I eventually decided that he was exactly right.

The thing about running with Bennett was that he always ran slightly too fast. He was a much better runner than I, he could have run me into the ground anytime, but that wasn't the problem. Running in the winter was supposed to be just to get in the mileage, keep our legs tuned up, but he always ran harder than that. He probably ran a lot harder, but I was so pumped up at the thought of running with him that I didn't notice. No matter how hard I ran, though, he was always a half step faster. I was never quite at his shoulder. He was running easily, speaking his long flowing sentences as if we faced each other in a couple of easy chairs, and I was gasping out inadequate replies because I didn't have the wind to say anything better. Even if I had run it as a race, I would never have pulled quite even with him.

One Thursday late in February, cold and wet and getting dark—it was probably too dark for us to be out on the roads—I finally said something to him. I'd had a hard week and had run hard all week, had stayed up late the night before studying for a history test, and I was stiff and tight and tired, my legs felt dead, so I asked him the question I'd been waiting to ask for years.

"Why do you push so hard?" I said.

Most of the time I could take it. It was just that I was so tired. Probably I shouldn't have come out with Bennett that night at all.

"What do you mean?" he said.

"You always go a little faster. No matter how hard I run."

"Who says?"

"I say. I've been running with you for weeks."

"Maybe you always run a little slower."

An interesting possibility.

"I run the best I can," I said. "It's never quite fast enough. No matter how hard I go."

We ran in silence awhile as he digested this information. Perhaps because of what I'd said my body felt leaden, as if I'd barely make another hundred yards.

"It's good for you to run with me," Bennett said. "It's good for you to push yourself. Have somebody always egging you on."

"That's not why you do it."

"What?"

"That isn't why you run that way. So I'll push myself and be a better runner."

It couldn't be. As if he were living his whole life for my benefit.

"Why do I, then?"

"You can't stand to be even with me. You can't stand for me to be as good as you."

It was one of those moments when—tired and irritable as I was—I said the first thing that popped into my mind, but as soon as I'd said it I knew it was the truth, the thing I'd always wanted to say to him.

I can still see the expression on his face. I would have expected stubbornness, a blunt refusal to admit the truth. What I saw, however, as I looked over at him, and he glanced at me, was blank surprise. Utter perplexity.

"You're not as good as me," he said.

It was almost funny, the way the first thing he said virtually proved what I was saying.

By that time I had practically slowed us to a stop, beside a long straight road roughly a mile from the school. To our left was a field, beyond it a woodsy hill.

"You never want me to be as good as you," I said. "You never let me be as good as you in anything. Like baseball. As soon as I got good at that you quit."

"I was never any good at baseball."

"I struck you out a few times and you dropped the bat forever."

"You struck me out. Everybody struck me out. I should never have played the game in the first place."

"I started to get good at basketball and you gave up that game too."

I shouldn't have brought that up. Bennett was far better at basketball.

"I told you why I gave up basketball," he said.

"I do some good work in English and you say my teacher's no good."

"I said he wasn't a first-rate intellect. I wasn't saying anything about you."

"I start to get somewhere at the newspaper and you say I'm not doing that right. I should be like you. Just write some great article and have them publish it."

"I wasn't saying you weren't good. I was saying just the opposite. You're better than you think. You don't give yourself enough credit."

"It'd be suicide for me to act like you at the paper. They'd throw me out on my ass. I'm not as good as you. I don't write as well. I've got to pay my dues."

I had cleverly reversed my field here. First I'd been saying he was always trying to look better; now I was saying he really was better.

"It's not as easy for me as for you," I said. "Nothing's as easy for me. But you always make it worse. You always push so hard."

"I just do what I do."

"It's inhuman the way you keep it up."

"Why don't you just ask me to run slower? Why do you make such a big deal out of it?"

"I'm talking about everything. Schoolwork. Running. Conversation. Why don't you ease up a little? Why don't you give everybody a break?"

We had stopped running entirely by then, were standing by the side of the road. We stared at each other, our faces flushed and sweating, hearts pounding, chests heaving. The field beside us was lightly covered with snow. It shone white in the gathering dark.

"You don't understand," he said.

"You're damn right I don't."

"You don't know what it's like to be me."

"I know what it's like to be me. Always running behind."

"They never expected anything of you."

"They sure as hell didn't expect me to be like you. No one on earth was as good as you."

Our parents had slipped into the conversation unnoticed.

"They let you get away with stuff," Bennett said. "Not doing your work. Not getting the good grades I did."

"Who ever got the grades you did?"

"Screwing around all the time. Running around with your friend Sam."

"You never wanted to do that kind of stuff."

"I was the older one. I had to be perfect."

I have no doubt that Bennett believed what he was saying. He was speaking with a great deal of conviction. I just don't know where he got such an idea. I'd never heard my parents push him. I'd never heard them say he was screwing around too much. If I'd had to guess, I would have thought they'd like to see him go a little haywire. Get away from that obsessive studying.

"Don't you think I'd like to do the things you do?" he said. "Lie around all night reading sports magazines. Never study for my tests. Then come home with a C and have them say that's okay, that all the brothers can't be students."

I didn't think he'd like that. I thought he liked the way things were.

"I act that way because I can't be as good as you," I said.

"You could be as good as me," he said. "If you studied as hard."

Now I knew he was lying. He didn't believe that.

I had obviously, however, touched on a subject which he had given a great deal of thought. He was bursting with views to express.

"When did they ever say you had to do all this?" I said.

"They didn't have to say. You just know. You've got a mother who can sing. Act. Paint. Sculpt. You've got a father who's a noted scholar. All these articles to his credit. Who values literature above all other things. You don't have to be told what to do in that family. You've got to be good. Preferably at the things they're good at, but certainly at something. You've got to be great."

Where had he gotten that idea? Susan wasn't too great. There was me. What about Teddy, for God's sake?

"What about Susan?" I wasn't going to lead with my best example. "She doesn't work like you."

"Susan's a terrible disappointment to them. Had a talent and didn't use it. She's afraid of competing with Mother. She's actually much better than Mother, if she'd let herself be. But she's stranded in mediocrity."

This was news to me.

"What about me? What about Teddy?"

"You got an exemption because you were so fat and soft. They coddled you. They like having one fat little child to coddle. With Teddy they seem to have lost it completely. He's way out of control. He's going to be the weirdest of us all."

The thing about Bennett was, he'd never change his mind. It was just like at night: once he had the hand cream on, his watch in place, the light switch tapped X number of times, that was the way it was. You couldn't change a thing. He couldn't rest unless things were just that way.

It didn't do any good to point out the huge holes in what he was saying, that Susan was mediocre, I was fat and coddled, Teddy was weird, we all in his description didn't amount to a hill of beans, yet we were just as much a part of the family as he was. His system was held together by a strange logic that only he could understand.

"There's no use trying to change things," Bennett said. "We are what we are. We do what we do. I'm the one who has to be perfect. Right at the moment I've got to finish this run. You can come with me or not. You can run behind me or beside me. It doesn't matter to me. But I've got to get going."

He still didn't understand. He hadn't answered my question. I couldn't run beside him. I could only run behind him. He'd die before he let me run beside him. I don't think he even knew it.

"You go ahead," I said. "I just don't have it today. I'll walk back."

He had never expected that. He had expected me to accept what he'd said, take my place slightly behind him and run along that road. We were to go through life like that.

"You sure?" He had looked surprised, then a little worried. He was actually somewhat protective of me.

"Sure."

"You'll be okay?"

"I'll be fine. You go ahead and run."

That was what he did. He went right back to the place where we'd stopped (I'm surprised he didn't step through the same footprints) and continued, at his steady pace, which you couldn't have altered with a hand grenade. I started walking, across the field, on a direct line to the gym. I had to go up some hills, and cut through some woods, and it was snowy, and wet, and got very dark, but I got there eventually, not long after Bennett, who had traveled much further.

That wasn't the last time we ran together. It was a little spat, much like many others we'd had, and by the next day, even, we'd forgotten all about it. But I still remember that evening, and the different ways we went—one set of footsteps through the snow and up over the hill through the woods, the other through the slush on the side of the road—and the one that seems burdened, the path that seems a little sad, is the one that was laid out in the road, the one that had been run so many times, and would never change.

III

Scott Hilton was the sports editor of the newspaper, a medium-built guy with large thick spectacles and hair the color of sawdust. He was basically good-looking but terribly rumpled: his clothes never matched and his hair was wild and stringy. He smoked incessantly, even when it wasn't permitted (he chain-smoked in the newspaper office, threw open a window on the most frigid of days), and he had a reputation as an enormous drinker. He looked more like a cloistered scholar. He was a terrific underachiever, who had somehow managed to flunk his sophomore year with one of the highest IQs in the class. The only subject he cared about was English, the only activity the newspaper. His fierce ambition was to become editor in chief and put out the greatest paper the school had ever seen.

He had almost no interest in sports, but had learned about them doggedly, the way a good journalist will study up on something like strip-mining. He had been given the sports page as a testing ground—if he did a good job there he might be entrusted with the whole paper—and he was a vicious editor, demanding perfection of anyone who worked for him. At the same time, he was oddly cynical about sportswriting. "It's all clichés," he would tell the young men who worked for him. "The key to writing a sports article is picking the appropriate clichés." He had combed magazines and sports pages for them, kept a long list beside the desk. "Hah!" he would shout when he found a new one, shrieking with soprano laughter and shaking the newspaper in his hand. "Look at this! Look at this!" With a flourish he would add it to his list. He composed his articles at the typewriter, pounding away furiously with his necktie loosened and a cigarette dangling from his lips; at regular intervals he stopped to select a cliché from his collection. The odd thing was that his articles were wonderful. He didn't really understand the phrases he was using, so he never used them in quite the right places. They gave his pieces a freshness that sportswriting seldom has.

It was he whom I approached a couple of weeks after my talk with Bennett, to ask for a better assignment. The other things Bennett had said passed right over me—I still thought Mr. Hirtle a great teacher and great intellect; I still planned to run the mile in track that spring—but what he had said about the newspaper stuck in my mind. The whole idea of working for the paper had been to give me a chance to write, to sharpen my skills and expand upon them. So far the longest thing I had done was a two-hundred-word freshman wrestling article. Every sentence was the same in such a piece. I had learned plenty about newspaper work, and had seen corners of the gym I never would have otherwise, but I hadn't done much writing. It had taken me two weeks to get up my nerve, but I finally approached Hilton one afternoon when he was going over some copy, sitting beside an open window, smoking. His hair looked as if a family of field mice had been living in it.

"What do you mean, a *better* assignment?" he said.

"I'm tired of writing up freshman sports. There's nothing to it. I get no space."

"I'm sorry, Wilder, but that's what the sports page is. You go to the stupid games. Write the stupid articles. Pick the appropriate clichés." He gestured toward his list.

"That's not all *you* do."

In addition to covering a varsity sport, Hilton wrote a feature article for every issue. He wrote on the guy who handed out towels in the gym, a powerlifting meet at the East Liberty Y, the collegiate career of the JV wrestling coach. His enormous feature articles sometimes forced cuts in my little hundred-and-fifty-word jobs.

"That's because I'm a big boy," he said. "I worked years to get where I am. I even did my sophomore year twice, just to make sure. When you're as big and smart and as good a writer as I am, which will be never, you can write big feature articles too."

"I don't care how big it is. But I want to write some feature. If I can't do it here I'm going to the news desk."

That was no idle threat. Spring was coming, when the number of sports jumped from two to four. He needed every sportswriter he could get.

He had blanched at this mention of the news desk.

"I'll tell you what I'll do. The last winter issue looks weak, and I was going to run a feature on the spring coaches. I *am* going to run the feature. I was planning to do it myself. But I'll give it to you, if you'll get it done early and give me time to go over it."

"Okay."

"If you screw up I won't print it. I'll kill it and do it myself."

"Right."

"This is an important thing. Not like an article on a game, that we print whether it's good or not." After making you rewrite it three times.

"I know."

"I'm doing this against my better judgment. You may not be ready for it yet. But don't go near the news desk. There's nothing but a bunch of assholes over there."

He should know. The next year, he'd be asshole in chief.

"Eight hundred words," he said.

I don't know what I had thought he would assign me. Maybe an extended feature article on the beaches of North Carolina.

My heart sank as Hilton wrote down the names of the teachers, the word count, the date the article was due. The idea had been to write more, not talk to people.

My first interview was with an English teacher named Champlin. He was new that year, scheduled to be an assistant tennis coach. He was almost a caricature of what a tennis player should be, or an English teacher for that matter. He had blond wavy hair, a face that seemed battered and much the worse for wear, craters under his eyes that belonged on the moon. He was the sleepiest-looking man I had ever seen. He chain-smoked Pall Malls (all of these people have since died of lung cancer); he wore slacks and subdued sport jackets that were in the best of taste. On his first day at the school, when no one had so much as seen him yet, he stepped to the doorway of his classroom, drew on a cigarette while he eyed his students wearily—looking like Bogart after a long night with the bourbon bottle—dropped his cigarette on the floor, and stamped it out. "I suppose this is the class I have to teach," he said. "Poor fool that I am." It was one of the strangest first-day entrances in the history of the school.

He was the only teacher who had ever snubbed Bennett outright; one day when Bennett found him walking to the dining hall and attacked him with his theory of *Hamlet*, Champlin frowned wearily and looked away. "While you've been sitting at home reading Shakespeare," he said, "I've been out in bars learning about life."

In other words, he didn't know beans about *Hamlet*.

The word was, however, that he was a different man on the tennis court. He was actually trim and muscular, and despite all the smoking remained in pretty good shape (he played tennis or squash every day), and once he took a racket in his hand was a virtuoso. His eyes lost their sleepy look, his feet their lazy shuffle; he was quick as a cat and extremely powerful. He could clobber anybody in the school, including the head coach. He was said to be extremely vain about his tennis game, as he was about almost nothing else, certainly not teaching, which he took at about half speed.

My interview with him was a disaster. I had three coaches to do, which gave me only a little over two hundred words per man, but in my nervousness the night before I had formulated enough questions for the *Paris Review*. As soon as I stepped in the room he said, "I can only give you fifteen minutes. I've got an appointment." This, despite the fact that I had approached him two days before and asked for plenty of time. He sat there impatiently, staring toward the back of the room, never so much as glancing toward me, and when I asked him a question—when he had first started to play tennis, or what his first coach had meant to him—he said, "No. Christ. Your readers don't want to hear about that. Tell them about the time I was the Junior Singles Champion of Southern California," or "Tell them about the time I hitchhiked around the country and stopped at tennis clubs. Hustling for money. If I'd hit a losing streak I would have starved." After delivering himself of a tidbit that was perfect for my article, he'd say, "Don't put that in. People will think I'm vain. Absolutely do not print that." Fifteen minutes of such exchanges and he said, "There. I've given you my time. Do you have enough?"

"I guess." Everything I'd written down had been subsequently crossed out. "I might have to come back to fill in a few things."

"Please. It's been all I could do to survive this ordeal." Ordeal? We hadn't even done anything. "Use what you have."

"I can't do this!" I shouted at Sam a few minutes later, as we stood at our lockers collecting our books. "I should never have taken this assignment." Taken it, hell. I'd begged for it.

"I told you not to join the newspaper," he said. "The literary magazine is the place to be."

I didn't tell him the newspaper staff's opinion of the literary magazine. We thought their writing sloppy and self-indulgent, their editorial board a bunch of arrogant shits. We scorned the fact that they came out only three times a year, spent days over a layout a good newspaperman could have done in an afternoon.

"You don't go through all this crap there," he said. "You just write."

Or don't write, as the case may be. Sit around and drink wine.

"That doesn't matter now," I said. "If I don't do this assign-ment I'll be in disgrace. I'll never get an article again."

"So what's the problem?"

I told him of my experience with Champlin. I showed him the list of questions I had spent half the night thinking up. My notes on the interview that had been all crossed out.

"I don't think you're going about this right," he said. "I had an uncle who worked for a magazine. He talked about inter-viewing. You ought to let me come with you next time."

Through the years I have come to think—and I was begin-ning to think even back then—that some people, in addition to having talent, have confidence. It is the way you say a religious person has faith, but some people don't have to work at it, they just have it, like curly hair. I don't know where Sam got it—from being an only child, or somehow from being the child of those parents (who hardly seemed bent on inspiring him with confidence)—but it was as important to him as anything. It was as important to him in sports as his great coordination. When I went for a ground ball I thought I could catch it; Sam knew he could. If he missed that one he knew he could catch the next one. If he wanted a girlfriend he knew he could get her. And part of the reason he did get her was that he knew he could, that he was so bold and brash, he asked the question that stuck in another guy's throat.

Anyway, he was a great interviewer. He went into the inter-view without an appointment—"It's better when they don't know you're coming. They don't have time to get their defenses up"—and without any notes, not even knowing what sport the guy coached. "Mr. Stein. We're from the *News*. Could we ask you a few questions?" While he talked to the man, just sat there having a conversation as if they'd met on a park bench, I sat in the background and took notes. Mr. Stein didn't even no-tice me. Sam asked the question that naturally flowed from the previous answer; he didn't try to cover ground. He did keep it in mind that I was writing for the sports pages. By the time he had finished, Mr. Stein was beaming, pumping his hand on the way out, thrilled to have met him. I had enough material to fill up the whole newspaper.

"That's how it's done," he said to me afterward. "You just

talk to the guy. Bring up whatever questions you think of. Can you do that?"

"Not as well as you. I think you'd better come to the next one too."

"I hate to baby you."

"Just one more. I'll give you credit in the article."

"Jesus. Don't do that. I'll never live it down at the literary magazine."

He did help me, and the next interview also went well, but somehow, when it came time to write the article, I couldn't do it. I was trying to do just the two good interviews, and I had a great deal of material, but I couldn't make it go together. I was picking and choosing details from entire lifetimes, whittling my sentences down so they included the smallest possible number of words (that way I could put in another detail or two), but when I put them together they read like a laundry list. All the sentences could have gone into the same paragraph, or they each could have been separate paragraphs. Next I tried to take the sentences I had and dress them up with fancy rhetoric (take a detail out here and there), add some clever transitions. No matter how I blew them out they remained ineradicably separate. I worked on them for a week, writing every day. At the end of that time, in despair, I took them in to Mr. Hirtle.

What with all the work I'd done (I'd written those sentences dozen of times) I secretly hoped that my article was superb and that I just wasn't able to see it. A part of me always thought that anything I'd written was by definition magnificent. I had a great deal of shy frightened hope as I sat beside Mr. Hirtle and he read, utterly impassively, the article I'd written.

"When is the deadline for the articles this time?" he said.

"Not for ten days," I said. "But this is a special assignment. It's due in two."

"Day after tomorrow."

"Yes."

"Because this just won't do. It doesn't hold together."

Unexpectedly—because I'd been working so hard that my nerves were shot, or because I couldn't imagine facing Hilton without an article, or because I greatly admired Mr. Hirtle and was humiliated in front of him—I felt my lower lip tremble, tears come to my eyes.

"I wasn't sure . . ." I started.

"It's all jumbled up. The sentences don't go together."

"I know."

"There's nothing to grab the reader at the beginning. No progression to what you say."

"No."

I would have admitted to anything at that point. Beat me, beat me if it makes you feel better.

"It doesn't sound like you. It doesn't sound like things you've written in the past."

"It's a feature article."

"A feature article still has to be written with good sentences."

"I tried to make the sentences good. I tried to make them especially good."

"I think that might be the problem. They don't sound natural. You're not trying to tell the reader something. You're trying to write good sentences."

"When Bennett writes a feature article . . ."

"God. Don't bring Bennett into this."

I looked up at him, startled at his tone. He frowned, looked away from me.

"You seem to have a thing about Bennett. At least Sam thinks so."

"I don't know. I guess I do."

"What's it all about?"

I looked away. He didn't seem especially sympathetic. Another day I wouldn't have said much, but all my defenses had collapsed.

"It's just the way I feel. All the time. He's taller than I am, and thinner, he's more muscular. Things are just easier for him. He could always run faster, and jump higher, and now out on the cross-country course he's got this easy stride that barely seems to touch the ground. While I flop-flop along. His brain works better than mine, he can memorize anything, and he can read things I can't begin to make sense of. He writes these sentences, he can put together sentences I can't begin to

think up, I'm not even in the same class. I don't know why I
thought I could do this article. Why I thought I could write
like him."

"Who said anything about writing like him?"

"I mean, write a feature article. I don't mean *like* him, exactly."

"You do, you do. That's the whole problem."

By that time I was sitting there crying. There were no two
ways about it. Tears were pouring out of my eyes, and my
breath was coming in little gasps, and now and then I let out a
sob. I was bawling in front of my ninth-grade English teacher.

"Henry." The word startled me. Mr. Hirtle was a man who
didn't use your name much, who didn't get personal (must
have been his patrician New England background). When he
did say your name he usually used both names, to keep it more
formal. "I want to tell you something. I know you won't believe it, but I want to tell you anyway. So it will have been
said. I want you to remember it. Twenty years from now, or
whenever you're ready, I want you to hear it again."

Mr. Hirtle's voice hadn't so much as wavered. He was sitting
there as if I weren't crying at all.

"You're a better writer than Bennett," he said.

"You don't have to say that. God." I let out a long sob, like a
foghorn.

"I know you don't believe me."

"It's okay to try to make me feel better. You don't have to get
ridiculous about it."

"You don't think you're better now. Maybe you aren't better
now. But you can be. You will be. Bennett has a marvelous talent with words. I'm sure he has a wonderful mind. No doubt
he'll be a brilliant scholar someday, and he may well make
himself a poet. But you're a better prose writer. Your prose is
more direct and focused. It's not just a bunch of beautiful
words piled elaborately one on another. You can be a fine
writer in your way. Better than he. But you've got to forget
about him."

"Forget about him? I live with him. He's there every day.
He's all over the school."

"I mean forget about writing like him. Comparing yourself

to him. You've got your own way. Whether you're doing feature writing or something else. If you try to write his way you'll ruin yourself. He could never have written this article. He couldn't go get the material and present it in a straightforward manner."

That was probably right. The material would have entered Bennett's brain and come out sideways.

Mr. Hirtle looked down at the pages in his hand.

"You've got to do this whole thing over. Throw out your notes and start again. You know the material at this point anyway. Tell what the teacher looked like when you went to see him. Or pick out the most interesting detail in his life and start with that. Imagine him in a sweatshirt and down on the athletic field. But don't try to cover his whole life. Just write the most interesting things. Put together an article out of the best details you have. Say what you'd tell somebody who stopped you on the street."

My sobs were diminishing. What he had said about Bennett passed right over me. Now, however, he was getting practical.

"What about Mr. Champlin?" I said.

"What about him?"

I told him how the first interview had gone, all the stupid questions I'd asked, the way Mr. Champlin had taken back everything he'd said.

Mr. Hirtle mulled it all over for a few moments.

"Do you remember the things he said?"

"Most of them. I've got some written down."

"You have a lot of interesting stuff."

"Sure. But all off the record."

"Write it up."

I gaped at him through a haze of tears. "Really?"

"He said the things. He must have wanted you to hear them."

"What if he says something about it? What if he tells me I shouldn't have done it?"

"I doubt that he will. It'll be too late anyway. If he says anything to you, send him to me."

I didn't at the time take what Mr. Hirtle had said about Bennett and me too seriously, and I certainly haven't since. For an

English teacher, and especially for a lover of poetry, he was an oddly cerebral person, who never let his feelings get the best of him. Bennett, on the other hand, lived by his feelings, wrote with them; he piled up image after image in his prose and poetry as if to begin to suggest the depth of his feelings. It was not the kind of writing Mr. Hirtle was likely to enjoy, or quite approve of. All literary judgment in the end comes down to taste, and taste is a matter of character.

What he said to me was important in a way other than the literal words. It was the first time anyone had suggested to me that, in some way, I might be superior to Bennett. It was a thought that had never occurred to me. And though I didn't believe it, though I didn't take it seriously—in fact it somewhat lowered Mr. Hirtle in my estimation that he would think such a thing—I didn't really think he had said it just to make me feel better. He wasn't the kind of man who did that. He believed in telling the truth, however it made you feel.

I did write up the article the way he had said. As he had talked, in fact—it was a strange sensation—I could see the article I would write, as if it were printed before me in the pages of the newspaper. I had been so obsessed with all the details I'd collected in my interviews that I hadn't seen the big obvious facts: that I'd interviewed three different men; that they all somehow went with the sport they coached; that the facts of their lives even matched their sports (Mr. Champlin would never make it as an English teacher; he was born to be a tennis bum). I could capture the essences of the men with almost any facts I included. But the article would have to be about their separate characters. I wrote it up that evening in a single rapid draft, rewrote and typed it the next evening. Hilton never even looked at me as he read it, frowned and squinted the whole time, but when he had finished he set it aside and said, "Okay. That'll do." That was the first article he hadn't made me rewrite. It had run to a thousand words, but he used the whole thing, at the top of the second sports page, with pictures of the three coaches. Everybody I knew read it. Far more people spoke to me about it than about my piece in the literary magazine.

For days afterward I consciously avoided the corner of the

second floor where Mr. Champlin had his classroom, but one afternoon about ten days after the article appeared I realized we were both walking toward the water fountain at the same time, in an empty hallway; there was no way to turn aside without being too obvious. At first he ignored me, as he did most students, then he seemed to remember who I was, and nodded and frowned. As he rose from taking his drink he said, "Incidentally, Wilder. I've been meaning to tell you. That was an excellent article you wrote. A superb article."

Mr. Champlin had emerged as the most interesting of the three coaches in the piece.

"Thank you," I said.

"It's made me quite famous around the school. Gained me a new respect in the classroom."

"Huh." An unlooked-for effect if there ever was one.

"I think you show a great deal of talent. I hope you'll continue in sportswriting."

He was backing away as he spoke those words, and by the time he had finished was walking back to his classroom. I never got to ask him—I probably wouldn't have anyway—what he had expected me to write in the article, since he had taken back everything he'd said. I never spoke to him again. He didn't return to the school the next year. The rumor was that he had become a teaching pro at a small tennis club in southern Florida.

IV

Spring break that year was a dismal week, cold and gray and wet. It always seemed to me that they scheduled that break a trifle early, or that the name they gave it was wishful thinking. Bennett and I had track practice every morning. We had to run in the outside lanes—usually with sweatsuits on, and a light shower falling—so we wouldn't tear the inside up. A couple of days we ran down on the cross-country course while the maintenance crew worked on the track. Our first meet was scheduled for ten days after break was over.

My afternoons were free, and I spent them with Sam.

The doctors had pronounced his leg better, as if by executive order. They hadn't done any treatment but rest it for six months, so it was hard to believe there was suddenly some difference. On Tuesday that week, during a few hours when it wasn't actually raining, we tried to go out and throw the ball around. The ground was still sopping, so our feet made loud splats as we stepped after the ball; when I tried to throw a grounder it hit with a thud, and almost immediately rolled dead; the footing was treacherous, not the best for a guy with wobbly cartilage in his knee. It all wasn't Sam's fault, but I couldn't help thinking of the year before, when a day like that would have been an occasion for wild hilarity—crazy lunges after the ball, off-balance throws before you smacked into the mud—when throwing the ball around had been a great way to be together. Now it was as if I were making Sam do it. In his tentative movements after the ball I saw the ghost of his former ability. Finally he said, "This is stupid. I can't move. Let's go to Cindy's."

The temptation to go to Cindy's was hard to resist that week. Her parents were in Florida.

"Why didn't you go?" I had asked her the weekend before. "Didn't they want you to?"

"Of course they did," she said. "They planned it for the week I was free. But it's just a drinking holiday for them. They're in bed half the day sleeping it off. Start in with the Bloody Marys as soon as they get up. I sit around alone on the beach all day. Pray my father won't kill us when he drives to a restaurant for dinner. Watch TV in a motel room at night while they drink themselves unconscious. I just told them I was sitting it out this year. I was old enough to stay alone. It was stunning how little fuss they put up."

They had left her alone in the house all week.

Having the afternoons that week, with nothing else to occupy our time, made me realize how different things were between me and Sam. We were more like former friends, who had in common mostly the memory of the way things had been. I was deeply involved in running and the newspaper, things he found of almost no interest. It was a problem just that I had passionate interests, while he, in his life, was marking time. Officially he scorned what I did, but I think a part of him was also envious that I enjoyed it and got so much out of it. There wasn't much to enjoy at the literary magazine—joining that group meant adopting a certain lassitude toward life— and he wasn't using himself in sports as he once had. My presence was a constant reminder of what he was missing. All the time we were together I felt an annoyance in Sam, a background of edginess.

The first thing Cindy said when she came to the door of her house was, "I found a bottle of wine."

At first it had sounded like paradise, nine days in that place with no parents around, but all the beer that had been left behind was three ponies of Rolling Rock, which Sam and Cindy consumed within twenty minutes of her parents' departure. They sampled various hard liquors, but couldn't persuade themselves they liked the tastes. Anyway, it wouldn't have looked too good if Cindy's parents had returned and found their liquor supply severely damaged.

"I was just rummaging around in the back of the cabinet," Cindy said. "There *had* to be something worth drinking in there. I found this big bottle of red wine. Some kind of Italian wine. They probably forgot it was even there. I was just working on it with a corkscrew."

"That gets pretty bad," Sam said. "Drinking by yourself in the afternoon."

"I was just trying to get the thing open. Waiting for you."

"Sure," Sam said. "We know."

She had the bottle on a table in the basement. It looked as if she had been trying to scrape the cork out bit by bit. All kinds of little pieces were sitting beside the bottle on the table. "I've seen Daddy do it hundreds of times," Cindy said. "I've just never noticed how." Sam, fortunately, had actually done it before—Mr. Golden considered that a proper function for a fifteen-year-old son at his table—and he had the cork out, at least what was left of it, in a few moments. Only a few chunks had made it down into the wine.

Soon we were sitting on the couch together, as we had so many times before, the radio playing, Cindy between Sam and me, our bodies pressed together (if you got further away Cindy pulled you back). I didn't always drink when they did, but it was a vacation, and the day was nasty, and it seemed so cozy on that couch in the basement. We had Old Fashioned glasses, but didn't fill them too full. I had never drunk more than a few sips of wine at a special dinner. It must have been good wine, because it tasted light, and went down easily. It wasn't long before I was pleasantly drunk, not to the point where you're no longer aware of things, but at that earlier moment when it seems your awareness is heightened, the lovely interval before the boom is lowered.

Sam was what would be called later in life a nasty drunk. For some people—like me—alcohol just gives a golden hue to the world, which gradually becomes goldener and goldener until you want to give everyone you see a big fuzzy hug. For others it releases a different inhibition, allows them to speak the wicked things they've been holding back. Sam said such things rather readily anyway. Drink only made it worse. As did, for some reason, the presence of a pretty girl.

We had been sitting in silence for some time, listening to the radio, when he said, "I'm surprised you're even drinking with us. In training the way you are."

"A little wine doesn't hurt a runner," I said. "He works it right off."

I had read those very words a few days before in *Sports Illustrated*. A French runner touring the States had said them.

"Better not let Wheel hear you say that." Wheel was our track coach. J. Ames "Wheel" Barrow.

"He's never touched a drop in his life," I said.

"He doesn't like his boys touching any drops either."

"Everybody does it. The captain's the biggest lush in the school."

I was actually quite uncomfortable at what Sam was saying. I was just enough of a Boy Scout to feel bad about breaking training, enough of a paranoid to think somebody might find out. I also happened to be the brother of a person who had never broken a rule—even a self-imposed rule—in his life. But it was a terribly lonely feeling to sit there sober with two people who were drinking. I wanted to be with them. I wanted to be with Cindy.

"I thought you guys at the newspaper didn't approve of drinking," Sam said.

"Talk to Hilton about that." Sam knew what he was saying was horseshit.

"I mean sitting around. Enjoying yourself. You've got all those deadlines to meet."

"We should go off and write poetry instead."

"You might be more interesting if you did. Learn a little about yourselves."

Sam had a way of backing me into a corner. I wasn't opposed to writing poetry.

"Maybe you *should* do another kind of writing," Sam said. "Other than those tight-assed little news articles."

"Maybe I should."

"Some long feature articles."

"I just did do a long feature article."

"You could do an amusing series on teachers. Just like your big bad brother Bennett."

"He's picking a fight," Cindy said.

"He has a way of doing that," I said.

"Have you ever noticed," Sam said, "that no matter what his big brother does, Henry finds a way to eventually do the same thing?"

"That's not true." I was staring down into my glass.

"Isn't it," Sam said.

"You said so yourself. One time to Hirtle. I avoid competition with Bennett." I had thought that very perceptive of him at the time.

"You're doing a hell of a job," Sam said.

"Let's listen to the music for a while," Cindy said. "Or talk about something interesting."

"This is interesting," Sam said. "Henry's interested."

"What do you mean," I said, "in particular?"

"Let's not get into some big discussion," Cindy said.

"There's school, for one thing," Sam said. "That's the biggest single thing."

"I should go to some different school. Jesus."

"Lots of people do. Public school. Some posh boarding school."

"I don't think we should be wanting Henry to go away," Cindy said.

"You've got to be compared to your brother at a school like ours," Sam said. "The teachers have him before they have you. And the particular person he is. Flitting all over the place."

Sam wasn't telling me any news.

"So what else?" I said. Changing schools seemed a trifle drastic.

"There's the little matter of cross-country," Sam said.

"You're the one that got me started in running! Dragged me out of bed every morning." He had been glad enough to take credit for it in front of Hirtle.

"I wanted to get in shape. See what it was like. I thought you could lose that grotesque layer of flab that was disfiguring your body."

"Shut up about that, Sam," Cindy said. "He did lose it. He's as skinny as you."

"In better shape too," I said. "I'll take you on for two miles anytime."

"Way to pick on a cripple," Sam said. "But we did a little running. Entered a meet for the hell of it. I didn't mean to create a fucking monster. You went away on what was supposedly a vacation and ran every day."

"While you drank every day."

"Came home with the brilliant idea of going out for the cross-country team. Where your brother Bennett was about to become a star. Now you're going out for the track team with him. Probably the same event."

I just didn't see it the way Sam was saying. I realized that was a possible viewpoint, but I couldn't believe he felt that way. I considered it an unfortunate accident that Bennett was on the track and cross-country teams. It was true that I'd gone a little overboard on running, but it felt good to transform my body and do things I'd never been able to do. I couldn't give up running just because Bennett did it. It had done everything for me.

"What does all this prove?" I said.

"Wait a minute," Sam said. "We can't leave out the newspaper."

"You were there when Hirtle recruited me for the newspaper. It had nothing to do with Bennett."

"He's on the newspaper. He's one of their biggest stars. So you join the staff."

"Hirtle practically begged me."

"He writes these big feature articles. You start writing feature articles."

"He's on the feature page. I'm on the sports page. It might as well be two different papers."

"To you maybe. To everybody else it's just the wonderful Wilder brothers. Running cross-country and writing for the newspaper. Loving their English teachers. They've each got their own little English teacher. They're even starting to look alike, now that fatso's getting thinner. It's so sweet."

I knew it all seemed that way to some people. People had mentioned it to me. But I'd had no idea Sam felt that way. Sam knew me better than that.

"By the way," he said. "That English teacher of Bennett's is queer."

I was so absorbed by what Sam was saying about me that I hardly took the words in. I didn't quite hear them.

"What do you mean?" I said.

"He's a fairy. He likes young boys. He sucks on their little cocks."

"How do you know?"

"I hear it around. Some guys on the literary magazine. A kid in the drama club."

"They say that about half the teachers in the school," Cindy said.

"I have it on pretty good authority," Sam said. "I'm not saying Bennett's queer with him."

"Of course he's not," I said. "Jesus."

"But he's hanging around with a fairy," Sam said. "Spends lots of time with him. People are going to think things."

"People always think things." Especially about Bennett.

I sat there in silence for a few moments. Sam certainly was full of news that day.

"So what's the point?" I said finally.

"About what?"

"This whole thing. What you're saying about Bennett and me."

"The point is you like it. You like being the little brother. Always coming in second. You love it."

"Sam," Cindy said. "That's a terrible thing to say."

"It's the truth, though," Sam said. "He eats it with a spoon."

"I'm sure Henry does the best he can," Cindy said. "He does the best job he knows how."

"That's the beautiful thing about it," Sam said. "As long as Bennett's around he can do his best and still fuck up. He can be very good and still lose. He can still feel bad."

"I *want* to feel bad," I said.

"Something as easy as that article you did," he said. "Talk to the guy and write down what he says. You were going to fuck that up. Fall to pieces in a puddle of tears. You had to come running to me."

Sam should have tried interviewing Champlin if he thought it was so easy.

"He did do the article," Cindy said. "It was a good article." Even she had read it.

"He did his best to fuck it up," Sam said. "That's what really would have made him happy."

"You're out of your mind," I said.

"But at least you have the satisfaction of knowing you're not as good as the great Bennett Wilder. You're not the best feature writer at the school. Not even at your own house. You're not the best feature writer in your own bedroom."

I figured Sam had finally lost it, was pulling out all the stops in a last-ditch effort to hurt me. I also think, looking back on it, that he may have felt deserted by me, that it seemed I had given up all my things with him to do things with Bennett. He hated Bennett, but he was also jealous of him.

"You'll do it all your life," Sam said. "Trail after your brother and do the things he does. Fuck up at everything so you can feel like the little brother. It's the way I saw you the first time. You brought him back to the school he'd graduated from just so everybody could remember he'd gone there."

It had been Bennett's idea to come that day!

"It'll be the way I see you the last time. When you're ninety years old and in a rest home. You'll both be in the same rest home. You'll live in the same room. Every day you'll play checkers. He'll always win."

"I want to say what I think," Cindy said.

"What do you know?" Sam said.

"I hear you talk."

"You don't go to the school."

"I know the things you two don't know. Because you're both too pigheaded."

"Oh," Sam said. "Pardon me."

"*You* two are brothers," Cindy said. "If you just knew it."

"He's not my brother," Sam said. "He's a goy."

He had said that because he was flustered. Cindy was speaking seriously.

"You're his other brother," Cindy said. "Who nobody knows about. And he's the only brother you've got. I wish you'd act like it. I wish you'd treat each other better."

There was a silence. Cindy had given us pause.

"This *is* the way brothers act," Sam said. "They fight."

"I wish they wouldn't fight around me," Cindy said. "It makes me feel bad."

Sam and I were embarrassed. It was the truth she had spoken, one it took a woman to see, or at least to say. The three of us sat quietly for a while as it all sank in.

"If the two of us are brothers," Sam said, "what are you?"

"Your sister."

"God. Don't be a sister."

"Your girlfriend. Your lover."

"Whose?"

"Both of yours."

She was just being nice, including me.

"If you're our girlfriend," Sam said, "you should show it."

"What?"

"You should kiss us."

I had been sipping wine as Sam made that suggestion, took a big gulp. It burned through me like whiskey.

"I'll kiss you. Of course I'll kiss you. If you'll stop fighting."

"We'll stop fighting," Sam said, "if you'll kiss us."

That was the whole thing in a nutshell. Half the reason Sam

was nasty when we were with Cindy was that he resented my presence, even when he didn't know that was the problem. He might even have said all those things just so I'd get mad and leave (he hadn't meant a word of it). Cindy wasn't his girlfriend, but he knew she was crazy about him and I figured he took advantage of it when he could. Who could blame him? Apparently he had just decided that if I wouldn't leave he'd approach the matter differently.

He leaned over to Cindy and kissed her, an absolutely endless kiss. I felt suddenly numb and fuzzy from the wine; it didn't bother me a bit to be beside them. I rather enjoyed it. I sat there with my glass, sipping from it occasionally, now and then glancing over at them. The kiss went on and on. Finally Sam pulled away, and Cindy looked over at me, her head rolled on the back of the couch. "Now Henry," she said.

Cindy was not embarrassed, but she was flushed and slightly breathless, almost limp. Her head just rolled over on the couch back to face me; she put her hand on the back of my neck as I leaned to kiss her. Strictly speaking, it wasn't as good a kiss as others she had given me. She wasn't in full command of it. But there was something terribly exciting about it. Her lips softly gave way as mine met them, and her mouth opened wide, wide; she probed my mouth deep with her tongue and let mine probe hers; we warmly breathed together, locked tight as we were. Our kisses before had been the breathless happy kisses of a boy and girl having fun, but this was different, this was adult, the kiss of a woman who has been drinking wine and who is becoming aroused. When I was older and a woman kissed me that way I knew what it meant.

Everything was hazy, moving like a dream. Sam would kiss Cindy, and Cindy kiss me, and the music kept playing, our bodies pressed together. When I wasn't kissing Cindy I might sip some wine, and Sam when he wasn't kissing drew on a cigarette and drank, and sometimes we stopped to give Cindy some wine, after which her mouth was cooler and tasted grapey. After a while I noticed, with some interest, that Sam's hand rested on her breast when he kissed her, and moved around gently, caressing where the nipple would be. After a few more kisses she took my hand and put it there too. I could feel her heart thumping, her chest rising and falling. At one point Sam didn't kiss her right away after I finished, started instead to unbutton her blouse. To my astonishment she let him, lay back on the couch with her eyes closed until he finished. He undid her bra, and there were her small white breasts, young and not quite formed, pink-nippled. He caressed them as he kissed her, and the next time I did too. They felt soft and smooth to the touch, the nipples taut. Her skin was hot, her heart pounding hard.

We must have been kissing for twenty minutes when Sam looked up and said, "I think it's time for Henry to leave."

I won't pretend I know how he should have handled it. "Jesus," he could have said, "we can't keep on like this," and everybody would have agreed. We could have talked for a while, gotten control of ourselves. Eventually he and I would have left and he could have come back alone. Something like that. He could have pretended he and Cindy were going somewhere. We were all so excited, all so—literally—close. I knew Sam and Cindy had something together that I didn't have with them, but they didn't have to hit me over the head with it. Sam could have put things more delicately.

"Henry doesn't want to leave," I said.

"I'm sure he doesn't," Sam said. "But it's time."

I sat there breathless for a moment. I couldn't believe he was doing this to me.

"Just let me stay here," I said. "Drink some wine."

"While we do what?" Sam said. "Watch you?"

"Why do I have to go now? If I didn't have to go before?"

It was as if I were asking him to spell out what he was going to do. Say the thing and hurt me with it.

"We like you, Henry," Sam said. "Cindy likes you. We're all big buddies. So we let you stay awhile. But now you've got to go."

He wouldn't quite say it.

"Cindy won't make me leave," I said. "It's her house. If she says I can stay you can't make me go."

Cindy was lying back against the couch, her eyes closed, her blouse still unbuttoned. Her mouth looked positively bruised.

She had pulled her bra down, though, and held her blouse closed.

"I don't know, Henry," she said, not opening her eyes. "I think you'd better go."

It was the meanest thing Sam had ever done to me. In a year and a half of crazy moods and dirty tricks, that was the worst. There was a weight like stone in my stomach. My eyes burned as if they would cry. I had to get up from that couch and walk by myself out of the basement. I didn't look back at Sam and Cindy. I didn't ever want to look at them again. When I was partway up the steps Cindy said, "Bye, Henry," and Sam said, "So long," but I didn't answer them. I walked through the silent upstairs and let myself out the front door.

A fine mist of a rain was falling, the air bitter cold. The rain was enough to soak me on my long walk home.

There wasn't much left to spring break at that point, and I didn't do much with it. Our track workouts got harder toward the end of the week, and lasted longer. In the afternoons I lay around getting over them. Bennett, as usual, was engaged in an elaborate reading project that took up eight or nine hours of his day. He was making his way through selected novels of Thomas Hardy. The track workouts that dominated my day and seemed an ample justification for my existence were just a small wedge of time in his. The rest of the day he was sitting upright in the easy chair in our bedroom or lying back against the pillows of the bed, staring with deep concentration at the print of a book. It was a feat of sheer will that few people could have matched. Bennett did it by second nature.

It took me several days to get up the nerve to ask him. Several times I walked into the bedroom to speak to him and ended up walking out again. I couldn't challenge that solid wall of concentration. There was an aura of reserve around Bennett, a line you didn't want to cross. It was the kind of line people often have with their parents.

The thing I wanted to ask him would cross that line.

On Friday evening I went into the bedroom determined to talk to him. I sat on the easy chair. He was lying on the bed. I pretended to read a magazine for a while, but I was barely looking at the pictures. I made a lot of noise turning the pages. Finally Bennett looked over at me and spoke. "Are you staying in here?"

If I was, he wasn't.

"I wanted to ask you something," I said.

"After you ask, are you going to leave?"

"After you answer."

"I hope this isn't too long. I've got some reading to do."

He had already lost thirty seconds from his nine hours.

"I wanted to ask you if Mr. Edmond is queer."

I didn't have to wait for an answer. I could have walked out without saying a word. The moment I asked, Bennett blushed from the top of his head to the tips of his toes. His whole body seemed to change color. His mouth took on a funny expression, as if he wanted to hold it a certain way but couldn't. Bennett had never been much of a blusher. He was such an eccentric all the time that it took a great deal to embarrass him.

"What makes you think so?" he said.

"I've heard guys talking."

"Like who?"

"Different guys. I heard some in the gym today."

If I'd told him my real source, the conversation would have ended right there.

"How would they know?"

"They wouldn't. So I thought I'd ask you."

"How would I?"

"You know him better than most people. You've been at the school for a while. Or I thought he might have tried something with you."

He was within about an inch of clamming up. That was the natural thing for him to do, he'd been doing it most of our lives, and I think that if we hadn't been closer recently, we hadn't had those talks a few weeks before, he wouldn't have said anything. But I also think that he may have been looking for someone to tell, that the whole thing had been weighing on him for some time and I happened along at the right moment.

"He is queer," he said.

There was a long awkward silence. I had stopped looking at

him steadily—it was too painful—but I glanced his way once or twice. He wasn't looking at me either.

"Did he try something with you?" I said.

"I didn't even know what queer was. I didn't know what was going on."

"I'm not sure I know now."

We were a pair of innocents. As artsy as our family was, it was funny the subject hadn't come up more. I understand that in other kinds of families people learn about sex sooner. But our family was so squeaky-clean and middle-class that we never heard much about the byways of sex. We hardly heard about the straight and narrow. Nobody here but us heterosexuals, boss.

"He's the smartest man I ever met," Bennett said. "I walked into his class last year and couldn't believe it. I was meeting the man I'd been looking for all my life. He knows everything about literature. British. American. He quotes from poetry all the time. He's got more poetry in his head than most people have on their shelves. And when he reads works aloud. Poetry. Stories. You hear things you wouldn't have heard any other way. I learned more in a month with him than I ever did in a year with anyone else."

You wonder in later years about those teachers you admired when you were young. What seems impressive at age fifteen can seem pretty small five years later. I'm sure Mr. Edmond didn't have all the learning Bennett thought he did. He probably wasn't as learned as our father. But he was one of those magnetic people. Students were impressed.

"He was the teacher I'd been waiting for for years," Bennett said.

"Do you still feel that way?"

"I still think he's a great teacher." Bennett seemed to be willing the words out. "I'll always think that."

"He shouldn't have tried something."

I was pressing Bennett too hard. I should have let him tell it his way. But that was the thing I wanted to know about.

"He waited awhile. Until I started working for the paper. I was beginning to do a series of articles. We'd get together to talk about them."

"What was it he did?"

Bennett's voice had been tight and strained the whole time, but when he said the next thing it sank into almost nothing. He could hardly speak the words.

"He told me he loved me."

"What?" I burst out as if with laughter. It was all I could do—I was so surprised—to keep from laughing.

"You don't know about this, Henry."

"I guess I don't."

"There's more to this than you would think."

I didn't know the first thing, of course. I didn't know the tip of the iceberg of that whole subject. I could have imagined being queer with someone at roughly your own level, like what Sam and I had done. Fooling around with your hands, making each other feel good. I had heard of guys sucking each other. But I couldn't imagine it with an older man. Who wore bow ties and was slightly balding and carried an umbrella and drove a Mercedes. I couldn't imagine lowering the barriers. Like undressing with him. And I couldn't understand what it had to do with love. Love was the heart-pounding sweaty-palmed feeling you had for a girl. Friendship was what you felt for a boy. Or a man.

I didn't perceive as love the feeling I'd had for Sam. And I didn't understand to what extent my whole relationship with Cindy—this was part of the problem—was a friendship.

"We were up in his apartment. We used to go up there to talk about my articles. I was looking at his books and he came up beside me and started to tell me these things. That I was a beautiful boy and he'd been in love with me as long as he'd known me. I was standing by the bookcase and he had me by the arm before I realized what was going on. You wouldn't believe how strong he is. I would have jumped away but I couldn't move. He said the feeling he had would poison our relationship if he didn't express it. That he knew I might not like the idea but he hoped I'd try it for him. I might end up liking it more than I thought."

The whole thing was strange to me, terribly strange. It was stranger than what Sam had told me about his mother, stranger than what we'd done afterward. That was what I was learning about sex, the thing they never told you in books on the facts of life but that should have been the first sentence in every one of them. Sex is strange.

Bennett was about to tell me he'd done this thing.

"I think I would have died," I said. "I would have collapsed on the spot."

"It wasn't like I had a choice. It wasn't like he asked me if I'd do this thing and then gave me time to decide. It was like he asked me and was already doing it, had ahold of me and was touching me and leading me into the bedroom. I didn't have time to think. I didn't have time to say anything. I guess I could have screamed and run, or tried to fight him off. But I didn't want to do that."

What a spot to be in. I couldn't believe it.

"What did he actually do?"

"He just touched me all over at first. Lay there and touched me all over. Then he took it in his hand. He did it with his hand."

That was the time, if there ever would be a time, to tell Bennett about me and Sam. It might have helped him to know I'd done the same thing he had. But I didn't tell him—something held me back—and I can't help thinking I was right. I think the idea—that something I'd done with Sam was like something he'd done with Mr. Edmond—would have insulted him. It would have stopped him right there.

"Did you do it to him?"

"He just kind of rubbed against me, against my side, the way I was lying there. He had his eyes closed and everything. I was trying to pretend it wasn't happening."

I could picture the scene, the awful awkwardness of it. One thing going on for him, and a completely different one for Mr. Edmond. It was bad enough just hearing about it.

"You could have told somebody."

"It crossed my mind. But that would have gotten him in terrible trouble. Thrown in jail or something. Fired from his job."

"Has it happened again?"

"It's happened. Not all that often or anything. There have been other times he's wanted to and I've made excuses. It's always just kind of there, whenever we're together. I wish I could get rid of it."

As a matter of fact, Mr. Edmond left the school at the end of the year. He didn't give Bennett any particular reason. He had taught in prep schools all his life, never stayed in one place too long. He may just have waited until some situation got to be too much for him.

"I still like him. No matter how queer he is, I like and respect him. I want to be his friend. I'd like to always be his friend. I just wish this other stuff would end."

In some ways that conversation was a turning point for me and Bennett. In years to come we would be much closer than we'd been up to then, and I think that conversation—that act of confiding—broke down some of the barriers. I also think that a lot of Bennett's intensity and secrecy in the past couple of years had had to do with what he'd told me. Not that he wasn't pretty intense and secretive anyway. But he'd had a lot on his mind.

"I did want to tell you," he said. "I wanted to tell you before. So you wouldn't run into the same kind of thing."

"Sure."

"I just couldn't get it out. It was too hard to say. But I'm glad I told you now."

"Thanks. Thanks for telling me."

It seems ironic that it was a chance remark of Sam's—a sneering, nasty remark—that led us to have that conversation at all.

EIGHT

You wouldn't have thought that a single incident, enacted under the influence of wine, could have destroyed a friendship built up over eighteen months. The seeds of the break had been sown much earlier, of course, in Sam's proclivity for saying things that hurt me, in the competition between us (hardly apparent when Sam was clearly superior), in the way he taunted me with Cindy, the way he lorded his sexual experience over me. Sam was headed down a path in life that he must have wanted to take, but I think a part of him hated himself for taking that path, or perhaps hated himself and then took that path. That part of him must also have hated me. He was trying to stifle a side of himself, and I kept reminding him of it.

The break was not obvious. We no longer sought each other out in our free time—I didn't go to his house after school or on weekends—but we didn't avoid each other at school. There was an uneasiness between us that felt like embarrassment; we were embarrassed to be around each other. We never mentioned that afternoon at Cindy's. We didn't mention Cindy, for that matter, or Renee, or that whole social group, which I didn't see anymore. I didn't seem to want to, without Sam as my friend. It would have been better if we had had it out, really shouted, screamed, had a bloody fistfight. It would have been better to be bitter enemies than to have that uneasy embarrassment between us. We let our resentments fester like hidden wounds.

There is really only one day left in our friendship, in that first time in my life when I knew Sam Golden. It is not a day when we were friendly, exactly. But it is the last time there was anything between us.

Our school's biggest rival in those days was a boarding school two hours east of us. The real rivalry was in major sports; track was rather minor and not much of a team sport anyway. The focus of attention that year was that they had, as we did, a hot sophomore prospect in the mile. Neither Bennett nor his opposite number, a guy named Capelli, would be a factor in the scoring—they would fight it out for third place—but track fans and coaches are obsessed with hot prospects and potential rivalries. Even the year before there had been talk of the two freshman milers, when they hadn't so much as laid eyes on each other. People were really anticipating a race that would take place in a couple of years, between two of the best milers in the state. They wanted to see that rivalry at its outset, see its tactics develop.

Bennett and Capelli had met twice, in track the year before and in cross-country that fall. Both times Capelli had won, though Bennett's best times were better than his. Both races had been unconventional. In the mile the year before Capelli had put on a big kick at the start of the third lap. Bennett had —wisely, it was thought—not tried to stay with him, had run his own race, but his kick in the fourth lap had fallen just short. In cross-country that fall they had run down from the track and across the stream together, but Capelli had taken off in a sudden sprint up the first hill, stunning everybody. Once again Bennett had run his race, and once again he had fallen short, though Capelli had come in wheezing and snorting, and pitched into the cinders as he crossed the finish line. In both instances everybody agreed that Bennett had run the smart race, that it was just a matter of time before his brains and strength won out over Capelli's sheer daring.

"He's such a wimp," Bennett snapped at me, the first time I mentioned Capelli's name. "He's about four feet tall, and he has an atrocious stride, and before the race he hangs all over you. He has to keep touching you. He doesn't know the first thing about strategy. He has no idea how a mile is supposed to be run. If he ever went up against a real runner they'd laugh him off the track."

He didn't run a gentlemanly race, in other words. He didn't run the way one was expected to.

The other possibility was that Capelli was a tactical and psychological genius. As I would eventually find out, it was disturbing to run a race in which somebody did the unexpected. It was disturbing to be entered in a race with somebody who might do it. For Bennett, of course, it was also disturbing to be touched, especially by a greasy little Italian. Did Capelli sense Bennett's reaction the first time, and from then on clasp his hand sincerely with two hands, touch him on the back and slap him on the ass, snuggle up to him and jockey for position at the starting line? He definitely did those things. Whether or not he knew the effect they were having I can't be sure.

He was certainly a different physical type from Bennett. As Bennett had suggested (though not to the extent Bennett had suggested), he was short, had the tight thick muscles of a wrestler, not a runner. He had a herky-jerky lopsided style of running that looked ridiculous. It looked as if he couldn't keep going for two hundred yards, but he kept it up for stride after stride, mile after mile. He was a phenomenon.

"He makes me tired," Bennett said to me late one evening, several days before the race. He must have been telling me because there was no one else to tell. An athlete was supposed to express only unbounded confidence, a limitless belief in his own abilities.

We were on our beds. He was lying on his back, staring at the ceiling.

"How do you mean?" I said.

"It's the way he runs. That weird wimpy way he runs. It looks so labored, so heavy. It makes me want to go to sleep."

"Why don't you run ahead of him?"

"You can't get ahead of him. No matter what you do. If you sprint like a hundred-yard dash he'll sprint right with you. Won't let you have the lead."

Sounded familiar to me.

"You're faster than him," I said.

"I know."

"So get out there and run faster. Take that first lap like a four-forty. Have you tried it?"

"I've got to run my own race."

"You'll be running your own race. You sure as hell won't be running his."

"I can't be pulled out of my plan. The way I run a mile best. I've got to run my best time. It's the only way to beat him."

That was Bennett's fatal flaw, the way he had to do everything the same. It was just like his jump shot. He couldn't bring himself to improvise.

"Try it just once," I said.

"No. I can picture this. I can see myself running my race and winning. Catching him at the end."

"You've got a great kick."

"He just makes me so tired. My muscles go limp. It's like running under an anesthetic."

Things didn't look good to me. Already, lying over on his bed, he seemed tense—you could have picked him up by the small of his back, like a piece of lumber—and the race was days away. I would have bet it was the tension that was making him tired. He kept picturing himself winning, running his race, but every time he did he also pictured the squat form of Capelli, that maddeningly awkward stride.

The weather in our track season was likely to be touch and go anyway—sometimes you looked back and realized there had only been two or three good meet days all season—but on that April day a cold front had settled over the city, and all day long a heavy stand of clouds kept blowing in and breaking up. Our rival school still brought several busloads of spectators, as always; a number of their athletes' parents showed up, since many of them lived in Pittsburgh; naturally some of our parents came. Mine, for instance. They wouldn't have missed a track meet for the world. Father stood up on the hill in his belted trench coat and gray fedora, holding his bugle; Mother was beside him in a bright-yellow waterproof poncho (for a moment it looked as if someone had pitched a tent there); Teddy was rolling down the hill through the bushes and running back up. My family was very much in evidence.

I must have been as nervous as Bennett that day. Possibly more so. All my life I had lived vicariously through him, but that day I was in the unique position—as I would be for the next two years—of being able to live through him and for myself at the same time. We were running the same race. The adrenaline that was pumping through me for his sake might come in handy for my own effort too.

The distance runners, out of some old custom, did their stretching together on the day of a meet, but after that we were on our own. Most of us jogged a very slow mile, possibly running a little harder at the end of it. We did strides, bouncing exaggerated steps to stretch our muscles out. We alternately loped and sprinted. Bennett had long since let me (and every other runner on the team) know that he preferred to warm up alone, already concentrating deeply on a race that might not start for an hour. I had pretty much lost track of him when, just as I was finishing my warm-ups, I thought of something I could do for him. I looked around the track and saw him nowhere. It was almost an accident that I looked toward the hill and saw him walking up the steps to the gym.

For days I had been trying to think of a way I could help Bennett in that race. I certainly couldn't run fast enough to box Capelli, or get out and upset the pace. I don't know why it had taken me so long to get the idea of just standing beside him at the starting line. Capelli could feel me all over, rest his warm body against mine, rub his greasy head on my shoulder. He could kiss me if he wanted. It seemed very possible to me, knowing Bennett, that he had lost the two previous races primarily because he had had germ attacks before they started. If I could keep the cooties off he might win going away.

At first I hesitated—you never knew how Bennett would react to anything—then went up the steps after him. It might be that his whole mind set before the race would be distracted by the thought of that vermin-infested body resting against his. I could set his mind at ease.

I had searched the whole first floor of the gym, looked through the locker rooms and even the bathrooms, when I realized he must be up on the gym floor. It was warm up there, I thought, warmer anyway than it would be outside, and it would be deserted. He could concentrate and do some easy stretching. There wouldn't be all the distractions that there were out on the track, dozens of people asking how he felt. For a few moments he could get some peace.

I hardly made a sound running up the steps in my warm-up flats. No lights were on when I got to the gym floor, and what with the cloudy day little light came in through the high caged windows, so it was quite dim in there, and colder than I had thought. I might as well have been walking into a mausoleum. As I stepped onto the floor I could see almost nothing. The floorboards, little used in the spring, cracked with my every step.

"Jesus," Bennett's voice said down to my right. "What are you doing here?"

He was standing alone in that near corner. There were some mats over there, and a light and heavy punching bag, and a thick rope hung from the ceiling for climbing, but he wasn't using any of that stuff. He had come up there to think.

"I want to tell you something," I said, walking in his direction.

"I came up here to be alone," he said.

"It'll only take a minute."

"I've only got a minute."

"I wanted to tell you before the race."

In the dim light filtering down through a window, he scowled. He probably would have preferred I hadn't mentioned the race.

"Tell me then, dammit, and get out of here."

I wished I had a different kind of brother. All my life I had wanted a brother I could confide in, be close to, who would do anything for me and let me do things for him. I had wanted that brother so much I sometimes thought I had him. But Bennett was not that way. People thought him arrogant, intellectually arrogant, but his arrogance was as much a shield as anything, a way to keep people distant, like his neuroses. He was so intense he would otherwise have swallowed people up. He listened with sympathy to what you said, but didn't confide in return, because he had a superstition that revealing his hopes and fears would make them come out the wrong way. His very existence was hemmed in by superstitions, neuroses, phobias. He was incapable of being the brother I wanted. Sometimes I forgot.

"I'll let Capelli stand beside me," I said.

"What?"

My words had sounded hollow and absurd.

"I'll see that he stands beside me. At the starting line."

"Oh." Bennett's tone softened. "All right."

"I thought you'd be able to concentrate better."

"I will. I wasn't going to stand beside him anyway. I'd have done anything to avoid it."

"I'll block him off."

"Okay. Great." Bennett sounded sheepish now that he knew I had meant to help him.

"I just wanted to tell you."

"Sure. Thanks."

We stared at each other awkwardly, trying to find the next thing to say.

"I'd rather you would leave now," Bennett finally said. "I've got to think."

His face, in the dim light, was a mask of determination. A great calm seemed to have settled over his body. I couldn't believe anyone would beat him that day.

As I was walking out the door to the stairs I looked back. "Good luck, Bennett."

He had already started to turn toward the corner. He raised his hand in a wave.

I walked down the stairs. If the race was half as hard as the conversation beforehand, it would probably kill me. I felt as if I could hardly run a step.

At the bottom of the stairs, in a black trench coat, a brown cloth cap, a bright-red tie, and large sunglasses, stood Sam.

"Have I entered the Twilight Zone?" I said.

The cap was pulled down to just above the sunglasses, his hands were stuck in the pockets of the trench coat, and his face wore a fixed grin, which was practically all you could see of it. He was standing very still.

"I followed you guys from outside," he said. "What's going on?"

"Bennett's warming up. I came to see how he was doing."

"Sweet of you. Did you tell him you love him? Did you kiss him?"

"Fuck off, Sam." I wasn't going to get confused about my brother that day.

"You guys kiss on the mouth? Or just on the cheek?"

Though his feet didn't move, he swayed slightly as he stood there. He looked as if a healthy slap would knock him down, as if he wouldn't even remove his hands from his pockets to break his fall. He removed one now, though. It held an open can of beer.

"Jesus Christ," I said.

Any connection with drinking at our school was hell in those days. You could be kicked out for stepping onto campus with liquor on your breath. Guys had been kicked out when they were picked up for driving under the influence after a school function. There was even a rule by which you could supposedly get kicked out for drinking at an off-campus party. We were prohibited, that rule said, from conduct anytime, anywhere, that was unbecoming a gentleman.

If a teacher had walked into the hallway right then Sam probably wouldn't even have been allowed to stay for the track meet.

"What are you doing?" I said.

"I'm having a drink. Having a beer. You want one? I got a whole six-pack on me here somewhere."

He started pulling them out of outside pockets, inside pockets, showing me. He only came up with four. One was empty, and he threw it into the corner with a loud clatter.

"Is this suicide?" I said. "Or what?"

"It's just a little party. A private little booze party."

"If anybody sees you with that beer you're gone. If anybody smells it on you." The closer I got to Sam, the stronger a possibility that seemed.

"I'm gone anyway. Didn't I tell you? I thought I told you."

He seemed to be frowning, genuinely puzzled, but it was

hard to tell behind all the paraphernalia. It was also hard to
tell how drunk he was.

"It must have been somebody else I told," he said.

"Yeah."

He took a long pull at the beer.

"Cindy's pregnant," he said.

"What?" I felt myself pale. "What are you talking about?"

"She's knocked up. In trouble. With child." He grabbed my
sweatshirt and pulled me close, breathing beer all over me. He
was wearing that grin again. "We've decided to start a family," he said.

I just didn't understand. The words wouldn't penetrate. I'd
heard of teenage pregnancy, of course, but thought it only occurred in lurid movies, or sex manuals. Sex was certainly a
moral question at our age, it was the one people brought up
most, but I'd never taken the part about babies seriously. Sex
among teenagers seemed too innocent to produce such compli-
cations.

No doubt that's why there are so many teenage pregnancies.

"How did this happen?" I said.

Now *there* was an intelligent question. I deserved the answer
I got.

"I dicked her," he said. "I thrust it deep within her. I did the
dirty deed."

"Shut up, Sam." I said. "Goddammit."

"We've been screwing since December. I've been careful
most of the time. But what the hell. You forget to take a rubber. Or you forget to buy one. You get it up one more time than
you thought. Or the fucking thing springs a leak. I don't know.
Something happened."

I hated Sam at that moment. Not just for the way he was
telling me—he was drunk, after all, and probably so scared out
of his wits that he was fighting to keep it casual—but for what
he had done, for the way I'd been taken. I loved Cindy, I loved
her more than he ever would, and now he was telling me he'd
been screwing her for months.

There was no way to satisfy my anger. He was standing
there like one of those plastic dolls with sand in the bottom.

You knock it down and it bounces back up, that same stupid grin on its face.

"What are you going to do?" I said.

"We find out tonight. We're going to tell her parents. I figured it would be easier if I was plastered. I'm sure they will be."

After the conversation, if not before.

"Then you can kiss my ass goodbye," Sam said. "My chapel seat starts collecting dust next week."

He was right. It was the same rule that covered drinking off campus. Conduct unbecoming a gentleman. Apparently a gentleman always remembered a rubber.

"Christ," I said. "You fucked up this time."

"I fucked. I didn't fuck up."

I should have gone ahead and hit him. For my own satisfaction. Bloodied his nose and smashed his glasses to bits. He probably wouldn't have felt a thing. But as I stood there staring at him, that broad unfathomable grin, I heard Bennett behind me. I hadn't heard him come down the stairs.

"Have a snort?" Sam held up the beer can.

"*Jesus!*" Bennett threw his head to one side in disgust.

I was ashamed for him to see me like that. One more incident in that raucous frivolous friendship. I couldn't even get serious before a race.

"Good luck in your race," Sam said. "The whole world's here to see it. Most of them got their money on the dago."

"I'm sure."

"Even your girlfriend's here."

Bennett had been heading for the door, but Sam's words made him just curious enough to stop for a moment. "Who's that?"

"Miss Edmond. Whatever you call him. Or maybe you're the girl. Maybe you take it up the ass."

What Sam was saying made so little sense that at first I didn't get it; it might as well have been nonsense syllables. About the time I did understand I saw the expression on Bennett's face, of real pain. He had gone stark white.

"Goddammit!" I shouted. I gave Sam a shove. He hadn't been expecting it, went flying across the hall into a trash bin that was standing there and almost knocked it over. Beer splattered onto the wall, and onto the floor; he dropped the can but snatched it up before it spilled much more.

"Jesus," he said. "Let's not waste good beer here."

He had darkened for a moment when he hit the wall, now flipped on that weird grin again. He raised the can in a toast.

"To love. To young love everywhere."

Bennett turned and walked out the door.

"You shouldn't have said that," I said. "It takes a real shit to say something like that."

"I didn't mean anything by it."

"Tell that to Bennett."

"Doesn't bother me how he gets his kicks."

He was eyeing the beer can judiciously, now took a long pull at it.

"You don't know what you're talking about," I said. "He just looks up to him."

"Yeah."

"He looks up to him as a teacher. And a friend."

"Then he's looking up to a faggot. But I'll tell you one thing. You're lucky it was you who pushed me." Sam didn't look in much shape to be making threats. "You're lucky you're a friend of mine."

"I wonder."

"And I'll tell you another. He'll never win that race today. He'll never win a big race in his life. He's too tight."

"He's ready."

"He was too tight the day he was born."

Sam finished off his beer as if finishing off the subject, dropped it into the bin.

"You're loose, Sam," I said. "You've been loose all along. But you can loosen up so much you fall apart."

I wasn't going to stand there arguing with him. That was a subject that could have gone on forever. Anyway, there was something I wanted to tell Bennett. I turned away from Sam and walked out the door.

I caught Bennett halfway down the steps. "I didn't tell him, Bennett," I said.

"Okay." He wasn't looking at me.

"He's the one who told me about Mr. Edmond. And he makes all those stupid jokes. But I didn't tell him anything. I haven't told a soul what we talked about."

"All right."

"He's just babbling away. He's drunk."

"I told you that kid would wind up no good."

"I know."

I still didn't want to think of Sam that way. It was getting harder and harder not to.

"If you keep hanging around him he'll drag you down with him."

By the time the starter sounded the first call for the mile, the clouds had moved in again and descended, it seemed, to just above the treetops on the hills beyond the lower fields. The sky was a deep gray, made a stunning background for the bright yellow of our jerseys, but the air was cold, so we all walked around skittishly like horses shy of the starting gate, waiting for the last minute to take our sweats off. Bennett seemed calm and determined, that combination of an intent mind and relaxed body that is the mark of any real athlete. I didn't agree with Sam. Bennett might have been tight at one time, but he had found his sport, the thing in the world he had been meant all along to do, and he had the same confidence about running that he had in the classroom.

The race that day, I think, was the key to the whole rivalry between Bennett and Capelli. The mile the year before had been a fluke, and Capelli had nearly died winning the cross-country race that fall, but on this day there wasn't a tactic in the world that would have surprised Bennett; he was in the best shape of his life and had been pointing toward the race for months. This was the day, I am convinced, that he would have gotten the monkey off his back forever, run Capelli into the ground, except for the fact that our coach, Wheel Barrow, stepped up and spoke to him before the race began.

"When Capelli goes out today," he said, "I think you should go with him."

He always preferred the succinct kind of statement that spoke volumes.

Wheel was a gray-haired man with small crinkly eyes and a long narrow jaw. He was trim and energetic, had been a track star himself and was still in superb shape ("Thirty minutes a day on the exercycle," he would tell anybody who listened. "And I always leave the table a little hungry"); he knew his sport and knew his athletes. He must have waited until then to speak because he knew Bennett brooded on things, figured it would be better to spring it on him at the last minute than to have him pondering it forever. Unfortunately, he had contradicted a mental picture that Bennett had already been pondering for weeks.

"I thought I should run my own race," Bennett said.

"Usually I'd agree," Wheel said. "But you've let him go out too far in the past. He gets a lead that's insurmountable."

"I've got a better kick," Bennett said. He thought his kick could overcome any lead.

"But you're strong too. You're as strong as he is. I just think you need to stay close enough to where your kick can do some good."

It was good advice. I agreed with it, as a matter of fact. I didn't necessarily think Wheel had chosen the perfect moment to deliver it. For the first time that day, I saw a shadow of uncertainty in Bennett's eyes.

Within a few minutes the milers were called to the starting line. Along the hill below the gym was a long line of spectators; at various places around the track—the jumping pits, shot-put circle—athletes had stopped to watch; around the outside of the track some JV baseball players had clustered, their coach knocking off practice long enough to see the mile; around the infield of the track was the usual mob of runners, coaches, hangers-on. My family was up on the hill, Father already having sounded the bugle a few times, to the scattered laughter of other spectators. Sam was in the infield, his hands stuffed in his trench-coat pockets and the grin still on his face. At least he had the good sense not to pull out a beer can. People must have wondered where the smell was coming from.

By common consent the top runners got choice positions at the starting line, so two seniors—who would finish first and second—had the inside lanes. Bennett was standing uneasily in the third spot, leaving some room, since by rights it belonged to Capelli. I was to Bennett's right. Sure enough, at the last minute, Capelli stepped out to the starting line to squeeze into that third spot. He was all set to cop a cheap feel off Bennett when, without a word, Bennett and I changed places. Capelli looked dumbfounded, stared at me for a moment. "You look just like him," he said.

"Sheer coincidence," I said.

I was feeling pretty loose at that point, pretty worked up. In addition to the race, I had what Sam had told me running through my mind. It gave me a certain recklessness.

Capelli had that short squat body—he was shorter than I was—and, though I wasn't particularly crowding him, was all over me. Clasping my hand, clasping my ass (it was definitely more than a pat), leaning up against me until I supported half his weight. I honestly think that if I had given way he would have maneuvered us right off the track, but I hung in there. I wasn't afraid of germs. Bennett had plenty of room to the outside.

"Why don't you just fuck me, Capelli?" I said.

He didn't even seem to hear. The kid had no sense of humor.

The thing that no one had mentioned—though as soon as I brought it up every cross-country and distance runner in the school wholeheartedly agreed—was that Capelli smelled as if he had already run about fourteen miles. He smelled as if he had been running workouts all week and hadn't taken a shower yet. He was overwhelming. He smelled worse than my French teacher, and I had never thought I would say that about a human being in my life. No wonder the guy was such a great runner. You couldn't get near him. I knew this fact must be disturbing to Bennett. He associated strong smells with especially virulent germs.

So although such things were strictly prohibited, when the starter began the commands I spoke quietly to the guy who was leaning so hard against me. "Try to take a bath sometime in the present century, would you, Capelli?" I said.

The gun sounded and the race was on.

In a way I'm making too much of it. What was it, after all,

a fourteen-year-old boy, two fifteen-year-olds, guys who weren't even shaving too often yet, whose best times were around 4:50. Mine was 5:15. The race was later recalled as something of a curiosity, but much more remembered were the legendary races in cross-country and track that Bennett and Capelli staged two years from then. They were two of the best milers in the state that year, record holders at both of their schools, captains in cross-country and track. Their races were more important than entire meets. They were running for the pride of their schools. Even I eventually ran more notable races. Though I was only third man on the team my senior year, I was captain of the cross-country team because I was such a dependable grind, and I was the best two-miler in track (okay, Bennett had been right). That little race we ran in our freshman and sophomore years can seem pretty insignificant. Probably it was only important to me.

With the crack of the gun Capelli sprinted out (perhaps my words had spurred him) and took the lead, even in front of the seniors who were certain to win. Again, in my opinion, he had made a brilliant move. Bennett had waited months to know what crazy-assed thing Capelli would do, and as soon as the race began Capelli did it, as if to say, "This is the way it's going to be. The whole race is going to be ass backwards." He not only took the lead, he went way ahead, as if he had forgotten we were running the mile. Behind him were the seniors who would finish first and second, and behind them, running alone, was Bennett. A pack of about six of us trailed far to the rear.

Capelli's tactic seemed to stun the crowd. People from his school were cheering, the usual shouts of encouragement at the start of a race, but our fans were silent. They didn't know whether to urge Bennett to go out and get him or not. That whole huge crowd was there, and hardly making a sound.

Toward the end of the first quarter, Bennett started to move up.

What I have always assumed is that Bennett had been torn; during the first lap he was deciding whether to follow his own strategy or do what Wheel had said. He had stayed closer to the seniors than he normally would have, run a faster pace than he usually did, but he hadn't gone out with Capelli. Sometime during that first lap he decided Wheel was right. As the lap was ending he moved up on the seniors, and in the middle of the straightaway he passed them. He was gaining on Capelli as he rounded the first turn.

The crowd livened up at the sight of this development. People on our side started to shout, and people on their side shouted louder; all around the track guys were yelling encouragement. Above it all sounded Father's bugle, in long loud blasts, letting Bennett know the family was behind him.

By the backstretch of the second lap Bennett caught Capelli. I have often thought he should have passed him right then (in the race two years later he did pass him right then), that he should have taken the lead so he wouldn't have to watch that maddening stride. Conventional track wisdom, however, dictates that the man with the kick run behind. Bennett probably thought he had broken enough rules already.

They ran together for a lap and a half. It was the most exciting six hundred yards of the race. Capelli looked as if he were about to keel over, he had looked that way from the start of the race, digging long with his lopsided steps. Bennett trailed him with that picture stride. The fans screamed; the bugle blatted. The only way you could tell their pace was slowing was by the fact that the seniors were moving up on them. Down the home stretch of the third lap, just about the time the gun went off, the seniors passed them.

At that point, as far as most of the crowd was concerned, the race ended. Bennett lost it. You couldn't believe, watching the strides of those two runners, that he would be the one to give in, but he was. It was as if the gun for the gun lap had shot him. "My body just felt like lead," he said to me later. "It was the hardest thing I had ever done in my life to run with him that way. I would rather have run twenty miles by myself. I couldn't keep it up another step." As if Bennett were caught in some invisible treadmill that kept pulling him back, Capelli started, at a surprising pace (especially considering the fact that he was slowing down too), to pull away. By the time they reached the one-ten mark Capelli had a ten-yard lead. You could see Bennett wasn't going to catch him.

I, of course, had not witnessed that titanic battle. It was all described for me later. I was running along in my clippety-clop fashion, back in the pack but feeling good; I was all pumped up for Bennett's sake and had maintained a strong pace. I had managed to stay loose in that third lap and had plenty left for the fourth. I felt I was running well, I thought I was running the best race of my life, but I had no idea, when I came up on that last backstretch, that I'd find myself gaining on Bennett.

Two other guys had already passed him, stepped around him as if he were standing still. He practically was. It didn't mean the same to them as to me, though. It was as if I were running up to a bed where I was expected to jump in and fuck my sister. There was no way I could avoid it; Bennett had nothing left at all. As I moved around him at the end of the backstretch I felt a sudden surge of speed, as if the act of passing him itself had given me new strength.

Sam went wild. Even from where I was, as intent on the race as I was, I could see him running to intercept me, bounding across the field with that slight limp, hands still in the pockets of his trench coat, his hat blown off and hair flying in the wind. "Beat the son of a bitch," he shouted at me as we hit the three-thirty mark. "Kill the dirty bastard. Beat that motherfucker for once." It was only when I heard Sam, when I caught the vehemence of what he was shouting, that I began to realize what I was doing.

Not that I had time to think. I wasn't exactly examining the situation, how humiliating it must be for Bennett to lose to Capelli, how much worse it might be to lose to me too. I didn't have time to decide if I should do that to him. I didn't have time to consider that this might be the only time in my life I had a chance to beat Bennett in a race, to wonder if it would be a tainted victory under the circumstances; I didn't realize the new strength I had found was leading me to the best time I would run all year, that I was ahead of two guys on our team I had never beaten and one on the other I never should have. All I knew was that I was running, I was running hard and feeling strong, and Bennett was behind me.

Two years later, the evening after he had beaten Capelli in the biggest race of his career, Bennett said to me in the quiet of our bedroom, "It was you that helped me beat him. That time my sophomore year when his stride put me into a trance, and everybody passed me. You passed me. My own little brother. It was when you passed me that I snapped out of it. I realized it was all in my head. If you hadn't passed me that day I would probably never have beaten Capelli in my life."

What a comfort it was that in my own small way I had helped to advance that great career.

I ran that last one-ten with Bennett on my tail, Sam trailing the two of us and limping along. It's illegal for somebody to run with you in the infield (you could be paced that way), but Bennett and I were both out of the scoring. Probably only Sam and my parents and Teddy were even watching the race at that point. I could hear the bugle blaring, Teddy's high falsetto cheers. God knows who my parents were rooting for. "We were just glad our boys were both doing so well," my mother said to me later. Teddy said he was rooting for me.

You could bat around the psychological factors forever. You could say I choked; that once I had actually passed Bennett— and despite the strength that gave me—it was all just too much; that I fell into a trance like Bennett's with Capelli; that the thought of being beaten by his brother gave Bennett super-human strength. I don't know about any of that. I came around the last curve still feeling strong, and the finish line was right there, officials holding stopwatches and gazing at them studiously. I didn't run out of control; I kicked with everything I had; and I ran through the finish line without slowing down at the end. In the last twenty yards, however, despite anything I could do—I could feel it happening first, then see it, right there within reach of my arm—Bennett moved beside me, then inched past. He finished a good two strides ahead. He had done it again.

As soon as he crossed the finish line people swarmed around him, consoled him for the tough loss against Capelli, praised him for the courage he had shown in going out after the man. You couldn't even get near him. I walked off toward the end of the straightaway. It was just beginning to dawn on me what had happened, how close I had actually come to beating Bennett. As always when I lost a close race, I was wondering if I could have run just slightly faster (it always seemed I could have). It crossed my mind that Bennett hadn't had to do that, it shouldn't have meant that much to him; he had lost the race that was important and could have let his brother win for once. A rage rose up in me, a fist twisting in my guts, a bitterness at all the times—as the younger, weaker brother—I had ever lost, when Sam came up beside me. He was still wearing the sunglasses, but the hat was long gone. His face was ruddy from the exercise, and he was more out of breath from his little run than I was from running that whole mile. His hands were stuffed back in his pockets. The strange smile had disappeared from his face. He wore around those sunglasses an expression of rage and disappointment.

"I knew you'd never beat him," he said. "You'll never beat that fairy as long as you live."

I hit him. I spun ninety degrees and hit him, the hardest punch I had ever thrown. He was tired from his run, I suppose, and woozy from the beer; the punch felled him as if I'd swung with a club. I jumped him when he was down and pounded with my fists, clawed with my fingers, pummeled with my knees; I didn't know what I was doing or who I was doing it to. "Hey!" I heard somebody shout from far away, and "Hold it!"; in a moment it seemed the whole crowd from the finish line had swarmed around us. Guys were leaning over me, pulling from behind; they hauled me to my feet and I hauled Sam, yanked him into an odd sitting posture. He was plopped there dumbly, his mouth bloody, sunglasses broken. Above one eye was a small open cut. His eyes were dazed; a trickle of blood ran down his chin. In his lap, spilling over his trench coat—he had finally managed to yank his hand from his pocket—was an open can of beer.

NINE

From the perspective of years, of what we call maturity, I can look back on those days and see what I should have done. Sometime during the weekend after the track meet I should have gone to Sam and said I was sorry, that he'd been drunk and we'd had a disagreement but it had been stupid to fight. I could have found out what was happening and seen if he was scared and asked if there was anything I could do. I could have gone to Cindy too, told her that no matter what had happened between us or what had happened in her life, no matter how people treated her or what she had to go through, I would always be her friend. Things had changed, and would change more, but the three of us would face them together.

Those were my feelings, I think, the deepest feelings in my heart, but I did not act on them. It is almost funny, remembering the boy I was, to think I might have acted on them. There was too much in the way. My anger at Sam for what he had done to Cindy, for the way he had betrayed me, for the truth he had showed me about myself that I didn't want to see. There was my shame at having been in that fight with him. There was the whole social stigma: he was the first person in anyone's memory or knowledge actually to have been kicked out of school for drinking at an athletic contest. At a school dance maybe, but never before had someone been caught drinking before the school day was over. He became a kind of legend around the school. There was also the story, which came to light in subsequent weeks, of what had happened between him and Cindy. There was a greater stigma in that than in the drinking. They might as well have been lepers, for all anybody wanted to have to do with them. It was as if, at the age of fifteen, they had been wrenched away from their friends and kidnapped into adulthood. There was no way we could get them back.

The truth of the matter was that for the rest of the time I was in high school, I never spoke to Sam Golden again.

I saw him now and then. I saw him around the neighborhood. For his sixteenth birthday his father bought him a bright-blue Triumph, and I saw him driving that. Once he came to an evening musical that our school gave, and I saw him in the audience, taller than he had been, thicker through the chest and shoulders, fuller in the face: he looked great. I could have gone over and sat beside him, talked to him—we would have laughed, I bet, laughed hilariously, at the huge joke of seeing each other again—but I didn't. I could have hurried to find him when the program was over. We would have caught up with each other in a matter of minutes. I kept watching him during the program, seeing him react to things, seeing him laugh—yep, he could still laugh—but when the evening was over I hurried out to my car and made sure he didn't see me.

My youth, my whole life, is a graveyard of things I might have done but didn't do. I am dazzled sometimes at the thought of what might have been, if I had had more courage or a little more daring. There were whole worlds I failed to explore just for the fear of taking a step or saying a word.

I did hear things about Sam, all through high school. The rumor was that he had not even been allowed to return to campus during school hours, that he had been told to clean out his locker on a Saturday afternoon and never appear on campus again. He finished the year at a small tutorial school in Shadyside where a number of flunkies and misfits went. In the summer his father got him a job as a busboy at a resort in the Adirondacks. He attended three boarding schools in his remaining high school years, finally graduating from the third after a stint in summer school. From the first of these schools he had been expelled for what seemed to me a harmless prank: on the last day of school before vacation the school served foot-long hot dogs as a special treat, and when the serving plate appeared at his table—Sam was the student waiter that day— one of the foot-longs was wearing a rubber. It is incredible what schools considered a grave offense in those days. From the second of the schools he had been expelled for calling up a town girl and saying vile things to her on the phone. He was dating the girl at the time. It has not been established that she thought the things he was saying were vile. Unfortunately, her mother was listening on another line.

I never heard how he was actually doing at those schools before he got kicked out. I never heard how his academic career was going.

The other thing I heard about Sam was that he had become an electric guitarist. That was hardly unusual in those days, when a rock group might form because four guys were sitting around on a rainy day with nothing better to do, but the word was, by the end of our senior year, that he was the best rock guitarist in the city. He didn't belong to any group for long, but played for a number of different ones, always lead guitar. He didn't sing, but stood slightly apart from the group, often with a cigarette in his mouth, and, while looking utterly impassive, performed virtuoso feats on the guitar. At breaks he would look up to find four or five girls standing around him.

Once a friend of mine was at a party Sam attended, and all Sam did was drink and smoke and listen to the music. He didn't socialize at all. He was with a tall blond girl who was extraordinarily beautiful, and who sat beside him doing nothing. Whenever she said anything, whenever she even started to make conversation, he would fix her with a threatening stare and say, very slowly, "I'm going to fuck you." No matter what she said, how casual or offhand she made the remark, he always responded in the same way—"I'm going to fuck you"— each time slightly louder, until finally she got out a whole sentence and he leaped to his feet, stood over her leaning down and shouting into her face, "I'm going to fuck you! I'm going to fuck you! I'm going to fuck you!" The whole party stopped and stared at them. Slowly he sat down, the people started to talk again, and the music played. She didn't say another word all evening.

Cindy similarly disappeared from my social circle, though she didn't as often pop up in rumor as Sam did. She just fell into a hole for a couple of years. She had dropped out of school as soon as her parents found out she was pregnant, had gone off to live with an aunt when she started to show, had had the baby and put it up for adoption the following year. When she returned to the city she started attending public school, apparently reflecting thereby her change in status. In my senior year somebody brought her to a dance out at school. The first thing you noticed was that she had gained weight; she was not unattractive or anything, but you wouldn't have turned to look at her if she walked by on the street. She seemed older than the rest of us, somewhat more mature perhaps, but she had lost a certain luster. She made a point of coming over to shake my hand—shake my hand, yet—as you might with an old acquaintance you were glad to see. There was no indication I was anything more than that. Neither of us mentioned Sam.

For a period of months, then, something under two years, I had those friends. We were terribly close but our friendship ended abruptly, more abruptly, I suppose, than most friendships end. It is odd, considering what we meant to each other, how abruptly it all ended.

Except that I haven't forgotten them. I haven't forgotten either of them. I don't know what it is about friendships when you're young; they are like no friendships you ever have again. I have never again fallen into a friendship so easily as I did with Sam Golden; I have never again gotten to know someone so quickly so well. I have never known anyone else I could spend time with that way, waking up in the morning and heading for his house with no other thought than just to be there, knowing it would be good if we just got together. I have never again known a friend I could ultimately depend on as I could—for a few months at least—on Sam, who might not approve of or like everything I did but was always behind me, and who knew me; he might wish I were another way, but he knew me.

I have been in love a number of times, but never again have I felt so pure and simple a love as I did for Cindy, never have I known another woman who was so much without guile and who gave of herself all she could with no strings attached. Her kisses were like the way she gave herself, and I never knew another woman who kissed like that. Never again have I been that way with two people, where we could be together and enjoy each other openly and like each other, where it was friendly and sexual and fun all at once, at least for a while.

Probably part of the reason I didn't pursue them after that spring was that I knew it couldn't be the same again, that it would be Sam and Cindy but not the same as before that afternoon on Cindy's couch. Things that we did changed our friendship; the changes didn't just happen. Even if it hadn't been the same, though, it might have been something. Who knows what our friendships might become if we let them go on after the things that end them?

The odd thing is that even in the eyes of some objective observers, the whole world has gone the way of that friendship. We think of those days as an innocent time in the history of America (though we know there are no innocent times), a boyish President full of hope, a people finally beginning to recognize the plight of their disadvantaged, a space program on the verge of exploring unknown worlds. Some months later that President was shot, and we fell into a spiral of disaster from which we don't seem to have recovered since. There was no real connection, of course. Sam and Cindy and I did not know we were living in a time of special innocence, and there were many things going on—as in any time—that were far from innocent. Public events, in any case, made no impress whatsoever on my mind. The newspaper might as well have been written in Swahili for all the attention I paid to it. Sometimes, though, it seems to me that my life—our lives—vaguely follow the pattern of the age, that Sam and Cindy were forerunners perhaps (as Sam was in everything), giving us warning of the disorder to come. They entered the sixties before the rest of us were ready.

All that seems coincidence. I don't think of it often. I do think often of Sam Golden. As far back in my past as he is, I think of him all the time. I see him as a kind of orphan in the city, privileged perhaps but as alone as if he were poor, with that clownish father, that cold and distant mother, abandoned in the streets to make his way. He wasn't probably as spectacular an athlete as I remember (he was only fourteen), but he played as if he were, played with abandon; he showed that often enough an athlete was successful just because he thought he would be. He extracted the essence from the smallest moments, could make a streetcar ride an event, an afternoon at the bowling alley a carnival. He had a way of approaching experience, walking right up to it and standing boldly before it. He did what he wanted. My memory of Sam Golden is a talisman for me. I pick it up and hold it and it brings me luck.

He was hardly perfect, could be moody and superior and vicious, but he had a knack for living that few people ever learn. When I think of how to live my life, not the things I want to do but the way I want to do them, I think of him. I picture him laughing at a story, eyebrows crinkled, jaw thrust out, chest gently shaking as he shook his head in disbelief; I see him asking me a question, staring into my eyes in expectation of the best answer I had; I see him poised to catch a punt as if the whole world were hurtling down into his hands. Whatever finally happened between us, whatever happened to him, however little I am able to echo the way he lived and however impractical it is—people are not comfortable with such intensity—I am glad I knew him. I am glad he lived. For a time in my life I was touched by one in whom the fire burned bright. In me he ignited perhaps only a spark. But the spark still glows.